MYSTERY WRITERS OF AMERICA
*presents*

# THE RICH
*and*
# THE DEAD

**MYSTERY WRITERS OF AMERICA**
*presents*

# THE RICH
## *and*
# THE DEAD

---

### EDITED BY

# NELSON DeMILLE

**GRAND CENTRAL**
**PUBLISHING**

New York    Boston

Grand Central Publishing
Hachette Book Group
237 Park Avenue
New York, NY 10017

www.HachetteBookGroup.com

Printed in the United States of America

First Edition: May 2011
10 9 8 7 6 5 4 3 2 1

Grand Central Publishing is a division of Hachette Book Group, Inc.
The Grand Central Publishing name and logo is a trademark of Hachette Book Group, Inc.

Library of Congress Cataloging-in-Publication Data

Mystery Writers of America presents the rich and the dead / edited by Nelson DeMille.
    p. cm.
ISBN 978-0-446-55587-6 (hardcover)
ISBN 978-0-446-55588-3 (trade)
  1. Detective and mystery stories, American.   2. Rich people—Crimes against—Fiction.
I. DeMille, Nelson.   II. Mystery Writers of America.   III. Title: Rich and the dead.
PS648.D4M965 2011
813'.087208—dc22

                                                        2010034196

# CONTENTS

# CONTENTS

# INTRODUCTION
## BY NELSON DeMILLE

I t is an honor and a pleasure to have been chosen as the editor of the 2011 Mystery Writers of America annual anthology.

This year's anthology is top-notch, and the stories collected here are in the finest tradition of the mysteries and crime stories that have appeared in this volume over the years.

The theme of this collection, as the title suggests, is rich people who are killed or who kill. And for fun, some of our authors also explore the illegal, illicit, and in some cases, immoral goings-on of the rich. For additional readings on this subject, I suggest any newspaper any day of the week. I think *everyone* had fun with this topic, and when the writer is having fun, the reader is having fun.

What is it that makes the criminal behavior of the rich and famous so fascinating to us? Often it's not the crime itself, which in many cases would barely make the news if committed by a lesser mortal. It is, I think, aside from the public's obvious fascination with the rich or famous, the idea that someone with so much to lose would risk so much in the commission of a crime. We are captivated by what drove this exalted person to the crime, and we want to know how the law and how society will deal with someone at this level. Will justice be done? Will the notoriety of the accused work for or against him or her? From O. J. Simpson to Bernie Madoff to every crooked politician and ditsy actress arrested for everything from DWI to murder that you've ever seen on the front pages of the tabloids, the answer is not always clear. But it *is* entertaining and engrossing to read about.

Some of the writers in this collection chose not to make the rich person the perpetrator, but to make him or her the victim. There is a saying in this business that it's hard for a writer to make the reader feel sorry for an unhappy rich girl on a yacht. True enough, but if the unhappy rich girl—or guy—is murdered, or blackmailed, or threatened, then we might feel some sympathy for them. In most cases, however, the rich person who is a victim usually got what he or she deserved. But still, a crime has been committed and now justice must be done. Or does it? Some of the stories to follow examine the moral ambiguities of getting rid of a rich, nasty SOB. Do we want to see this crime solved? Yes. But do we want the perpetrator brought to justice for ridding the world of that rich, nasty SOB? Maybe not.

———

I WANT TO take this opportunity to thank all the writers who put so much time and effort into this year's anthology, though I won't thank them by name—they're in the Contents. But I do want to thank by name Barry Zeman of the Mystery Writers of America (MWA), with whom I had the pleasure of working on this project for the last year. Barry did a lot of the heavy lifting and kept me from getting a brain hernia. Thanks, too, to Margery Flax, administrative manager of the MWA, who was of enormous help to me when I was president of MWA and who was truly the administrative manager, par excellence, for this anthology. I also want to thank John Helfers of Tekno Books, who coordinated all the pieces of this project and did a fantastic job of editing. Thanks, too, to Celia Johnson of Grand Central Publishing (GCP) for pulling it all together. GCP is the publisher for my novels, and I'm happy to be working with them on this anthology.

This book would not have been possible without the hard work and dedication of the panel of judges, who read nearly two hundred submissions from fellow MWA members and who had the difficult task of choosing the best for me to pick from. Many, many thanks go to Libby Hellmann, Daniel Stashower, Persia Walker, James Lincoln Warren, and Carolyn Wheat.

And finally, I also want to thank the Mystery Writers of America, one of the finest professional organizations in the publishing business, for inviting me to edit this year's anthology. As a thirty-five-year member and former president of MWA, I can say with some authority and experience that the MWA has been instrumental in keeping the mystery story in the forefront of all writing genres and has assured mystery readers a continuous supply of the first-rate stories we love—up to and including this year's extraordinary anthology.

If you love crime and mystery stories, you will love this collection from the men and women who have proven themselves to be masters of the genre.

Enjoy!

—Nelson DeMille

MYSTERY WRITERS OF AMERICA

*presents*

# THE RICH
*and*
# THE DEAD

# DEATH BENEFITS

## BY NELSON DeMILLE

On a pleasant Friday afternoon in June, best-selling author Jack Henry sat in the study of his Upper East Side townhouse. He had put his creative writing aside and was now focused on his finances—bills, income projections, royalty statements, and pending deals.

After a few hours, he was coming to the realization that he was on the brink of insolvency. Bankruptcy. "Holy shit."

It just didn't seem possible. He was rich and famous. How could he be broke?

Well, because the money going out was greater than the money coming in. That's how. Actually, he'd known about this problem for some time. But through a process of denial, disbelief, and maybe a little arrogance, he'd put off the inevitable conclusion, which now stared him in the face. "You're broke," he said aloud. "You have no money. You're screwed."

He opened the lower left drawer of his desk, pulled out a bottle of Rémy Martin, and took a swig.

He sat back in his leather chair and stared blankly out the window of his East Sixty-fourth Street townhouse. How did this happen? Well, two financially ruinous divorces had not helped the bottom line. Not to mention that his last two novels hadn't been well received by the critics or the public and had also been turned down by the book clubs. And then there were the movie deals that had never materialized, and the foreign translation deals on his last two books that had dwindled to a few lowball offers from thieving publishers in countries that he couldn't even locate on a map. Lithuania? His agent, Stan Wykoff, wanted him to accept *any* translation deal, like the thousand bucks just offered by the Bulgarian publisher for his latest novel, *Into the Dark Waters*. Stan had told him, "I'll see if I can get you a paid trip to Bulgaria to publicize the book." To which Jack had replied, "*You* go to Bulgaria. See if you can get me another thousand."

Jack took a second swig of cognac. "How are the mighty fallen."

His biggest financial problem seemed to be taxes—federal, New York State, and New York City. A letter from his accountant informed him that his tax obligations—past, present, and future—totaled slightly over half a million dollars with interest and penalties. How did *that* happen? Well, apparently he'd made enough money to owe taxes, but he'd been spending his gross income as it came in and had not set aside money for his government partners. That wasn't too smart, but he didn't believe he'd been too extravagant in his spending...except of course he had high fixed and necessary expenses, like the two top floors of this townhouse, which cost him ten thousand a month. Then there was his secretary and his housekeeper. And, of course, there was the summer rental in East Hampton at...how much was that? He found the entry in his checkbook. One hundred and forty thousand for the season. Maybe he should have spent this summer in the city. But how could he do that? *Everyone* was in the Hamptons.

Then there were his incidental expenses like the catered dinner parties; the BMW lease; his club, the Knickerbocker; his clothes; dining out; and a few vacations. Paris in the fall, for instance. St. Barths in January. A few bucks here and a few bucks there, and before you know it, it adds up.

And on top of all this were his necessary business expenses. Typewriter paper. Printer cartridges. Lots of paper clips. Plus a new dictionary. It adds up.

The problem, he was convinced, was not the expenses— he'd always had these expenses. The problem was the income. Expenses were steady; income was down. *That* was the problem. *That* was what had led to this alarming gap in his cash flow chart. Or whatever his accountant called it.

And was this declining income *his* fault? No. It was the fault of his publisher, who couldn't sell crack cocaine to a junkie. And they damned sure couldn't sell books. Not *his* books, anyway.

The other reason for this income crisis was Stan Wykoff. Laziest literary agent on the planet. And for doing nothing, Stan took 15 percent of everything that Jack made, which, admittedly, had not been as much in the last few years as it had once been. Yet there had been a time when Jack Henry pulled in two or three million a year, and Stan Wykoff skimmed his 15 percent right off the top. How much, Jack wondered, had Stan made off him in the last ten or twelve years? Jack did a quick calculation in his head and came up with about three million dollars. "Bastard."

If Jack thought that Stan Wykoff was sharing in his financial distress, he would have taken some satisfaction in that. But the Wykoff Agency had dozens of authors who Stan ripped off at 15 percent, and as long as half of them produced, then Stan could actually live better than his highest-paid author. For doing nothing.

Jack Henry looked at his watch. It was close to 4 p.m., and he wanted to get on the road and drive out to his summer rental. He needed a break from this depressing reality and a break from his writing, which was not going well. He needed to sit on his back deck and stare at the sun setting over Georgica Pond, a drink in his hand, and his mind on something else. Like fishing or getting a tan. Or the new cocktail waitress at The Palm.

Something would turn up that would get him out of this predicament. It always did.

As he tidied up his desk, he came across a bill that his secretary had marked "Important." It was an annual premium notice from the National Life Insurance Company. Five thousand two hundred and thirty dollars. It took him a few seconds to recognize what this was. It was, in fact, the bill for a policy that he had taken out on the life of Stan Wykoff. The death benefit was five million dollars and the beneficiary was Jack Henry.

Jack stared at the premium notice, recalling better days when he was doing well financially and he and Stan had a substantial insurable interest in each other's lives. Stan, he knew, had a similar policy on him. In fact, he recalled, they had taken their insurance physicals together, then gone out for drinks and later playfully pretended to push each other in front of moving vehicles. He smiled; then the smile faded as he thought about Stan getting his premium notice and paying it without a second thought or a second notice.

As for their present insurable interest in each other, Stan would not suffer a significant loss of income if Jack died, so the five million was all gravy for him. And if Stan died...well, Jack's income would go up. Five million. And Stan, who had seemed so irreplaceable when the policy was taken out, was now easily replaceable. In fact, Jack would have a new agent before the embalmers finished with Stan Wykoff.

Meanwhile, however, this was a term policy and the premiums were rising faster than Jack's and Stan's ages. And Stan, with nothing to do all day, went to the gym a lot and kept fit. Jack on the other hand was tied to his desk sixty hours a week, and perhaps he drank too much. In fact, he realized that Stan had a much better chance than he did of cashing in on the five million dollars.

*Bottom line here*, he thought, *this is a good place to save some money*. He threw the premium notice in the wastebasket, stood, and walked toward the door.

He stopped. Then turned, walked back to the wastebasket, and retrieved the bill. *Five thousand two hundred and thirty dollars*. That's what it would cost him to make five million if Stan died in the next twelve months. But what if Stan didn't die? Why would Stan die? *How* would Stan die?

Jack stared at the bill. His lottery ticket. The solution to all his money problems was pressed between his thumb and index finger. Stan was healthy . . . but even healthy people had accidents.

Jack came to his senses, then laughed silently at the crazy thought that had formed in his mind. "This isn't a novel by Jack Henry. This is real life. Real people don't murder people for insurance money." Actually, they did. *Desperate men do desperate things*. But he wasn't a murderer. He *was* a financial idiot, but not a killer. He threw the premium notice back in the wastebasket and left his office.

He called the garage for his car and began packing a few things for his long weekend in East Hampton.

His life, as he knew it, was coming to an end, and he tried to be philosophical about it. "Better to have had money and lost it than never to have had money at all." Better to be poor and honest than to be rich with a crime on your conscience. *Behind every great fortune is a crime*. He looked at himself in the bedroom mirror and said, "I can live without this townhouse, without the BMW, without the house in the Hamptons, without Paris or St. Barths. I can clean my own small apartment in a cheaper neighborhood and do my own laundry and my own secretarial work. I don't need to dine in expensive restaurants—I can learn to cook.

And I don't need all the women that money can buy. And if I never get laid again..."

He went quickly back to his office and fished the insurance bill out of the trash.

———

JACK HENRY SAT in a rocker on his cedar deck and faced west. The big red sun was sinking into the wetlands around the large tidal pond. He sipped his gin and tonic—his third—and felt relaxed, but also tense. He had the means to turn financial ruin into financial gain. The five million dollars—a tax-free death benefit—would pay off the government and his creditors and buy him three or four more years of comfort, and also buy him time to turn out a few more best sellers. The last two books, written perhaps too quickly under the stress of financial pressure, had not been up to his usual high standards. He could do better than that with a five-million-dollar cushion. He owed that to his readers.

And, of course, he'd have a new agent. Someone who believed in him. Someone who could negotiate a high advance for a three-book deal with a better publisher. "Someone," he said aloud, "younger and hungrier than the late Stan Wykoff." *The late Stan Wykoff.* He liked the sound of that.

Or he could liquidate everything here, take the five million, and move to St. Barths or the Bahamas. Maybe the Cayman Islands. He pictured himself in a nice beach house with servants. He smiled.

Then he frowned. Yes, he had the solution—but did he have the will to...well, do it?

In his younger days he had been a risk taker, but the risks were always calculated and the reward was always worth the risk. What he was contemplating might not be worth the risk, even with a five-million-dollar reward. But...well, what was the alternative? Poverty. No more nights at Elaine's. Cleaning his own toilet.

In his early writing career he'd written a number of police procedural novels—crime novels—and he'd done a lot of research on the subject of murder. A homicide detective by the name of John Corey had once told him, "*The perfect murder never looks like a murder. It looks like an accident. Right out in the open. And the murderer calls the cops right away. The best accident is the victim falling off a boat. Off the cliff is good, too. Gun went off by accident is a little dicey, but it can work. Everyone knows it wasn't an accident, but how you gonna prove beyond a reasonable doubt that it was murder?*" Corey had added, "*Have a good story and stick to it, and make sure there are no witnesses.*"

Detective Corey had given him some good inside tips on the perfect murder, and Jack remembered all of them and had incorporated some of them into his novels. His fictional detectives always got their man, of course, but Jack had always wanted to write a book where the killer outsmarted the law. "That happens in real life," he assured himself. "Smart killers get away."

A big crow sat on the railing of his deck and stared at him closely, waiting perhaps for him to move off and leave his bowl of peanuts. *The crow*, he thought, *must be a literary agent.* He grabbed a handful of nuts—about 15 percent—and flung them at the big black bird. The crow flew off, then circled back, and landed on the lawn where the nuts had fallen and began pecking at them. "Vulture," Jack said. "Bloodsucking parasite." Which reminded him to call his agent. He pulled his cell phone from his pocket and dialed Stan Wykoff.

Wykoff answered, "Hi, Jack. What's up?"

"Not much. I'm out at the beach, and I thought I'd catch up with my old pal and agent."

"Okay. Well, not much to report."

"How's the deal going with Columbia?"

"The country or the movie studio?"

"The *movie studio*, Stan."

Stan replied, "There is no deal, Jack. Just some interest in *Into the Night*."

"*Into the Dark Waters*."

"Right. They like it. It got good coverage, but—"

"Don't take less than half a mil for a two-year option."

"Let's see if they offer."

"I want points and a screen credit no smaller than the producer's."

"Okay...I'm in the middle of something, Jack. Can I call you back?"

"What are you doing this weekend?"

"I'm not sure."

"Come on out. I have a great place this year. Plenty of room. Pool and tennis court."

"Sounds tempting, but—"

"I'm going to the Southampton Library fund-raiser tomorrow afternoon. Fifty, sixty big authors under the tent, all signing their latest for a good cause. You can poach."

"I don't *poach*, Jack."

"You can make their acquaintance, buy a signed copy of their book, and leave your card on their table. They all hate their agents, anyway."

There was a short silence, then Stan said, "Well..."

"Take the train out. I'll pick you up at East Hampton station, we'll go to The Palm for a few drinks and a steak, then maybe we can prowl. Call me with your ETA."

"Well..."

"I can't promise we'll get laid, but I can promise we'll get drunk. And tomorrow you'll have fifty potential victims under one tent. Plus a cocktail party afterwards with lots of top editors who you'll know. See you later." He hung up.

Jack sat back in his rocker and finished his gin and tonic. *Well,* he thought, *this story is going to have a twist.* Author bites agent. Plus a happy ending. Author keeps a hundred percent of what he makes.

———

Jack met Stan Wykoff at the East Hampton train station, and by 8:30 p.m. they were at the bar in the celeb-studded Palm restaurant. The Palm in Manhattan and the one here in East Hampton were Jack's kind of place: overpriced, which kept the riffraff out, great steaks, Alpha male clientele, waiters who knew who he was, and women who appreciated all of the above. And if things went right this weekend, he could continue to be a regular at both Palms. If things did not go right, he'd be getting his beef at Burger King.

Jack had a scotch and Stan had white wine. Jack chatted up the lady bartender who was young enough to be his daughter. Stan played with his BlackBerry, probably, Jack thought, texting his ex-wife, imploring her to come back. Stan Wykoff was the antithesis of the macho male characters that Jack Henry created in his novels, and the antithesis of Jack Henry himself. And yet, they'd once been friends and still called each other friend. The truth, however, was that they'd grown to dislike each other, and the only bond that remained was professional. And even that had been weakened when they'd stopped making money for each other. It was like a bad marriage—worse, actually, because they both secretly feared they might be worse off without the other. So they continued the charade.

Their table was ready and they sat. Stan had a salad and fish, and Jack had a bloody red steak and more scotch. This, Jack thought, was why he hated Stan Wykoff. The man ate like a bird, drank like a worm, and took care of himself like he was going to live forever. Plus, Stan was cheap and never picked up the tab for anything. Agents were supposed to give back a little of the 15 percent. Like send a limo now and then or maybe buy a goddamn lunch once in a while.

Jack Henry was a generous man, and he had the Amex bills to prove it. Cheap people pissed him off. He wanted to remind Stan that he couldn't take it with him. But he *could* leave five million behind.

They talked about the publishing business, and Jack realized, not for the first time, that Stan Wykoff was not current on the new challenges facing the industry. Nor was he up on any good gossip. In fact, Stan had no clue about what was going on along Publishers Row. Stan did not read the trade journals or online publications or go to seminars or trade fairs or do many lunches with editors. In fact, Stan Wykoff mostly sat in his Upper West Side apartment doing who knew what all day. Meanwhile his midtown agency was run by two clueless, underpaid recent college grads whose most outstanding attributes were their tits. *How*, Jack wondered, *did this guy survive?* Well, partly on his past reputation and mostly on his stable of authors who hadn't fired him yet. In fact, most of his authors lived out of town and weren't around enough to figure out that Stan Wykoff was lazy and out of the loop. The editors knew this, of course, but they liked Stan Wykoff because he never drove a hard bargain. Jack Henry could attest to that.

And to add insult to injury, Stan Wykoff's reputation, such as it was, was enhanced by his being the agent of best-selling author Jack Henry. It occurred to Jack, perhaps because of the alcohol, that *both* their careers and reputations were in decline and that this relationship—symbiotic or parasitic—was no longer working for them. They were both dying. The writer couldn't write, and the agent couldn't agent. And that, Jack knew, was the truth. *In scotcho veritas.*

But one of them could survive if the other was dead. Thanks to the National Life Insurance Company.

The bill came and Jack said, "I'll get it."

"Thanks," Stan replied.

Bastard.

———

STAN DID NOT want to go club hopping, and Jack was just as happy about that. Stan was not a good wingman. In fact, he had a knack for driving the women away, especially when he told them the long, sad story of how his wife had left him for a dweeby college professor—English literature—who she'd met when taking a class at NYU. As Jack liked to tell people, she got an A in the course and Stan got an F.U. Jack had always wanted to use that in a book but thought Stan might be offended.

They drove to Jack's rental house, a big contemporary on Georgica Pond. Jack pulled into the long gravel driveway and said to Stan, "Do me a favor. I like to garage the car. Can you move that bicycle?"

Stan got out of the BMW and walked toward the bicycle that Jack had left in the driveway.

There wasn't another house in sight and no traffic on the dark road. In fact, no witnesses.

Jack put one foot on the brake and pressed slightly on the accelerator. The engine revved, and the car strained forward.

*Do it! Now!*

Just as Jack was about to hit the gas and release the brake, a thought flashed into his mind. *What if the impact doesn't kill Stan?* He'd have to back up and run him over again. Then he'd have a lot of explaining to do to the cops: *Well, Officer, I... I don't know why I backed up and ran him over again. I was distraught.*

*Do it!*

Jack realized he was pressing harder on the brake and the accelerator, and the engine was roaring.

Stan turned and looked back at the car, and Jack saw him staring at him like that proverbial deer caught in the headlights.

Jack slumped in his seat and took his feet off the pedals.

Stan hesitated, then wheeled the bicycle onto the grass.

Jack pressed the remote and the garage door lifted—revealing a garage filled with sporting equipment, bicycles, storage boxes, and other junk. Not much room for a car.

Stan stared into the garage, then turned and looked back at the BMW.

Jack took a deep breath, killed the lights and the engine, and got out of the car, forcing a smile as he walked up the driveway. He glanced into the garage and said to Stan, "I thought I cleaned this out."

Stan didn't reply. They made eye contact in the dim light of the lamppost. Jack forced another smile and said, "Too much to drink."

Stan walked back to the car, retrieved his suitcase, and both men entered the house.

It occurred to Jack that this would have been far from the perfect crime. His enthusiasm was interfering with his judgment. He wouldn't write a scene with so many illogical mistakes. And if he did, he could write it over again. But in real life—real murder—there were no rewrites. *You get one shot at this, Jack. If you get it right, you get five million; if you get it wrong, you get twenty years to life.*

He noticed that Stan was standing in the middle of the living room, looking at him. Stan seemed to be disturbed about something. *In fact,* Jack thought, *Stan, who was not usually a very imaginative man, may have imagined that his author was trying to kill him.* Not good.

Jack smiled widely and waved his arms to encompass the big

cathedral-ceilinged room, saying, "Isn't this a great place? Boy, I could get some good writing done here. You gotta come out for a few weeks. You work too hard, buddy. I want to run a few proposals by you. We'll sit by the pool. Tennis in the morning. Hey, I have a bottle of Chateau Montelena in the wine cooler. How 'bout a nightcap?"

Stan replied, "Where's my room?"

Jack maintained his smile and good cheer and replied, "Terrific room. Overlooking the pond."

He carried his agent's suitcase up the stairs and showed him to a big guest room, saying, "If you need anything, I'll be out on the back deck."

Jack went downstairs and poured himself a scotch from the bar, then went out through the sliding glass doors to the deck and collapsed into a chaise lounge.

Stan definitely looked a bit...troubled, but Jack was sure that Stan would conclude that he had misinterpreted what happened in the driveway. Jack was drunk and Stan had also had a few. Plus, Stan was still alive, so that was proof enough that Jack— his author and pal—was not trying to kill him. Jack recalled the night when they had pretended to push each other in front of moving vehicles. Just a little drunken fun. Maybe that's what Stan was thinking now. In fact, maybe that's how Jack should have played it. Well, he couldn't rewrite that, but he could write the next chapter.

He put his creative mind in gear and thought about ways for Stan Wykoff to have an accident.

"*Killing a friend, wife, or acquaintance is easy,*" Detective Corey had told him. "*You have access and trust. What you also need is balls and brains. And a plausible story. You need imagination.*"

"Got all that," Jack said to himself.

Detective Corey had cautioned, however, "*The only thing the cops and the D.A. will have on you is your motive. A strong motive equals a strong presumption of guilt. But motive is not enough to build a case.*" Right. The five million dollars would look like a good motive, but the policy was over ten years old. It wasn't taken out last week. Right?

He felt that he was starting to vacillate. Maybe he was just fantasizing about killing his agent. All authors fantasized about killing their agent. Maybe that's what had happened in the driveway. A half-played-out fantasy.

Jack stared up at the starry sky. This could be his last summer in the Hamptons. His financial future—his entire life—rested entirely on what he did or did not do this weekend. He looked back at the big house and stared at the light in the guest room window; then the light went out.

In the morning, he'd know if Stan had let his imagination run wild—especially if Stan called a taxi to take him to the train station. But if everything seemed okay, then Jack would suggest taking the boat out for some ocean fishing.

———

THE MORNING DAWNED bright and sunny. Good boating weather. "Good day to drown my agent."

Jack got out of bed and headed for the bathroom. Little Scotsmen were playing bagpipes in his head and he took an aspirin, then washed up while he listened to the maritime weather channel. Seas were calm with one- to two-foot waves; winds were from the south at three to four miles per hour. Perfect day to take the twenty-eight-foot Sea Ray out on the ocean. Five miles should do it. In fact, since Stan Wykoff couldn't swim, five feet should do it. But he needed to be away from witnesses. Five miles.

Jack slipped on a ratty flannel bathrobe over his boxer shorts and went downstairs.

He found Stan in the kitchen, already up and about, having a cup of coffee and reading the *New York Times*, which was delivered each weekend morning.

Stan glanced up from his newspaper, and Jack greeted him with a smile and a hearty good morning. He inquired of his houseguest, "Did you sleep well?"

"Yes, thank you."

Jack thought Stan seemed subdued, but he wasn't dressed, packed, and waiting outside for a cab. So, as Jack had hoped, Stan had forgotten or dismissed the driveway incident. People rarely took that long leap from suspicion to absolute belief—from reasonable doubt to conviction. That was why juries returned verdicts of not guilty and why murder victims rarely saw it coming.

Stan was wearing stupid yellow pajamas—silk or synthetic—with idiotic bears on them. Probably a gift from his wife. Jack hated men who wore pajamas. And open-toed slippers. *Wimp.*

Jack poured himself a cup of coffee and noticed that Stan had found a frying pan and had scrambled some eggs in a bowl, and he'd also found some chives in the kitchen garden. Stan was one of those men who liked to cook. Jack disliked men who liked to cook. Skinny men, like Stan, who sliced and diced and made horrible healthy things to eat. The only green thing in Jack's refrigerator was the mold on the cheddar cheese.

Jack sat at the round table and sipped his coffee. He asked Stan, "Is this decaf?"

"Yes."

*That*, Jack decided, *is a capital offense punishable by drowning.*

The Saturday *Times* had the Sunday Book Review section included, and Jack picked it up from the table and flipped through it. None of the ads for other authors' books included a blurb from Jack Henry, and he realized he hadn't been asked for a blurb in almost a year. He noticed, too, that many of the reviews were of novels by hot new authors who Jack considered terminally cool or effete or just plain incomprehensible. But the *Times* loved them for "taking chances" or "making us rethink how we see the world" or some other cliché. Bottom line, the culture had changed, and Jack Henry's fictional heroes—men who were men and women who were women—were no longer in fashion. In fact, his career was in a death spiral.

Stan put down his paper and asked, "Would you like an omelet?"

"Sure."

Stan went to the stove and began puttering. Maybe Stan should write a cookbook, Jack thought. *Cooking for Lonely Losers.*

Stan was now pouring some liquids into the blender—orange juice, apple juice, milk—plus ice cubes and a powdery nutritional supplement from a can.

Jack said, "We don't have to be at the Southampton book signing until three. I want to take you fishing this morning. This house came with a twenty-eight-foot Sea Ray."

Stan flipped the omelet. "All right."

Jack had thought Stan might find a reason not to go out in the boat, but Stan was making it easy for him.

Georgica Pond was actually a tidal basin with an inlet that went out to the Atlantic Ocean, and he'd tell Stan they were going for big game fish. *Maybe,* he thought, *I'll also chum for shark, and Stan will be the chum.* But maybe a shark wouldn't eat Stan out of professional courtesy. He smiled.

Stan Wykoff, for all his physical fitness, couldn't swim, as Jack knew. And the life jackets, which should have been aboard in the sea locker, were still stored in the garage, as Jack had discovered last weekend and as Stan would discover if he happened to inquire about a life jacket, which was something prissy Stan might do.

One thing Jack would not forget to bring aboard was binoculars to look for other boats. *Make sure there are no witnesses.*

He thought about his statement to the police: "Well, Officer, I was at the helm with the twin engines roaring, making about forty knots, and Mr. Wykoff was sitting aft—or maybe standing—and a rogue wave hit the port side and the craft rolled, and the bow went up and slammed back into the water. I turned to see if Mr. Wykoff was okay, and...he was gone." Add an appropriate facial expression. No smiling.

There would be questions, of course, and though he was in shock and distraught, he'd do his best to answer. "Yes, of course, I came around, but I didn't see him. No, I don't know if he knew how to swim. Apparently not. And unfortunately, there weren't any life jackets on board. It's not my boat. I circled and called out; then I got on the radio and called the Coast Guard as I continued my search." He'd make sure to add, "This is all in the Coast Guard report." *Word for word with no inconsistencies.*

*Sounds good*, Jack thought. *Tight and to the point. No rewrites necessary. No plot holes. Murder on the high seas. Perfect crime. Just make sure not to mention that I pushed Mr. Wykoff overboard, waved, and yelled, "Fuck you!"* Jack smiled.

Stan put a plate in front of Jack and asked, "What are you smiling about?"

"Oh...I just had a thought about...I forgot."

Stan poured the contents of the blender into two tall glasses and set them on the table. He said, "This will clear your head."

Stan sat and took a long swig of the foamy drink.

Jack sipped it. Not bad. Cold and sweet. He took another drink, then dug into his eggs.

Stan said, "There are actually a few things I wanted to speak to you about."

Jack glanced up from his eggs. "What?"

"Well, your career."

Not Jack's favorite subject, but he was relieved that Stan didn't want to talk about Jack asking him to get out of the car so he could run him over. Jack replied, "I've hit a rough patch." He added, "What I'm working on now is a blockbuster."

Stan reminded him, "You said that about your last two books."

Jack was totally pissed off, but he kept calm. Why argue with a dead man?

Stan assured him, "I'm here to help."

"Good. Go write me a few chapters." He knocked back the rest of the smoothie and finished his eggs.

Stan said to him, "I need to be very frank with you, Jack, and I need you to just listen."

Jack had the feeling that Stan was about to fire him, which, last week, would have been fine with him and would have saved him the trouble of firing Stan. But now, he didn't want any unpleasantness—he wanted to get Stan on that boat. Jack said, "Let's save it for later."

"No. There will be no later."

"Stan—"

"Listen, Jack. We're *both* in trouble." Stan explained, "To be totally honest with you, all my authors are either drunks, senile, lazy, burned-out, talentless hacks, has-beens, dropouts, or pending suicides."

Jack stared at Stan but didn't reply.

Stan continued, "I'm broke and in debt, and I know you are, too."

"I...I'm not..." Suddenly, Jack didn't feel well. His stomach was tightening, and his chest felt heavy.

Stan continued, "We've worked all our lives and now we face poverty, and worse—professional embarrassment and personal humiliation."

Jack tried to reply, but he felt a tightening in his throat.

Stan said, "Don't try to speak. I know it's difficult." He continued, "A few days ago I received a bill in the mail that you also received." He inquired, "Did you see it?"

Jack stared at Stan, but his sight was getting blurry and tears formed in his eyes.

Stan said, "Bills coming in, no money in the bank, and no prospects for the future. It's very frightening. But where there's life, there's hope. Don't you agree? No, don't answer that. It was rhetorical."

Stan finished his smoothie and went on, "So, when I saw the bill...well, you're a bright man, and you have—or once had—a great imagination. So you can imagine what passed through my mind. But then I said to myself, 'No, I can't do that. Jack and I have been through thick and thin together. We go back almost fifteen years.' You were there for me when Cindy left and I liked you for that—even after I heard about that joke you were telling everyone. The one about Cindy getting an A and me getting an F.U." He frowned. "Not funny."

Jack felt his throat constricting, and he tried to stand but fell back into his chair. Heart attack?

Stan glanced at his watch and said, "Just a few more minutes." He let Jack know, "Cindy is considering coming back. Part of our problem was money, but I think I have that straightened out now." He asked, "Isn't that good news? Jack?"

Jack was concentrating on trying to breathe, but it felt like someone was sitting on his chest.

Stan watched him for a few seconds, then said, "Hang on. I'm almost finished." He leaned across the table and continued, "Anyway, as I said, when I saw that life insurance bill, I had a bad thought, an evil thought, and I felt very guilty about it. So, when you invited me here, I thought this would be a good opportunity for us to reconnect. I actually have some good news for you about a movie deal I'm working on for two hundred thousand for one of your older and better books. I was going to tell you about it when we got back here last night." Stan looked at Jack, frowned, and said, "But you tried to kill me."

Jack managed to shake his head.

Stan seemed annoyed and impatient, then snapped, "Well, you

were *thinking* about it. But Mr. Macho got cold feet. Or maybe you realized how stupid your plan was." Stan added, "You're losing your balls *and* your brains."

Jack felt a flood of acid rising in his stomach and he thought he was going to vomit, but nothing came up except a stream of sour-tasting bile that made him gag.

Stan seemed not to notice and said, "So, I thought to myself, if Jack wants to kill me for the insurance money, then maybe I should kill Jack for the same reason." He looked into Jack's eyes and asked, "Do you see my point?"

Jack noticed that the backs of his hands were turning purple and swelling.

Stan noticed, too, and said, "I think you're having an allergic reaction. Like anaphylactic shock. Did you eat something that you're allergic to?"

Jack managed to croak, "You...bastard..."

Stan stood and retrieved the can of nutritional supplement and read the ingredients. "Vitamins...minerals...uh-oh... ground oyster shells." He looked at Jack and asked, "Aren't you allergic to shellfish? Deathly allergic?" He put the can down and gave Jack a look of contrite concern. "Oh, Jack, I'm so sorry. I put this stuff in the omelet, too. Oh, my God, Jack, I think you're going to die." Then he suddenly smiled as though just realizing something and said, "But it's not all bad news. The good news is that I'm going to make five million dollars. That's the best deal we've ever done together."

Jack managed to stand and stagger to a kitchen drawer. He opened it and withdrew an EpiPen filled with adrenaline, the antidote to the deadly allergic reaction.

Stan snatched the device out of Jack's hand and said, "You don't need that. I'll call an ambulance. Right after you stop breathing."

Jack felt his knees buckling and slumped against the counter.

His eyes were so swollen he could barely see, but he did see the chopping board that Stan had used to cut the chives, and on the board was a knife. With all the strength that remained in him, he grabbed the knife with his swollen purple hands and plunged it into Stan's chest.

Stan looked at the knife in disbelief, then staggered back, blood spreading over his yellow silk pajama top.

Jack Henry and Stan Wykoff stood staring at each other; then Jack slumped to the floor, followed by Stan.

They lay side by side on their backs, each of them in respiratory distress—though for different reasons—and each on the verge of cardiac arrest. Jack felt his airway closing and the room was getting dark. Stan's chest wound was bubbling frothy blood, and wheezing sounds came from his mouth.

Jack drew a final gulp of air through his constricting windpipe and got a single word out of his mouth. "Bastard."

Stan felt himself drowning in his own blood but managed to reply, "Has-been."

Both men lay on the cool terra-cotta floor, staring up at the rotating ceiling fan.

Jack's last thought was of a silly cartoon he'd stuck over his desk—horned demons with pitchforks driving a crowd of people through the gates of hell, and there was a sign over the gate that said, "Authors *Must* Be with Their Agents."

# THE PIRATE OF PALM BEACH

## BY TED BELL

**W**ell, Barney, I suppose the Palm Beach Social Season is now officially under way," Charles "Cholly" Forsythe IV said, breaking the staid silence. Observing the harbor through binoculars, Cholly was addressing a small, podgy, and (at best) middle-aged man to his left, both rocking away beneath the paddle fans on the Reading Verandah of the Marlin Club.

Heads swiveled, not because Forsythe's comment was particularly earth-shattering, but because anything one decibel above a whisper was frowned upon. Abuse this rule and expect a black-edged card from the social secretary. Wouldn't be pleasant reading, either.

Ill-behaved members up at the Hobe Sound Club got even more chilling communications. Fall into disfavor there, and you soon discover a discreet white box in your mailbox, containing a black sweater. No note attached because the meaning was clear: the dreaded black sweater meant Mrs. Nathaniel Knickerbocker had decreed you were no longer welcome at the club.

The Marlin Club stood on the island of Palm Beach's northernmost tip, not facing east to the blue sparkle of the Atlantic, but rather west to the placid waters of Lake Worth. Established in 1894, the venerated old club provided docking and harbor facilities, a safe haven for the members' yachts, down from Newport or New York for the Season.

The club's lofty location afforded a crow's-nest view of the comings and goings of the long white yachts steaming into and out of Palm Beach. An ideal spot to keep track of whose yacht was down this year and whose yacht was not. Thus, Forsythe's constant use of binoculars on the verandah.

Cholly Forsythe, you see, kept an eye on things in Palm Beach. In fact, Cholly kept an eye on *everything*. Forsythe was the society editor of the *Palm Beach Breeze*. Had been for years, writing under the nom de plume of Winnie the Pooh. The column was an island institution; most everyone jump-started the day with Cholly's acidic musings before turning to the ho-hum *New York Times*, also known in town as the *Daily Worker*.

Forsythe—a somewhat reptilian, Capote-like figure, sixtyish—wrote with a biting, tongue-in-cheek snobbery that was simply outrageous, but people loved hearing him say in print the very things they fervently wished they could say, or had said themselves at dinner last evening. Victims of Cholly's mighty poison pen had many things to say about him, the kindest of which was, "At least the son of a bitch stabs you in the front."

The Marlin was a fishermen's club, and Cholly did a lot of fishing. But he was a bottom-feeder, his prey salacious tidbits, not the finny denizens of the deep. One of Cholly's early columns had stated that there were only three types of men to be found bellying up to the Marlin's boat-shaped bar of an afternoon: the rich, the famous, or the merely alcoholic. Needless to say, he got the black card.

He also dug for dirt strolling the pristine velvet greens and fairways at the Palmetto Club off Worth Avenue. Also, Mrs. Post's formerly fabled Mar-a-Lago; McCarty's eponymous saloon; and, especially, Taboo, a hot-spot gin joint on Worth where, after hours, the old boys went looking for the young girls and vice versa. Taboo was Palm Beach's very own gossip particle accelerator.

One bright December morning at Taboo, Cholly, brunching alone, heard nature's clarion call. Making his way back to the loo, he heard half the fire trucks and EMS vehicles in town screech to a stop outside, sirens wailing. Firemen and policemen barreled inside, elbowing through the crowded bar. People screamed, thinking the joint was afire.

"Hell's going on?" Cholly asked the barkeep.

"See that woman seated four stools down? In the pink sequined Scaasi halter top?" he said. "You know who she is, don't you?"

"Breathes there a soul on this island who *doesn't*?"

"Well, she's naked."

"*What?*"

"From the waist down. Went to the ladies', took off her skirt and panties, made her way back through the crowd, and now she's perched totally bare assed atop that stool. Ordered another martini, I refused, she made a stink, and I called the cops."

Strapped to a gurney, her modesty covered with a blanket, and with six firemen acting as pallbearers, the smashed socialite sailed out gaily, wishing everyone a Merry Christmas and a Happy New Year.

Winnie knew them all, of course. The truly, the merely, and the nearly rich. The demigods, the semigods, and the gods. The swells and the ne'er-do-wells. The antisocials and social climbers (referred to as "Alpinists" in his column); the poseurs; the pathetic; the penniless European "counts of no account," who drove ancient, monogrammed Rolls-Royces in vile colors up and down the avenue.

He knew, too, the elderly, elegant ladies of old Palm Beach, silently sipping tepid tea behind their thick silk draperies, the Last Victorians, the women who *truly* ruled this roost, but whose names or pictures were never, ever seen in the *Breeze* or anywhere else until the day they died.

"I'm just a hound who loves the smell of bloodlines," Cholly had once said of himself in a Social Diary interview.

Winnie the Pooh's true identity was one of the best-kept secrets on this small, tight-lipped barrier island. Here, family secrets were hidden, nurtured, and protected like hothouse orchids. Secrets existed in great profusion and many of them, thank heaven, followed their keepers into the grave.

But not all.

Occasionally, like naughty faeries on gossamer wings, flitting in tropic breezes, Palm Beach whispers escaped captivity to captivate the nation. Like those awful Kennedy or Pulitzer affairs many, many years ago; those were the explosive national bombshells that gave Cholly his big break in the gossip business.

"Season under way, you say, Cholly? Good lord. You silly ass, it's not even Halloween yet," Barney Dodge whispered, the *Wall Street Journal* spread across his expansive lap.

Dodge, a native of this verdant paradise, who'd sent his kids and grandkids to the Day School, had retired some years ago after a long and distinguished career in the "inheritance business," sometimes referred to sub rosa as the "lucky sperm" club.

As a card-carrying member of the Old Guard, Barney Dodge knew precisely when the hell the damn Season started. And it certainly wasn't a week before Halloween!

"What on earth makes you think the Season has started anyway?" Barney asked Cholly.

"Well, for one thing, my dear boy, take a look at whose yacht just dropped anchor in the middle of our little pond," Cholly said, ordering two more iced mint teas from a hovering waiter.

Dodge raised the binoculars hung round his neck and said, "Well, I'll be damned, Forsythe, you're right for once. He certainly is early this year. Last I heard, he was cruising that beautiful yacht of his off Saint-Tropez with some French starlet or two."

"Hmm."

Two iced teas in chilled glasses with sprigs of mint appeared, the tray set upon the wicker table. Swizzling his drink with the long silver teaspoon, Cholly said, "Is the yacht's notorious owner aboard, Barney? Have another look."

When Dodge raised the binoculars, Cholly, seeing all his fellow readers deeply engrossed, quickly slipped the long thin spoon inside the pocket of his silk jacket. The club's iced-tea spoons were sterling, and Cholly had about twenty of them at home, been taking them for years. Not that anyone noticed this petty thievery. And if anyone ever did, blame would fall upon the help, not the members.

Like a lot of Palm Beachers, Cholly had his own little secret (actually quite a *big* secret) and he guarded it ferociously. At age twelve, Charles Forsythe IV had discovered that he was a raging kleptomaniac. Caught a few times and arrested as a kid, he'd been sent to a psychiatrist and all that foolishness.

But he wouldn't, couldn't stop, and he'd quickly learned how not to get caught. An old bachelor who'd always found sex exceedingly unpleasant, he loved the thrill of his private little game, the *frisson* of pleasure he got from stealing. The delicious, almost erotic secrecy of it all.

And who knew how to keep a secret better? Cholly Forsythe had all the keys to all the closets where all the skeletons on the island were hidden. Tremendous power, he often thought with a shudder of pleasure, sitting by the fire in his small Moorish palace on El Vedado. Because of this treasure trove of intimate knowledge, he had unlimited power over these powerful people, whenever he chose to wield it. The island was littered with the social remains of the once mighty who'd dared to cross swords with Cholly Forsythe.

And most of them never even saw it coming.

Meanwhile, Barney Dodge eyed the newly arrived yacht. The *Narcissus*. A gorgeous black-hulled schooner, she was an annual source of some irritation to Barney. Unlike his own oceangoing behemoth, *Cut Bait*, the *Narcissus* had been designed in the twenties by the famous New England yacht designer John Alden. And she looked the way a yacht ought to look: *Yar.*

He gazed at *Cut Bait*, grimacing. He kept her at the club and lived aboard her year-round. Two crewmen were varnishing her teak rails. Yar? Hardly. What she was, was a giant fiberglass bathtub, designed by Kohler of Wisconsin.

The *Narcissus* was a 130-footer with teak decks, Sitka spruce spars, a gleaming mahogany cabin house, and a lot of history, too. The movie star Errol Flynn had owned her back in the forties.

She was called *Zaca* back then and had been requisitioned by the Navy during World War II. She'd been fitted with antiaircraft machine guns for coastal patrols. After the war, so the story went, Flynn flew to Washington and asked the naval chief of staff if he could keep the machine guns. Request denied.

Aboard *Narcissus*, a buxom blonde in a skimpy thong bathing suit was lounging in the cockpit with the famous yacht's owner, an extraordinarily good-looking, mysterious, and somewhat controversial character with the unlikely name of Blackford Blaine.

"You know everybody in society, Cholly," Barney said. "What's the story with this Blaine character, anyway?"

"Just what everyone else knows. Wealthy Chicago family, meatpacking, like the Swifts and the Armours. St. Paul's. Harvard. Olympic medal for sailing. Got bored making millions on Wall Street and decided to become the playboy of the Western world. Frankly, Dodge, I don't like the cut of Mr. Blackford Blaine's jib. Never have."

"Chicago, huh? That's odd. Harry Fiske once told me he went to kindergarten in Tuxedo Park with a tough little kid named Blackford Blaine."

"Did he now? That *is* odd, Barney," Cholly said, delighted, making a mental note.

———

"LOOK LIVELY ON the foredeck!" the *Narcissus's* owner and skipper shouted to two of his crew, a pair of Dartmouth kids, racing forward to secure the yacht's mooring buoy. "Steady now, lads, ease the main halyard, drop the foresail. Ready about!"

There was a rustle and snap of canvas as both the mainsail and the jib came fluttering down, the mainsail collapsing in a heap on the great wooden boom and the foresail puddling on the foredeck. No longer under sail, the *Narcissus* ghosted to a stop dead abaft of the chosen mooring.

"Nice piece of sailing, Skipper," the leggy blonde said, slathering more sunscreen on her sumptuous pneumatic bosom. Blackie had met this southern belle in Savannah at a swell dinner party given in his honor by Mrs. Georgia Barnwell, one of Blackie's wealthy "benefactors," on his way south. Ended up inviting her aboard for the last leg of the voyage to Palm Beach. A cute little hell-raiser, already married three times, each one richer.

A good girl, though, loads of fun. But a little too hyper. Never seemed to feel the need for sleep. Did the *New York Times* crossword puzzles all night long, scratching away. Middle of the night, she'd shake him awake and say, "Blackie, what's a three-letter word for sex?"

"Sex," he'd reply before rolling over and going back to sleep.

And she was always damnably wide-awake when he roused himself, usually around the crack of ten. Propped up against the pillows, the prow of her magnificent bosom barely obscured by some scanty gown, smoking cigarettes, gulping oceans of black coffee, and constantly underlining things in some kind of book or other.

"Blackie, you finally awake?"

"Yes, my sweet," he replied, raising his crimson silk sleep mask, cracking one eye, silently pressing a button that would bring Naga, his Japanese houseboy, running from the galley with Blackie's daily eye-opener, an elixir known as a Bloody Bullshot. "Breakfast of champions," he called it.

Blackie was no health nut, but he had read somewhere or other that beef bouillon was good for what ails you. Chock-full of vitamins or minerals or something of that nature.

"You drink too much," the kid sniffed as he tipped the cup. He gave her a wink.

"Stopped drinking once, baby. Most boring twelve hours of my life."

"You're funny."

"*Domo arigato*, Naga," Blackie said, draining the potion gratefully and returning the silver julep cup. He looked over at her and said, "Naga here has a great voice, but he only knows one song. Like to hear it?"

"Why, I'd just adore to hear it!" she said with her southern lilt, putting down her book of Tibetan folklore.

"Let 'er rip, Naga," Blackie said.

Naga smiled, puffed himself up and sang.

> *"Hot ginger and dynamite,*
> *There's nothing but that at night,*
> *Back in Nagasaki,*
> *Where the men they chew tabaccy*
> *And the women wicky wacky wooooo . . ."*

"Bravo, Naga!" she cried, clapping her hands as Naga bowed deeply and left the stateroom, pulling the door closed behind him.

"A quiz," she announced a few minutes later. "Which is closer, the moon or London?"

"Haven't a clue, baby. You tell me."

"The moon, silly. You can't even *see* London!"

"Come here and give us a kiss," Blackie said, feeling much restored by the restorative.

"Why should I?"

"This is a love story, baby, you have to say yes."

———

BLACKFORD AVERY BLAINE, or Blackie as everybody (who was anybody) called him, had a way with women. And it wasn't just his money, his yacht, his broad shoulders, or his dashing good looks and flashing white grin, either.

Last year a cute reporter from *Vanity Fair* had been assigned to follow him around New York for a few days and then write an article about him. Blackie knew she was digging for dirt, and he'd decided to dish out a little here and there, just to keep things lively.

She asked him what he thought about older men and younger women. Blackie pretended to think.

"Let me put it this way, honey. My next wife hasn't even been born yet."

"Good one," she said, jotting it down. "Could you explain your much-vaunted success with the opposite sex, here in New York and abroad?"

He considered.

"Well, you see, kid, it's like this. Most rakes can have a strong effect on certain women," he'd said earnestly. "That's because when a guy like me falls in love, even for that brief period, he gives himself over to the woman in a certain manner, a *complete* one, one that is very rare for a man. And this, I've found, is devastatingly seductive."

Shortly after the *Narcissus* was successfully moored, a uniformed member of the crew appeared from below, carrying an overstuffed Louis Vuitton duffel bag. He went to the rail and handed the bag down to a crewman waiting in a Zodiac tender, recently arrived along the yacht's port side.

"Oh!" the blonde cried upon seeing her luggage departing without her. "Am I leaving so soon?"

"I'm afraid so, sweetheart. Terribly sorry, but it can't be helped.

My dear mother lives here in Palm Beach, and she's terribly ill. Conjunctivitis. I've asked her to come stay aboard the *Narcissus* so I can look after her. Won't be with us long, poor dear."

"Conjuncti-whatever. Is that fatal?"

"Acute conjunctivitis? Oh, yes. Always."

"I'm so sorry, Blackie. Must be very hard on you," she said and made wriggling into a pink and green Lilly Pulitzer shift some kind of erogenous hula dance.

"Ah, well, as the poet says, 'For in that sleep of death, what dreams may come when we have shuffled off this mortal coil.' With me on that one, sweet potato?"

"Huh?"

"Look here, one of the lads will zip you over to the yacht club docks in the Zodiac. My chauffeur Wolfgang's waiting there, take you anywhere at all. Rolls Corniche convertible. White. Can't miss it."

"You're a sweet guy, Blackie, you know that?"

"You're not so bad yourself, kid. Maybe I'll see you around sometime."

"Gee, that would be swell." She gave him a peck on the cheek before boarding the waiting tender.

"Know an eight-letter word for good-bye?" she said as she stepped down into the gently bobbing Zodiac, the crewman holding her hand.

"Farewell?" Blackie said.

She laughed, and the Zodiac roared away, throwing a wide white wake to either side.

———

A FEW DAYS later, Blackie Blaine pedaled his bike down the flower-bordered Lake Trail, south to the western end of Worth Avenue. His PB attire consisted of a long-sleeved navy blue shirt of Sea Island cotton, pleated white flannel trousers, and a pair of scuffed white bucks, no socks. Socks, Blackie had learned the hard way, were anathema on this island. A tourist might as well put a pair of fake antlers on his head as stroll down Worth Avenue wearing socks.

He slowed at a discreet arched entrance to the island's oldest golf club. No signs even indicated the club's existence. The Palmetto Club's uniformed sentries stood up as Blackie wheeled under the Moorish arch and into the club designed by the island's first architectural genius, Addison Mizner.

"Afternoon, Mr. Blaine." The boys all smiled. "Welcome back."

"How's it going, fellas? Good to see ya," Blackie said. He biked to a stand of trees next to the croquet lawns and dismounted, leaning his bike up against the trunk of a huge jacaranda, the ground covered with its purple petals. Then he sauntered back to the Avenue.

He was well-known at the club, a good single-digit handicap golfer; a member in good standing, as they say. So the ensuing exclamations of "Hiya, Blackie, good summer?" and "Oh, Blackie! I'm having the most divine dinner party Friday and you absolutely must come!" were met with his wide grin and a hearty "You betcha, kid!" barely breaking his stride. Again the young men seated to either side leaped up, a tradition accorded to all members.

"No need to salute, gentlemen," Blackie said to the boys, sounding like a rear admiral. "I'll be on the bridge for the remainder of the afternoon."

The kids were still laughing when he stepped out onto that shining sunlit street of dreams so appropriately called Worth.

First stop, Tiffany's.

Blackie, let it be said, loved jewelry. Had loved it since the day, as a boy of about ten, he'd accidentally witnessed his mother examining a magnificent diamond bracelet his dad had purchased from some man in New York named Harry Winston. His father, who worked on Wall Street, took the train out every evening to their home in Tuxedo Park.

Lingering in the shadows, he saw his mother go into her

walk-in closet, stand on her tiptoes, and deposit the glittering bracelet inside one of her countless pairs of high-heeled shoes. Hiding it, the boy figured, from all the burglars out there, thieves in the night, second-story men, boogeymen, and the like. Blackie was still of an age where he looked in his closet and peeked under his bed before tucking in every night.

"Now you listen to Mamie and behave yourself, Blackie Blaine. No more shenanigans. Your father and I will be home around nine or ten. You'd better be sound asleep, do you hear me?"

She bent over and kissed him on the cheek, then walked out of her dressing room, a little gold evening bag swinging from her shoulder. Downstairs, his father was waiting in his favorite chair, sipping a whiskey sour, reading the day's *Wall Street Journal*.

The shoes were up on the highest shelf, and he had to shove the round satin stool at her mirror-topped vanity into her closet in order to reach them.

He was always afraid of getting caught, surprised by his mother. She was unaware that she'd been observed hiding the bracelet. But fear of discovery—well, that just added to the fun. He'd take the shoe, the left one, off the shelf and shake it to make sure she hadn't moved the bracelet to a new shoe.

Then he'd climb down off the stool and take the prized object over to a nearby window where sunlight was streaming in. Turning it over and over in his hand, the brilliant, many-faceted stones caught fire, igniting his imagination and sealing his fate.

———

BLACKIE STROLLED INTO Tiffany's, winking at all the pretty young things behind the glass counters who smiled in recognition. He was hardly Tiffany's biggest or best customer, but Blackie spent time in jewelry stores the way some men go to Ferrari or Porsche dealerships on Saturday mornings. They seldom buy, but how they do love to kick those tires.

"Look out, girls, Blackie's back in town!" he said, headed to the rear of the store.

"Mr. Blaine! What a surprise!" the petite and not unattractive manager, Caroline Biddle, said, rising from behind her mahogany desk and offering him her hand.

"Miss Biddle," Blackie said, bowing slightly from the waist. "It seems I require your services." He bent forward and gave her a peck on the cheek, which made it turn bright red. The thing was, he'd asked her to dinner at Renato's one night years ago, mainly to talk jewelry. She'd gotten the wrong impression that evening and never quite got over it.

"Buying or selling, Mr. Blaine?"

"Buying."

"We don't usually see you here this early in the season."

"Got run out of Newport on a rail, I'm afraid. Tarred and feathered and one step ahead of the sheriff."

She smiled. "Nothing's changed. What can we do for you?"

"Want to buy a present. An old friend is throwing a big shindig in my honor at her home tomorrow night. Like to get her a little something."

"Not Mrs. Guest's party at Casa Cielito Lindo?"

"Now, how would you know about that?"

"Winnie the Pooh was gushing about it this morning. 'Kick-starting the Season at Cielito Lindo.' The column said the Donald and Melania are even flying in from New York."

"And who are they again?"

She laughed. "So, Mr. Blaine? Necklace? Bracelet, earrings, a beautiful brooch, perhaps?"

"Earrings. Betty does love diamond earrings."

"She certainly does. And lucky to have a husband as generous as Mr. Guest, as you well know. Let's go take a look," she said, leading the way to the private paneled room where they brought out the heavy artillery. It looked like a little French sitting room with a kidney-shaped walnut desk in the center of the room, and three spindly gilded chairs pulled up to it.

"Have a seat and I'll be right back. Something to drink? Fiji water? A glass of champagne?"

"I'm fine, thanks."

Blackie felt silly sitting all alone on the poofty little gold chair, but what the hell was a guy supposed to do? Business is business. And, technically anyway, Blackford Blaine *was* in the jewelry business.

Returning with a large rectangular box covered in black velvet, she took the single chair opposite Blackie, used a key, and lifted the lid.

"What do we have here? Oh, these are pretty." She held up a pair of earrings that looked like two large diamond chandeliers. Blackie examined one under the halogen lighting.

"You think she'd like these?"

"Any woman would. I warn you, Mr. Blaine, they are quite expensive."

"Really? What's the most expensive pair you have?"

"Well, that would be Tiffany's Extraordinary Diamond Drop earrings, pear shaped and set in platinum. Aren't they lovely? E-Flawless. They weigh in at 30.1 carats together. Do you want the good news or the bad news, Mr. Blaine?"

"Let's get the bad out of the way," Blackie said, picking one up and examining it carefully.

"The cost of these earrings is well in excess of one million dollars."

"And the good news?"

"Mr. Guest gave his wife these exact earrings for their twentieth wedding anniversary just last month."

"Darn the luck!"

"Sorry."

"I'm not. How much are these diamond studs?"

"Those are twenty-five thousand, Mr. Blaine."

"I'll take those, I think."

"Perfect for daytime wear. Shall I have them gift wrapped?"

"Please. I've got to make a few more stops along the avenue. Say, half an hour?"

"Delighted, Mr. Blaine."

———

BLACKIE SPENT THE afternoon hitting balls on the Palmetto Club's driving range. When the sun got so low he couldn't see where his drives were going, he biked over to Michael McCarty's joint. An old-fashioned saloon for regular guys who never asked about your kids or where you'd "summered." Good steaks, too, and he joined a couple of pals for a late dinner before heading back to the *Narcissus* around midnight.

Blackie wheeled his slightly wobbly bike into the deserted parking lot at the Marlin Club. Couple of lights still on, only one or two cars parked under the trees. He walked to the seawall, paused a moment to enjoy the sight of the *Narcissus* riding the swells, her masthead light twinkling, towering above the smaller yachts in the harbor. Just another beautiful night in Paradise.

The moon threw a ghostly road across the water. Times like these, under the tropic stars with the soft rustle of wind in the palms, he would come close to serenity. Times when he'd think, *You made it, kid. Had to crawl across a thousand miles of broken glass to get here, but by God, you made it.*

He shook out a cigarette and lit up.

He heard a noise to his left, a grunt, and looked over to see a very heavy man on his hands and knees, crawling around the rear of an old Bentley, which was parked along the seawall, peering underneath it. The car was as black as the shadows; he hadn't even noticed it.

Blackie flicked his smoke into the water and strolled over.

"Need a hand? What seems to be the problem?"

"Lost my damn car keys. Sure I had 'em in my pocket. Must a dropped 'em. Damn, these pebbles hurt!"

"Let me take a look. Got a handy-dandy little flashlight on my key chain."

He went around to the side of the car, dropped easily to the ground, swinging the beam from side to side. "There they are. Right beyond the rear axle."

"Yeah, yeah, I see 'em but I can't—damn it—slide under there to—"

"Don't worry, pal, I'll slip under there for you."

Blackie stretched out, snatched the keys, got to his feet, and dropped them into the man's hand.

"Awfully sporting. But, look, you got your white trousers filthy. Least I can do, send 'em to the—"

"Buy me a nightcap, and we're square."

"A drink. Splendid idea."

Weaving a little bit, the grossly overweight man climbed the steps leading from the docks up to the bar with Blackie right behind him, ready to catch him if he stumbled. Guy'd had a snootful.

The man collapsed in a chair, saying, "Bes' table weren't for that damn plug ugly *Cut Bait* blocking half the view."

"What'll you have?" Blackie asked, walking toward the bar.

"Brandy. Jus' put it on my account."

The bartender, glad to see Blackie, said, "Yes, sir, Mr. Blaine. Last call, though." Back in his sportfishing days, Blackie had won the Rybovich Cup for the biggest blue marlin caught since the late fifties. The large silver trophy stood on the mantel in the Members' Room, and the record still stood, too, with Blackie's name on it. The Rybo, they called the old cup.

Blackie got a beer and a brandy and sat down opposite the bleary-eyed fat man. He'd seen him around the club over the years but had never felt any overwhelming desire to meet him.

The fellow took a swig, then shot his hand out across the table. Blackie shook it, meaty and damp as cold ham.

Staring at Blaine from beneath heavily lidded eyes, glassy in the light of the red ship's lantern flickering on the table, he said, "You look vaguely familiar, sir. I'm Cholly Forsythe."

"Blackford Blaine."

Forsythe dropped Blackie's hand almost as fast as the smile dropped from his jowly red face.

"Blaine, huh?" he said. "Well, well, well."

"Something wrong?"

"I'll say."

"What?"

"You."

"Sorry?"

"I look into things. Recently, I've been looking into you, Mr. Blaine, into your shadowy, wholly invented past. Google, you know. A phony bum like you cannot hide from Google. Sources of mine 'round the country, too. A few phone calls. Universities, the Racquet & Tennis, other clubs in New York and Long Island. The IOOC in Geneva, et cetera. No Blackford Blaine anywhere. All is not as it appears, is it?"

"A parallel universe, perhaps?"

"A fake and a *liar*," he hissed wetly, his protuberant Hitchcockian lips quivering. "Your kind come down here all the time. Common as dirt. Lowlife poseurs playing at a gentleman's game. Seducing the innocent, young and old, living off their kindness. But we always uncover you; lift enough rocks and we find you."

Blackie was slow to anger, but he was starting to seethe. "What's your name again, pal?"

"Forsythe."

"You're drunk, Forsythe, or I'd ask you to step outside."

"Les' see," the fat man said, ticking off the items with his stubby little sausage fingers. "St. Paul's? Hmm. No record. Harvard grad?

No Blackford Blaine in the graduating class of seventy-nine. Racquet Club in New York? Never heard of you. Odd. Nor has the On-on—wensh—"

"Onwentsia Club?"

"Onwen-sha-ma-call-it Club in Lake Forest, any membership record of the much vaunted Blaine family. Was a Blaine from Tuxedo Park, I discovered. A partner at Dillon, Read & Co. Jumped out a window on the thirtieth floor after millions went missing. Your esteemed father, I take it, the noted embezzler?"

The words were razors through raw nerves. His father's tragic death had wiped out his family, caused Blackie to drop out of Harvard, to take a job to support his devastated mother and his siblings.

Blackie stood up, reached across the table with his right hand, and grabbed Forsythe's shirtfront, lifting him straight up six inches, like a doll out of its high chair.

"The hell do you want, you ugly son of a bitch?"

"Only the satisfaction of seeing you squirm when your sordid little tale appears in the local papers."

"Guys like you make a whole lot of enemies, I'm sure. But remember this, Forsythe. I'll be the very worst one you've *ever* made."

"Don't you dare threaten me. You can't afford the publicity, Blaine. B'lieve me."

"Good night, Forsythe. Do your worst."

"No worries about *that*," Forsythe sneered, a strangled laugh in his voice, throwing back his brandy. Like any serial killer, he loved closing in for the kill.

Blackie dropped him like a sack of manure and strode out into the moonlight, taking a calming breath of fresh air. Walking down to the floating dock, he saw the Zodiac where he'd left it that morning. He stepped under a dock light and lit a smoke, leaning against the pole.

His chest was heaving with anger. He didn't give a hoot in

hell about the rumors, stories, and myths that had attached themselves to him over the years. True or false, he'd heard them all. But to survive, he depended on those myths for access to the world in which he operated. To sue some fat snob for libel in the local courthouse would be bad for business.

He must have stood for a few moments, the wind slapping the halyards about in the rigging of the sailboats, when he heard the door to the bar slam open. Stepping into the shadows, he saw the silhouetted figure of his new pal, Cholly Forsythe, swaying precariously at the top of the steps. If Cholly saw Blackie, he gave no hint of it. He had a large object in his hands, and as he staggered down the steps, Blackie saw that it was a large silver trophy. Not just any trophy, either.

The Rybo.

The man giggled childishly as he tiptoed across the manicured lawn bordering the parking lot. He made his way to his Bentley, set the trophy down, and popped the trunk. Tossing the trophy inside, he slammed the lid, got into his car, and sped crazily away into the tropical night.

———

THE ENTRANCE TO Cielito Lindo on Billionaire's Row, overlooking the Atlantic, resembled the famous arch at Paramount Pictures in Hollywood, but more elegant. Wolfgang steered the white Rolls through an army of valets busily parking cars for those without chauffeurs and stopped under the porte cochere. Blackie climbed out and smiled. Some joint.

The Ivor Guest residence, at some forty thousand square feet, wasn't anywhere near the largest on the beach. Still, Blackie always thought it looked like some fabulous Mediterranean hotel set amid a gorgeous jungle.

Blackie took a flute of champagne from a bare-chested waiter in a traditional Hawaiian *malo*, or loincloth, who looped a lei of pungent white flowers around his neck. Then he made his way through a high hallway with a frosted wedding cake ceiling, past endless rooms that seemed to bloom with rosy light. Reaching the loggia with arches opening onto the gardens and the gleaming sea beyond, he headed outside in search of his hostess.

———

THE TERRACED GARDENS below were a wonderland of Japanese lanterns, reflected in many illuminated pools and cascading fountains. He leaned against the marble balustrade and took in the lovely vista, which included in its sweep acres of tropical jungle; a sunken Italian garden; a half acre of deep, pungent roses; and the silvery ocean sliding off to the deep blue horizon. Somewhere hidden in the gardens, a full Hawaiian orchestra was tuning up. Blackie smiled. He and Betty Guest had first met at the Surf Rider Club in Honolulu twenty years ago.

He found his old friend standing near a bush of flaming hibiscus, the silver sequins of her gown flickering in the lantern light, the fascinating planes of her face reflecting the soft glow. Betty Guest had at one point been on the cover of every fashion magazine in London, New York, and Paris. Now in her sixties, she was still alluring, flirtatious, and gracious to a fault.

Betty had been the first of Blackie's "benefactors," as he called them. Over the years, the number had grown. Beautiful women, extremely wealthy and extremely lonely, who enjoyed Blackie's company, even for a brief while. Women who were always happy to see the black-hulled *Narcissus* sail into Newport, Martha's Vineyard, the Hamptons, and other ports of call from Hilton Head to Key West.

After Palm Beach, the *Narcissus*'s next port was the Lyford Cay Club in Nassau; then she'd sail the eastern coast of South America, making calls at Buenos Aires and Rio. A combination of shrewd investments and the generous donations of these wonderful, extremely grateful gals kept Blackie living the lifestyle to which he'd become happily accustomed. The fact was, he truly loved them all. And they all loved him.

Betty opened her arms and embraced him.

"Oh, Blackie, darling, how are you? It's been ages! You look divine, of course, no one does more for black tie than you do."

"Betty, it's awfully nice of you to do this. . . . You look positively gorgeous by the way. And the house, the flowers, it's really a bit ritzy for an old beach bum like me."

"No date tonight?"

"Guests of the Guests may not bring guests, remember?"

She laughed at their old joke and took his arm.

"Before this turns into an absolute mob scene, let me take you around and introduce you to some wonderful new people. Do you need another drink? You might."

"Probably. But first, I wanted to give you this," he said, handing her the small robin's egg blue box.

"Now, Blackie, you know you're not supposed to— Oh, darling, they're exquisite, that is so sweet, I can't begin to tell you. Every time I wear them I'll remind myself that Blackie is a girl's best friend."

"Not every girl, Betty, just you."

"I bet you say that to all the girls."

"Matter of fact, I do."

She laughed at his honesty. Since Blackie had always been completely honest with all his benefactors, none of them had ever had cause for jealousy.

"One dance, Blackie? For old times' sake? Sounds like the Honolulu Hepcats are in full swing." They set off, arm in arm, through the lush gardens.

———

LATER, WHEN BLACKIE made his way to the main house, it seemed to have swollen with humanity. Laughter bubbling with champagne; groups forming and re-forming, swelling and shrinking with arrivals and departures; a constant social diaspora as natural and regular at parties in this town as breathing rarefied air.

"Excuse me," Blackie said to a young white-jacketed houseman. "Both of the bathrooms seem to be occupied, and I've a bit of an emergency."

"Not at all, sir. Just use that main staircase to the second floor, take a right, and use any of the facilities in any of the guest rooms along that hallway."

"Great, thanks."

It was the work of a minute to find himself in the tower suite dressing room of Mrs. Ivor Guest. On her glass vanity stood a miniature mirrored chest of drawers. Sitting on the small satin stool, he carefully went through each velvet-lined drawer until he found what he was looking for. Yes. The glorious Diamond Drop earrings Ivor had bought Betty for their anniversary.

He picked them up, looked lovingly at the pair of them. A million dollars right there in the palm of his hand. But he put one back into the drawer, and slipped the other into the side pocket of his tuxedo trousers. He slid the drawer closed, winked at himself in the silver-framed vanity mirror, and returned to the fray downstairs in time for dinner, feeling much better about his immediate prospects.

———

As GUEST OF honor, he was seated to Mrs. Guest's right. Twenty tables of ten were scattered throughout the gardens. Directly opposite him sat Mr. Charles Forsythe, swilling champagne. Blackie took no end of delight in the man's obvious discomfort, seething at seeing Blackie toasted by Mrs. Guest and many others in the most fawning terms.

At one point, Betty passed him a note below the table. He was just able to read it in the flickering candlelight, holding it in his lap.

*Darling, I've been waiting so long. Please meet me in the pool house by the Venetian Grotto at eleven. I'll be waiting....*

The table was set with blue and white china once used at Peterhof, Peter the Great's Russian summer palace. And then the gleaming golden vermeil tableware. Blackie had seldom seen true vermeil used anywhere in America except the White House. Vermeil flatware is made of sterling silver covered in 14 karat gold and is very hard to come by.

As dinner ended, Blackie clinked his wineglass and stood to thank his hostess, saying, "When one looks back upon another star-studded season in Palm Beach, they shall remember this one brilliant night and our lovely hostess, someone whose radiance outshines the brightest of stars above. On behalf of all your countless friends, Betty, I raise my glass to your charm, your beauty, and your inimitable style...."

There were resounding "Hear, hears!" from every corner of the garden, and Mrs. Guest's eyelashes fluttered as she raised her glass to her guest of honor, her brown eyes never leaving the face of Blackford Blaine, the only man she'd ever loved.

Blackie started to sit, paused, and said, "Oh, and one more thing before I shut up." His blue eyes lasered on Cholly. "Do try to refrain from stealing the spoons, Mr. Forsythe. Be a good boy and put them back, won't you?"

———

TWO HOURS LATER, only a few hardcore guests remained. Mr. and Mrs. Ivor Guest had long slipped upstairs and were preparing for bed when Mrs. Guest uttered a sharp cry. She was at her vanity, pawing frantically through her jewelry drawers.

"What is it, dear?" Ivor said, buttoning his silk pajamas.

"The Diamond Drop earrings! Our anniversary! Please call the police, Ivor. They've been stolen!"

"Stolen?"

"Well, one of them, anyway."

"*One* of them?"

"Yes."

"Betty, darling, please. You must have lost one or misplaced it. Nobody steals just one earring."

"I did not!"

"You simply cannot call the police and tell them that a thief, upon discovering a pair of million-dollar earrings, has stolen just one."

"And why not?"

"And deliberately left behind a half million dollars? I wouldn't buy it, and the police certainly won't buy it."

"What shall I do?"

"I'll buy the match, pet."

"Would you really, dearest?"

"Of course. Now, out with the lights. It's time for bed."

Betty reached up and turned out the bedside lamp. Her weary head against the pillow, she looked over at her gently snoring husband and smiled. Her beloved would return to the *Narcissus* tonight, half a million dollars richer. She'd have her favorite earrings back. And sweet Ivor? Well, husband number four wasn't getting any younger. Maybe one day—

———

THE AFFAIR WAS long over, the tables and chairs packed away, when the hardcore party boys moved to the beach terrace for stogies and brandy. Blackie saw Pete Benchley standing alone, puffing away, and gazing out to sea. President of the Marlin Club, Pete was Blackie's oldest fishing buddy and he said hello. Benchley offered Blackie a Montecristo Torpedo, held a lighter to it, and the two men caught up quickly.

"Well, Blackie, you won't believe what the hell has happened at the club. Simply unbelievable."

"Try me," Blackie said.

———

TEN MINUTES LATER, Benchley found Cholly Forsythe standing at the beach bar, uproariously drunk like everyone else. Pete took the man's elbow and leaned in toward his ear.

"Got a minute, Cholly? How 'bout a little stroll down the beach?"

"Sure! Cigar?"

"Got one going," Pete said, puffing.

After a hundred yards or so on the hard-packed sand, Pete stopped and looked Forsythe in the eye.

"Cholly, you don't have anything at home that doesn't belong to you, do you?"

"What? Of course not! What are you talking about?"

"I'm talking about the Rybovich Cup, Cholly. The Rybo, the trophy you stole last night."

"Me? Preposterous! How dare you accuse me of *stealing*! Really, Benchley, you are way out of line. Don't care who you are, nobody gets away with speaking to me—why, I'll—"

"Someone saw you do it, Cholly. Eyewitness."

"Who? Lying son of a bitch. Why—"

Benchley sighed and looked out to sea, no longer able to stand the sight of this wretched man.

"Two options, Cholly," he said. "I can call the police right now, have them get a warrant to search your house. Or the club's service door can be left open tonight, and you can sneak in and put the damn trophy back where it belongs. This is a onetime offer. Do the right thing, and in light of our family's long friendship, not to mention the enormous embarrassment this would cause you in town, I'll keep this between us. Otherwise—"

Forsythe was staggered.

"Don't know what came over me, Pete. Only had a few pops, ran into that phony bastard Blackie Blaine, and suddenly the idea of our trophy sitting up there with his name on it just made me crazy, y'know?"

"No, I don't know. I saw him catch the fish."

"Can you just tell me who told you? I'd like to apologize to them, too. Keep it under the rug, you know, hush-hush, for the good of the club."

"You know I can't tell you that."

"Barney Dodge, right? *Cut Bait* moored right off the damn bar, sits up on deck drinking half the night. Had to be—"

"Doesn't matter who it was, Cholly. But I will tell you something he mentioned to me."

"Yes?"

"He said, and I quote, 'Tell Forsythe this: If he never wants to see Winnie the Pooh's multiple arrest records for robbery in Duckbill, Alabama, in the newspapers, he'll keep his fat mouth shut and mind his own business from now on. Period.'"

Pete Benchley turned away from the simpering, nearly blubbering Forsythe in utter disgust and walked back toward the brilliant glow of the gardens and the rhythm of ukeleles rising into the sapphire sky above the eternal sparkle of Palm Beach.

What a town.

# THANK GOD FOR CHARLIE

## BY PETER BLAUNER

E very time she looked in the mirror now, it felt like faith had been broken and the terms of a contract had been violated.

She had always been the pretty girl, getting all the attention whenever she walked in a room. Kindergarten teachers, high school quarterbacks, feminist art critics, and presidential candidates had nodded, openmouthed and glassy-eyed, at her most trivial utterances and shallow insights. But at fifty-eight, the game was ending. The closing studio gates had left lines on her face, and chemo had taken her hair a few years back. What grew back was silver and coarse; even with tinting and highlights, most dye went on like furniture shellac these days. The knowledge of how things could go wrong had pushed her eyes deep into her head, creating a slight shadow under her brow that chemical peels and Botox could not lighten, and though she tried to tell herself sometimes that maturity could give a woman character, all it took was a few steps down Madison and a young man's glance straying over her shoulder to remind her that her powers had been diminished.

Thank God for Charlie. If it wasn't for him, she might have been tossed out of her East Side sublet months ago, residuals from the old TV shows dwindling even as her ex-husband, "the talent manager," accumulated more and younger ex-wives and had to dice alimony payments into ever-shrinking slices. But Charlie, with his graying comb-over, his bridge-and-tunnel accent, and his bulky shapeless sweaters, had become her rescuer, helping with the rent and groceries, taking her out to dinner, even arranging limos to bring her to her doctors' appointments. Charlie who never had a date in high school and had spent the years when she was in Laurel Canyon collecting favors from the clubhouse politicians and local fixers in southeastern Queens. Charlie with his grubby job soliciting investments from union pension funds, his frumpy wife in Jamaica Estates dragging her feet about the divorce, and his three spoiled kids begrudging their hardworking father every moment of joy in his life. Charlie who treated her like she was still a slim-hipped, gossamer-haired prime time princess, the Undercover Co-Ed brandishing a fake Beretta and a golden thigh on the cover of *TV Guide*, and not just a washed-up starlet living in obscurity among the retired garmentos and aging Poodle Ladies on First Avenue.

Yes, sometimes it seemed wrong that she had to spread herself like a stunned chinchilla under his girth and endure his chemically invigorated exertions. But when he'd make an omelet for her afterward and serve it to her with a vitamin supplement and orange juice while they watched some old Ingrid Bergman movie on cable, her skin freshly moisturized and her feet warm in bunchy wool socks, she felt her tender gratitude shade into something closer to love than she could have ever imagined.

But then two weeks ago, she found him close to tears in her kitchenette. A federal grand jury had just indicted him for defrauding the roofers' union out of $250,000—most of which went to her rent and medical expenses, he said. They could send him to prison for eight years unless he gave them a bigger fish. So how could she refuse when he begged her for help?

She put on a fresh coat of lipstick and then tugged down the front of her white ribbed turtleneck, worrying at first that the transmitter taped to her stomach was conspicuous and then worrying that it wasn't because of the weight she'd gained. Back when she was Christie Ball ("undergrad by day, undercover by night"), there would be a scene every week requiring her to strip down to her bra and panties so the pimply, bespectacled tech wizard J.T. could affix a tiny Japanese microphone to the sleek alabaster curve of her back or, if standards and practices was feeling lax, the marble quarry of her Maidenform cleavage. Now she was wearing wires down her Spanx and a digital recorder from the prosecutor's office in the ugly, fake Navajo amulet dangling before her once-perky breasts, a chunky little piece of turquoise that looked like it had been handled by a sweaty Chinese food delivery boy. She pulled up her collar to cover more of her neck, gave a chilly smile to a young brunette walking into the bathroom wearing a cocktail napkin and stilettos, and then forced herself to march bravely back out into the restaurant.

It was one of those vaguely Mediterranean-themed midtown places just at the tail end of a Reagan-era reputation. A pair of middle-aged Wall Street sultans looked at her from a side booth with harem-like swags, dull glimmers of recognition in their rheumy eyes; she realized they might have been kids when the series was first on the air. The girls they were with—long legged, pearly toothed, and honey shouldered—were young enough to be the daughter she never had. It was almost a relief to head back toward the table by the kitchen where her target waited, gazing admiringly, as if she were still the little blonde with the cornflower eyes just off the bus from Minneapolis.

Martin, the man Charlie had set her up with, was a ruddy, rough-hewn type, with knuckles like walnut shells, thinning slicked-back hair, and cheeks that filled up when he smiled. On the show, he might have been cast as a second-act heavy, someone for Christie Ball to take seriously. But his herring-bone jacket, open-collared Oxford shirt, and steel-banded Patek Philippe chronograph smoothed the edges considerably. And as the business agent for something called the Northeastern Service Workers Union—though the sooty sound of it made her want to spend a weekend at a spa—he represented a pension fund worth a half-billion dollars. "A whale compared to a guppy like me," Charlie insisted. But even better, a big fan of Christie Ball's from the old days, who'd been dying to meet her ever since Charlie connected with her at a Cancer Trust event three years ago. Now the prosecutors were counting on this Martin being so excited about having dinner with her that he might speak incautiously enough to incriminate himself on tape.

She nestled back among the pasha-style cushions and leaned into the candlelight, hoping the flickering of shadows would be kind to her softening jawline.

"I was worried you weren't coming back," he said with what sounded like a slight Jersey accent carefully policed. "They came back so many times to take your salad away, I had to threaten to break the waiter's fingers."

"So what were we talking about?" She saw that her half-drained glass of Chateau Petrus had been replenished.

"I can't believe I'm having dinner with Christie Ball." He shook his head.

"Please call me Jackie," she said, using the name she'd had since she was sixteen.

"I'm sorry I keep staring, Jackie. I just remember what a crush I had on you back then. Your posters were everywhere."

"My goodness, Martin." She covered her mouth, self-conscious about her gums. "How young are you anyway?"

"Oh, I'm sure I'm older than you. But you know how it was. You made working men feel like schoolboys."

"You're a liar, but I love you for saying it."

She sized him up as basically a complacent type with a wife, four kids, and a McMansion in Short Hills. A hands-on type who figured out there was more money to be made behind a desk. There was something attractive about the way the corners of his eyes crinkled up when he listened. Most women her age would consider him fairly good-looking, she realized, but then most women her age had never gone screaming down Mulholland Drive on the back of a Triumph Trident with their arms and legs wrapped around Warren Beatty and their flaxen locks rioting in the wind.

"Anyway, the union pension fund," she said. "What are we going to do about it?"

His eyes narrowed, and his nostrils twitched ever so slightly as if he had just caught the odor of a gas station on an August morning.

"Jackie, you need to understand that I represent the interests of fifty thousand men and women who have dedicated their lives to public service," he said seriously. "I don't know how much exposure you had to that in Hollywood, but there's no glamour in it. These people work the midnight shifts at city hospitals and haul hazardous waste to the dumps. They expect to be taken care of in their old age. And you're asking me to gamble their life savings with this investment company. Why should I do that?"

"Martin, you're right to be careful," she said, going into the spiel she'd practiced with Charlie's prosecutors. "It *is* risky. But L. B. Thompson is the fastest growing firm of its kind. Last year, the real estate portfolio earned twenty-two percent in just..."

She started to reach into her Chanel bag for the brochure Charlie had given her, but Martin took hold of her wrist.

"It's okay," he said, slowly turning her hand over as if to force the palm open. "You can show me that later. But right now, there's something I'm more interested in."

His liquid brown eyes roamed across her features appreciatively. With Charlie, it was different, she had to admit. He gorged on her greedily, like a boy stuffing himself with pizza after football practice, ravenous and indiscriminate, glad to have a woman who weighed less than him across the table. But this Martin studied her more like a connoisseur, taking his time savoring her vintage, noting the care she took in putting herself together. The pressure of his thumb was velvet gentle but steady on her quickening pulse.

"You want to know how you'll be taken care of," she said.

The crinkle lines dispersed, and she realized she'd sounded too eager. "Let the conversation unfold naturally," Charlie's handler had said. But timing had never been her strength. In fact, she'd never been that good at simulating emotion. Her value was as an object to be looked at, riding on her looks until they would take her no further, vaguely hoping some commensurate skill would eventually kick in. But now that she had put the line out, she had to "commit to it," as they said in the acting classes that never really helped her get work.

"Obviously, the company wouldn't pay you back directly for investing the fund with them, because that would be a kickback," she said. "But there's another way."

"Okay." He cocked his head to one side, seeming receptive.

"A movie."

"You want me to invest union pension funds in a *film*?"

"No," she said, slowing herself down to remember the money laundering scenario she'd been given. "You would invest a very small amount of your own money first...."

"*My money.*"

His eyes half-disappeared when he smiled this time. There was nothing remotely threatening in his expression, but she still found her hamstrings tightening for some reason, as if he'd just casually mentioned an interest in dismemberment.

"It's not as scary as it sounds," she said a little breathlessly. "Thompson will put up most of the financing. So when the movie comes out, you're guaranteed at least double your money back."

"So it's like a side deal, where the money gets washed?" He lowered his chin. "I guess you can play these games moving cash around in film accounting, but I have a more practical question."

"Yes?"

"What's it going to be?"

"Hmm?"

His hand moved up her arm. "This movie. For there to be any budget to put money into and any revenues to take out of it, there has to be an actual film. Doesn't there?"

"It's going to be my comeback," she improvised.

"Really?" He raised his eyebrows.

"Why? Is that a problem?"

Even though they were talking about something fake, she still felt a clutch in her heart. Not that he would hurt her physically, but that he might start laughing in her face.

"So is there a script?"

"We're working on it. It should be done in the spring."

"And what's it about?"

She exhaled too sharply, almost blowing out the candle on the table. Who knew he would ask so many questions? Did Charlie and his handlers think this would be easy for her, making things up on the spot? She wasn't some theater workshop veteran who was used to riffing. She was a former model accustomed to having her lines highlighted for her in each week's script.

"It's about a girl like the one I played on the show," she began to embroider. "But more . . . mature now, of course."

"As we all are."

"I think there's a hunger for these kinds of stories out there," she went on, encouraged by the way he nodded. "Anyway, she's just gotten out of prison for something she didn't do, and now she's going to get revenge on the guys who set her up. . . ."

Not bad for a former airhead who only started reading seriously ten years ago. Maybe the passage of time had given her something in exchange for everything it had taken.

"So who's going to be in it?" Martin hunched forward, staring deep into her eyes.

She felt a knot in the back of her neck as she tried to remember the names of some contemporary stars. "It's going to be a whole retrospective thing." She crept farther out on a limb. "I've already talked to Warren about it, and now Dustin's interested...."

"Wow...."

"And Harrison Ford wants to see the script." Her ears popped as if she were climbing too quickly. "So we're already talking to people on the West Coast about dividing the costs of theatrical distribution with someone in Europe."

"It sounds great, Jackie," he interrupted. "I'd love to help you...."

"You would?"

"Yes, I've always thought you were wonderful. And just sitting here, talking to you, brings me back to another time in my life. People haven't appreciated how special you are, and I think that's a shame."

"Martin, that's *so* nice of you."

"Well, I mean it. Whatever you had then, you still have now. But even more so..."

She leaned farther toward him, into the candlelight, almost singeing her hair. Oh, *yes.* This was what she wanted, to be taken seriously, to be believed in again. She almost regretted using whatever allure she had left to guile him.

"So tell Charlie that we'll work out the details with investing the pension fund," Martin said. "But there's something more important that we need to discuss."

"What's that?"

"That I'd like to spend more time with you."

His hand covered hers. She wondered what the men listening in the van outside were making of all this.

"What would you say about that?" he asked.

"Well…" She raised her Bordeaux, trying to collect herself.

"Please. I don't mean to pressure you. It's just that I'm going through a divorce, and I heard Charlie is getting back together with his wife, and…"

*"I'm sorry?"*

"You didn't know?" He tucked down his chin. "I thought that was part of the reason he set us up tonight."

"Martin." She tried to smile, but some of the muscles in her face were restricted. "I don't think I'm following you."

"My lawyer's wife is friends with Estelle, Charlie's wife. She says they withdrew the papers because neither of them could face the financial fallout. So that meant you were available."

*"Available?"* She pictured herself like an empty chaise lounge by an old swimming pool.

"I thought you knew…."

Her hand closed up under his as it began to dawn on her how she'd been used. Dear, sweet Charlie had dangled her as bait to attract a shark, and now he was cutting the line on her. This fat, greasy man had played her for a sap like Barbara Stanwyck two-timing Fred MacMurray in *Double Indemnity*. Wasn't it supposed to be the other way around? Wasn't she supposed to be the femme fatale here? How could he have done this after she'd lowered herself for him? After she'd lowered her standards just by *being with him*? Hadn't she allowed him to love her? Hadn't she tolerated his bad breath; his sagging jowls; his stupid jokes and boring anecdotes; the endless rubber chicken dinners and charity dances with state legislators, lobbyists, and investment managers in Albany and White Plains?

But then she turned and caught a glimpse of herself in a wall mirror, and the thought reflected back that maybe it was her fault for not being a good enough actress to fool him. Maybe he'd sensed that in the back of her mind she was already moving on, writing her memoir of overcoming disease and an addiction to diet pills, in which he'd be a minor footnote, not worth mentioning in her talk show appearances.

"I'm okay," she said numbly.

"You sure? You look a little pale."

"I'm fine." She recomposed her smile. "I guess he just wanted to share the wealth, right?"

"It's not like that." The leathery folds of his face opened up like a wallet. "I'm sure Charlie just wants you to be taken care of."

"To be taken care of." She swirled the dregs around the bottom of her glass.

"If you're uncomfortable, I'll take you home right now."

She finished her drink and set it down with a loud *thump*. The sultans and their dates in the side booth stared at her, as if some crazy old woman was about to make a scene. She stared back defiantly, daring them to say something. Fame had come and gone, millions of dollars had run through her fingers, and her face was starting to resemble a rain-soaked orchid, but she was still here, wasn't she? Maybe there was still time to adapt, to become a husky old good-time broad, indomitable and undaunted, dragging her mink on the rug on the way out and taking pride in the simple fact of not giving a damn anymore.

"Order me another round," she said.

"Really?"

"Yeah, I'm just getting started."

She kissed him full on the mouth. Didn't she deserve to be with a man who could *really* take care of her? Then she sashayed back to the bathroom, giving the men in the side booth an eyeful and their dates a lesson in how to carry yourself with what used to be known as class. She waited for the ladies' room door to close behind her before she tore off the wires and tossed them in the trash. She was sure she hadn't given Charlie or the prosecutors what they needed. Then she went back out to enjoy the rest of her evening.

———

THE CLOUDS OVER Beverly Hills were pulling back as the new development girl, twenty-five and just starting to pay off her college loans, finished the morning pitch session.

"And then there's this one," she said, sliding over the news story she'd pulled off the web last night. "I thought it was interesting."

The vice president in charge of production leaned over the conference table to study it, confounded that Pilates had not kept him from developing a gut before forty. "Former TV Star Killed in New York," the headline said.

"Just give me the coverage." He rubbed his eyes.

"This girl who used to be the star of a police show in the seventies got shot five times coming out of her apartment building. The story says she'd been subpoenaed to testify against some mob guy in a pension fund scandal. Her boyfriend roped her into it to get himself off the hook, and the prosecutor went along with it for the publicity value. Instead they got her killed. I thought it had some potential as a fem-jep story—"

"All right, wait a minute." The vice president grimaced. "First of all, as soon as you say 'pension fund scandal,' my eyes glaze over. Second of all, she's dead at the end, so that's a bummer. And third of all, this story says she was *fifty-eight*. How are we supposed to care about someone that freaking old?"

"Right." The D-girl nodded. "I should've thought of that."

"It's okay, you'll learn." The vice president took a quick glance at the old file photo accompanying the story. "You know, it's too bad, though."

"What?"

He pushed the picture back across the table. "She really used to be a nice-looking girl."

# THE SADOWSKY MANIFESTO

## BY KAREN CATALONA

It may have started with a seven-figure inheritance, but for Max Bergen, the literary agency had never been about the money. Great-aunt Mildred's bequest meant Max could pick his office from the best commercial real estate in New York, fill it with expensive furnishings, and then focus on what he really cared about: experimental, opaque literature. Whether any of those projects brought in the type of money to support his lifestyle seemed inconsequential. But after years passed, bills mounted, and his inheritance dwindled, Max Bergen began to look at his slush pile in an entirely new light.

That morning was like most. Nibbling on one of Edna's home-baked goodies, he skimmed through the query letters that Edna had left open and neatly stacked on his desk. The queries went into three piles: the maybes, trash, and the wall of weird.

"There's a lovely one on cat training," Edna noted, using her cane to walk the short distance out to her desk.

Max, his mouth full of her moist apple crumb cake, nodded and waited respectfully until she was out of sight before tossing the pitch into the trash. Book queries involving pets were some of the worst, although a howler he found last week, *Life Lessons from My*

*Parakeet*, with its earnest Hallmark sentimentality, had earned a spot on his wall of weird.

Max started reading through the queries and was able to make some quick decisions. A query for poetry. Trash. Personally, he liked poetry, but it didn't sell. Query with three misspelled words. Trash. Query for a comic novel featuring a talking dog. Trash. Query for a "fiction novel." Trash.

Max sipped his coffee and had the vague memory that there was a talking-dog movie that did really well last year. He contemplated the potential existence of a market for talking-dog novels. He lifted the query from the trash and put it in the maybe pile.

The phone rang, and Max heard Edna's friendly "Hello?"

He had told her a few dozen times to answer the phone with: "Max Bergen Literary Agency," but she often forgot so editors thought they had misdialed and got someone's grandmother. Edna Bloomgarten entered the job market for the first time shortly after she entered her seventies. Only after her husband's death from a heart attack did she learn about his gambling addiction and the two mortgages and that most of their savings was gone. Edna couldn't type and the fax machine gave her a lot of trouble, but she ran a tight ship and her cinnamon-marbled coffee cake made up for a lot.

Max returned to his queries. The next was a mesmerizing pitch for a literary novel with a daring theme and abhorrence for punctuation. He wasn't sure he understood the concept but suspected it was genius. With a heavy sigh, he tossed it into the trash. He had stacks of brilliant literary novels he couldn't sell piled up in his apartment; if he wanted to keep his agency afloat, he could no longer afford to follow his own tastes. After all, somebody had to keep Edna in flour, sugar, and eggs.

Edna peered around the door at him, tightly grasping the doorframe. "You've got a call." The fear and urgency were plain in her tone.

"Who is it?"

Edna looked stricken and whispered, "I'm not sure if I'm allowed to tell you."

Feeling a flush of worry, Max wanted to ask more but Edna looked like she might keel over. He waved her away so she would go sit down.

"Hello," he answered tentatively.

"Max Bergen?" The voice was clipped, authoritative.

"Yes, that's me. What can I do for you?"

"Agent Keating of the FBI. I have a few questions. I was wondering if I might take a few moments of your time."

The tone made it clear that it was a request in form only.

"Sure, of course."

"I'm assuming you heard about Donald Sadowsky?"

The name sounded vaguely familiar, but Max couldn't quite place it. "You know, I'm not sure." Max's mind continued to race, trying to think of anything he had been involved in that could possibly lead the FBI to contact him. Some of his college buddies sold a little weed, but that was years ago. Were any of those guys named Donald Sadowsky?

The FBI agent sounded surprised, and his voice had a flat edge of disbelief. "You haven't heard of Donald Sadowsky?"

Max's fingers sprang across his computer keyboard, typing the name into a search engine.

Agent Keating sounded annoyed. "The mall shooting with the assault weapons? In New Jersey?"

Max scanned the articles on his computer that popped up in connection with Donald Sadowsky and a few phrases jumped out at him: *mass murderer, record killing, forty-two dead.* This wasn't about a college buddy with weed.

Max's mouth was so dry he could hardly speak. "Oh yeah, yeah, that guy. I did hear about that."

"Were you in contact with him?" Agent Keating asked.

"No!" Max blurted out, feeling some inexplicable and vague sense of guilt.

"Has he contacted you by mail?"

Max surveyed his office that was awash in paper even with Edna's tidiness. Every flat surface had papers or manuscripts stacked on it. The table next to the wall of weird easily had twenty to thirty manuscripts stacked precariously on it alone.

"Wow, he may have. I'd have to check. I get hundreds of letters a week."

Agent Keating said, "I need you to search your office and see if he sent you anything at all."

A thought knocked the wind out of Max. "Is it poisoned? What's that white powder stuff, and you breathe it, and then you drop dead?"

Agent Keating offered coolly, "Anthrax?"

"Oh my God, did he send me anthrax?"

Agent Keating started to sound annoyed. "No, we aren't concerned for your safety. Just look and see if you can find any correspondence from him."

"Why? What's going on?"

"We have reason to believe that he corresponded with you. Actually, we don't have any evidence you wrote back, but based on some notes we found in his home, we believe he sent you a package containing his manuscript."

"He wasn't trying to kill me?"

"No, he wanted you to sell his book."

Max sat back in his chair and took a few seconds for this to settle in.

"Look, Sadowsky killed himself, and we have no reason to believe he wanted to hurt you. But the Behavioral Sciences Unit at Quantico—what you would probably call profilers—want to have a look at what he wrote. They have this idea his book could help them gain insight into the mind of a killer, that sort of thing. We can't find a copy of his book anywhere in his home. No notes, no rough draft, no anything, so you might be our only chance. I'd appreciate if you could look for whatever writings he sent you and turn it over to us. Quietly, of course."

Max agreed, and after the phone call was over, he sank down into his chair. He felt a little dizzy.

A madman had selected him for special attention. Insight into the mind of a psychopath was stuck somewhere among his piles of paper, sandwiched between stacks of manuscripts.

He stared out across his office, feeling troubled and humbled all at the same time.

After a few dark moments, he looked up and saw Edna watching him from the doorway, dabbing at her eyes with a newly moist handkerchief.

"Max, my dear Max," she croaked. "Why didn't you let me know you were in trouble?" Then she whispered, looking around the room as if she expected it to be bugged, "In trouble with the FBI?"

"Oh no, Edna. It's not like that. It's okay." Edna still looked stricken. Max got up and led her to a comfortable chair in his office. As he helped her take a seat, she gripped his arm, leaned in close to his ear, and whispered, "I can help you hide the evidence. I know a place where stuff stays hidden."

"Edna," Max said, looking at her with new eyes. "There is no evidence; everything is okay."

"Of course there's no evidence," Edna said in a conspicuously loud tone, one suitable for an FBI bug or the hard of hearing. Then her voice dropped to a whisper. "Before my Dudley passed, he knew people. He worked for certain people, if you catch my drift. Let me help you. I know a place where you could hide the stuff, whatever it is, before the FBI gets here."

Max felt a rush of affection for his bespectacled secretary. "Edna, the FBI isn't investigating me, they are investigating this guy named Donald Sadowsky."

"The terrible man that's all over the news?"

"Yeah, that guy."

"Oh, dear."

"The FBI says this madman may have sent us a manuscript."

"Oh my." Edna sat next to him on the expensively upholstered love seat.

The two of them sat in silence; the sound of traffic below was like the rushing of a distant river. Max glanced back at the computer screen, staring at Donald Sadowsky's eerie DMV photo, an image that stared out from every news website he had checked. For a mass killer, Sadowsky looked the part. He had white blond hair that stood in uneven tufts around his scrawny face, and his washed-out blue eyes were lit up with a malevolent kind of amusement. The guy's face was all over the Internet. Max looked at his face again and felt a shiver. No wonder the public was so fascinated by this guy.

Then Max abruptly sat up and walked over to the wall of weird, knocking over one of the piles of manuscripts stacked on the floor next to his desk.

"Max, what are you doing?"

Max turned to Edna, looking a little sheepish. "The FBI wouldn't be the only people that would want to get their hands on this book. I feel bad for what he did to all those people, but this manuscript could be worth a lot of money."

———

AN HOUR LATER, Max had Edna seated on the comfy chair next to the window, sorting through the stacks on top of the radiator, while Max was on the floor, piling and unpiling the manuscripts collecting dust underneath the table next to the wall of weird. Other than the sounds of New York street traffic five stories below, the shuffling of paper, and the occasional clank of the aged radiator, Edna and Max worked in silence.

Then Max found it. A thick package wrapped in brown paper, with "D. Sadowsky" on a white return address sticker on the upper left-hand side.

"Edna?" Max said, hoping she didn't notice the tremble in his voice.

He held the package gingerly, but it was heavy and he almost dropped it. She walked toward him to help.

"No! Stay back. Who knows what that nutjob put in here." Max shook it gingerly and let out a breath of relief when nothing rattled inside. "I don't think there's a letter bomb or anything in here, but just in case there's anthrax, I want you to keep your distance. Go back to your desk. I'll open it over here by the window."

Edna, her eyes wide, shuffled to her desk.

"How about this, Max: I'll dial the nine and the one and just put my finger over the one, and if something is wrong, you holler, okay?"

"Okay, Edna," Max said as he tugged on the folded flaps underneath the manuscript. After some gentle tugging, he slid the manuscript onto the radiator next to the window. It was a stack of almost three hundred printed pages. No white powder.

Max's breath burst out of his chest. He didn't even realize he had been holding it. Edna peered at him around the doorframe, a bumpy arthritic finger poised over a button on her cordless phone.

"Is everything okay, Max?"

"Edna, we still got that champagne in the mini-fridge?"

Edna nodded.

"This is the novel of a madman, a mass killer, and quite possibly a future *New York Times* best-selling author."

Edna's eyes beamed from behind her bifocals, and a few minutes later, they toasted each other with champagne in clinking coffee mugs.

They sat next to each other on the couch, both a little giddy but fascinated at what would be in the book.

"*Death Robots from the Secret Underside of the World*," Max said, reading the title page with reverence before he passed it to Edna. "Sounds interesting."

Max dove into the first page. The narrator, presumably named George ("Call me George" was the first line of the book), woke up in the morning and ate a breakfast of oatmeal. Max quickly read the first ten pages. No death robots. George worked in a toothpaste factory, and his daily routine was described in excruciating detail.

Fifty pages further and still no death robots. Every few pages, George ate oatmeal for breakfast.

An hour later, Max sighed. "He's a little dry."

Edna shook her head decisively. "Dull as dirt. When the robots showed, I thought it would get exciting." Edna sighed. "Who would have ever guessed the death robots were as boring as George?"

"Who knew that I would be rooting for the death robots to kill George?"

Max put down the manuscript and dropped his head. His fingers began massaging his temples.

"Do you think this book would ever sell?" Edna asked.

"It would get interest because of the whole morbid fascination the public has with Donald Sadowsky, but that would only go so far. As soon as an editor actually got a chapter into this thing, any hopes for a dream deal would be over."

"Maybe you could edit it? You are such a talented young man. You could rewrite it a little to make it less bad," Edna said.

"It's terrible. Literary Ambien. The only people that could manage to read past the first chapter would be those FBI profilers."

Max shook his head. The dream of the big paycheck saving his trust fund literary lifestyle was growing dim. He was doomed to sell the talking-dog book and hope it covered the rent.

Edna looked sad. "You work so hard. This Sadowsky guy is all over the TV, the magazines, and everywhere. People are obsessed. Think of all the fuzz this book would get. It could make you a bunch of money."

"Edna, I think you mean buzz. Yes, this book would get a lot of buzz, but that only carries you so far." Max went over to his desk and pulled out a letter from the maybe pile. "This talking-dog novel might go somewhere; please write a letter to this guy and request a manuscript. Tomorrow, we mail the Sadowsky manuscript to the FBI."

Edna took the news without argument; her blue, rheumy eyes were pools of disappointment behind her thick glasses.

Max decided to spend the night getting drunk.

———

THE MAX BERGEN Literary Agency was a small operation: Max, Edna, and whatever college intern was foolish enough to work for him for free. The latest intern, Kimberly, was there the next morning when Max rolled in late and more than a little hungover. He was glad she was there. The phone was ringing off the hook, and Edna was nowhere to be seen.

After she got off a phone call, she looked up at him. "Dude, you have like twenty-eight voice-mail messages. Don't you ever check this thing?" Kimberly said, smacking on some gum.

"I checked my messages last night, and I didn't have any. It must be a mistake."

"No, dude, it's twenty-eight messages, and for some reason, they think you are working with the Sadowsky guy, the one who offed all those people in Jersey. I thought the dude killed himself."

Kimberly handed Max the pages of messages, and Max

recognized some familiar and surprising names. Where was this coming from? Publishers who hadn't returned his calls in years had left friendly messages.

"Sadowsky sent me a manuscript. It's complicated. If anyone calls, just tell them I'm in an important meeting and I can't be disturbed."

Edna walked in with an iced orange bundt cake and a triumphant smile. "Are you getting a buzz?" she asked Max coyly.

"Oh, Jesus," Max said, and he gently walked Edna into his office and closed the door so Kimberly couldn't hear.

"Edna, what did you do?"

"I might have mentioned to three or fifteen of the people I know in publishing about your latest acquisition. I told some of the big gossips, so I knew the info would make the rounds fast!"

"Edna, this is a disaster. I have all this interest in a manuscript that is not publishable."

"But now you have all the buzz. People will get excited about it."

"They'll be excited until they actually read the thing; then they will be napping."

"Max, I know it's bad, but—"

"It's worse than bad, it's boring! If it was just bad writing, there is still hope to get it published, but boring writing is DOA."

Edna blinked at him.

"DOA means 'dead on arrival,' Edna," Max said, sighing. "Bad writing could potentially be published, but boring can't. There's nothing that can be done with this manuscript. I'm going to wait a day or two, then tell people that I was ethically obligated to turn it over to the FBI. Let people think that's the reason why it won't be published; maybe I can save a little face that way."

Max heard the phone ring again. Kimberly was already on the other line.

Max rubbed his face. The hangover was fast warping into a

migraine. "And now everybody in the world knows about the manuscript. This is going to be embarrassing."

Edna bit her lip and cut Max a generous slice of the bundt cake. She got up to go to the mini-fridge to pour him a glass of milk.

Max's voice was soft. "You know, the thing that drives me nuts is that, based on what this guy was, you'd expect some wild, violent, frenetic tale, but it's just nothing. It's completely flat. I mean, where's this guy's crazy? Where is the violence?"

"You do get lots of crazy," Edna added, handing him the glass of milk.

Max forked a bite of the bundt cake, trying to ignore the growing sense of nausea.

"You deserve this break; you're a good boy." Edna's eyes surveyed the room, and she stared hard at the table bordering the wall of weird. "Nobody knows exactly what Sadowsky sent you, right?"

"The FBI thinks I have the only copy." Max's eyes darted over to Edna, searching her face. She gave him a crooked smile, and soon he was thinking what she was thinking. "We could say something else is the Sadowsky manuscript. Something interesting, crazy violent, and what people think Sadowsky would write."

"*The Devil's Cupboard,*" Edna whispered.

*The Devil's Cupboard,* written by Sigmund Cerletti, was a manuscript that occupied prime real estate on the table pushed up next to the wall of weird. A copy of it arrived on the eighth of the month, every month. It was a single-spaced manuscript with 8-point typeface and margins a millimeter from the paper's edge, giving the impression that some feverish brain had crammed thousands and thousands of words on each page. Just the thought of slogging through the first page made him feel tired. But he had skimmed the manuscript, and the little he had seen of it scared the hell out of him. He had never read a manuscript so fascinated by the topics of entrails, gurgling blood, or crushed skulls. He put the bite of cake down. Just thinking about *The Devil's Cupboard* had that effect on him.

"Edna, why don't you take a look at the first few pages and tell me what you think."

Edna looked down through her bifocals at the pages and finally lifted a page a few inches away from her face.

"Oh, my," she said, her mouth pursed in distaste. After a few more pages, she looked positively ill and a little faint.

"It's okay, Edna, I'll take it." Max gently lifted the pages out of her hand.

Edna blew her nose into her handkerchief as she collected herself. "It's so disturbed and twisted."

"So it's a perfect Sadowsky book, right?" Max said, giving her arm a squeeze. After a deep breath, he looked at the manuscript again. It almost seemed as if the tiny letters were vibrating with weirdness, twitching, winking, contracting as his eyes followed them on the page.

"So should we start a big auction with the publishers?" Edna asked, starting to smile again.

About fifteen minutes later, Max frowned and said, "Wait a second, how are we going to talk this crazy guy into letting us use his manuscript to pass it off as Sadowsky's?"

Edna shrugged. "This book will make lots of money. Most people like money."

"Yeah, but this guy is twisted, and if his main character is anything like him, he's incredibly narcissistic. This guy's ego would never let us pass off his book as Sadowsky's."

"We can talk to him. I will convince him," Edna said, her grandmother's face still hopeful.

"Yeah, just call a guy out of the blue and ask him if he's up for a little literary fraud? Maybe show up at his door with a big check in hand. Where does this guy even live?"

Edna hobbled over to the table to check the envelope's return address.

At that moment, Kimberly walked in without knocking, carrying an oversized bouquet of red roses from an editor who had previously never returned his calls.

"Whoa, dude, look at what you got from the Neville Publishing House."

"Thanks, Kimberly. Edna, where does this guy live?"

Edna looked uncertain about answering in front of Kimberly, but said softly, "His return address is from Atascadero, California."

Kimberly laughed. "Ah, is that manuscript from a crazy dude?"

Max thought about the manuscript. "Well, yeah."

"That figures," Kimberly said, walking off.

"Wait, why? What figures?"

"Atascadero has a big mental hospital. I grew up in Templeton, less than ten miles away. Half the town's employed in the hospital. Well, I guess it's kind of a prison, too. Like, if somebody kills somebody, but it's because they are crazy or the voices told them to do it or something, that's where they send them. It's like the criminally insane or whatever."

Kimberly shrugged, dropped off some more mail, and walked out. Max and Edna didn't say a word until she had closed the door on her way out.

"What's the return address on the manuscript?" Max demanded. Edna checked and read it off while Max compared it to the address he found on the Internet for the Atascadero State Hospital.

"It's a match! Sigmund Cerletti is locked up at some prison psych hospital. This is perfect! We can pass off the manuscript as Sadowsky's, no problem."

"What if he gets released someday? Maybe some technicality

or he does all his time or something. He'll come out and then say that he wrote the book and the Sadowsky thing is a fraud."

"That's why this whole situation is so perfect. Even if this guy ever gets released from the psych ward and claims he wrote the book, who is going to believe him? He just got out of the psych ward!" Max, still grinning, shot a questioning glance at Edna. "Come on, Edna, why are you worrying?"

Edna was thoughtful. "I can hardly read more than a page or two because it's so frightening, the way that man's head works. What if they release Sigmund Cerletti, and he comes after you?"

"Edna, you read it for yourself. No state mental hospital would ever be stupid enough to release a guy like that. We have nothing to worry about."

———

A YEAR LATER and a month before the *Sadowsky Manifesto*'s release date, Max strolled into the office. Buzz, as Edna liked to say, was huge. The public outcry over the sale of a killer's manifesto had been dampened by the fact that all "author" profits were being donated by his estate to survivors, the victims' families, and crime victim charities. (Sadowsky's sole surviving relative was an elderly, financially secure aunt, who as sole executor of the estate wanted nothing to do with the book, Sadowsky, or the money.) As the agent, Max wrangled a hefty commission, but any percentage of the ungodly advance was still a lot of money.

He bought a Porsche. He started paying the intern.

"How was your client lunch?" Kimberly asked.

"Great! This guy has been slaving away for years, and I am the first to discover him. He's completely brilliant, and his novel is amazing."

"What's it about?"

"Well, there's this guy, and there's this grid of humanity. There's this anorexic porpoise, but I think it's symbolic. Probably an indictment of man's spiritual pillaging of the natural world? Anyway, the whole work is really deep. Humanity is represented by dots and despair is a rectangle, but joy is a circle. It's very subtle how he draws everything out."

Kimberly stared at him blankly.

"It's hard putting into words the kind of brilliance this guy is capable of." Max turned to Edna, who was pulling from an oversized UPS box an object with large wooden levers that intersected with a large wooden bulb at the end. "Whoa, Edna, what is that thing? It looks like some medieval torture device."

Edna beamed at the object that upon closer inspection looked a little like an enormous garlic press. "It's a vintage spaetzle press! And there's more." Edna pulled out an intricately carved wooden club. "It's for baking Springerle, these fancy cookies. You need this special rolling pin to make them."

Now that Kimberly worked full-time hours, Max let Edna work part-time hours for her full-time salary. She signed up for French pastry classes and had mastered the chocolate croissant. Recently, she was returning to her Bloomgarten roots and exploring German baking. She would bring in spicy pfeffernusse cookies or cakes with names he couldn't pronounce, like the one she brought in the day before, a delicious and dense chocolate cake studded with sour cherries.

"Oh, yes," Edna added, "the UPS also brought you a certified letter. I signed for you."

Max dug out the letter from under the spaetzle press while Edna tried demonstrating the Springerle rolling pin for Kimberly whose gum smacking had slowed, a sign she was paying attention.

Max opened the certified letter and felt a wave of fear, then nausea, when he read its contents:

Attention Mr. Bergen,

You, sir, are despicable. I know (and can PROVE) who truly authored the *Sadowsky Manifesto* and will rejoice in exposing your fraud. I will be stopping by your office on January 14 at 8 a.m., so that I can see you with mine own eyes while I inform you, in detail, how I will destroy you.

I expect you will want to clear your schedule.

> Very truly yours,
> Dr. Edwin Rickman
> Staff psychiatrist
> Atascadero State Hospital

As soon as he read the letter, Max had to get out of the office. Edna and Kimberly looked so happy, still enveloped in the bubble of success and excitement the *Sadowsky Manifesto* had generated. He didn't want them to know their joy was on borrowed time. The taint of literary fraud would poison his business, ruin his career, and probably land him in court. Did people go to jail for those sorts of things? Would he go to the nicer white-collar jail or the rapists' and murderers' kind of jail?

He mumbled something, and soon he was out of the office and out the front door of the building. The January New York air was frigid, and a gust of wind hit him like a bucket of ice water. He could feel the cold seeping into his skin and he was shivering uncontrollably, but it was nothing new.

He had been shivering ever since he read the letter.

———

THE IDEA SEEMED brilliant at 3 a.m., when he was a little drunk and very desperate. A big bag of money, a gym bag bursting with crisp packets of tens and twenties, might be the kind of visual spectacle to win Dr. Rickman over to the potential benefits of keeping the origins of the *Sadowsky Manifesto* a secret.

While it sounded good in drunkenness and in theory, the reality was trickier, especially running around getting all the money before their 8 a.m. meeting. Max learned that ATMs limit how much money you can withdraw at a time, and after you make lots of withdrawals while schlepping over fifteen city blocks of Manhattan, the bank thinks the ATM card is stolen and cuts you off. Max switched to cash withdrawals from every credit card he had in his wallet. The big bag of money was heavy, and he was winded from lugging it around in the skin-tingling cold.

Getting to the office building early, the fifth floor was deserted, the fluorescent lights shining rectangles of cold light in the darkened hallway leading to his office.

A sharp, angry voice pierced the silence. "Max Bergen?" Max stopped, trying to determine where the voice was coming from. A wiry man with a long, pinched face like a Doberman slipped out of a darkened doorway and stepped in front of Max. They were face-to-face, only inches from each other. The man's eyes stared into his with an eerie intensity, and his lips curled in distaste when he said, "I've been waiting for you."

"Dr. Rickman?" Max took a step back, trying to gain his equilibrium.

The man stepped forward into Max's personal space, so close that Max could smell oatmeal on his breath, see a stray flake of it in the man's twitching mustache.

Max backed away again and hurried toward his office. "This is my office; please come in."

The presumed Dr. Rickman followed close at Max's heels into the darkened, empty office. Considering the nature of the meeting, Max had given Kimberly the day off and told Edna to come in late. It was a mistake, Max thought, looking over at Dr. Rickman, a man he was standing alone with, a man radiating a barely contained, malevolent kind of glee.

"After I see you, I go to the police. I brought all the

documentation with me," Rickman boasted, gesturing to an overstuffed briefcase. "Every single shred of paper I need to prove the so-called *Sadowsky Manifesto* is a fraud and that you have robbed credit from the true brilliant and talented artist."

"Please let me explain, I—"

Rickman brought a fist down on Max's desk, a loud echoing boom filling up the silence of the empty area.

"I'm not done yet. After I go to the police and have you arrested for fraud, then I will go to the *New York Times* with my personal copies of the papers proving your intellectual theft, exposing you for the huckster you really are."

Max propped his head up with his hands. He thought he should say something, but fear had sucked the breath out of him.

"Then I will take the documentation to a lawyer, the most ruthless, cutthroat, greedy lawyer ever who will take every dime you have, plus some you haven't even earned yet."

Max stared mournfully at Rickman, a man whose face was lit up with his cause, who spoke with such force and conviction that spittle landed in little drops on the manuscripts covering Max's desk.

"I don't care if it will destroy you; that's the plan, so no begging. There's only one thing I want to know: how did you think you could get away with it?"

Max was weakened, melting under the weight of Dr. Rickman's vitriol. He thought about pleading with him, but opted instead for the truth. "Sigmund Cerletti is locked up in some hospital for the criminally insane. He's not going anywhere, and it sounds like he shouldn't be going anywhere. You know the guy. Is he locked up for a murder or something? I mean, clearly he's a violent nutcase, right?"

A strange expression passed over Dr. Rickman's face: incredulity, fear, outrage, and white-hot anger. Rickman plastered his arms close to his sides, his fists balled. Max desperately wished he had some sort of weapon for protection. Two words slipped from behind Rickman's clenched teeth.

"Pen name."

"What?" Max asked, confused.

"Pen name!" Rickman roared, his angry bass filling the room. "Sigmund Cerletti? Didn't that sound funny to you? Probably not, you uneducated cretin. It's a pen name; I took the Sigmund from Sigmund Freud and the Cerletti from Ugo Cerletti. You know, Cerletti? The guy who invented electroshock therapy? I wrote the book! I wrote the *Sadowsky Manifesto*, and I deserve all the credit."

Lines from blurbs Max had arranged, printed on the back of the book, flashed through his head: "horrific insight into the mind of a madman," "compelling and viscerally repulsive," and the star blurb, "the most peculiar and disturbing read to emerge in decades."

Dr. Rickman was standing, ranting now. "I want the world to know the man behind the genius. I want my name up on the *New York Times* best-seller list."

Max tried to speak calmly, reasonably. "The reason the book has captured popular imagination is because the public thinks it's the work of a crazed killer. Some books are well received because they are brilliant; some are more about fame. Once the public knows it's written by you, they won't be interested anymore."

Rickman startled and looked at Max as if he had just struck him, his face flushing red. "I am a genius. My work will be appreciated on its own merits."

"It will be," Max said soothingly. "People will be amazed and impressed by your words, yours, but it will reach thousands, maybe millions more, if they think it is written by Sadowsky. And you will make lots of money if it's got his name on it."

"I spent fifteen years of my life working on this book. I have poured my heart, my tears, my blood, my soul into this work only to be ignored. My genius will not be ignored. It is time that the world knows the truth about me." Dr. Rickman had slipped out of ranting stance and back into his chair across from Max. He looked Max in the eye. "My integrity is not for sale."

Max sat staring at Dr. Rickman, who remained in focus as the rest of the room shifted and circled around like a kaleidoscope. Max felt dizzy, like the ground was starting to tilt up, or maybe he was sliding down. Everything was slipping away. Dr. Rickman would see to that.

Then he remembered the money. He could hear Edna's words from their discussion the day before: "most people like money." It seemed futile, but what else was there?

Feeling sheepish, Max put the bag on his desk, letting it sag open so packets of the bills tumbled out.

Max looked up with hopeful eyes. Dr. Rickman stared at the bills with such intensity, his body was almost vibrating.

"Let's work this out," Max said, pleading.

Dr. Rickman's head snapped up, and like the sudden burst of a jack-in-the-box, his fist shot out and smashed into Max's forehead. It stung like nothing Max had experienced before. Blood trickled down from above his left eyebrow, wetting his cheek and tickling his neck.

"Why did you do that?" Max sputtered, his fingers pressed to his forehead.

Dr. Rickman pursed his lips, opened his mouth to say something, then shook his head before lunging toward him and landing another solid blow, this time to Max's cheek. It happened so fast, Max didn't even see it coming.

When he saw Rickman's arm pull back, like he was aiming another punch, Max raised his arms to block the blows and his mind flashed to a scene from the book, a particularly disturbing chapter in the *Sadowsky Manifesto* involving a fatal beating and a page-long description of brain matter on the carpet.

Despite his arms, Rickman's fist found Max's cheek with another solid blow, and Max felt something collapse and his eye started tearing from the sharp, burning pain.

A loud crack split the air. Max immediately thought of gunfire, his hands jumping over his body, feeling for a gut shot.

Then there was silence, the eerie, hollow kind of silence that follows an explosion. Max looked at Dr. Rickman, whose body was motionless, his eyes staring into something that the living couldn't see. He teetered for a moment before dipping at the knees and dropping to the ground like a felled tree. Standing directly behind where Rickman had been was the shaking five-foot-one-inch frame of Edna Bloomgarten.

"What happened?"

Edna looked frazzled but sheepishly held up a heavy wooden object.

"You hit him with a bat?" Max asked.

"It's a Springerle rolling pin," Edna whispered, correcting him.

Edna got a handkerchief from her purse and started to dab at the blood on Max's face. Max waved her away and squatted down to get a closer look at Dr. Rickman's crumpled shape.

"I know where to hide a body," Edna whispered.

Max frowned at the man at their feet. "Edna, I think he's still breathing."

"Oh."

"We've got to call an ambulance. Wow." Max looked at the back of Rickman's head. He would have never imagined a single hit could do so much damage. "Edna, he looks really bad."

Edna's snowy eyebrows arched with particular meaning. "I know where we could hide a body."

Max thought about it. A few seconds later, he sighed and picked up the phone.

———

Minutes later, EMTs and police circled around Dr. Rickman while Max stood behind them, pacing.

The quiet was too much for Max, who after a time commented to no one in particular, "He looks like he's in really bad shape."

A few minutes later Sergeant Williams turned back to him and said with the dry, dark humor of someone who's stood by on one too many crime scenes, "He is in real bad shape; he's dead."

While they waited for the medical examiner, the EMTs began attending to Max, cleaning off the blood, checking his face for fractures. Edna tearfully recounted the tale to Sergeant Williams while cutting him a big slice of her cinnamon-marbled coffee cake. Max watched Edna, her sweet, bespectacled, grandmotherly face, and imagined how she must be spinning things to Sergeant Williams. Edna was good on her feet. She had managed to shred the entire contents of Dr. Rickman's briefcase in the few minutes before the police had arrived.

After Sergeant Williams's second piece of coffee cake, he walked over to Max, who was sitting on a chair as an EMT flashed a light in his eye, looking for signs of a head injury.

"I talked to Ms. Bloomgarten, and I'd like to hear from you. How did this whole thing get started?"

"He came to confront me." Max took a breath, working up the nerve to tell the truth. "He came to confront me about being the true author of the *Sadowsky Manifesto*."

Edna touched the sergeant's shoulder, offering him another cup of coffee. "Can you imagine? What a crazy man—delusional, really—thinking he wrote Sadowsky's book."

The sergeant nodded, smiling up at her. *Believing her,* Max thought. He decided confession may be good for the soul, but it would do terrible things to his lifestyle.

# KIDDIELAND

## BY TIM CHAPMAN

The second-to-the-last time I saw Robert Teague Junior alive was the day my mother decided to hand dye the living-room carpet. Bobby was a kid I would never have chosen to play with except that our families were close so we saw a lot of one another. It wasn't because he was boring and spoiled, a lot of kids in the sixth grade were like that, but Bobby was sneaky. If you didn't keep an eye on him, he'd pull some stunt, and if it backfired, he'd try to blame it on you. He was in my class at Eldridge Elementary because he had been kicked out of several private schools, including the local military academy. "Those boys are just playin' soldier," he liked to say. "Most of 'em wouldn't know their ass from a teacup." The kids in my class were wise to him; he hardly had any friends.

Even though she was just dropping us off, my mother put on a sundress and makeup and fixed her hair. She put my sister in her blue shift, the one she said made Meg's eyes the color of cornflowers. It was a long ride across town from our little red ranch house to the Teagues' house, but I enjoyed it. It was a hot day, so I hung my head out the window like a dog to catch the breeze. The air was moist and heavy and smelled green. It was a cicada year, and their drone was relentless. Every few blocks we'd drive through a cloud of them, turning a couple dozen to paste under the wheels of our old Buick, and I'd have to pull my head in to keep from getting one in my mouth. Meg was curled up, napping, on the backseat. When we pulled into the long driveway leading back through the elms to the Teagues' house, my mother snapped at me, "Get your head in here, and sit up straight. And brush the hair out of your eyes, you look like a beatnik. Megan, honey, wake up. We're almost there."

My father and Mr. Teague had been in the army together, an experience that made them friends for life. The way they talked about it you'd think they'd won the war by themselves; killing Krauts and "keeping Rommel on the run." When they came home from Africa, Mr. Teague took over his family's Cadillac dealership. My father went to work on the night shift at the tool and die company. The difference didn't seem to bother the two men, but my mother was very aware that compared to us the Teagues were rich.

"Now, don't do anything to embarrass me this time," she said, pulling up in front of the pillared porch at the end of the circular drive. "And eat whatever Dolores gives you for lunch"—she looked hard at my sister—"whether you like it or not."

Bobby was sitting on the steps, waiting for us, and he pushed himself to his feet and walked ahead of us to the door. "Let's go," he said. "Mom didn't want to start fixing lunch until you guys got here." The front door was enormous and had a brass knocker shaped like a lion's head. Bobby pushed the door open with his butt and bowed low to let us enter.

We marched Meg down the hallway to the big, sunny kitchen where Bobby's mom was standing at the counter, stirring something in a mixing bowl. She didn't look like anybody's mother; she looked like Princess Grace. She wore slacks and a silk shirt, open at the throat. She was cool and lean, and I had to look away to avoid staring at her.

At last, I said, "Hi, Mrs. Teague. We're here."

"Well, if it isn't Bryan and Margaret." She stopped stirring long enough to click off the little radio sitting on the kitchen counter. "I'm just starting a batch of cookies for us to enjoy after we have some lunch. Margaret, why don't you come over here and give me a hand. We'll let the boys go play their boy games." She looked at Bobby. "Lunch in an hour, dear. I'll call you when we're ready."

I looked at Meg. She hated the name Margaret and usually barked at anyone who made the mistake of calling her that. She'd been sent home from school last year for punching a boy who called her Margaret. She'd broken his nose. I saw a scowl slide across her face and disappear. She walked over to Mrs. Teague, looking up at her reverently as she went.

Bobby elbowed me in the ribs. "C'mon," he said. "I've got stuff to show you."

We went upstairs to Bobby's room. It was twice as big as the room Meg and I shared, and I wandered around, checking out his toys and looking at all the clothes in his walk-in closet. "Why do you have all these suit coats?" I asked. I turned and saw Bobby across the room, on his hands and knees, pulling something out from under the bed.

"I dunno," he said. "I never wear them. C'mere. Take a gander at this."

He pushed a red metal box toward me on the floor. There was a piece of window screen over the open top held in place with clamps. I went over and looked. Inside were half a dozen small lizards sitting on sticks and crawling through a bed of wood shavings.

"These are chameleons," he said. "I got them at the parade in Lombard last Memorial Day. The man said they'd change color to match whatever they're sitting on, but it's really just different greens." He unscrewed the clamps and inched the screen back a little bit. I sat down to get a closer look. "You have to be careful when you take them out. If they get away, you'll never find 'em again. They're too fast." He slid his hand into the cage, cupped it around a sleeping lizard, and picked it up.

"Think fast!" he shouted and tossed the animal at my face.

We were both surprised when I caught it. Based on past experience, I had expected something like that. Bobby was obviously disappointed. I hadn't jumped or screamed or anything. I just sat there, holding the little creature in my lap. I grinned at Bobby, proud of my cool. He glared back.

"Nice catch," he said, "but check this out." He took another chameleon from the box and held it up, his fingers gripping it under the front legs. "Their tails grow back," he said. He glanced at the open bedroom door to make certain we were alone. Then he gripped the lizard's tail with his other hand and jerked it off. The chameleon's mouth snapped open in a soundless scream. Its tongue bulged out of its mouth, and it closed its eyes. Bobby tossed the writhing lizard back in the cage and handed me the tail. It twitched on my palm.

"Doesn't that hurt them?" I asked. "It looks like it hurt."

"I dunno," he said. "You can keep the tail. I've got others."

I put the tail in my pocket.

Lunch consisted of bologna sandwiches and potato chips, followed by the chocolate-chip cookies Mrs. Teague and Meg had baked. As she was walking around the table, refilling our empty milk glasses, Mrs. Teague paused behind Bobby's chair and rested her hand on his head. Bobby closed his eyes and leaned back, pushing the back of his head into her palm. The corners of his mouth turned up in a little smile, and he let his arms hang down at his sides. They stayed like that for a moment, and then Mrs. Teague ruffled his hair. "Go and play," she said.

The three of us kids went out back. Meg sat in a little chair on the porch and watched while Bobby and I set up a battlefield under a massive willow tree. I asked her if she wanted to come down and play with us, but she just waved. When Meg was in one of her quiet moods, she could go a whole day without speaking.

Bobby had dozens of soldiers, but he had the wars all mixed together. His army was mostly little green army men and a few medieval knights. My army was composed of Civil War soldiers, cowboys, and a few spacemen. We each had one model tank. Bobby went back inside, and when he came out again, he pulled a can of lighter fluid and a book of matches from underneath his shirt.

"Your mom's here," he said. "We'd better get crackin' if we're going to napalm these soldiers."

Fortunately our battlefield was mostly dirt; hardly any grass grew in the shade of the ancient willow. Bobby squirted lighter fluid on all the soldiers and connected the puddles at their feet with streams of the pink liquid. He took a couple of Black Cat firecrackers out of his pocket and stuck them under the tanks, then shot a thin stream of lighter fluid around their fuses. "You can't soak 'em," he said, "or they won't light."

He pulled a match out of the book and scraped it across the striker, cupping his hand to shield the flame from the wind. When he touched it to the lighter fluid, there was a gentle *whoosh* and blue flame spread from soldier to soldier, weaving across the ground until all were enveloped, and lastly, the firecracker fuses lit. The tanks blew apart spectacularly, hurling plastic shrapnel across the yard. I got hit in the neck with a piece of a turret. The soldiers didn't burn long, and when the flames had gone out, we surveyed the damage; legs sagged, facial features were smoothed to shiny nothingness, rifles and hands had melted to dripping blobs.

We got the devastated armies back in their shoebox just as my mother and Mrs. Teague stepped out onto the porch. They were holding half-empty bottles of beer, but I could tell my mother was ready to leave. She kept passing her drink from hand to hand, looking for a place to put it down. Finally, she set it on a table that held some potted plants and called to us.

"Meg, Bryan, let's go." She put her hands behind her back and turned to face Mrs. Teague. "Thank you so much for letting the kids come over. I managed to get all my little chores accomplished."

"Happy to help," Mrs. Teague said. "And Margaret and I had a nice time baking cookies. Didn't we, Margaret?"

Meg smiled up at Mrs. Teague, and my mother's mouth fell open. She must have thought Meg had been hypnotized. I clambered up the steps to the porch and fell in behind my mother, and as I did, I noticed her hands. They were covered with brown dots, some smudged and some perfect little circles.

———

THE NEXT TIME we saw the Teagues was on a visit to their vacation home on Lake Geneva. Mr. Teague picked us up in the big Greyhound bus he had bought and turned into a motor home. There was another family on the bus, a man who had been in the army with my father and Mr. Teague and his wife and daughter, who sat at the dining table in the middle of the bus with Mrs. Teague. The man sat up front with my parents so they could talk with Mr. Teague while he drove. The man was in a wheelchair, and even though he had the brakes on, he kept a grip on one of the fixed seats to keep the chair from moving around. My father rested one of his hands on the arm of the wheelchair, just in case. All the adults were wearing shorts, and you could see that the man in the wheelchair was missing his right leg from the knee down. I had never seen an amputated limb before. The skin looked taut and shiny, more like plastic than flesh. I must have been staring, because suddenly my mother smacked me on the back of the head. "Be polite," she said.

"That's okay," the man said. "I lost my leg in Africa when I was over there with your dad. We looked all over for it, too, but we just couldn't find it." He laughed a little, with a high-pitched, nervous sort of laugh.

I stumbled to the back of the bus and sat down next to Meg on a bench that could be turned into a bed.

"I thought you'd be sitting with Mrs. Teague," I said. We both looked over at the dining table. The wheelchair man's wife and daughter were giggling at something Mrs. Teague had said.

"She's got her fan club," Meg said and turned to look out the window.

I spent the rest of the trip trying not to stare at Mrs. Teague, then trying not to get caught staring at her. I memorized the bounce of her hair, and the way she tilted her head when she was saying something serious, and the bend of her thin wrist when she was gesturing with her cigarette, and especially, her openmouthed laugh when she found something funny. I was so entranced that we were halfway to Lake Geneva before I realized Bobby wasn't on the bus.

We spent the afternoon on the private beach behind the Teagues' A-frame vacation home. My father helped wheelchair man hop across the sand to one of the beach chairs where the adults were sitting, sipping whiskey sours, and talking. I curled up on a lounge chair near my mother, who was putting on suntan lotion. Her face was already turning red, but it wasn't half as red as her hands. She had scrubbed them raw trying to get the carpet dye off.

Like most of my mother's projects, she had dyed the carpet without consulting my father first. She liked to surprise him. He was surprised all right. He came home from work to find the light gray living-room carpet covered with black polka dots. My mother had filled a shaker bottle with dye and walked back and forth across the room, camouflaging her cigarette burns. When he came home that evening, my father just stood in the doorway, staring at the carpet. He didn't say anything for several minutes. Meg and I watched from the kitchen and waited for the fireworks. Finally, my father looked at my mother, smiled, and said, "Hi, honey. What's new?"

Mr. Teague went inside for a minute and came out with a scuba mask and snorkel. He tossed them to me.

"Here you go, Bryan, old man. These are Bobby's, but he won't mind if you use them. See what you can see at the bottom of the sea."

"Thanks, Mr. Teague," I said. "Where is Bobby? I thought he'd be here today."

Mr. Teague didn't say a word. His lips got tight, and he turned and walked back to the house. Mrs. Teague waggled her fingers at me, and I went to sit in the sand at her feet.

"Don't mind him," she said. "He's just worried about Bobby." She took a sip of her cocktail and looked out across the lake. "Bobby's trying out another military academy this weekend." She chuckled. "Or should I say, they're trying him out. Anyway, Bobby may not be going to your school next year." She reached out and tousled my hair. "I'm sorry there's no one your age to play with today, but I'm sure a boy with your imagination can find something fun to do."

I sat there for a minute, aware of my skin. A tremor had started on my scalp, where her fingers touched it, and flowed down my spine and out along my limbs. Then she shooed me away with a gesture. "Go play now," she said. "Scoot."

Meg and the other little girl built sand castles. Meg's was on one side of the beach, and the girl's was on the other. Occasionally the girl would walk over, look at Meg for a minute, then go back to the other side of the beach. Meg never said a word to her. The only time she acknowledged her presence was when a big speedboat tore past. It was closer to shore than it should have been and its wake roiled up onto the beach. Meg looked up from her work and pointed to the girl's sand castle, which was crumbling in the surf. The girl squealed and ran back to survey the damage.

I hid underwater, floating facedown at the edge of a tangle of weeds and cattails, breathing through the snorkel. There were some frogs and a few sunfish hanging out in the little submerged forest. I did my best to catch one, but they were too fast for me. By the time my mother called me for dinner, my back and the backs of my legs were aching and scarlet.

Two weeks after the trip to Lake Geneva, the Teagues threw Bobby a birthday party. Most parents would have made a pizza and a birthday cake and invited a few friends over. Bobby's parents rented Kiddieland.

Kiddieland was an amusement park filled with games and rides and vendors selling hot dogs and popcorn and cotton candy. It gave kids an opportunity to eat too much; ride some spinning, zipping, whirling machine; vomit; and start the cycle again. Even with the potential for that kind of fun, Bobby was only able to get about a dozen kids to show up. Most of them were like me, kids whose parents were friends with Bobby's parents. Mr. Teague paid the owners to close the park for the day, so we could have the place to ourselves.

Some of the kids brought their parents with them. My mother dropped me off with instructions to be out in the parking lot at 3 p.m. sharp, when she would return to pick me up. My father had to work, and my mother had had enough of the Teagues' "profligate exhibitionism." My parents had discussed this over dinner the night before.

"I will not subject myself to another afternoon of watching people fawn over those two. And I don't know why you insist Bryan go. He doesn't even like Bobby, he just tolerates him for your sake."

"Whatever happened to showing people a little kindness?" my father asked. "They're having a difficult time. Rob was really upset when Bobby was expelled from this latest military academy."

"He tried to burn the place down, for heaven sakes. What do they expect?"

"Bobby tried to burn down a school?" I asked.

My father turned and looked at me like he just realized I was in the room. "You can't repeat any of this to anyone. Is that clear?"

"Yes," I said. "How did he do it? Burn down the school, I mean."

"He didn't burn it down. He piled up a couple of mattresses in his dormitory and set them on fire. Someone smelled the smoke, and the fire was put out before it did much damage."

"And the dean or the general or whoever kicked Bobby out," my mother said. "His father tried to buy them off by donating a new gymnasium, but they figured if Bobby was going to end up burning it down, there wasn't much point."

"The point for us," my father said, "is that they are all very upset and could use our support." He kept looking at me; I think he was afraid that if he looked at my mother, he'd start yelling.

"I'll go," I said. "I don't mind."

"Really?" my mother asked.

"Really," I said. "It might be fun."

The whole group was waiting for me just inside the entrance. I was the last one to arrive. Mrs. Teague was all in white—blouse, skirt, and tennis shoes. She smiled at me, but when she turned around, Bobby punched me in the arm. "You're late, man," he said. "I didn't think you were coming."

We were really too old for most of the rides—they were designed for kids about Meg's age—but we made the most of it. There were games with prizes like ring toss and pitch out, and there was plenty of food. The best part was that Bobby's father had paid for it all in advance. There were no lines, either. If you wanted to go on a ride, you just walked up and rode it. Bobby spent most of his time throwing darts at balloons. The man who ran the game must have been paid off, because no matter how many balloons Bobby popped, he always won a big stuffed animal. I divided most of my time between the Tilt-A-Whirl and the roller coaster. These were the only two rides for older kids in the park, and they were good ones. The Tilt-A-Whirl could easily make you lose your lunch, and the roller coaster had a sharp turn followed by a sixty-foot drop. It was called the Big Dipper, and I had been afraid to ride it up until I was ten years old.

I took a break for lunch and got a hot dog and a root beer. I saw Mrs. Teague sitting alone on a bench, watching Bobby play the ring toss game. I sat next to her, but she was watching so intently, she didn't notice me at first. I followed her gaze to see Bobby hurling rings at the pegs. He never got a ringer. The wooden rings hit the table with a *whack* and bounced up in the air or caromed off and landed in the midway. The man running the game just stood and watched. He looked confused. Bobby hurled ring after ring, as hard as he could. I turned to say something to Mrs. Teague, but she was crying. She didn't make any noise, but her cheeks were wet and she clenched her purse while she rocked back and forth on the bench.

When Bobby ran out of rings, he looked around and saw us watching him. He left his pile of stuffed animals in front of the ring toss and came to sit with us. He was breathing hard, and his cheeks were flushed.

"Scoot on over," he said, sliding in between his mother and me. "Man, did you see that? I swear, that game is fixed."

Mrs. Teague took a handkerchief out of her purse and blotted her eyes. "Well, dear," she started, "perhaps an underhand toss might have been more—"

Her mild scolding was drowned out by the arrival of the rest of the group. Mr. Teague and the other parents and kids were having a popcorn battle. They were laughing and tossing handfuls of popcorn at one another. When they saw us sitting on the bench, they attacked, hurling fistfuls of the fluffy stuff in the air over our heads. It was a salty, imitation-buttery blizzard. I started eating popcorn off my lap, which cracked everyone up.

"Hey," Mr. Teague shouted, "who's up for one last ride on the Big Dipper?"

I looked at my watch. It was almost three o'clock, but I couldn't pass up one more ride. Only a few of us wanted to go. We hurried over to the loading ramp and paired up. Mr. Teague sat in the front car with one of the girls. She was frightened and wanted to ride with an adult. I looked for Mrs. Teague, but she was leading Bobby toward the last car in the line. I wound up sitting with a kid I had never met before. The attendant went from car to car, lowering the lap bar and telling us to stay seated. The lap bar was hinged on one end, and after he pulled it across our laps, the attendant secured the other end with a big metal pin. When he was finished, he stepped back, released the brake, and we were off, clattering up the track, past the crisscross of wooden beams and braces.

The roller coaster ran through a series of small dips and turns before it began the main ascent. On the straightaways, we thrust our hands into the air. We screamed and yelled as the ground changed places with the sky. On the curves, we snatched our hands back, anxiously gripping the lap bar when it felt like inertia would hurl us off into the void. But we were quiet as we approached the top of the highest run. I looked up at the blue and felt the wind ruffle my hair. There was a shriek from someone behind me, and then the drop. We dove toward the earth, and the kid next to me was clutching my arm and I couldn't tell if I was laughing or screaming. And then it was over. The cars glided up to the platform and stopped, but someone was still screaming.

Bobby had fallen out at the top of the roller coaster.

Mr. Teague rode with Bobby in the ambulance to the hospital. Mrs. Teague stayed behind to wait with the children whose parents hadn't come to pick them up yet. I went out to the parking lot and asked my mother for another ten minutes, then went back to wait with Mrs. Teague. She was sitting on the same midway bench where we had watched Bobby at the ring toss booth. Dressed in white, encircled by the white popcorn that still covered the ground, she looked like a very sad angel. One of the girls was lying on the bench with her head on Mrs. Teague's lap. I sat on the grass behind the bench and waited. After a few minutes, the girl's father arrived and waved to her from the entrance. She ran to him, and they walked out together toward the parking lot.

Mrs. Teague looked at me and stood up. "Is your mother here yet, Bryan?" she asked.

I nodded.

"All right, then," she said. "Tell her I said hello." She turned and walked away toward the bathrooms. I watched her go. Her shoulders were slumped, and her arms hung down at her sides. As she walked, she reached into the pocket of her skirt, pulled something out, and dropped it in the grass. I waited until the washroom door closed behind her and then went to see what she had dropped. It was a big metal pin. The kind used to secure a lap bar on the Big Dipper.

I never saw Bobby Teague or any of the Teagues again. Bobby died on the operating table. My father said the brain damage had been so severe that it was just as well. It was a little over a month after the funeral that Mrs. Teague went to live with her mother, somewhere on the East Coast. She filed for divorce shortly after that. My father still got together with Mr. Teague, usually for drinks and dinner with wheelchair man, but that eventually ended, too. Mr. Teague sold the Cadillac dealership and moved out to Los Angeles.

I kept the metal pin. It's in a box, along with a desiccated chameleon tail and a few other childhood mementos, on a shelf down in the basement.

# ADDICTED TO SWEETNESS

## BY LEE CHILD

The man calling himself Socrates said to the man in shackles, "White powder has always made money."

The shackles were nothing more than regular handcuffs, four pairs, latched separately to the guy's wrists and ankles, with the empty ends locked into an iron loop set in the floor. As a result, the guy was squatting like a fakir in a pool of liquid, half on his ass and half on his feet, with his knees up and his arms pulled down between them. His head was raised, and his hair was wet and plastered to his skull. He was trying to keep the conversation going, obviously.

He said, "Always?"

"Well, okay, not always," Socrates said. "Not during the Stone Age, maybe. Or the Bronze Age or the Iron Age. The Middle Ages, I'm not sure, either. But certainly for the last three hundred years."

The man in the shackles said, "Sugar."

"Yes," Socrates said, pleased with the response. He was Brazilian by nationality, but ethnically he had all kinds of blood in him. Mayan, Aztec, Carib, some Spanish, some Portuguese, and a long strain of West African from slaves on the island of Antigua. He said, "In the West Indies, sugarcane was grown on every square inch of available land. There was insatiable demand from Europe. Huge fortunes were made. Hard work, though, for those involved."

The man in the shackles said, "Slavery."

"Exactly," Socrates said. "Hoeing, planting, weeding, and harvesting was backbreaking. Boiling and crystallizing was skilled. But it was all done by slaves."

The man in the shackles was white and American, so he said, "Sorry."

Socrates said, "Not your fault. In the West Indies, the owners were British."

The room the two men were in was the ground-floor living room of a suburban house, unoccupied as of an hour ago. The residents had been told to take a long walk, and Socrates had overseen the iron bolt being screwed into the floor, and then his men had taken a long walk, too, but not before bringing in five gallons of gasoline in a can. The guy in the shackles was soaked in it. The liquid that had plastered his hair to his skull was gasoline, and the pool he was sitting in was gasoline. Less than a gallon so far, but a little goes a long way.

Socrates said, "The plantation owners had one fieldworker for every two acres, plus skilled labor for after the harvest, plus domestic staff. As a result, they were heavily outnumbered, twenty to one at times, and they were mistreating their people very badly, working them too hard in the sun, and abusing them in their houses. Especially the females. They had their way with the pretty ones and worked the ugly ones relentlessly."

The man in the shackles said, "Uprisings."

"Yes," Socrates said. "They lived in a permanent state of fear. Quite rightly, I might add. They deserved to. They were always listening out for plots against them. Which were few and far between actually, but they happened."

The man in the shackles didn't speak. Socrates was walking

slow circles around the gasoline pool, clockwise, declaiming, enjoying himself, like he imagined his ancient namesake had in the marketplaces of old Athens. He said, "What do you suppose they did when they discovered a planned move against them?"

The man in the shackles said, "Examples."

"Exactly," Socrates said. "They made examples of the ringleaders. They had two favorite methods. Do you know what they were?"

"No."

"The first was breaking on the wheel. Do you know what that was?"

The man in the shackles did know, but he wanted to keep the conversation going obviously, so he said, "No."

Socrates said, "A man would be stood upright and tied by his wrists and his ankles to a large wagon wheel. Then a fellow slave would be made to break all his bones with a heavy iron bar. All of them, but slowly and in sequence. Possibly an arm first, and then the opposite leg, and so on. The victim would be reduced to a bag of jelly, just hanging there with no effective skeletal support. The agony must have been terrible."

The man in the shackles said, "Yes."

Socrates said, "The second method was to burn them alive. They would be tied to a stake, and a bonfire would be built around them."

The man in the shackles said nothing.

"The power of example," Socrates said. "Very effective. There was trouble, but surprisingly little of it, given that for a long time an overwhelming majority was suffering hideous torment."

The man in the shackles said, "Bad."

Socrates smiled. "But there were enormous profits to safeguard. Then as now. White powder and insatiable demand. Incalculable wealth, something that had never been seen before. Should I burn you alive?"

The man in the shackles said, "No."

"But you stole from me."

"No."

"Half a million dollars is missing."

"Mistake."

"Sloppy bookkeeping?"

"Yes."

"Crystallizing the sugar was an art. The cane was crushed in the mills, and the juice was drained and boiled, and the molasses was skimmed off, and the resulting pure liquid was dried in the sun, and lime was added, and the powder just appeared. That is, if everything was done right. If it wasn't, then money was lost, and the skilled man was beaten severely, often flogged, even though he was a skilled worker and even though the process was difficult and his mistake might have been entirely innocent. Sometimes the victim had a limb cut off, usually a leg. Sometimes he was castrated."

The man in the shackles said nothing.

Socrates said, "It was about the power of example."

The man in the shackles shifted his weight and said, "Pocket change."

"Whose?" Socrates asked, interested. "The plantation owners' or mine?"

"Either one."

"True," Socrates said. "One hogshead of sugar didn't amount to much. A tiny percentage really. Almost invisible, just like a bag of cash is to me."

"Well, then."

"But the big owners had hundreds of slaves. Suppose they all slacked off, just a tiny percentage each? A hogshead here, a hogshead there, weeds in the fields, crops planted too late to get the rain? Then what?"

The man in the shackles didn't answer.

Socrates said, "I have more than hundreds of associates. I have thousands ultimately. Suppose they all made small mistakes?"

"Can't help it. I try hard."

"I'm sure you do. But what if all of you were as sloppy?"

"It was a small amount."

"As was a single hogshead of sugar."

"That's my point. And it was a genuine mistake."

"So you want me to show mercy?"

"Please."

"But then what about the power of example?"

"It was a mistake. That's all."

Socrates stepped over to the corner of the room and picked up the gas can. It was made of red metal, and it had an angled spout. The liquid inside sloshed and moved and exhaled vapor and made thin keening sounds as tiny waves broke against the inside walls. Socrates hefted it high and stepped back to the shackled man and tipped it like a teapot and drizzled a thin stream over the man's head. The man moved, and the stream bathed the hollows above his collarbones and his neck and his back. The man gasped, like the gas was very cold or like he was very afraid or both. Socrates kept it going a full thirty seconds, the best part of another gallon. Then he returned the can to the corner of the room and started walking circles again.

He said, "It was my money, not yours."

The man in the shackles said, "I apologize."

"For what?"

"For the mistake."

"Do you think an apology is enough?"

"Yes."

"Convince me."

The man in the shackles took a deep breath, fully aware that what came next would be crucial. He said, "Any process has inefficiencies at the edges. With the sugar, you know, some of it must have gotten spilled. Some of the liquid must have leaked. It's inevitable. You can't drive yourself crazy, looking for perfection."

"Now you're worried about my spiritual welfare?"

"I'm just saying. There are going to be losses. And mistakes. You can't worry about all of them."

"I don't," Socrates said. "Not all of them. Because you're right. One hundred percent perfection is impossible. Therefore, I set realistic targets."

"Then we're okay."

"No," Socrates said. "We're not okay. Because you exceeded the target. Three hundred grand, maybe four, that's within the margin. But you took five. That's outside the margin."

"But you've got billions. You're a very rich man."

"Actually, I'm an unbelievably rich man."

"So a mistake about half a million is like losing a dime under the sofa cushion."

Socrates took a pack of cigarettes from his pocket, took a cigarette from the pack, and put it between his lips. He held his lighter in his hand. It was a plastic Bic, shaped like a cylinder, disposable, nothing fancy. He didn't spark it up. He just played with it, rotating it fast between his fingers, like a tiny twirling baton. He said, "One assumes that physiologically sugar is important to the human organism in small quantities, but that those small quantities were extremely hard to find in nature so that the craving had to be correspondingly huge and permanent. That's what those old British plantation owners found, anyway. They sold all the sugar they could produce. Demand didn't fall away, even after people were getting enough. They became addicted to sweetness."

The man in the shackles smiled, trying to be a pal. He said, "People are addicted to what we sell, too."

Socrates said, "No, they're addicted to what I sell. There

is no 'we' anymore. An hour from now, you won't even be a memory."

The man in the shackles didn't reply. Socrates said, "My point is that those old primeval nutritional urges seem to have hard-wired us for addiction. For a million years, we were compelled to seek things out, and we can't stop now. We can't just flip a switch after all of evolutionary history."

"But that's good for us. For our business, I mean."

"Generally," Socrates said. "But specifically it's bad for you. Because people get addicted to being rich, too. I mean, look at me. I had to work very hard in the past. That's like my own evolutionary history. I can't just flip a switch now."

"But you are rich. You'll always be rich."

"So I should stop now? Is that what you're saying? Does a person stop eating cookies because he's had enough sugar for the day? No, he keeps on reaching for that packet until they're all gone."

"It was a small amount."

"My small amount."

"You've got enough."

"I need more. Because you're forgetting something else. Being rich doesn't mean anything unless other people are poor."

"You need me to be poor?"

"I like the comparison. It makes me feel better."

"I thought this was about the power of example."

"Well, that, too."

And at that point, the man in the shackles just gave up and waited. Socrates sensed the surrender. Entertainment was over. He stepped back to the corner of the room and picked up the can of gas. He poured more over the guy's head while the guy bucked and struggled and cried. Then he trailed a wet line all the way to the door. He held the can upside down to chase out the last drops. He put the can on the floor and crossed the hallway and opened the front door. His guys were back from their walk. They were waiting in the cars.

There was a breeze outside, enough to make a draft inside, enough to stir the gasoline vapors and spread the smell. The wind was blowing parallel with the front of the building, creating a slight Venturi effect, sucking air out of the house the same way a spray gun sucks paint out of a reservoir. Socrates figured the whole house would burn, but he didn't care. It wasn't his.

He clicked his lighter.

It didn't work.

The serrated wheel spun free and then jammed. The flint had broken, and the fragment had seized up the mechanism. He dropped the lighter and pulled his gun. He aimed at the floor from a foot away, right at the wet line. He figured the muzzle flash would do the trick or, failing that, the heat of the bullet itself.

The breeze gusted, the vapors stirred; he pulled the trigger, and the air itself seemed to catch fire all around him, blue flames dancing and curling and twisting, connected to nothing, then connected to his clothes, to his hair, to his skin. He stood up slowly, moving, turning, ablaze, stamping a meaningless circle inside an envelope of fire. The breeze fed the flames and pulled more vapor out of the house, which fed the fire even more. Socrates made it out the door and two steps toward his car, and then he went down heavily on his front, and the wind caught the door and slammed it shut behind him.

The guy in the shackles heard the screaming, and then he heard cars driving away, and after that he heard nothing, until an hour later the occupants of the house got back. They didn't call the cops. No one thought that was a good idea. They called the shackled man's friends instead, and four of them arrived another hour later with bolt cutters. Then all five men left, stepping over the blackened lump on the driveway.

# BLOOD WASHES OFF

## BY MICHAEL CONNELLY

LAPD Interview Transcript
March 4, 2010
Subject: Elyse Conover (EC)
Interviewer: Detective Harry Bosch #2997 (HB)
Location: PAB Seventh Floor, Robbery-Homicide Division
Case No. 10-0067

*(begin tape)*
*(4:45 a.m.)*

**HB:** Okay, we're going to begin the interview now. It will be recorded and transcribed, and you will be asked to sign the transcript after verifying its authenticity.

**EC:** I understand.

**HB:** Can I get you anything? Coffee? Water? I realize that you have been up all night.

**EC:** I'm fine, thank you.

**HB:** I also know that you've been through a traumatic event. Can I ask if you are on any sort of medication at this time?

EC: No, nothing.

HB: Okay, then let's start. My name is Harry Bosch. I am a detective three with the Robbery-Homicide Division of the Los Angeles Police Department. I am sitting with Elyse Conover in interview room three on the seventh floor of the Police Administration Building. The date is March fourth, 2010, and the time is 4:47 a.m. Mrs. Conover resides at 8771 Mulholland Drive in Los Angeles. This is Mrs. Conover's formal witness statement. She has agreed to discuss the events surrounding the fatal shooting that took place in her home earlier this morning. She is here voluntarily and has not requested the presence of an attorney. Do you agree with what I have just said, Mrs. Conover?

EC: Yes, I do. But please call me Elyse.

HB: Elyse then. It is standard procedure for me to ask if you wish to have an attorney present during this interview. Would you like me to arrange that, Elyse?

EC: No, I said that won't be necessary.

HB: If at any time you change your mind about that, you tell me and we'll get you representation. If you don't have an attorney, we can get you one.

EC: Thank you. It won't be necessary.

HB: Can you give me your birth date, Elyse?

EC: I'm sixty-three, born January third, 1947.

HB: And how long have you resided at the house on Mulholland?

EC: Since 1987.

HB: Just you and your husband? Are there any children?

EC: We decided not to have children. Mark didn't want them.

HB: Why don't you describe in your own words the events of last night? Start with your arrival at the house.

EC: Yes, well, my husband and I had just returned from Lake Tahoe, where we have a second home on the lake. We've been spending a lot of time there lately. But on Monday, there is a court hearing, and so we came back for that. We had not been home in almost a month.

HB: The hearing on Monday is in regard to the charges your husband is facing?

EC: Yes, involving the fraud allegations and IGE.

HB: That's the International Gold Exchange bankruptcy case, correct? Your husband Mark was the founder of that company?

EC: Yes, and they charged him with defrauding the public.

HB: Are you familiar with the details of the charges?

EC: Taking in one hundred ninety million in gold futures contracts when the company had less than thirty million in secured gold. What the prosecutor called a classic Ponzi scheme.

HB: And you are not charged with any crime in that case?

EC: No, I had nothing to do with the business. I didn't know what he was doing. I had to read about it in the newspaper.

HB: And do you know what the hearing on Monday is about?

EC: It is a status conference, but my husband believed the district attorney's office was going to drop the criminal charges and proceed civilly.

HB: Do you know what made him think that?

EC: His attorney and other things that were printed about the case in the paper. The evidence to convict my husband is not there.

HB: So going back to last night, you said that both of you returned from Lake Tahoe. Was that to LAX?

EC: No, Van Nuys. We flew in on a private charter because we had our dogs.

HB: Your dogs?

EC: We have two Labs, and if we took a commercial flight, they would have to be placed in cargo. I couldn't do that to them. They don't do well in that situation. So we have an account with Elite Air, and we flew down on a charter jet.

HB: So it was just you two and your two dogs on the plane?

EC: Yes, plus the pilot and copilot.

HB: Do you know what time it was when you landed?

EC: We landed about nine thirty.

HB: And you drove to your house on Mulholland?

EC: We had a limo take us. Our cars were at home.

HB: You arrived at the home at about ten fifteen?

EC: Yes, and we knew something was wrong as soon as we opened the front door.

HB: Why is that?

EC: Because we could smell food. Like someone had been cooking. And we hadn't been there in almost a month. We had a caretaker checking on the place, but she only came by once a week and she certainly wouldn't be cooking in the house. We put the bags down by the door, and Mark told me to stay there with the dogs while he looked around.

HB: Why didn't he take the dogs to look around?

EC: They're both old dogs. They're our companions. They're not guard dogs. We always said that if we had an intruder, Mickey and Minnie would lick them to death. They're no threat to anyone.

HB: What about an alarm? You didn't have an alarm on the house?

EC: We did, but we never used it. It seemed to go off all the time for no reason. The slightest earthquake or tremor. We stopped using it long ago.

HB: Okay, I'm sorry to deviate from the story. Go on. What happened when your husband started to look around the house?

EC: Well, I heard a commotion and then voices. I could tell Mark was startled by something. I called out to him, but he didn't answer at first. I wasn't sure what to do, and then he called out. He said, "Elyse, you better come here." So I went into the kitchen, and there was a man there. He was holding a gun pointed at my husband.

**HB:** Where in the kitchen was he?

**EC:** He was sitting at the table, and he had made himself something to eat. He had defrosted one of the steaks Mark flies in from Montana.

**HB:** Did you know this man?

**EC:** I had never seen him before in my life. Neither had Mark. After being initially startled by the intruder, Mark recovered his usual bluster and yelled, "What is this?" and "Who the hell are you?" And the man said, "I'm one of your victims." He pointed the gun and told Mark to sit down in front of him. He told me to sit down, too, but at the end of the table. He said, "You're going to watch this, too."

**HB:** Okay.

**EC:** Detective, do you have any tissue?

**HB:** Yes, I can get that. I'll be right back.

*(pause tape)*
*(resume 5:06 a.m.)*

**HB:** Can you continue with the story now, Elyse? You said the man told both of you to sit down and that he threatened your husband with the gun.

**EC:** Yes, and so we did. My husband asked him his name, and he said it was Eric Anderson. I could tell Mark didn't recognize the name. All the victims, there were more than five hundred of them. He didn't really know them because they were voices on the phone or website customers. Most of his investors he never met. He asked Eric where he was from, and he said he drove over from Phoenix. He said he had been living in our house for a week. Eating our food. He had been waiting for Mark to come home.

**HB:** Did he specifically say why he had come to the house?

**EC:** He said he lost everything. He had a home and a wife, and they were planning to have a family. He put everything he had into IGE. He had a friend at the office who was also an investor, and he had gotten a twenty-four percent return. So Eric put everything he had in, and he lost it all. Then he lost his house, and his wife left him. He blamed Mark, and he was outraged by how it looked like we hadn't lost anything and that we were protected because it was the business that went bankrupt. He had gone through all our things while he had been waiting. For a week. He knew what we had. The steaks, the cars in the garage, the clothes. He was wearing my husband's watch. The Breitling. He found it in a drawer in the bedroom. He wanted to know how it could be that he lost everything, and we didn't lose anything. He pointed the gun and told Mark to tell him how this could be.

**HB:** Did your husband respond to this?

**EC:** My husband is an arrogant man, Detective Bosch. The money made him that way. I saw it long before this. It changed him. He thought he was bulletproof. That he could say and do whatever he wanted because the money protected him. I think that is why he stole. At some point, millions were not enough for him. He wanted more. He wanted tens of millions, and he believed he could just take it and there wouldn't be any consequences. He was an honest man when I first met him. But that was a long time ago.

*(phone ring)*

**HB:** Sorry, let me take care of this.

**HB:** Bosch?

**HB:** I'm in the interview with her. I told you not to—

**HB:** Okay, I understand. Thank you.

**HB:** Sorry about that, Mrs. Conover. Let's continue. What did your husband say to Eric Anderson?

**EC:** He tried to turn things around so that he was the one who was wrong. He told him he was a victim of his own greed. That he should have known that the IGE investment was too good to be true. He said he got what he deserved. He told Eric that if he wanted to shoot anybody he should go ahead and shoot himself. He said it was his own fault that he lost his home and his wife left him. Because he was a fool.

**HB:** What did Eric do or say?

**EC:** He started to cry a little bit, and he called my husband a monster. He said that he preyed on people who were just trying to make a better life for themselves. My husband laughed at him then and said that it was people like him that made the world go around. Eric called him a liar. He said they spoke once. He said that when he heard the rumors about the company folding he called and said he wanted to talk to somebody about his gold. He talked to my husband, and my husband went into the vault and told him his gold was safe, that he was looking right at it on the shelf and Eric had nothing to worry about. But Eric now knew that that was a lie.

**HB:** And what did your husband say to that?

**EC:** He laughed. He said that Eric wasn't the only one who called. He said dozens of people called, and he told them all the same thing, that he was going into the vault to check on their gold reserve. But there wasn't any gold—he had already cashed it out—and there wasn't even a vault. That was just a picture on the website. What he would do is get down and crawl under his desk, and it sort of echoed like he was in a vault. And he laughed because the people always believed him because they thought he was in a real vault. He told Eric that he was a sucker and that suckers were born every minute to feed the rich. He taunted that poor man, Detective. He told him that on Monday the charges were going to be dismissed because there was no evidence against him.

He had guaranteed nothing to his customers. The small print on the futures contracts didn't even guarantee that they were secured with actual gold. He told Eric that greed had made him blind and that he deserved every bit of his misery. By then, I could see the tears on Eric's cheeks. He was defeated. He was a beaten man.

HB: What happened next?

EC: That was when Eric fired the gun.

HB: Mrs. Conover, I need to know as much detail about the shooting as you can remember. The paramedics—

EC: Elyse.

HB: Right, Elyse. The paramedics who treated and transported your husband to the hospital said your husband appeared to have been hit by at least three bullets in the upper chest area. Do you recall exactly how many times Eric Anderson discharged the weapon and whether he was sitting when he did this?

EC: He only fired the gun once.

HB: Are you sure?

EC: Yes, I'm sure. He looked at my husband and said, "My blood is on your hands." He then held the gun to his head and pulled the trigger.

HB: You mean after he shot your husband?

*(no response)*

HB: Elyse? You mean after he shot your husband?

EC: No, he didn't shoot my husband. He shot himself. And my husband laughed. He was relieved and...proud. Yes, I think he was proud that he talked this poor man into killing himself. Then he looked over at me, and he said, "Don't worry, blood washes off. With enough money, anything washes off."

HB: So what happened next?

EC: It was strange. When Eric shot himself, the gun popped out of his hand and skittered across the table. Right to me. So I picked it up. It was heavy. I pointed it at my husband. Then I shot him. Three times I shot him.

HB: Mrs. Conover, I think I'm going to stop you here and inform you of your constitutional rights.

EC: I don't think you have to.

HB: You have the right to remain silent and to refuse to answer any further questions. Do you understand?

EC: Yes, of course.

HB: Anything you say may be used against you in a court of law. Do you understand that?

EC: Yes. But is this really necessary?

HB: You have the right to consult an attorney and to have an attorney present during any questioning now or in the future. Do you understand?

EC: Yes.

HB: Okay, knowing and understanding your rights as I have explained them to you, are you willing to continue this interview and answer my questions without an attorney present?

EC: Might as well.

HB: I need a yes or no answer to my question, Mrs. Conover.

EC: Yes, I will continue to answer. Please call me Elyse.

HB: Elyse, I also need to tell you that the phone call I took a few minutes ago was from my partner at the hospital. I'm afraid your husband has succumbed to his wounds. They couldn't save him. He is dead and I am now placing you under arrest on suspicion of his murder.

EC: I understand.

HB: Do you want to call an attorney now?

EC: I don't think so. I want to explain what happened. So the victims will know.

**HB:** I understand. Why did you do it, Elyse? Why did you shoot your husband?

**EC:** Because Eric was right. He was a monster and I saw it right then. I killed the monster and I'll wash off his blood. You watch. I have the money now. I'll wash the blood off.

**HB:** Okay, Mrs. Conover. We're going to go over to central booking now. We can continue this afterward. They'll have a doctor there who will want to talk to you to determine your mental facility.

**EC:** I'm fine, Detective. I feel good about myself for the first time in a long time.

**HB:** Okay, Mrs. Conover.

**EC:** Call me Elyse.

**HB:** Let's go, Elyse.

*(5:29 a.m.)*
*(end tape)*

# THE GIFT

## BY FRANK COOK

Why is he rockin' and holdin' his head like that?"

"I dunno. Doc says he's got something in his brain he's tryin' to get out."

"You know who he looks like? That guy...you know...that rich guy...What's his name...?"

"That is him."

"That's him? You're shittin' me. That guy whose company makes all that stuff?"

"That's the guy. It was all over the papers."

The orderly put his hands flat on either side of the door's wire-reinforced window to get a closer look. "Wait'll I tell Louisa. Crap, man, how'd he end up in a place like this?"

"Told you. Went loony. Somethin' in his head's bad."

"No, I know that, man. I mean, how'd he end up here? I mean 'here.' Rich people, ya know, they go to private places. How come he's here?"

"All I know is that his big fat company exploded. Stock was worth like a zillion dollars one day and worthless the next. They threw his ass out."

"Yeah, but these guys…these guys got money stashed, man. Like all over the world, ya know."

"Nope. Ex-wives. Stockholders. TV said they got it all. As soon as he started going bonkers…they got themselves a court order. Got all his money taken away for themselves. Dumped him here."

The orderly stepped back from the metal door. "Guess it's not like he knows the difference. Look," he whispered. "He's cryin' again. He's screamin' and cryin' at the same time. Lordy, what can be inside that man's head?"

―――

"*O Canada!*
"*Our home and native land!*
"*True patriot love in all thy sons command….*"

Bryson looked in the rearview mirror, not believing what he saw in the backseat of the limo: J. Christian Hanrahan actually moving his head up and down to some song he was singing. And he was smiling. New Yorkers didn't smile on their way to work.

Bryson knew better than to comment but flicked on the compartment speaker to hear Hanrahan softly finish.

"*O Canada, we stand on guard for thee.*"

"Sir, there's an accident on the FDR this morning. Things are backed up. I was thinking of taking the Parkway and then crossing back."

"Whatever you think, Bryson."

Bryson switched off the intercom. No argument. No orders. No anger. Somebody had killed his boss and replaced him with this mellow guy.

The car reached the Hanrahan Worldwide Building, and Bryson flashed a rare thumbs-up to the security guard who opened the rear limo door. Behind his back, the guard flashed the same signal to the guards at the lobby information desk, who relayed it to the young woman standing at attention at Hanrahan's private elevator to the fifty-second floor.

The elevator girl breathed a sigh of relief. It was her first day on the job.

"Good morning, sir," she said crisply as he crossed into the elevator. She didn't expect a response and didn't get one. Beyond "Good morning," the rule was to speak only when spoken to. Still, he was humming the Canadian national anthem.

"Going to Canada, sir?" She smiled, facing the front of the elevator.

He stopped humming, and there was an icy silence behind her. She closed her eyes and wilted.

Came an intimidating drawl, "And what concern would that be of yours?"

———

BY THE TIME Hanrahan stepped off the elevator, the song had evaporated from his head and his mood had deteriorated. On his way to his office, he neither greeted nor acknowledged the VPs hovering on either side and slowed only as he barreled toward the desk of his executive assistant.

Maryann Shannon gathered the newspapers and mail on her desk, rose and pushed open his office door so he wouldn't have to break stride, and followed him inside.

"Fire the elevator girl," he said.

"And a good morning to you, too, Christian. Why would I do that?"

"Too chatty."

Maryann rolled her eyes. "I'll move her to the mailroom."

"I said fire her. It's my company."

"And if it wasn't for me, no one would work here. I'll get you another elevator operator."

He tried to stare her down. "I can get another executive assistant, you know."

"No, you can't." She smiled sweetly, putting the mail on his desk. "But I can get another job...and I will if you're not careful."

He looked at her a moment longer, angry at her response and angrier still that she was probably right.

"What've we got?" he said.

With a movement practiced and polished over twenty years, she put today's *Wall Street Journal* in the center of his desk, *Barron's* on top of it, and *Investor's Business Daily* on top of that. "Dollar is up against the euro this morning but down against the yen," she said. "We were up eight points on the close yesterday but lost some ground in the aftermarket...."

"Why?" he stopped her.

"Rumors...distribution problems in China."

"True?"

"No and yes," she said. "Dockworkers' strike in Argentina delayed some headphone pins. More an assembly problem than a distribution problem."

"Fixed?"

She shrugged. "Extra shifts at the Hanoi plant. We'll make it up."

Hanrahan said nothing, which Maryann knew was a bad sign. "Don't screw with it, Christian. The SEC's got eyes everywhere, and you don't need the money."

He blinked, then looked away. "Just a thought," he said dismissively.

The routine continued. He asked. She answered. He ordered. She took notes.

Finally he said, "Anything else?"

"Two things. Larry...your golf buddy?"

Hanrahan nodded.

"He called to say he's getting married this weekend."

"Again?"

"Apparently. Some nice waitress from the country club. He wants to know if he can borrow the Gulfstream and a flight crew."

"Where the hell is he getting married?"

"Italy," Maryann said. "Odescalchi Castle. Where Tom Cruise and Katie Holmes got married. He wants to impress his new bride."

Hanrahan looked at her in disbelief. "That's stupid," he said, then paused and shrugged. "Tell him to consider it my wedding present. What's the other thing?"

Maryann hesitated. "Doug's executive assistant called this morning. Doug wants to know if you got his present."

Hanrahan gave her a quizzical look. "Present? From Doug?"

She returned his confusion. "No idea."

"Did something arrive?"

"Not that I'm aware of."

He looked down at the newspapers and absently tapped his left index finger on his desk. "Well, if something shows up, send it back. I don't want anything from the boy genius. Besides, what can he give me that I can't buy a dozen of myself? Whatever it is, I don't want it."

"Aye-aye," she said as she closed the door behind her.

He swiveled to look out at the skyline, a children's choir singing in his head.

"*O Canada…*"

———

DOUG SEARCY FROWNED. The sun behind him was getting higher but the waves in front of him weren't. There were some things money couldn't buy. He checked his BlackBerry again. No response. He dug his bare feet into the sand.

"Elvis, please," he said aloud and the handheld lit up. The "please" wasn't gratuitous. His more promising research suggested higher-order machines could develop emotions. Be nice to them, and they'll be nice to you.

A voice sprang from the BlackBerry. "Yo, dude! What's happenin'?"

Doug cringed. "Would it kill you to say, 'Yes, sir,' just once? Or maybe, 'Good morning, boss,' or something like that?"

"Screw you. My McMuffin's getting cold. Whaddaya want?"

Not for the first time, Doug wished he had stayed at Cal Poly long enough to take a business course on How to Fire Your Mother's Friend's Son Named Elvis, Who You Shouldn't Have Hired in the First Place, but he hadn't. "Did Hanrahan call?"

"Whaddaya mean, 'call'?"

"He wouldn't text. He'd call. Probably on a telephone...from his desk. Did he call?"

"How the fuck should I..."

"All I need is a yes or a no."

"No."

"Thank you, Elvis."

"I got a headache. Can I go home?"

"No," Doug said and took a wild guess. "And Elvis, don't smoke that stuff in the office." There was an audible gasp as his assistant clicked off.

Doug pressed the End key. Last night's computer code should have worked. Something must have gone wrong. He announced aloud, "Paul, please."

"Hi, Doug," came a voice. "How are the waves?"

"Not so hot, actually. Thanks for asking. Hey, did the program run all right last night?"

There was a moment's silence. "Yes, I think so. I don't see any anomalies."

Doug rocked forward in the sand and stood as a young man with a surfboard brushed by. "Dougie boy, you coming in?"

"Can't. Gotta go to work."

"What?"

"Work," Doug repeated.

"What?"

"Work...where they give me money."

The shirtless man shrugged and ran into the waves. Doug watched and longed for irresponsibility. "Paul, you still there?"

"Still here."

"Can you give me some Mozart?"

"Sure. What would you like?"

"Something calming. Piano Concerto No. 21."

As Doug carried his surfboard back to his car, his head filled with the Netherlands Chamber Orchestra.

———

HANRAHAN'S INTERCOM BUZZED.

"Lunch, Christian?"

"I'll take it here, Maryann. By the way, did Doug's present show up?"

"Not yet. His freak assistant called back a little while ago asking the same thing."

"Did he tell you what's coming?"

There was a long pause. Hanrahan could tell Maryann's finger was still pressed down on the intercom. "Maryann," he repeated, "did he tell you what was coming?"

"A bug."

Now it was Hanrahan who paused. "A bug?"

"Elvis said it was a bug."

A moment later, Hanrahan opened his door and frowned down at his assistant. "He's sending me a bug? Some kind of creepy-crawly thing? Are you kidding me?"

Maryann shrugged. "Why don't you just call Doug and find out what's going on. What's it been? Fifteen years? Come on. You guys used to be friends."

"We weren't friends. You were there, Maryann. We were partners. We all were. Hell, we still are, on paper anyhow. We worked together...then we didn't. End of story. If he wants to talk to me, he can call me."

"Well, he obviously wants to interact with you, or he wouldn't be sending you something. Want me to try to get him on the phone?"

"No...and I've changed my mind. I'm going out to lunch. Tell Susan, Chuck, and Amir they're coming with me and bring their reports."

"None of them are ready with their reports, you know that."

Hanrahan allowed himself a small smile.

———

THE SCENT OF something illegal hung over his assistant's desk, but that didn't bother Doug nearly as much as what he was hearing.

"For God's sake, Elvis, you said I was sending him a bug?"

"Well..."

"Earworm, Elvis. Or *orhwurm* to be more precise."

Elvis flashed a malicious smile. "Right...one of those things that crawls into your ear and starts eating your brain."

Doug stared with dismay, wondering again why Elvis was on the payroll. "That's an earwig, Elvis. And it doesn't eat your brain, and it usually doesn't even go in your ear and, oh, for Christ's sake, never mind."

Doug retreated to the other end of the vast warehouse floor, nodding to coworkers as he went. There were no walls or cubicles at AudioNeuroTech—commonly known as ANT—nothing to limit creativity or interchange between the CEO and even the lowest member of the staff. "Ideas can come from everywhere and everyone," he reminded his "collaborators," who he refused to call "employees."

ANT was a place of open spaces and open minds—with the possible exception of Elvis...and, of course, when Christian Hanrahan had worked there.

Doug walked back to his Thought Center (not his "office"), thinking Hanrahan probably assumed he was crazy—just as he had, what, could it really have been fifteen years ago?

It was a match made on Wall Street. Doug, a touted West Coast genius with unlimited potential. Christian, a small-time East Coast manufacturer with a knack for making money. What could go wrong? Everything.

Doug was young and liberal and invested in social purpose. Christian was older, conservative, and invested in the Fortune 500.

The memories haunted Doug even now. "This isn't working out." Hanrahan came to him. "We've got millions in venture capital tied up here, but I just don't think you—we—can deliver a product."

In the end, and in a voice louder than Doug had ever used before or since, it was decided Christian would stay long enough to secure mezzanine financing; then the company would divide.

Christian would spin off the hardware division. Doug would stay and develop software.

"Hanrahan's going to build stereo speakers for the rest of his life," Doug had laughed to his friends.

Christian had warned his golf buddies, "That guy's going to give people brain cancer someday."

Fifteen years ago. Since then, Hanrahan's speaker-manufacturing business had evolved into headphones and earbuds, multiplex cinema speaker systems, and Broadway soundstages. Hanrahan speaker components were in car radios and televisions, laptops and telephones. There were deals with Japanese consortiums and assembly plants around the world. Hanrahan Worldwide was worth $15 billion and change and going up.

ANT had grown, too, of course, but differently. Doug's research papers had found their way into all the scientific journals, and there were ever larger research grants from the National Science Foundation. There were lectures at prestigious universities worldwide and, of course, more than a few lucrative patents here and there.

Doug shook his head at how far they had both come separately. He collapsed onto his green oversized beanbag chair. Aloud, he said, "Maryann Shannon, please."

———

Maryann's smile carried coast to coast. "Way too long," she said. "Are you in . . . Oh, still out there? No, I was hoping for a free lunch. . . . Oh, you know. He's surly as ever. . . . No . . . no . . . Actually he should be back in a few minutes. . . . Nope, no scions today, just a couple of newbies on the accounting team. . . . Yes, he'll probably make them pay for their own lunches. . . ."

Doug came to the point, and Maryann barely kept from laughing.

". . . Yes, a couple of times this morning. . . . Well, I'm sure Elvis means well. . . . Yes, a bug, that's what he said. . . . Of course, I'll take a message. . . . That's it? That's all? That's a little cryptic even for you, isn't it . . . ? Okay. No problem, as soon as he walks in. . . . You want me to have him call you. . . . All right, if you say so. . . . Okay, bye."

Maryann looked down at the message. Boy genius, indeed. From the far side of the office, she heard the distinctive *ding* of Hanrahan's private elevator. Like a wake behind an ocean liner, Hanrahan moved toward her, barking orders to subordinates as he bulled by offices. Apparently, lunch hadn't gone well.

She pushed open his office door, Doug's message in her hand, and stood aside as he approached.

He stopped abruptly. "What are you smiling at?"

"I just talked to Doug. He left a message."

"What? No present?"

"I guess not."

"What's the message?"

She handed it to him and watched him read, expecting a smile or even a chortle. But nothing.

"Anything else?" he said.

"No. Just that."

An irritated look came over his face.

"Christian, I don't understand. First a bug. Now this. What's going on?"

Hanrahan lifted his eyes toward her, wondering how much she knew and how much she could figure out and how long it would take her. In a deadly calm and controlled voice, he said, "What's going on is that you need to cancel my appointments this afternoon. And make sure I'm not disturbed."

Maryann watched him go into his office, softly closing the door, taking the message with him.

All it said was, "O Canada."

————

FOR A LONG time, Hanrahan stared out his office window at the skyline, seeing nothing but his own thoughts. If he called his personal financial manager right now . . . but no, he couldn't do that. The New York attorney general's office would have a record of the call within two weeks, and he'd be in jail within two years. Insider trading. Not a good solution.

Or he could call Doug and congratulate him on his breakthrough. Doug might even invite him back into ANT—office of the CFO, just like the old days. Young science genius in the number one job, older money guy down at number two.

Hanrahan studied the skyscrapers around him and Wall Street down below. Doug could never survive here, he told himself.

From nothing, Hanrahan had built his company into an international giant. He had battled the barracudas and won. He had worked for it. He deserved it.

In one corner of Hanrahan's office, there was an antique stock ticker machine given to him by the president of the New York Stock Exchange. On the walls were pictures of himself with the world's great leaders—Bush Senior, Clinton, and Bush Junior; Thatcher and Blair; Gorbachev and Putin; Jiang Zemin and Hu Jintao; and more.

Now Doug was back in the picture, and he wondered how long it would take to unravel. He read the message again. "O Canada." An inside joke between him and his Canadian-born partner from years ago. Former partner, he corrected himself.

There was a rap at the door, but Maryann didn't wait for a response to enter.

"I think I've got it," she said, holding a dictionary in her hands. "Elvis kept saying ear bug, did you get the ear bug. But you know what I think he was talking about? I think he meant to say earworm. Christian, you know what an earworm is?"

Hanrahan knew but let her talk.

"It's a song that gets stuck in your head. You know, when you wake up in the morning, and you start humming a song for some reason and can't get rid of it. I didn't even know it had a name. Earworm."

Taken from the German *ohrwurm*, Hanrahan knew, but still said nothing.

Maryann closed the dictionary. "Christian, Doug was really excited when he called this afternoon. He said he had finally done it. After all these years, he said he accomplished what he set out to do."

Hanrahan took a deep breath. "Possibly." He shrugged. "Hearing loss. Deafness. He believed—well, he had a theory—that he could cure deafness. Conquer it. That's what he used to say.

'Conquer deafness.' That was the original purpose of Audio-NeuroTech."

"I remember," she said. "His father, right?"

"Yes. His father."

Maryann looked puzzled. "What do earworms have to do with deafness? And how could anybody 'send' you an earworm? Usually songs just pop into your head for no reason. Or you hear one and can't get rid of it."

Hanrahan turned his palms up. "I don't know. You'd have to ask Doug."

"Was there a song in your head this morning?"

Hanrahan shook his head and lied. "Nothing. If he intended to send me something, I'm afraid I didn't get it."

Maryann's excitement dimmed and she turned to leave. "Conquering deafness," she said, closing the door. "Noble goal."

Hanrahan turned back toward the skyline. How many times had Doug attempted to explain the science to him? Sound waves move into the outer ear and cause the eardrum to vibrate. Vibrations go through the three smallest bones in the body—the hammer, the anvil, and the stirrup—and then pass to the cochlea, filled with hairlike nerve endings that send signals through the auditory nerve to the cerebral cortex.

"But it's all so delicate," Doug would rave. "Heredity. Measles. Meningitis. A loud noise. Some medicines. Aging. Hearing can be destroyed so easily. But"—Doug's eyes would go wide—"what if you could bypass that whole auditory structure? What if you could implant sound right into the brain?"

Back then, Doug made it seem so plausible, so hopeful, so... noble. Hanrahan was there to keep Doug's feet on the ground.

The reality was that the burn rate for Doug's research was a half million dollars per month and going up with nothing to show for it. Venture capitalists put up another $10 million, but it seemed to vanish overnight. ANT moved from a small lab to a giant warehouse. The company went from Doug, Christian, Maryann, and a few technicians to dozens of additional collaborators.

But Doug couldn't get his idea to work. Finally, Hanrahan agreed to stay through the second-tier financing and even put together a red herring for the IPO. But if ANT couldn't show something to the FDA soon...if it couldn't bring something tangible to market, then...

They decided to separate, Christian going back to the East Coast and Maryann going back, too. She'd stay with her family until she could find a job, or maybe Christian would hire her if he ever got his stereo-manufacturing business going.

Doug insisted they remain partners, if only on paper. He promised they'd be happy someday that they did.

———

There was a knock on the door, and Hanrahan looked up at the clock. How did it get to be six o'clock? Maryann appeared with her coat over one arm and leaned against the doorframe.

"I've been thinking about it all afternoon," she said. "If he did it...'conquered deafness'...you get Nobel prizes for stuff like that."

Hanrahan nodded. "But that's a pretty big 'if.' I don't know where the line is between science and magic, but a lot of Doug's ideas seemed to cross it."

"A lot of science is crossing that line these days," she said.

Hanrahan said nothing, wondering again how long it would take her to figure out the rest of it.

Maryann moved to leave. "I think you should call him. Maybe he'd like to renew the partnership. Might be nice to be part of the company that came up with something like that." She closed the door.

Maybe tonight, maybe tomorrow, Hanrahan knew she'd figure out the rest.

She'd figure out that if Doug's theory worked for the deaf, it would work for those who could hear, as well. And if sound could be sent directly to the brain, of what importance were things like speaker systems, headphones, and earbuds?

Hanrahan's mood darkened with the night.

*Cure deafness? Hardly*, he told himself. Yes, it could allow the deaf to "hear" and also restore hearing to the sick and the elderly, he supposed, but that could hardly be called a cure. Just an expedient alternative.

But what about when the nondeaf wanted it, too? And they would. The bright boys in marketing called it the youth demographic. Kids. They'd buy anything and spend billions. And now, Hanrahan believed, those billions would go to ANT.

Hanrahan's entire multibillion-dollar company was built on the reality that people needed ears to hear—that before getting to the brain, sound had to travel through the outer ear and through those bones and nerve endings that Doug always complained about. *That's how God created man*, Hanrahan repeated to himself, *to hear through ears, not the brain.*

Doug's breakthrough would make Hanrahan Worldwide obsolete, and it wouldn't take years to do it. His investors would vanish at the first scent of trouble.

Doug had to be stopped. Hanrahan could feel a swell of righteousness in his chest. He wasn't thinking just about himself. What about his employees? Thousands of them worldwide. They considered him their father, and he considered them his family. *A father protects his family*, he told himself.

Doug had to be stopped. And it wasn't just God and Hanrahan Worldwide that were insulted by Doug's breakthrough. What about the telephone companies and phone manufacturers?

All those people who depended on sound moving from one mechanical device to another and then through the human ear? How many millions of jobs and trillions in investments would be lost if Doug managed to refine his discovery?

And even worse, what about the enemies of the United States? If Doug could put a song directly into a man's mind—"O Canada" for God's sake—what would happen if America's enemies got hold of the technology? Could they put an idea into the head of the president or members of Congress? Or other leaders of the free world?

To Hanrahan, the mere fact that ANT was based in California meant the technology was halfway into the wrong hands—liberals who wouldn't know what to do with it.

Doug had to be stopped; Hanrahan nodded in the darkness. And in the name of all that was great, Hanrahan knew at that moment that he was the one who had to do it.

A determined look came over his face. Over the years, he had dealt with many kinds of people, not all of whom possessed thousand-dollar suits and handmade silk ties. Sometimes suppliers were undisciplined. Sometimes distributors got greedy. Sometimes Hanrahan had to employ hard people to handle hard situations.

He picked up the telephone on his desk, then put it down. He opened the bottom drawer of his desk and found a disposable cell phone that he kept for emergencies such as this. He punched in a number and a few seconds later heard a flat voice on the West Coast say, "Yes."

"I have an ANT problem," Hanrahan said. "I need an exterminator."

———

By 3 A.M., the batteries fed by the solar panels on the warehouse roof were nearly drained and Doug had turned off everything in the building except his desk lamp and his computer. He pretended to work but was brooding.

Why hadn't Hanrahan called? And why was it so important to him that he should? Why did he feel he had to prove anything to Hanrahan at all? Why was it so important that he hear Hanrahan say the word *congratulations*?

Because Hanrahan never believed. Never believed Doug was more than a spoiled California surfer boy. Never believed in his genius. Never believed in the goal. All Hanrahan cared about was the money.

Somewhere on the other side of the warehouse, Doug thought he heard something fall in the darkness. He looked up, but at almost the same moment, his BlackBerry vibrated on his desk.

A smile spread across his face as he looked at the caller ID. He was elated and hated himself for it.

"Christian!" he answered it. "Awfully early on the East Coast. Well, what did you think? 'O Canada'! Did you hear it all right? Are you excited? I always told you that when we got our breakthrough, I'd make you listen to 'O Canada'! There it was!"

He stopped talking and waited, and when Hanrahan said it—"Congratulations, Doug"—Doug silently leaped out of his chair and jabbed a fist into the air. Victory!

The word had been said evenly and without enthusiasm. Hanrahan sounded somber, and Doug thought there might even be a hint of jealousy. But the word was all he needed.

"It was Ohashi at Keio University in Tokyo who had the answer," Doug bubbled. "And the people at Weizmann in Israel. They had a big piece of it. Then Columbia and the University of New Mexico. I mean, they built the computer and—they played tic-tac-toe, Christian—and when they did that..."

"Doug, what are you talking about?"

Doug tried to calm down. He knew he was rambling and nearly yelling, the excitement overwhelming him.

"DNA computers, Christian. That's what they did in Tokyo. They were able to re-engineer bacteria DNA and inject binary code into it. Then the Weizmann Institute built a biomolecular computer. And when Columbia and UNM built a DNA computer that could play tic-tac-toe, it dawned on me. Tic-tac-toe, Christian. That's digits. Zeros and ones. Computer code. We could map our technology into DNA, digitize it, and transmit it to receptor cells with cerebral cortex characteristics. Of course, then we had to develop an interrupter code so it wouldn't replicate and keep looping and looping and..."

Hanrahan was lost in the science, but it didn't matter.

"The DNA was the key," Doug said. "I had figured out how to bypass the ear, but I couldn't figure out how to send sound so it would be received by just the person it was intended for. DNA was the answer. Everybody's DNA is different. Just like everybody's phone number. Just like you call from one telephone number to another, we can transmit DNA to DNA. 'O Canada'! Eh, Christian!"

Out of the corner of his eye, Doug thought he saw a movement in the shadows, but when he peered into the darkness, there was nothing.

"How did you get my DNA?" Hanrahan said.

"I tried it on my DNA first, of course," Doug said. "And when we got it to work—well, I wanted you to be second. I'll do Maryann next. I mean, we're all partners, remember? Did you know we still have your old desk here? It took a long time, but you know what I found? One of your gray hairs. That's all I needed. And we've got Maryann's desk, too, and I think we found one of her long blonde hairs."

There was a motion off to the left, Doug was sure of it. He kept talking to Hanrahan, but something was wrong.

"The point is, Christian, we can implant sound into the audio nerve or straight into the cortex. We can circumvent hearing loss. And who knows, with a little more research, maybe we can bypass the optic structure—no more blindness. . . ."

Doug abruptly stopped talking. A large figure emerged from the darkness, and Hanrahan could hear the fear on the other end of the phone.

"What the . . . ? Who are you . . . ? We're closed. . . . How did you get in . . . ? What are you doing . . . ? Don't touch that. What . . . what . . . what do you mean a present . . . Mr. Hanrahan? . . . What are you talking about . . . ? I'm talking to Mr. Hanrahan right now."

Doug's voice was suddenly loud into his BlackBerry. "Christian . . . there's a guy here. . . . He broke in. . . . He says you sent . . ."

Sitting in his office in New York, Hanrahan heard the gunshot. Victory.

———

MARYANN HADN'T BEEN in for two days. There had been no phone call, not even an e-mail. Hanrahan was concerned but not worried. Such a tragedy. She needed time to deal with it.

The story in the popular press was minor for most of the world—young genius, working late, shot in a bungled burglary. Building set ablaze to try to cover the crime. No suspects. Police investigating. "Wrong place at the wrong time." These things happen.

It was a bigger story in the financial press, if only for a few days. ANT stock plunged, but then recovered on the basis of a pipeline of royalties from existing patents. Plus, ANT's surviving partners stepped forward to assume control—globally known entrepreneur and financier J. Christian Hanrahan and a relatively unknown woman named Maryann Shannon.

Hanrahan was contacted by a few Wall Street reporters. "Yes," he lamented, "we started out together years ago. . . . Yes, incredibly bright . . . a loss to the entire world."

Then, "Yes," he confirmed, "ANT's research was destroyed

in the fire," and "The company will be absorbed by Hanrahan Worldwide. Yes, of course, the revenue stream, too."

He hung up the phone and swiveled to take in his view of New York, pleased that all had worked out so well. Then he heard it, inside his head, softly, a children's choir.

"*O Canada!*

"*Our home and native land!*"

Then it seemed to get louder.

———

TEN MONTHS LATER on a sunny beach in the Caribbean, Maryann Shannon watched the waves lap the shoreline and run up almost to her toes. It had taken a few weeks for the stockholders to realize that Christian was incapable of running the company any longer—a constant, loud singing inside his head, he pleaded, put there by a dead man.

Obviously he had gone mad.

The bottom fell out of the stock. He was ousted by the board of directors and replaced as president and CEO.

It took a few months more to have Christian declared mentally incompetent and to convince the courts to seize his personal assets and bank accounts and move them to the protection of his family—a collection of snarling ex-wives.

And that was all okay with Maryann.

On the day she had returned to work those many months ago, she found a package on her desk to be delivered to Hanrahan. It was an ANT box from California. But impossibly, the postmark was the day after the fire.

Inside was a Personal Auditory Ultrawave Launcher (PAUL) with instructions on how to use it. Then she figured it out—she figured it all out. The package never made it to Hanrahan's desk.

She took all the money she had and borrowed more, and

shorted Hanrahan stock. Then she pressed the *on* button. She harvested millions.

On the beach in the Caribbean, she lifted her sunglasses and smiled down at the device.

"Paul," she said aloud.

"Yes, Maryann, can I help you?" the device answered.

"Current assessment?"

"Christian's DNA continues to replicate," Paul said. "I'm afraid it's becoming quite loud. We should send an interrupt code."

"No," she said. "Not just yet."

She took a sip of margarita, then said aloud, "Elvis, please."

"Yo, babe."

"Could you put a little more lotion on my back?"

"Sure thing, babe," he said.

———

IN A GRAY hospital just outside New York, an orderly stepped back from a heavy metal door, still peering through a wire-reinforced window.

"Look," he whispered. "He's cryin' again. He's screamin' and cryin' at the same time. Lordy, what can be inside that man's head?"

# BLING, BLING

## BY DAVID DeLEE

Mighty Mo' Mac was not his real name. It was Myron Epps. He wasn't born or raised in South Central LA. Not even in the South Bronx. He grew up in Granville, Ohio, a small, rural college town thirty-five miles northeast of Columbus. No, his mom wasn't a crack whore selling herself out of a double-wide. She was a professor of English at Denison University. And no, his dad wasn't serving five to fifteen in prison. He served on the Granville Board of Trustees.

But being a young man growing up in a well-to-do family in Middle America did not sell rap albums. And ever since before he could remember, all Myron Epps ever wanted to do was be a rap star. And not just any rap star. Myron wanted to be the biggest, the baddest rap star there ever was.

Rap stars grew up in LA and New York, even Detroit. Not places like Granville, Ohio. They had names like Tupac and Snoop Dogg and 50 Cent. Not Myron Epps. Most of all they had street cred. They had reps. They had juice.

Mo' Mac had credibility; he had a reputation. He had the juice. So what if it was all a lie. "Who's this?" he asked.

I offered him my business card. It read simply:

Grace deHaviland
Bail Enforcement Specialist

Mo' turned from the wall of windows where he stood, staring out at an Olympic-size pool surrounded by a landscaped patio with rock outcroppings and flowing waterfalls and tropical plantings with flowers and a wave slide and tiki torches and strung with lantern lights and a wet bar and a smoking BBQ pit, all overlooking the forested banks of the Scioto River below. Good-looking people in barely there bathing suits frolicked and drank and ate, all to the booming beat of rap music with bass so heavy it vibrated the glass and the whole house. It sounded like N.W.A. or maybe Public Enemy, but what did I know, rap's not my thing.

A short, rotund figure, Mo' Mac took the card with pudgy fingers full of gold. He wore an open silk shirt with the sleeves rolled two turns up his arms and sweat rings darkening his armpits and enough gold draped around his neck to make King Midas jealous. Oh, and diamond studs the size of nickels in each ear.

He scrutinized the card with a furrowed brow. I wondered if maybe he couldn't read. Finally he looked to the man standing beside me, his attorney, Saul Rosenfeld. Rosenfeld answered the door when I rang, had led me into the vast living space in the rapper's palatial mansion nestled on the banks of the Scioto River, north of Columbus.

"Bail enforcement. What's that?"

I told him, "Bounty hunter."

He arched a thick black eyebrow. "Really?"

I nodded. "Really."

The eyebrow still raised, he said to Rosenfeld, "She's the one's gonna get Jimmy?"

An older, conservative fellow, Saul Rosenfeld wore a dark blue suit with a white shirt and red tie. A man with a thin build and darkly tanned features, he had a full head of white hair and sparkling white teeth. He shrugged. "I guess."

Mo' grinned. "No shit?"

"No shit," I said. "I'd like to ask you a few questions. Get some background information on Jimmy Dolens."

"A sweet sista like you, darling. Ax me anything."

Being half Latina, I have dusky brown skin, long, wavy, black hair, and my eyes are dark brown like my mom's were, so I get that sista stuff a lot. I didn't bother to correct him.

Mo' hooked an arm out, aiming to drape it over my shoulder.

I sidestepped out from under, smiling politely.

He frowned, not amused.

But his wife was. LaKendra sat on one of two facing couches by the fireplace. She flipped noisily through a copy of *Variety* magazine draped on her lap, snapping her gum, and snickered. Big, gold hoop earrings dangled from her ears. She wore silver, glittery short shorts and a white sleeveless shirt tied between her notable boobs to reveal her bare, brown belly and the diamond stud in her navel that exactly matched the one in her nose.

LaKendra had a music career of her own before teaming up with Mo' Mac a few years back. A duet that led to a tumultuous marriage: think Whitney and Bobby on that one. By all accounts, neither the marriage nor the partnership had done anything to stop the tailspin their careers were in. Not unlike the rest of hip-hop and the music business in general.

"You better watch yourself, Mo'," LaKendra said, nodding at me. "This cat's got claws, baby. And a bite, too. Am I right, honey?"

"Ain't you got something to do?" Mo' asked. "Paint your nails or something equally as important?"

"Better than watching you make a fool of your own damn

self?" She snapped her fingers and shook her head. Her gold hoops caught the light, winking. "I don't think so."

Mo' raised his arms, then slapped them down to his sides, gazing around the gargantuan living room, as if looking for help. He settled on Rosenfeld. "Saul. Do something with her, wouldcha?"

They were like squabbling siblings.

Rosenfeld tried to not look put upon. He failed. "Kendra, perhaps now would be a good time to look at those contracts the studio sent over. I have them in the kitchen."

LaKendra slapped her magazine down. "Fine. Whatever."

Rosenfeld put a hand to the small of her back, hovering just above her glittery spandex-encased bubble butt, and guided her out of the room.

"We don't pay you enough for what you put up with, Saul," LaKendra said. "You know that?"

Rosenfeld sighed. "I know it."

If Mo' heard the exchange or cared, he didn't show it. He led me toward the front foyer. The ceilings throughout the house were twelve feet high, the walls painted a creamy white with expensive-looking blond wood trim and bleached wood floors. The foyer was laid with tile so white I thought about putting my sunglasses back on. We started down a hallway. Memory lane. The walls were covered with framed CD covers and professionally shot photographs of Mo' and LaKendra on tour in various concert venues. Each cover and each photo was individually lit with its own spotlight.

"Whaddya wanna know about Jimmy? Besides he's a thieving, slimy, backstabbin' dawg. That he ripped me off for over forty million bucks. That he left me high and dry with egg turd on my face. That if I ever got my hands on him, I'd choke him 'til his eyes popped and his sockets bled. That's what I know about Jimmy Dawg Dolens."

Colorful.

What I knew about Jimmy Dolens was that he was a financial management guru by trade, specializing in the entertainment industry. That he spent the last seven years as Mo' Mac's business manager until Mo' fired him for, among other things, negligence, breach of contract, misdirecting funds, and dereliction of fiduciary responsibility.

I also knew that the state's attorney general's office had him arrested six months ago, charging him with fraud, theft of services, and grand larceny.

Now out on bail and countersuing Mo' Mac for hundreds of thousands of dollars, his criminal trial was scheduled to start next week. The day before yesterday Jimmy Dolens missed a pretrial court appearance. That caused the judge to issue a bench warrant. The ink on the warrant wasn't dry before Dolens's bail bondsman—on the hook for a hundred thousand dollars—called me to "track his worthless ass down."

"That's all well and good," I said in response to Mo's rant. "But I'm more interested in where he might've gone. Who he might contact? Who might help him now that he's on the run?"

"Man, I wish he'd come to me." He slapped a fist into his palm. "I'd help his ass all right."

I was getting nowhere with and a little tired of Mo's pseudo-gangsta act. I grabbed the crook of his arm, pulling him to a stop. "Look. You want Dolens to get what he deserves. I get that."

"You do, do you? Tell me. Whaddya think he deserves, huh? Prison? Jail time? That's for pussies, girl. Justice ain't no prison cell. For me, justice is you cap his ass."

"Really? For stealing money, he deserves to die?"

Mo' took a moment to think on that. Once he did, he shook his head, like something he ate didn't agree with him. "Grace? It's Grace, right? You any idea how many cribs I got?"

I shrugged. "A few."

He liked that. "Yeah, a few. I got me seven right here in the

U.S. of A. This one and two more here in Ohio. I gots a castle in Scotland. Cost me twenty-seven million bucks to renovate it. I don't even know how much to buy it. I've stayed there twice. You wanna talk about cars?"

I didn't.

He waved a hand in the air. Every finger had a ring on it, all of them sparkling gold and silver and diamonds. "More 'an I can count. Bentleys, Mercedes, Ferraris, Maseratis. Cars I ain't even driven yet. I even owns an island somewhere down in the Caribbean. A whole island. All mine, you dig?"

I started to say I didn't give a—

But he waggled a finger in front of me.

"That ain't all. I gots planes and boats and them Jet Ski things, and I gots me a record collection that's sick. Old stuff on vinyl, on tape. CDs. Thousands of 'em. Hundreds of thousands of 'em. And you know what?"

Bored, I was forced to shake my head.

"Two of my cribs? They in foreclosure. The feds? They say I ain't paid taxes in over two years. Six million dollars I owe them. Plus interest and penalties. Dolens was supposed to do that for me. I got liens on my properties. I got liens on my assets. I got liens on my motherfucking ass. All 'cause of Jimmy fuckin' Dolens."

"Then tell me where to find him."

Mo' looked around the hallway, frustrated, like I hadn't been listening to him. He shrugged. "How the hell I know where he's at? He ain't talking to me. Ain't talking to none of my people, you know?" He looked around some more. "Ain't nobody out there gonna help him. He's burned all his friends. Ain't got no family. No brothers, no sistas. His ex-wife, maybe. Mindy. You talk to her yet?"

"I went to her house before coming here. No answer. Left messages on her cell."

"Yeah. Well, anyone knows where Jimmy's at, maybe it'll be Mindy."

From behind us, Saul Rosenfeld said, "I have an idea that might help."

In tandem, Mo' and I turned. I wondered how long he'd been standing there, listening. "Jimmy kept a small office downtown, leased by Mo' and Kendra's corporation. I have the keys. Could something there help you? I can take you if you'd like."

"That would be great."

Rosenfeld stepped to one side and waved us toward the front foyer. He looked at Mo'. "Kendra's in the kitchen. You two need to talk."

"Right." Mo' stuffed his hands in his pants pockets and walked away from us. His head bowed like the weight of a world was on his shoulders. I guessed it was. His financial world. He stopped at the foyer, turned back.

"Grace, you don't like me much." At my protest, he held up a hand. "It's cool. You don't get to where I'm at without reading people, and fast. Now I know, you're looking at me and saying to yourself, I ain't got no sympathy for ole Mo' Mac. He ain't raking in forty million a year like he used to but so what? He's foreclosed on two cribs, but he's got five more he can live in. He can maybe sell off a few of them, too, or that castle of his in Scotland or his Caribbean island to settle up with the IRS deal. His shit ain't so bad. Not like he'll be on no unemployment line any time soon. You be thinking that, and you'd be right."

He swallowed hard. "But it ain't all about the bling."

"What's it about, Mo'?"

"It's about the work. It's about drive, pouring your heart all in your art. It's about what I do and how I do it. It's about delivering product to the people. It's about me being me. The whole package. It's about—"

"Your rep."

He smiled. I was getting it. Getting him. "That's right, girl. It's about the rep. I ain't like other people. Never have been, never will. I do what I do 'cause I love it and people respect me 'cause of it. The bling? That's just icing on the side. But to do what I do? People's got to respect me. That's what Jimmy Dolens took from me. That's what he stole. You dig?"

I nodded. And maybe I did, a little.

"Good. So do me a solid."

Skeptical, I said, "Ask, but no promises."

"Fair enough. What I'm axing is this. When you bag Jimmy D's, you call me."

"Why?"

"I wanna see him going down. I need that. You feel me?"

I nodded. "I feel you. But no promises."

Jimmy Dolens's downtown office was on Gay Street, next to the old Modern Finance Building. It had two large windows and an alcove for an administrative assistant. I sat at the big oak desk while Saul Rosenfeld sat in one of two director's chairs, watching me. He looked grateful to be able to sit and just relax. I let him.

Several metal filing cabinets lined one wall, there was a small coffee table, and two low overstuffed chairs sat off in the corner. The walls were filled with dozens of pictures of Jimmy with rap stars (Snoop Dogg, Lil Wayne, 8Ball, Eminem); Jimmy with movie people (Denzel Washington, Danny Glover, Spike Lee, Russell Crowe); and Jimmy with rappers-turned-movie-people (Ice Cube, Mark Wahlberg, Ludacris, Will Smith).

"What are you hoping to find?"

Tossing the desk drawers, I said, "Hard to say. Client lists. Contact information of people he knows. Places he's known to frequent."

There was no computer in the office. It had probably been seized by the authorities when they arrested Dolens. There was no BlackBerry, no Rolodex. Even his files had been picked through and cleaned out. The trip to the office was beginning to look like a waste of time.

Because Rosenfeld sat there, staring, I felt obligated to say something, to talk. "Most people are creatures of habit. They have a comfort zone. They do the same things, eat at the same restaurants, go to the same movie theater, buy their cigarettes at the same corner market, their lattes at the same Starbucks. Change makes people jittery. They avoid it, and that makes my job easier."

I closed the last drawer in the desk. It, and the office, was a bust.

"Tell me more about Mo' and LaKendra."

"What's to tell?" he said. "Mo' and Kendra are into the IRS for millions in unpaid back taxes. When they started calling, Jimmy's... shortcomings surfaced. They've foreclosed on properties that are underwater, unsellable. They've defaulted on dozens of loans. Their credit's been stretched to the limit with Jimmy taking out loans to cover old loans. It's a mess."

He shook his head like a disappointed father. "They're blaming it all on Jimmy, of course. Accusing him of stealing millions over the years while keeping them in the dark about risky business investments he's entered into, using their names to get in, exaggerating the value of their assets to get credit, defaulting on payment due dates even after they've been extended. And of course, finally, not paying their taxes."

"And did he?" I asked. "Do all those things?"

Rosenfeld shrugged and looked at the carpet. "It's like a messy divorce. There's blame enough to go around. Jimmy took advantage and did things he shouldn't have, hid things from them he shouldn't have. When the gravy train started to sputter, he scrambled to stay ahead. As is inevitable in these cases, he couldn't."

Sensing his reluctance to go on, I prodded, "But there's more."

"Mo' and Kendra didn't do anything to help their situation.

They kept buying cars and houses and planes and jewelry and clothes. You want to talk about vacations and parties? Would make you sick the money they spend. Mo' and Kendra kept acting like nothing was wrong. Like Jimmy didn't tell them a thing." He sat up and sighed. "That's a crock, too. He warned them. I warned them. We haven't had a new record contract in over three years. With nothing new in the pipeline, sales tanked. The tours weren't selling out. Then they weren't even getting booked. Anyone could see the income stream was drying up. All they had to do was look."

He sat back heavily. "They figured something would come up. It did. The houselights, and the bill was due." He looked past me out the window to the street below and maybe even farther than that. "You ask me? Sure, Jimmy's a thief, but Mo' and Kendra were as complacent as if they were co-conspirators."

I got up, stretched, and wandered over to the window to contemplate my next move. I looked to the street below. Middle of the day traffic was light. Across the street, the outdoor tables at Café Brioso were filling up with the early lunchtime crowd. Just another day.

I watched for a few minutes then turned away. "You just said they hadn't had a new recording contract in years, but back at the house, you took LaKendra into the kitchen to discuss new contracts the studio sent over. What was that all about?"

Rosenfeld shifted in his seat, suddenly antsy, his lips pressed into a thin line. Stalling, he got up. He buttoned his jacket, tugging at the cuff-linked, powder blue sleeves underneath. I wondered how hard Mo' and LaKendra's recession was hitting him. Then I saw the Rolex watch. Maybe not so hard. He cleared his throat.

"Arco Records has made an offer. A deal for a new album and tour dates."

Good news I would've thought, but Rosenfeld looked like

he'd just swallowed a guppy. I asked the natural but apparently stupid question. "That's good, isn't it?"

"Normally, sure." He cleared his throat. "Here's the thing, and you can't repeat this to anyone. There is a deal on the table. A lucrative one. But there's a catch."

And I guessed it. "They don't want Mo'."

He nodded. "It's Kendra and only Kendra. She's got to cut Mo' out, or there's no deal."

"She going to do it?"

He shrugged again. "Has to. No choice."

"Mo' know yet?"

Rosenfeld consulted his watch. The Rolex. "Probably by now. I went over the financials with Kendra while you were talking with Mo'. The two of them are incorporated. Partners. Fifty-fifty. She's got to get Mo' to relinquish any involvement or no deal."

I whistled. "That'll be hard to take." I thought about street cred and reps. About juice. "How's he going to react?"

"In a word? Badly. With all this, I'm afraid it'll crush him."

"You have some nerve!" The voice came from a petite blonde woman who appeared at the office door. "What are you doing here, Saul Rosenfeld?"

Rosenfeld spun around. "Mindy?"

Mindy must be Mindy Dolens. Jimmy's ex. Dressed in a cream-colored trench coat, cinched tight around her impossibly thin, stick-figure waist, she had mousy blonde hair and pinched features. She carried a large black bag wedged between her arm and side, the straps high on her shoulder.

"You have no right to be here. This is Jimmy's private office."

Rosenfeld took a step toward her. "Mindy..."

"You have no right, Saul." Her eyes brimmed with tears. Fighting them back, she pushed an errant lock of hair off her face. "Why? Why are you here?"

"We're looking for Jimmy," I offered. "We could use your help."

Her eyes flicked to me, murderous in their anger, wide in their shock at my audacity. "You can't be serious?" She turned her attention back to Rosenfeld. "I won't help you hurt Jimmy, Saul. How could you? You were his friend."

He seemed to melt a full suit size under her stare. "Mindy, I..."

"You are unbelievable." She spun and bolted down the hall.

I ran to the door, called out, "Mrs. Dolens. Please."

She was already at the stairwell and pounding down the steps. To Rosenfeld, I said, "Stay here."

"Where are you going?"

"To get Jimmy Dolens."

I raced to the top of the stairs, then paused, waiting, listening to Mindy's heeled shoes banging down the steps below me. I counted to ten. I didn't want to stop her anymore. I'd decided instead to follow her.

The door downstairs opened. I slowed. It swung shut with a click. I picked up my pace, reaching the door—an old glass and wood frame thing—and stood off to one side, glanced out, first to the right, then to the left. I spotted Mindy walking at a brisk pace, crossing the street, already half a block away.

I stepped outside, keeping to the left side of the sidewalk, staying close to the buildings. If Mindy glanced over, I could turn and pretend to window-shop. Unfortunately the buildings were mostly vacant, only a large auction banner in the window to catch anyone's attention. It would have to do.

But my luck held, and Mindy dashed across High Street without a glance back. She continued west, a woman in a hurry. I jogged across the intersection against the light and cursed the horn-blowing idiot who tried to run me down, more worried it would catch Mindy's attention than for my own safety. My heart thumped as I speculated where she might lead me, hoping it would be to Jimmy Dolens.

Both pedestrian and vehicular traffic picked up on the other side of High Street. That worked to my advantage. Keeping Mindy in sight, I zigzagged through the crowd, closing in on her but using them to conceal my approach.

Settling in behind two men in business suits, I shrugged off my Just Cavalli leather jacket. When I emerged from behind them, I had my jacket draped over my arm; my thick, black hair wound in a tight ponytail; and my cell phone trapped between my ear and shoulder, carrying on a one-sided conversation.

Mindy had come to Jimmy's office for a reason. What it was, I had no idea. I thought about calling Rosenfeld and asking him to look around to see what I'd missed, but I nixed that idea. If she led me to Jimmy, it wouldn't matter.

Tired of talking to myself, I snapped the phone shut in time to see Mindy making her way to the next intersection. Wall Street. Unlike the one in New York, this Wall Street was an alley at best, and the only transactions taking place here happened after dark and involved drugs or sex.

At the corner, she glanced back.

I turned my back to her, dropping two quarters into the nearest parking meter for cover. I waited a heartbeat, then glanced over my shoulder. She was gone. I jogged the half block to Wall Street, stopped at the corner of the Diamond Exchange Building, and peeked down the alley.

Mindy was the only person in sight. A block down, heading away from me.

I waited until she reached the end of the block, a three-story red brick building. Across the street, there was a single-story building with a large, open bay door. Cars were parked inside. I could hear tools clanging and the loud blast of an impact drill. Beyond it was Elm Street, then the parking lot Mindy appeared headed for.

I ran, threading my arms back into my jacket. There were

probably a hundred cars parked in that lot. If she climbed into one of them before I got there, I'd lose her. I reached the end of the building and the parking lot beyond it. I stopped, poked my head around the corner, hoping to see her threading her way between cars, maybe getting into one. I didn't.

Damn it.

A sea of cars, gleaming hot in the noontime sun. Out of options, I entered the lot, feeling exposed, walking along the first row, stooping so I could look through rear windows, listening for the telltale sound of a car door opening or closing, an engine starting up.

I reached the end of the row, nothing. Fearing I'd lost my best lead, anxiety soured my stomach. I told myself patience was the key and started down the next row. A dark blue SUV, a red Miata, a banged-up late-model Civic. My heart tripping. If a car suddenly started up and shot out of the lot, I was powerless to stop it. With my car three blocks away, still parked at the curb on Gay Street, she'd be gone.

Walking. I stooped, looked. Walked on.

A gray Lexus. An old Mercury Sable station wagon. A red Volkswagen Beetle. There. In a late-model green Corolla, pulled in grille forward, sat two figures. I bent low using the VW Bug for cover. Even with my dark sunglasses, I had to raise a hand to further block the intense sun. The passenger in the Corolla had straight, mousy blonde hair.

Had to be Mindy.

And in the driver's seat: Jimmy Dolens!

I drew my weapon, a Kimber .45, and my badge case. With the .45 in my left hand, I held my shield visible in my right, my wrists locked, one over the other. I duckwalked behind the Corolla, low, came up along the driver's side, and tapped the glass with the heavy barrel of the .45. Dolens jumped like I'd zapped him with a Taser.

"Bail enforcement!" I yelled through the glass. "Step out of the car! Keep your hands where I can see them!"

He twisted some more, then reached for the door handle. The lock disengaged with a click; the door opened.

I tensed. "Slowly!"

From inside the car Dolens was yelling, "—led her right to me. Jesus Christ!"

Mindy protested weakly, "I didn't."

He banged the door into the car beside it. Jimmy Dolens rolled out through the narrow opening. Tall and lanky, he came up all arms and legs. His skin was dark as crude, a string bean of a guy in an oversized gray sweatshirt, jeans, and sneakers.

I took a step back. "Get your hands where I can see them. Raise 'em!"

"Yeah, yeah." Jimmy Dolens stood up to his full six-foot-four-inch frame, his hands raised in the air, his eyes darting around, running through his options. He had none.

The passenger door slammed open, and Mindy jumped out. "Don't hurt him! Please!"

My eyes darted to Mindy, but I kept the .45 trained on Jimmy. "Stay where you are, and no one'll get hurt. Just stay calm, and do exactly what I tell you." I tucked my badge into the back pocket of my jeans and waved Jimmy toward me.

"Put your hands behind your head, and face the car."

Jimmy did as he was told. I holstered the .45 and swung his arms behind his back, cuffing him with flexicuffs. Mindy watched us over the roof of the Corolla, worry in her eyes. I turned Jimmy around. In his eyes, I saw a strange mixture of anger and resignation.

"Is there anything I can offer you?"

I shook my head.

He slumped against the car trunk, resignation beating out anger. "Didn't think so." Mindy rushed over to be with him, stroking his arm and muttering, "I'm sorry." Watching them, I made two phone calls.

The first was to Suzie Jensen, a deputy sheriff and my best friend. We'd joined the sheriff's department together ten years ago, just a few years out of high school. She was still with them, a road supervisor now. I didn't last two years.

When she answered, I told her what I had and asked if she'd provide transport to Police Division Headquarters. She agreed. Of course she agreed. She's my friend. Besides, she'd get credit as the arresting officer, help beef up her stats.

While we waited, I made my second call, this one to Saul Rosenfeld. I told him I had Jimmy in custody and would be bringing him to Division shortly.

"That's great. Great news. What happens now?"

I told him. Once we got Jimmy to headquarters, we'd take him in and let the desk sergeant know what we had. At that point Suzie—as the arresting officer—would escort Jimmy through the booking process. Photos, prints, the whole works. Then he'd be put in a cell and wait to be arraigned. He'd be re-charged, and if the D.A. wanted to play hardball, additional charges would be tacked on then.

What I didn't tell Rosenfeld was that while all that was going on, I'd be on the phone with Jimmy's bail bondsman, making arrangements to have the bounty payment deposited into my account. This gig meant ten thousand dollars to my positive cash flow.

"What about Mindy?" he asked, interrupting my thoughts.

She could be charged: aiding and abetting, conspiracy, harboring a fugitive. That would be up to the D.A. But I told her and Jimmy that if they stayed cool, I'd forget to report her involvement.

"Good, good," Rosenfeld said approvingly. "Kendra called. She told Mo' about the studio's offer."

With a held breath, I asked, "And...?"

"Like I expected, he blew up. A lot of screaming and shouting, throwing things, making threats."

"What kind of threats?"

Rosenfeld pooh-poohed it. "Words. A lot of yelling. Nothing more. Mo's all bluster, no bite."

"You sure?"

"Yeah. I've known Mo' a long time. All talk."

"And LaKendra? She okay?"

"She will be, but boy, did she go for broke. She cut Mo' out completely. Told him the partnership, the marriage, all of it was over. A clean break."

I winced. "That hurts."

"I guess. Wasn't much of a marriage to begin with."

"Still," I said, "have his wife send him packing while she goes on to do a new album, leaving him teetering on the edge of bankruptcy. Where's the street cred in that?"

"Yeah. Well, you've got Jimmy for him. That's something. He could use some good news today. I'll call him and let him know."

"No!" Damn it.

Rosenfeld hung up before I could stop him, tell him that was a really bad idea.

Deputy Suzie Jensen drove us up Ludlow Street to the back entrance of Division Headquarters. She pulled her cruiser up to the curb across the street. I sat in the back with Jimmy; Mindy followed close behind in the Corolla. Once we parked, Suzie flipped the emergency lights on, got out, and opened the back door, all the while scanning the street for problems neither of us expected. Old habits.

I climbed out and did the same, then leaned over and urged Jimmy out. Cars lined one side of the street, and farther down, there was a parking lot full of cars and people milling around.

The police lights piqued their interest. A few stopped to watch, hoping to see something exciting.

"Let's get him processed." Suzie smiled, relaxed. "Then you can thank me with a drink at the Wooden Nickel. First round's on you."

I smiled back. "Goes without saying." To Jimmy, I said, "Watch your head."

I held a protective hand out. When he'd fully emerged from the backseat, I took hold of his arm. Suzie slammed the door shut and did the same on his opposite side.

"Ready?" Suzie asked.

I said, "Ready."

But we weren't.

We spun, hearing the sudden screech of tires coming from a car fishtailing around the corner, spewing thick white clouds of smoke behind it. It was a black Maybach, a $400,000 luxury car made in Germany. The car righted itself, then slammed on the brakes, sliding to a stop a dozen feet from where we stood, leaving Suzie and me feeling a bit flat-footed.

The driver's door flung open.

I can't say I was surprised seeing Mo' push his bulk up and out of the driver's seat. What did shock me was the Glock in his right hand.

Suzie shouted, "Gun!"

We both drew weapons while Suzie pushed Jimmy down to the ground.

I shouted, "Mindy! Get down!" Then I took a step toward Mo'. "You don't want to do this." I whispered to Suzie, "Stay with Jimmy; I can talk him down."

I stepped wide, circling away from Suzie and Jimmy, drawing Mo's attention to me. I held my .45 in a classic Weaver stance.

From my peripheral vision, I noticed a couple of cops a dozen yards back moving quickly toward us from the headquarters building, while several people in the parking lot surged to the curb eager to watch, to see something go down.

"Motherfucker stole from me. He needs to pay."

Mo' lined his pistol up on Jimmy, holding it sideways, gangsta-style.

"You don't want to do this, Mo'," I said.

"I can't let 'im get away with dissing me. I can't. He's gotta pay."

Suzie crouched over Jimmy, her 9mm in her hand, tracking Mo'.

"It's not going to be Jimmy who pays, Mo'. Not if you do this." I moved slowly, closing the gap between us.

"You don't know what you're talking 'bout. Man fucked my rep. Needs to be put down like a dawg."

"You try putting him down," I nodded toward Suzie, "one of us is putting you down. We can't stop that, Mo'. Only you can. Now put the gun down."

He glanced over to the crowd gathering at the edge of the parking lot, watching us. It had swelled to a dozen people or more. I felt the presence of the cops moving up behind me. If I couldn't talk him down soon, this was going to end badly. Very badly.

From the crowd, someone yelled, "Hey, dat's Mo' Mac!" A young black man in cargo pants two sizes too big for him. "Can't let 'em get away with that, dawg!"

Jesus. My skin was prickly with sweat. "Don't listen to that shit, Mo'. Jimmy's going to pay for what he's done. I promise he'll be going away for a long time."

"Jail? That don't mean jack shit."

Again from the crowd: "Give it to 'im, Mo'!"

Suddenly another car wheeled around the corner. A black Beemer, coming on fast. The car stopped. Both front doors flung open. Saul Rosenfeld came out of the passenger side. LaKendra popped out of the driver's seat.

"Mo' fuckin' Mac! What the hell you doing?"

Rosenfeld moved to the edge of the car door. "Kendra, don't."

But she'd already cleared her door and was marching toward Mo'. Her hands on her ample hips, fisted. Her bitch full on.

I called out, "LaKendra, stay back!"

She didn't listen.

Mo' had pivoted when the car first came around the corner. Now he turned full on. His gun aimed squarely at LaKendra. His pudgy face glistened with perspiration. His eyes were wide, jumping around. I wondered if he was on something.

LaKendra said, "Put that damn gun down, fool. You ain't shooting nobody. 'Cept your own damn self you ain't careful."

Mo' took a step toward her. His brow hooded, his anger palpable. And his arm rock steady holding the gun. "Who you think you is coming here, telling me what to do? You crazy, bitch. You gonna stop me from doing what's right?" He waved a hand at Jimmy. "After the shit you pulled today? You gonna go stepping out on me"—he slapped his chest with his hand—"then come here and tell me not to cap this lowlife motherfucker here?"

LaKendra's paced slowed. Something in her face told me she wasn't so sure about what Mo' would or wouldn't do. That maybe he had been pushed too far, pushed past his limit.

She held up her hands. Her voice suddenly soft. "Mo', listen, no…"

Behind me, I heard Suzie. She saw it, too. "Grace…"

I took off running. "Mo'! No! Don't!"

Mo' Mac turned the Glock straight up and down in his hand, now properly gripped to shoot. I shouted again, still running, close now. The two cops behind me were charging hard. I leaped.

He pulled the trigger. The recoil lifted Mo's hand.

The bullet struck LaKendra in the stomach. She staggered

back, clutching at her gut. Blood leaked through her fingers. She looked up, wide-eyed.

I crashed into Mo'. His large puffy body fell forward. We hit the ground. The Glock flew out of his hand and skidded across the pavement. One of the cops dropped down beside us. He grabbed Mo's arms and pushed me away, flipped Mo' onto his stomach. He wrenched Mo's hands up and back, his knee grinding into Mo's back as he cuffed him. He wasn't gentle doing it.

I climbed to my feet as the cop hauled Mo' to his.

The other cop and Rosenfeld were on the ground beside LaKendra. The cop was shouting into his shoulder mike for a bus. Rosenfeld gripped her hand. She coughed. Blood bubbled up out of her mouth.

Suzie came up behind me and put a hand on my shoulder. "You okay?"

I glanced behind her, saw more cops had arrived. Two of them were walking Jimmy Dolens toward Division Headquarters, Mindy in tow, crying.

The cop with me held Mo' by the arm, firm. The ambulance sirens were already in the air, getting closer. The cop with LaKendra was doing CPR. There was nothing I could do.

Mo' had a confused look on his face. He was staring at LaKendra, watching her die. I stared at Mo'. "What were you thinking? Now you've lost everything."

Hearing my words, he turned to me. His expression shifted. From confused to serene.

Then a smile spread across his face. "I didn't lose nothin'. I fixed it." His smile grew wider. "I finally fixed it."

It was my turn to be confused. "Fixed it? How?"

Mo' didn't say. It was the crowd that gave me the answer. It had grown to twenty, maybe twenty-five people. Young people mostly. Blacks wearing their baseball caps sideways, their britches low, to expose their boxers. And Latinos in their wife-beater

T-shirts and their plaid work shirts tied around their waists, and a few Latinas and a couple of young Asians.

"That was righteous, bro'."

"Yo, you rock, dude."

"Way to put that bitch down, man! That was wack."

"Mo' Mac! You the best."

"We loves you, Mo'."

I stepped back, shaking my head. But Mo', he was grinning.

"You hearing that? That's what I'm talking about." A second cop joined the first. They pulled him away from me, but Mo' kept shouting, "I gots it all going on now, dawg! Who's da baddest nigga on the block now!" To me, he called out, "You watch. See how much my records be selling now, bitch!"

And the crowd cheered.

# MURDER IN THE SIXTH

## BY JOSEPH GOODRICH

P aris, Graves told me, was the finest city he'd ever seen. It had the best coffee and the most beautiful women in the world—and he considered himself a connoisseur of both. But to enjoy either of them, to really enjoy them, required the kind of money he'd never had and never expected to have... until the Durands changed all that.

Graves had been in Paris for six months by then. His French was, to put it charitably, imperfect. Anything beyond the rudimentary imperatives of food, directions, and toothpaste was a locked door, a linguistic barrier he despaired of ever crossing. The chatter in the street and in the Métro, in the cafes and *tabacs*, made him feel isolated and awkward and ashamed.

He was lonely. Desperately lonely.

And toward the end of July of that year, he was just about broke.

By then, he was down to one meal a day. He still had his room at the Palace Hotel, a narrow rectangle of faded carpet and peeling wallpaper, but he couldn't expect the management's patience to last forever. Madame Isabelle, the concierge, still had a pleasant word for him when he dropped his key off in the morning and picked it up again at night, but Monsieur Claude was another matter. A native of the Auvergne, he had the suspicious nature of a provincial. Poor Madame Isabelle was torn between her feelings of compassion for one of life's *orphelins* on one hand and her husband's dour officiousness and absolute faith in cash-in-hand on the other. And Graves was caught in the middle. So as August's rent approached, he spent as much time away from the hotel as possible.

He walked mostly: through the marvels of greenery in the Jardin de Luxembourg and the Parc des Buttes-Chaumont; along the ancient gray streets of the Latin Quarter and the twisting, downhill spiral of the rue Mouffetard; beside the Seine, where he'd linger at one of the bookstalls and page through books he couldn't read; anywhere, really, fate and his feet led him. And when he wanted to rest—away from the noises and voices—he'd turn to the sculpted silences of the cemeteries. He particularly loved the Cimetière de Montparnasse. The feeling of peace that came to him there was something he found nowhere else in Paris. He drank from the well of the dead and was refreshed.

He wasn't the only one. He began to recognize the cemetery's regular visitors. The young woman in section twelve, making notes in a broken-backed *cahier*; the old woman in the faded Chanel suit, perched on a bench near the crematorium, fingering the strand of pearls around her neck and gazing at the apartment buildings that loomed above the graveyard walls; the old man with the withered arm, forever keeping the rusted tin containers at the base of a war monument full of fresh, bright flowers—Graves knew them all and others, though not a word had ever been exchanged; and they knew him. After a while, he told me, he began to think of them as friends—almost, really, as family.

But they never spoke. Never.

Until the day a large, immaculately tailored older gentleman rose from his habitual bench, walked slowly past Graves with a slight, courteous nod, and collapsed on the path.

———

THEY SAT ON the *terrasse* of the Faucon d'Or.

"I'm very glad you were there," the old man said in stiff but serviceable English. "In this heat, you know, a man of my age and...stature must be careful."

Graves silently agreed. The old man's face was a flabby, sallow white with dark purple pouches under the eyes; he was too heavy for his own good, regardless of the weather, and older than Graves had thought at first. It was obvious the old man had money. The expensive suit, the Cartier watch on a thick wrist, the rings on the plump fingers testified to that. The old man gestured at the glasses on the table.

"My friend, another drink—yes?"

Graves hesitated, calculating the strain on his wallet.

"You must allow me," the old man said. "I wish to express my gratitude."

Graves quit calculating. "Well...all right, yes...thank you."

"Thank *you*, my friend." He turned to the *patron*. "*Monsieur!*"

———

THEY TALKED AND drank for hours. Little by little Graves opened up, and eventually words were pouring out of him faster than the alcohol was pouring in. He felt fine and fuddled and expansive in the afternoon sun. The old man was the first person Graves had spoken to—really spoken to—in God knows how long. The old man nodded sympathetically, asked the right question at the right time, was never shocked. For the first time in months, Graves didn't feel as if he was being judged—by others or by himself. He'd always felt, he told the old man, like a witness called to testify in the case of the world versus himself....A hostile witness, at that. Disappointment and remorse would inevitably arrive with the hangover, but for the moment all was well. He looked at his reflection in the rusting mirror over the sink in the men's room and laughed at the blurred and smiling face he saw there.

———

DISAPPOINTMENT ARRIVED SOONER than he'd expected, for when he stumbled back to their table, the old man was gone. The café was deserted. Had the old man ever been there at all? He must have been. Who'd paid for the drinks? Well, the old man had paid—or had he?

What if the old man hadn't paid?

"Monsieur?"

Graves swung around woozily.

"The lady ask me," the *patron* said in heavily accented English, "that you should have this."

"...The lady?"

"She say this is for you, monsieur."

Graves took the rectangle of colored paper. When he unfolded the thousand-euro banknote, a smaller paper rectangle fell onto the bar. He picked up the calling card with clumsy fingers. He focused his swimming eyes and read the words engraved in fine black script: M. Serge Durand, 11 rue St.-Sulpice, Paris 75006.

On the back of the card someone had written: "We show mercy to God when we show mercy to his creatures —P. D,"

———

HEAD SPLITTING, NAUSEATED, he lay wrapped in his dirty bedsheets. God, had he been drunk! No matter how hard he tried, he couldn't remember what he'd told the old man or how deeply the old man—M. Serge Durand—had probed. He kept to his room for the rest of the week, waiting to see if there'd be any repercussions from his meeting with M. Durand.

What had he said…? What the hell had he said?

After four or five days had passed and nothing had happened, he felt secure enough to venture out into the streets again.

He didn't admit it to himself, but he knew where he was going.

————

HE TOSSED HIS cigarette into the gutter, pressed the buzzer of 11 rue St.-Sulpice, and waited.

The door opened onto heaven. That was Graves's first thought: heaven.

Barefoot, tall, and willowy, with long dark hair that set off the most remarkable sea blue eyes, a young woman dressed in a matelot's blouse and charcoal slacks blessed him with a perfect and perfectly heart-melting smile.

"*Oui?*"

"*Je—Je voudrais…,*" he began haltingly. "*…Je voudrais—parler—avec Monsieur Durand…s'il vous plaît.*"

"We can speak in English," she said. "If you would prefer it."

"God, yes. Thank you." He held out the calling card. "Monsieur Durand gave me this, and I…"

When she saw the handwriting on the back, she smiled again, and sunlight poured out of the heavens. "You are Monsieur Graves! He told me about you."

"Is he home? May I see him?"

Clouds drifted into her sea blue eyes. "I'm afraid that isn't possible."

"Is something wrong?"

She bit her lip and looked at the parquet flooring of the foyer. "My father is not well."

"I'm…I'm sorry."

She looked up at him. Her eyes were stormy and pain racked. "What the doctors say is not good."

"What is the—the problem?"

"His heart. *Comme toujours*, his heart."

"I see."

She started to say something, then stopped. Graves waited.

"—*Alors*," she said, stirring. "I'll tell him that you called. Papa will be pleased. Thank you."

She turned to go into the house.

"Would it be all right—," Graves blurted, and she turned back to him. "Would it be all right if I called in a couple of days to see how your father's doing?"

She thought it over. "Yes. That would be all right." She started in again. The door began to close.

"Who should I ask for?"

"*Pardon?*"

"I don't even know your name."

"Pauline," she said and closed the door.

Pauline Durand. P. D. *Oh, my God*, he thought as he walked toward the Métro, *Pauline Durand*.... Miracles do occur, he decided. Angels do appear on earth.

———

SHE HAD GOOD news for him when he called.

"He is much better, and he wants you to dine with us this Friday evening. Is that all right for you?"

He thought he could manage it.

———

PAULINE CROSSED TO the library door and took his hands in hers. She was lovelier than ever, if such a thing was conceivable. Her dark hair was up, exposing the line of her long white neck, bare but for a thin chain of silver. "I'm so glad you could come," she said. "Papa, look who's here."

Pale and massive, Monsieur Durand shifted his gaze from the French windows and the garden beyond and nodded. He'd aged considerably since Graves had seen him last. His face was pinched, diminished; his breathing labored.

"Papa's doing much better," Pauline said brightly. "Aren't you, Papa?"

Durand lifted a shoulder, let it drop.

Pauline turned to Graves. "Doctor Branchet is dining with us. You don't mind, do you?"

"Not at all."

She knelt beside the old man's chair. "Papa, I'll leave you with Monsieur Graves. You'll call if you need anything?"

He waved a tremulous hand in the direction of the door.

As she passed Graves, she whispered, "Don't give him anything to drink."

Graves watched her exit, then fixed himself a scotch and soda.

The old man's eyes glittered greedily. "...How is it?"

"You have very good taste, Monsieur Durand. It's marvelous."

The old man sighed. "Someone should enjoy it."

Graves crossed to the French windows and looked out into the garden. The red and yellow and orange flowers glowed in the dying light of day.

"I was quite worried about you, Monsieur Durand. How have you been since last we met? Better, I hope?"

"I've been making my will," Durand said. "I am preparing to die."

"Monsieur Durand, don't say that. You'll outlive us all."

Durand laughed, but there was no humor in it. "I doubt that....All this talk about my heart. My heart is what it has always been. A problem. Nothing more than that." He pointed at a photograph of Pauline on the desk. "She is what will kill me."

"I'm afraid I don't—"

"She is her mother's daughter, Monsieur Graves. Very smart

and very cold. I managed to outwit and outlive Ariane, but I will not have such luck with Pauline."

"Monsieur Durand, you don't mean that."

The old man brought a meaty fist down on the desk with surprising force. "Please do not contradict me! Ariane tried to destroy my soul, but she couldn't do it. I was young then—strong. But Pauline...Pauline is smarter than her mother ever was. She knows her greatest friend is my greatest foe—time. All she has to do is wait, and in time she will have won the battle. She will have won—and I will have lost."

"Monsieur Durand, please—"

He slammed his fist down again and continued with mounting anger: "I—will—have—lost!"

The old man gasped. He pointed at one of the desk drawers. A key was in the lock, but the drawer opened easily. Graves took out the bottle of nitroglycerin tablets and placed one, then another of the tablets under Durand's tongue.

Durand sat back in his chair. He wiped the sweat off his forehead and temples with a silk handkerchief.

"...Once again you have saved my life, Monsieur Graves," he said weakly. "Now—if you'll be so kind—please ignore my daughter's advice, and for the love of our immortal Savior, give me a scotch and water."

Graves had no difficulty disobeying Pauline's request.

———

DURAND SAID NOTHING about his attack, and neither did Graves. He did his best to concentrate on the twists and turns of the dinner conversation—a good portion of which was conducted in French, as Doctor Branchet spoke little English. Pauline served as translator, doing her best to keep Graves *au courant*. He appreciated the effort, and when he recalled the old man's

outburst in the library, Pauline's charm and vivacity and sheer
beauty almost always cleared away his doubts. Almost always...

Monsieur Durand watched them but seemed to be listening
to someone—or something—else. He joined in the conversation
only when the subject turned to painting. Branchet insisted that
a certain Braque had been painted in a certain year; Durand just
as vehemently denied it.

"Why don't we look in one of your books, Papa?" Pauline
said. "Wouldn't that be better than guessing and fighting over it?
You must be careful not to get excited."

"I know when it was painted, *ma petite*—1910."

"Nineteen fourteen," Branchet corrected.

"There's one way to settle this." Pauline strode off to the
library and returned several minutes later with an oversized art
book. She placed the volume in front of her father, who slowly
flipped through its pages.

"Here it is: Nineteen ten!" the old man crowed at Graves.
"You see, young man, I was right."

Doctor Branchet graciously conceded the point.

That was the old man's last victory.

————

TOWARD THE END of the meal, Durand's limited energy was
visibly flagging. He thanked the men for coming and kissed Pauline on the cheek. Refusing all assistance, he shuffled away to the
library to replace the book. They watched him leave the room
and, a few moments later, heard the library door open.

"...Do you think he'll be all right?" Pauline asked. "Should I
go see if he is all right?"

"He'll be fine," Graves said. "He just needs to rest."

"*Un autre café, Pauline?*" the doctor asked.

"*Merci, non.*"

"Monsieur Graves?"

"Yes, thank you. *Oui.*"

The doctor poured Graves a fresh cup of coffee, then one for himself. He lit a cigar and unbuttoned his jacket. "Tell me, Monsieur Graves. Have you ever been to 'Ollywood, California?"

"No, I haven't. Someday, though—"

"He hasn't come out yet," Pauline said. "I'm going to check on him. Excuse me." She rose and hurried away, heels tapping on the parquet flooring.

"...A lovely woman," the doctor said.

"Very."

Branchet leaned forward earnestly. "Monsieur Graves, I must ask you something."

"Yes?"

"Have you been, perhaps, to Denver, Colorado?"

The doctor would never know. Pauline's scream cut off any answer Graves might have given.

———

GRAVES SAT WITH Pauline in the library. Grief lacerated her— if only she'd accompanied her father to the library, if only she'd kept an eye on him...

Graves listened, he soothed, but his mind was churning over something else. Something he'd rather not think about. She was so beautiful, after all. So kind. And in the not-too-distant future, so very, very rich. She'd make someone a lovely wife. Maybe him if he played his cards right. They could lead a golden life together. A life of love and wealth and happiness... No, the old man deserved better. There was no way to avoid it. It had to be said.

"He knew this was going to happen, Pauline."

"We all knew it. But who thought it would happen so soon?"

"He did." Graves took a deep breath, let it out slowly. "You killed him, Pauline."

She looked at him, stricken. "How can you say that? How can you possibly say that?"

"I know what I saw."

"You saw me stick a knife in his heart, is that what you saw?"

"Practically." He stood up and crossed to the old man's desk. "Your father had an attack earlier this evening. After you'd left the room."

"I—I didn't know that."

"He didn't want you to. I got his pills out of the desk drawer for him. This drawer," he said, pointing.

Ice entered the blue of her eyes. "Did you?"

"And I noticed something then. The drawer wasn't locked. The key was in the lock, but the drawer could be opened. Now the key is missing. And I'll bet the drawer is locked."

He reached out, grasped the drawer handle, and pulled.

The drawer didn't open.

Pauline's tears had stopped. She watched him intently.

"In a situation like this," Graves went on, "I have to ask myself, who locked the drawer so he couldn't reach his pills? And the answer to that is another question: who was in the library between the time your father and I left it and the time he went back to replace the book? . . . I didn't go in. Neither did Doctor Branchet. Neither did your father. But you did, Pauline. You're the only one who did. So it's only logical that you're the one who locked the drawer. . . . You killed him. It's as simple as that."

He poured himself a stiff shot of scotch at the bar, then turned to the silent Pauline.

". . . Well?"

"You're very smart," she said quietly. "But not quite smart enough." Her eyes shone with hatred and triumph. "I know about you. Father told me everything you said to him that day. I know what you did in America. I know why you're here in Paris and why you can't go home. And I also know the last thing you want is to have the police brought into this."

"You're sure about that?"

"Very sure."

Graves reached for the phone on the desk. "Let's see just how sure you are."

"Who are you calling?"

"The police."

"You wouldn't dare."

"Wouldn't I?"

Graves waited for the connection to be made.

"*Allô?*" Madame Isabelle said.

"*...Bonsoir,*" Graves said into the receiver. "*Parlez-vous anglais?*"

"*Oui—un peu,*" Madame Isabelle said. "A leetle beet, yes. You are for a room?"

"Inspector, I'd like to report a murder."

"*Comment?*" said a puzzled Madame Isabelle.

"No." Pauline tore the phone from his grasp, slammed it into its cradle. "We don't want the police here."

"And why is that, Pauline?"

He could hardly hear her answer. "You know why."

Graves sat in the old man's chair. "Things aren't as bad as you think." He gestured to the chair in front of the desk. "Sit down, Pauline. Let's talk."

After a long moment, Pauline sat down.

———

"I DIDN'T PRESS my luck," Graves said. We sat in the lobby of the Palace Hotel with cigars and an almost empty bottle of very good scotch. "I didn't bleed her dry, and I never asked for more. I could have—I held all the aces. But I didn't. I bought this hotel, settled in, and that was that. In fact, I haven't seen her since that night. I have no desire to. No desire at all…Another—yes?"

I nodded.

"I'm not a greedy man. I just wanted enough money to enjoy some of the finer things this life has to offer. Give me a good cup of coffee, a beautiful woman, and I'm content." He dusted cigar ash off his blazer, glanced at his wristwatch. "My God. I had no idea it was so late." He hoisted himself to his feet.

I rose unsteadily. "Thank you for a pleasant evening."

"The pleasure's all mine."

He accompanied me upstairs, "Just to make sure you get there all right." We shook hands outside my door. My key was in the lock when a question struck me. "Graves?"

He stopped at the head of the stairs. Swaying slightly, he steadied himself with a hand on the banister. "Yes?"

"…What was it you did in the States? Did you kill somebody?"

"I did nothing that hasn't been done before," he said, and began his descent.

I followed after him groggily. "But you've got to tell me. I want to know. Did you kill someone?"

Before I knew what had happened, I was dangling backward over the banister. His grasp on my shirtfront was all that kept me from tumbling to the lobby below.

"Careful, *mon ami*." His eyes locked on mine. "We've had a lot to drink, and a fall down these stairs could be fatal. One slip and—"

"I was only asking…for God's sake…."

His features slackened. The ice melted in his eyes. He pulled me back to safety and grinned. "You see what I mean about these stairs?"

"…I see."

"Sleep well. I'll make sure Madame Isabelle brings you breakfast in the morning."

Smoothing my rumpled shirt, I started up the stairs.

"You're in thirty-seven, isn't that right?" he called out after me. "I'll leave a note for her at the desk."

I'd reached the third-floor landing and could only hear his voice by then.

"That's my old room," I heard him say. "Number thirty-seven. You're going to have a very good time in Paris, I can tell you. It's the luckiest room in the hotel."

———

THE DAY THAT Madame Isabelle found Graves's body at the foot of the stairs, I switched hotels. I took a cab to the Ritz and was glad of the change. I feel best at a place like the Ritz. I always have.

Gazing out at the Place Vendôme, I drank a toast to Graves's memory. Then I put the bottle of scotch away. Too much whiskey will kill you.

As will a sudden, unexpected jab between the shoulder blades at the top of a steep and rickety old staircase.

Graves had covered his tracks well—changing his name, altering his appearance, burrowing into an obscure hotel on an anonymous side street in an unfashionable *quartier*. It had taken me four years to find him.

But I'd found him.

Because Pauline had asked me to. And I love Pauline.

Besides, I'd never much cared for our dear papa, either.

# THE PRECIPICE

## BY DANIEL J. HALE

I woke up on a wooden floor in front of a rough-hewn lime-stone fireplace. The flames made me squint. I felt drunk and hungover at the same time. My platinum Rolex—the last remnant of a life taken for granted—read three fifteen. I still wore my tuxedo.

It took a few moments to realize where I was and a few moments more to remember I was under court order not to be there. The trip from the mansion to the cabin would have taken over an hour. I'd been in no shape to get behind the wheel when I left my cousin's wedding reception. The brunette in the metal-lic green dress must have driven. Her name was Chloe or Zoe or something like that. Chloe sounded right. I needed to find her. We needed to leave before someone found us.

I tried to stand. My head was an anvil. I caught myself on the lip of the hearth and sat with my back to the fire. A shapely blonde in a black cocktail dress lay on the white fleece rug in the middle of the room. Her long golden tresses covered her face. Unless she'd changed clothes and put on a wig, it wasn't Chloe. As I crawled across the flokati, I saw a Mustique-shaped birth-mark below the blonde's left knee. Then I noticed her comically large feet and chartreuse-painted toenails. "Dizzy?"

She didn't answer, but she was warm, and she had a pulse. I brushed back her hair—translucent complexion, patrician features, determined chin. Karen Altenbaumer was the paragon she'd been two decades ago, when we graduated from high school and she dumped me for Keith Fallon. I hadn't fared as well; I'd turned doughy, my skin was sun damaged, and worry had salted my black hair with gray. The days of girls like Karen going for me were long gone. I shook her awake.

She looked at me for a moment, then she let out a piercing scream.

I covered my ears. "Softer, please."

Karen kicked me in the chest and sent me sprawling toward the fireplace. "Stay away from me!" She scooted backward across the flokati.

I pulled myself up onto the hearth. My cummerbund cut into my waist. The coppery taste in my mouth told me I'd bitten my tongue.

She stopped and stared. "Trip?"

"Hey, Dizz."

She pulled back her hair. The large diamond studs in her ears caught the firelight. "What am I doing here?"

"I don't even know why I'm here."

Karen gave me a suspicious glare.

"Believe what you want." I rubbed my temples. "Just keep your voice down. My brain's about to explode."

"Okay." Her words softened to a whisper. "I feel like I've been hit in the head with a baseball bat." Karen looked around and said, "This place is familiar. We used to come here in high school."

I nodded. "It's my family's old cabin."

"How did we get here?"

"No clue. The last thing I remember is leaving the party with that dark-headed girl in the shiny green dress."

Karen tilted her head to the side. "Wasn't she a bit young for you, Trip?"

"That's not really the point right now." I paused. "What's the last thing you remember?"

"The car service had just picked me up at the mansion."

"Car service? I thought billionaires' wives had chauffeur-driven time machines."

"My husband's selective cheapness is also not the point right now." Karen ran her fingertips over her lips. "I took a drink from the bottle of Evian they always leave for you in the backseat. We turned onto Turtle Creek. Everything went black. The water must have been drugged."

I stood and reached into my pants pocket. I was relieved—then horrified—to find my car key there. Chloe hadn't driven. I must have. I hoped no one got injured in the process. I walked over and offered Karen my hand.

She held my wrist and looked at my watch. "I've lost over five hours."

"Me, too." I pulled her to her feet. "I don't know what's going on, but we need to leave." I tried to guide her to the front door.

Karen stood her ground. "I'm barefooted…and I need my mink."

I looked for her shoes and coat, but the fire's glimmer faded as it reached the corners of the cabin's great room. I headed for the archway that led into the kitchen.

"Where are you going?"

"Lights." I flipped one switch after another. Nothing happened. I looked back at Karen and said, "They must have shut off the electricity."

" 'They'? Didn't you inherit this place from your father?"

"I lost it. I lost everything." Thinking I might be able to see by the glow of its screen, I pulled my cell phone from the breast pocket of my dinner jacket and hit the power button. It was dead. "Bring your phone?"

"It's in my evening bag, wherever that is." Karen looked around.

I cut across the flokati. "I'll go warm up the car. There's a flashlight in the glove compartment. I'll bring it back, and we'll find your things."

She grabbed my hand and pulled me to a stop. "You're not leaving me alone."

"Fine." I slipped out of my alligator tux shoes and nudged them over in front of her. "These'll be a little tight, but they should get you to the car."

She gave a frown that on any other woman would have been a pout. Coming from Karen, it was a warning, a look of "Don't you dare say another word."

I winked at her. "It's not that you have big feet, Dizz. Mine are just small."

Karen rolled her eyes, then she held on to my shoulder as she slipped on my shoes. I caught a whiff of Caron's Poivre. My second wife had worn it back in the days of charity balls and exclusive islands and flying private. It seemed a million years ago. I wanted to go back in time. I wanted to go back to being the guy who gave away money, not one who needed it.

We hurried onto the front porch. The cedar planks felt rough beneath my socks. Wood smoke tinged the cold, dry Texas air. A crescent moon shone down from a dome of stars. Flat, bluish light covered the scrub oak–covered slope that ran from the high ridge on which the cabin sat to the highway far below. Halfway between here and there, the old limestone quarry loomed like a black hole in the center of what had been my grandfather's thousand acres. Its void threatened to gobble up the land the way it devoured our caretaker when I was eight. A serpentine break in the trees delineated the driveway as it curved far around the quarry and down the hill.

Karen shivered in her little black dress. I draped my jacket over her shoulders, then we hurried down the steps and through a copse of trees to the parking area. I was horrified—then relieved—to see the ancient Mercedes sedan sitting undamaged in the pea gravel–paved clearing. At least I hadn't smashed into another car. Walking gingerly across the tiny stones, I pulled the key from my pocket and hit the remote unlock button.

The interior of the car filled with light too pale for comfort. Karen opened the back door as I slid into the driver's seat. I turned the key in the ignition. The interior went from softly lit to dark. The engine didn't make a sound. I released the key. The lights glowed again. I tried again with the same result. I stepped out of the car.

Karen stood before me in her fur coat and a pair of black satin pumps. "My things were in the back." She handed me my jacket, pointed at my shoes on the ground, then said, "Car won't start?"

"Battery's dead. Find your purse?"

She shook her head.

I put on my jacket and my shoes. "Cell phone in your coat?"

She slid her hands into her pockets. "No."

"If there's not a power pack in the emergency kit, we're going to have to hoof it to Dinosaur Valley. Let's hope there's a park ranger on duty." I opened the trunk. The compartment filled with anemic light. A large crocodile handbag sat in the center of the floorboard. I picked it up. The thing must have weighed over ten pounds. It didn't seem appropriate for evening wear. "You took this to the party?"

"Of course not. I carried my Devi Kroell clutch, but..." Karen looked at it carefully. "I think that's my Birkin."

I handed her the purse.

"It's so heavy." She ran her fingers along one of the handles. "It is mine—I can feel my nephew's bite marks. I can't imagine what I could have left in it that weighs so much."

"I hope your phone's in there."

She opened the bag.

"Well?"

Karen looked at me; then she looked past me. Her voice a whisper, she said, "There's something behind you."

I turned to see only shadows. "There's nothing—"

Footsteps on gravel moved swiftly away. I looked back to see Karen disappearing into the trees. I started after her, but I tripped and fell palms-first onto the pea gravel. I brushed off the pebbles imprinted in my hands, then I looked inside the handbag Karen had left on the ground. The stones inside sparkled so intensely, they seemed to amplify the moonlight. I didn't know how a handbag full of diamonds had ended up in my trunk, and I wasn't sure why the sight of them prompted Karen to run away, but if I knew her—and I'd known her almost all her life—she would head straight downhill toward the highway . . . and the quarry.

I dove into the woods. The moon's light dimmed to near darkness. A branch snagged my bow tie and pulled it from my neck. Limbs clawed at my hands, neck, and face. It didn't matter. I had to keep moving. The trees grew right up to the edge of the quarry. Karen would have hardscrabble ground beneath her feet one moment, sixty-five feet of nothing the next.

I yelled, "Dizzy! Wait!"

When I was eight, my dad and I spent Thanksgiving at the cabin. Our caretaker joined us for lunch. He brought a bottle of Jack Daniel's; he drank more than he ate, then he wandered off. When he didn't come back, Dad and I went looking for him. We found our caretaker at the bottom of the quarry. I didn't want to find Karen there, too.

My tux shoes' smooth soles were made for dancing; they weren't good when it came to keeping traction on a rocky hillside. I snagged my ear on a branch. Blood dribbled down my neck and under the collar of my shirt. It didn't matter. I had to catch Karen before she stepped out into thin air.

As I scrambled down the slope, I heard something moving through the trees off to my right. "Dizzy?" There was no answer. I came to a halt. Fast footsteps—it sounded like a heavy man in heavy boots—hurried past just out of sight on my right. A moment later, another set of substantial footsteps passed on the left. Karen and I had company. I had a feeling they weren't there to help us.

None of this made sense. I hadn't spoken to Karen in twenty years. In that time, her welfare boyfriend had become her billionaire husband, and me the playboy philanthropist had deteriorated into a pathetic charity case. Tonight, after seeing each other across the room at my cousin's wedding, Karen and I woke up together in the cabin I'd lost a month earlier. The trunk of my car was full of diamonds. The sight of them caused Karen to run. I chased her. Now, other people were chasing us.

The situation was surreal, but it wasn't a dream. Karen was drawing ever closer to the quarry. I knew I wasn't going to catch her in time. Even if it tipped off the men in the boots, I had to warn her before she plunged into oblivion. "Dizzy! Stop right now! There's a cliff in front of you!"

A breaking branch jolted the still air. The Doppler fade of a man's scream in free fall ended in an abrupt *whump*. Whoever the guy was, he'd fallen into the quarry. He was surely dead.

"Dizz? Are you all right?"

There was no answer. The second man had probably already gotten to her. I was nearing the void, but I couldn't slow down. There might still be a chance to save Karen.

Feet skidding over limestone chaff, I pushed through the closely spaced limbs. There was another scream nearby, but it was cut short by a gun blast. Moments later, I heard a sound like a sack of potatoes hitting solid ground.

"Dizzy..."

I didn't know if I'd end up dead, but if Karen was alive, I had to help her. I hurried down the embankment. I broke through the trees. I stepped into a void. I grabbed a limb. I swung out over nothingness.

Heart racing, adrenaline pumping, I struggled to regain my footing. Once back on solid ground, I held to the tree and looked out over the pallid quarry floor. In the muted light, it looked as if it might have been only a couple of yards to the bottom. The distance amounted to death. Dreading what I might see, I looked straight down. Two figures lay at the base of the cliff. Both appeared to be men in camouflage pants and jackets.

"Dizzy?"

A weak voice called out from my right. "Trip."

A white figure in a black dress dangled over the precipice a few yards away. Karen glanced at me and said, "Help."

I rushed through the trees to where she hung to the base of a small oak that itself clung to the brink.

She looked up at me, her face scratched and bleeding. "Please don't let me fall."

I flopped down on my stomach, arms hanging over the edge, and hooked my feet around the bases of two small trees. I was going to tell her to kick off her shoes, but she was already barefoot. "Swing your legs up to me."

"If I die, Keith will hunt you down."

"Stop talking and swing your legs!"

She twisted her body and raised her knees. I reached for her. Her left leg came within inches from my grasp. My watchband's safety clasp snapped open.

"I'm slipping!"

"You have to hang on." I took a deep breath and gave thought to trying to refasten my watch. There wasn't time. "Try again."

She swung one leg up. I reached for it and missed. The Rolex slid down around my hand. I couldn't extend my thumb, which meant I had no grasp. I bunched my fingers and let the watch slip free. As the last tangible piece of my old life fell away toward the limestone floor, I said, "Give it all you've got." The watch crashed to the ground. Karen swung her left leg toward me again. I grabbed her at the knee and pulled her to safety.

A few steps from the rim, I noticed a camouflage canvas backpack and a mink coat near a large oak. I lowered Karen to a seated position against the tree's trunk, then I covered her with the fur and sat beside her. The backpack contained a black ski mask, a matte-finish handgun, an ammunition magazine, a cylinder I assumed to be a silencer, and something that looked like a bulky cell phone.

"Satellite phone?" Karen was staring up at it.

"Yeah." I pulled out the sidearm. It looked like a SIG Sauer Pro, except it had a manual safety. The weapon was cold, and it didn't smell as if it had been fired recently. "There must have been another gun."

She nodded. "It went over with the second man."

I inserted the magazine, checked the safety, and placed the firearm on my lap in case the dead men in camouflage had brought reinforcements. "What happened?"

"They tried to throw me into the quarry." Her voice was steady. She didn't cry.

"How did you...?"

"Survival defense training, in case someone tried to...do what those guys tried to do. I've been taking classes for the past year. I planned to surprise Keith with a demonstration on our fifteenth anniversary." She drew a quivering breath. "Next week."

"Why did you run when you saw the diamonds?"

"Keith kept them in the safe in case one of us got held for ransom." She drew in a slow breath. "Your cousin brokered the deal for the lot of them."

"So you thought I knew about the diamonds? And I *kidnapped* you?"

Karen looked down.

"I didn't, and I didn't."

"I realize that now." She gave me a hard stare, then her face softened. "Someone abducted us both and brought us here. Why?"

"I don't know exactly, but..." I paused. "Remember how I told you I'd lost this place? The bank foreclosed on it last month. The property wasn't even mortgaged."

Karen shot me a confused look. "Which bank?"

"Dinosaur Valley National."

Her jaw went slack. "Keith bought it three months ago."

"His name doesn't show up in any of the records."

"His name never shows up when he doesn't want it to." She shook her head. "Keith has hated you ever since high school."

"I never understood that. What did I ever do to the guy?"

"It wasn't what you did—you were consistently kind. It was what you represented. Keith was a scholarship student with bad teeth and a worse home life. You, William Harrison Gilford III, were the smiling prince who'd had the world served to him on a platinum platter."

"And you dumped me for him." I gave a sarcastic chuckle.

Karen placed her hand on my arm. "You were going to Princeton. Keith and I were headed to Austin. And..."

"What?"

"He had something you didn't."

I dreaded to hear what she might say, but I had to know. "Say it."

"Ambition. He wanted it all. You lacked for nothing. You'd had everything given to you. Speaking of..." She pulled up my sleeve and said, "Where's your watch?"

I motioned toward the drop-off.

"Oh, Trip. I'm sorry. I'll buy you another." She paused a moment. "When you got that Rolex for your eighteenth birthday and Keith found out it cost more than the Porsche you'd gotten for your seventeenth birthday, his hatred went into overdrive."

"I didn't even know it was valuable."

"Because you didn't care, Trip. You were wonderfully oblivious. The watch was a gift from your father, and that was all that mattered to you. Keith has one like it now, except his is encrusted with diamonds. It was the first thing he bought when he made his first million. He never takes it off."

I looked at Karen and said, "Back to the question of why..."

"There's only one way to get to the bottom of this." Karen stood. "And that's to get to the bottom of the quarry."

I thought back to when I was eight. When we found our caretaker, my dad shielded my eyes, but not before I'd already taken in the horror. He'd landed so that one leg was folded underneath him. His eyes were wide-open. Blood oozed from every orifice. The most gruesome thing was that his fly was wide-open, leaving him exposed. In his inebriated state, he had apparently thought it was a good idea to urinate into the quarry from the top of the cliff.

I rose to my feet and said, "It's not going to be pretty."

"I don't care. Besides, my pumps are down there."

I gave Karen my shoes, and I helped her on with her coat. Gun in hand, backpack over my shoulder, I led her along the rim, then down the slope. The limestone chaff gnawed at my feet, but I had a lot more traction in my socks than I had had in my tux shoes.

When I'd put on my tuxedo ten hours earlier, I was looking forward to one final hurrah, an evening of dining and dancing and drinking and having the tab picked up by my still-wealthy cousin. The Gilford name had already been written in the Book of the Risen and the Fallen. My cousin's wedding was the last big affair I'd ever be invited to, and I intended to enjoy it before I faded away. I had no idea the night would end with someone trying to make me fade away permanently.

We reached the point downslope where the quarry had been gouged into the hillside. The bottoms of my feet were raw. I looked across the expanse of limestone floor toward two dark masses near the sheer face. "Stay here, Dizz. I'll get your shoes and see what I can find." As I limped away, I noticed her beside me. "Have you ever not been the most stubborn girl on the planet?"

"I'm not a girl anymore, Trip."

"Yeah. I noticed."

The first man lay flat on his back; he had a dark hole in his chest. The other was faceup as well, but he was bowed by the backpack on top of which he'd landed. Their arms and legs were strewn in directions that were horrible and cartoonish at the same time. The tang of feces cut into my nostrils. Both men stared unblinking at the night sky. Their blood looked like oil in the moonlight. Their flies were zipped. I slipped the gun into the backpack and said, "Recognize either of these guys?"

"No." She squatted and picked up one of the pieces of silvery metal strewn around the body of the first man. "The gun he pulled on me got smashed to bits."

There among the shrapnel, I noticed a large section of onyx and ebony pistol grip. "Uh-oh."

"What?"

"That's my handgun." I paused. "At least, it was. I sold it to a private collector last month."

"Was his name David Binder?"

"Yeah." I tingled all over. "How did you know that?"

"Someone's setting you up, Trip, and I think I know who it is." She approached me and pulled the sat phone from the backpack. "Let's find out for sure."

"What are you doing?"

She extended the antenna. "Hitting redial." She punched a button.

"Dizzy! No!"

"It's ringing." She held up her hand. "Shh..."

I heard a man's voice, but I couldn't tell who it was or what he said. Karen hung up and retracted the antenna. "It was Keith. He said, 'Is it finished?'" She looked like she'd been hit in the stomach with a cannonball.

I pulled her into my arms. I wanted to hold her forever, to breathe her in and keep her safe from the world. I wished I could.

She spoke in whispers. "It all makes sense now. You lose everything. You kidnap me. I try to escape. You chase me through the woods. We struggle on the edge of the quarry. We fall to our deaths. Nice and neat, just the way Keith likes it. Except it didn't turn out to be very nice or very neat."

I pulled away. "Chloe must work for him."

"Who's that?" Karen wasn't crying.

"The girl in the green dress—the one who was too young for me."

Karen nodded. "Keith probably owns the car service, too."

I approached the cliff wall. Fragments of platinum Rolex surrounded a pair of red-soled pumps. The day before she left me, my last wife went to Neiman Marcus and spent the last of my trust fund on Louboutins. Karen's were scuffed and scratched, but the heels were still firmly attached. I thought about collecting the pieces of my watch, but there wasn't enough to salvage.

Karen and I exchanged shoes. She handed me the phone. I extended the antenna again.

She shot me a confused look. "What are you doing?"

"Calling the sheriff."

"Are you insane?" She looked around. "How could we explain any of this to the authorities?"

I shrugged and said, "All we can do is tell the truth." I began to walk away.

She pulled me to a stop. "Keith isn't just powerful. He's lethal. Honesty will only land you in jail and, eventually, on a table with tubes running into your arm."

"Well, what do we do? You hung up on him. He'll know something's wrong. He'll send more people."

"No, he won't." She held out her hand. "I'm going to call him."

"Are *you* insane?"

"I know how to put a stop to this." She looked me in the eye. "Trust me."

I handed Karen the phone. She punched in several digits; then she stared at the keypad.

"Forget his number?"

She looked up at me. Tears flowed down her wounded cheeks.

"Dizz." I put my hand on her shoulder.

She waved me away, then she pressed one final button. Phone to her ear, she half sobbed, "Oh, Keith!" She let out a gut-wrenching wail. "Trip Gilford kidnapped me. He was holding me in his family's old cabin. I tried to get away, but he chased me through the trees." Her voice quivered. "Then there was this man in camouflage who tried to throw me into the quarry. I grabbed his backpack and pushed him over the edge."

I heard Keith speaking, but I couldn't tell what he said.

Karen sniffled. "Survival defense training—it was going to be a surprise. I tried to make a run for it, but I twisted my ankle. I found a gun in the backpack. I shot Trip in the woods. Another man in camouflage came after me. I shot him, too. He fell into the quarry."

He spoke more soft words.

"I can't walk, I'm cold, and I'm so scared. Trip threw a party here our junior year of high school. Do you remember where this place is?"

Keith's voice was audible but not intelligible.

"Thank God you're nearby. Please hurry. I'm at the top of the cliff."

Keith said something else. I still couldn't understand, but his words sounded soothing.

Karen let out a softer sob; then she said, "I love you. Focus on getting here safely—I'll call the police."

Keith was in mid-no when Karen punched the end button. She powered off the phone, collapsed the antenna, and handed it to me. She wiped away the tears and, voice unwavering, said, "He'll be here in ten minutes."

I found myself following Karen up the hillside. My feet were so sore, I winced with each quick step. It amazed me that she could move so quickly in heels. It amazed me even more to find that she was intact—even energized—after learning her husband had tried to have her killed. Some people crumble in crisis. Others summon deep reserves of strength that disintegrate when the tribulation is past. Karen obviously fell into the latter category.

As we hiked up the slope, I said, "What's the plan?"

"Negotiate."

"You have completely lost your mind, haven't you?"

Karen shook her head. "This whole thing boils down to money. Everything Keith's made, he made while we were married. Fifty percent of what's his is mine. He doesn't want me to have my half. I'll tell him I'll walk away with twenty-five percent if he clears your name."

"What if he decides to kill us both and keep a hundred percent?"

"He thinks I called the police, and he thinks you're dead. He won't try anything. He won't even be armed. He'll just be thinking about regrouping and waiting for the next opportunity."

We threaded our way through the trees until we reached the spot on the rim above the dead men. Karen and I stood facing each other. I'd never felt so close to or so distant from her.

She smiled and said, "Am I as much of a mess as you are?"

I brushed off the front of my tux with my hands, but it was a lost cause. Karen opened her coat, looked down at her ruined dress, then closed it. I noticed blood oozing from a scratch on her forehead. I wiped it away with my thumb. "Did you have any idea things with Keith were this bad?"

"Not *this* bad, but…" For a moment, she looked something close to her age. "On our twelfth anniversary, we were having one of our usual arguments. I said I would've been better off if I'd stayed with you. He was so angry, I thought he was going to burst into flames. I've tried to make it up to him, but he hasn't been the same since then."

"So that explains…"

"What?"

"Over the last three years, the wealth my father and my grandfather worked so hard to accumulate has been systematically erased. For a while it seemed like a string of bad luck, but nobody could be that unfortunate that consistently. I always suspected someone was behind it. I guess I was right."

She put her hand on my arm. "I'm sorry. I never intended for that to happen."

"It's not your fault." I ran my hands back through my hair. "You didn't know what Keith was going to do. And I was a novice when it came to financial matters. I mean, I got a degree in Romance languages and literature. My dad felt so bad about me losing my mom at such a young age, he took care of everything so I could enjoy life. After he died, I tried to follow in his footsteps, to be a good person, to be a thoughtful philanthropist, but I trusted the wrong people. Those people apparently worked for Keith." I heard car wheels on gravel. Through the trees, I saw headlights climbing the driveway. "It's showtime, Dizz."

As the sound of the engine grew louder, Karen pulled me into a close hug and whispered into my ear, "You're the best man I've ever known. I really should have stayed with you."

I wanted to tell her she had shattered my heart so completely when she broke up with me, I'd never gotten over it. I wanted to tell her no woman had ever compared to her. I wanted to tell her she was the real reason I'd been divorced three times. There were so many things I could have said, should have said. I kept my mouth shut.

Karen backed away, hands in her coat pockets. "You better get out of sight."

"Shouldn't you be sitting down? Since you twisted your ankle?"

"It won't matter. Now go."

I hobbled away through the trees. A car door slammed. Fast, heavy footsteps trudged through the woods. Keith knew exactly where to go. He should—he'd planned the whole thing. Even if Karen didn't think he'd try anything, I decided to be prepared. I reached into the backpack for the handgun. It wasn't there. I wondered if I'd dropped it on the hike back up the hill.

Voice loud and firm, Karen said, "Stop right there!"

"It's me, Dizzy." The voice was unmistakably Keith's, but it had taken on a tone of supreme composure; three billion dollars could buy a lot of self-confidence. "You can put the gun down now."

*The gun?* I mentally cursed at myself for not anticipating this. I was naive about business, and I was naive about women. I hurried back through the woods along the rim.

Voice steely, Karen said, "You really thought you could get away with it?"

"Get away with what?"

I broke through the trees. Keith stood hands up, back to the brink, the band of his Rolex gleaming in the moonlight. Karen faced him from a couple of yards away. She had shed her coat and shoes. Keith was dressed in a suit and tie. His clothing appeared well tailored, his reddish hair meticulously clipped. He looked every bit the robber baron. He also looked like he'd seen a ghost.

Eyes wide, Keith glanced over at me and said, "Dizzy. To your left."

Gaze fixed on her husband, she spoke in a mocking tone. "Surprise!"

Keith gave a nervous smile. His teeth were straight and white. He'd obviously invested some of his fortune into his appearance.

My looks had been marred and my wealth had been decimated, thanks to him. Two charities that depended on me had ceased to exist. I'd never felt such spite for another human being as I did for Keith at that moment. I wanted to shove him into the quarry.

His eyes darted between Karen and me. "Is this some sort of a joke?"

Karen kept the handgun aimed at him. "Is your plan to frame Trip for kidnapping me a joke? Is your plan to have us both murdered a joke? Is your plan to marry that little trollop...." She glanced over at me. "What was her name again? Chloe?"

*Chloe was his mistress?* Confusion replaced contempt. I took a step toward Karen. "What's going on, Dizz?"

Focus steady on her husband, she widened her stance. "Is your plan to marry Chloe a joke?"

His smile disappeared. "Dizzy, your imagination's playing tricks on you."

"The recordings I've downloaded from that obnoxious watch of yours aren't imaginary."

He glanced up at his Rolex. Its diamond bezel flashed fire. *She'd hidden a recording device inside?*

"It's the only thing you never take off." Karen took a step forward. "You wore it to bed with your mistress. You wore it in the pool while you and your financial advisers figured out how to ruin Trip. You wore it in the steam room when you gave your hoodlums the kill order."

Keith looked like he was on the verge of passing out. "Dizzy…"

As I tried to get my head around the fact that Karen had known Keith was setting us up, she dropped the gun and said, "You should have been more careful." She leaped forward and grabbed an overhanging branch. Her legs swung in a long, fast arc. Her feet struck Keith in the chest with such force, it sounded like a basketball exploding. Keith disappeared over the edge of the cliff. He didn't utter a sound. A sickening thud told me it was ended.

Karen released the limb and dropped to the ground.

My whole body went numb. I fell to my knees. "What have you done?"

"It was self-defense." She approached me. "He would have killed me eventually."

I looked up at her. "Are you going to kill me, too?"

She chuckled lightly. "You're the last good man on earth. I want to spend the rest of my life with you."

The words wouldn't come. Even if they had, I wouldn't have known what to say. I loved Karen. Being with her was all I'd ever wanted. But at what cost? The life of a man who'd tried to kill us both, a man I'd wanted to kill myself? That and possibly my soul.

"Just one thing—I'll handle the money." Karen extended her hand. "Now come on. We have work to do."

# THE ITINERARY

## BY ROBERTA ISLEIB

Detective Jack Meigs knew he'd hate Key West the moment he was greeted off the plane by a taxi driver with a parrot on his shoulder. He hadn't wanted to take a vacation at all, and he certainly hadn't wanted to come to Florida, which he associated with elderly people pretending they weren't declining. But his boss insisted, and then his sister surprised him with a nonrefundable ticket: he was screwed. A psychologist had once told him that it took a year for grief to lift and that making major life changes during this time only complicated the process, which was why he'd gone to work directly from the funeral and every day in the three months since. There was no vacation from the facts: his wife Alice was dead, and she wasn't coming back.

The driver packed him into a cab that smelled like a zoo and lurched away from the curb. Then the bird let loose a stream of shit that splattered off his newspapered roost and onto Meigs's polished black leather loafers. The cabbie hooted with laughter.

"That means good luck, man," he said, gunning the motor and grinning like a monkey in the rearview mirror. "Mango doesn't do that for just anybody."

The parrot screamed during the entire ten-minute ride to Meigs's hotel, and the driver never shut up, either. Would everyone connected with this damn town want to give him a travelogue?

"I'm takin' you down our main street, give you the flavor," the cabbie said as he turned off Truman Avenue onto bustling Duval Street. He veered around a stumbling bum and a covey of fat, sun-crisped cruise ship escapees carrying plastic cups of beer. Were open containers legal in this town?

"Hemingway got soused here every afternoon after writing." The cabbie pointed to a shabby-looking bar, drinkers spilling out onto the sidewalk. "And Jimmy Buffett wrote 'Woman Goin' Crazy on Caroline Street' right down there in Margaritaville." He pointed to yet another bar, lit by palm trees and flamingos in flashing neon, also crammed with boozers.

The whole scene was a police officer's nightmare.

The cab driver swerved onto Caroline Street and pulled over in front of Notre Paradis, the bed-and-breakfast that Meigs's sister had chosen for him. A thin man wearing a tight white shirt and copper sparkles on his glasses bounded off the front porch to greet him.

"I'm Laurent, your host. This is your first trip to Key West? You're going to love it!" He struck a theatrical pose and then paused to look Meigs over—his khakis with the worn cuffs and pockets, the gray turtleneck on which he'd spilled his Coke during the turbulence from Miami to Key West. Laurent lowered his voice to a whisper and winked. "Yes, there is a lot of money in this town. But there's plenty to enjoy without piles of cash, too."

After unpacking, Meigs changed his shirt and went to explore Duval Street on foot. Laurent had dismissed his protests and insisted this was a must-see; had actually escorted him down Caroline Street and watched like a mother seeing her firstborn off to kindergarten until Meigs turned to salute good-bye.

On Duval, Meigs stepped over two bums stretched out on cardboard in front of an empty storefront and skirted another playing bad guitar next to a dog dressed in sunglasses and Mardi Gras beads. Every few minutes, the dog lifted his snout and howled along with his owner. A handful of tourists stopped to take photos.

"Cruelty to animals," Meigs muttered to himself. Neither the cops nor the residents in his small Connecticut town would have tolerated sleeping bums and singing dogs.

In front of Fast Buck Freddie's tropical window displays, a petite woman in a lime green tube top and a heavyset man with a florid complexion were going at it in hissed whispers. Meigs couldn't help catching "give me some space" followed by "but I paid for the goddamn cruise." Then the big man grabbed the girl's wrist and started to yank her across the sidewalk.

Meigs moved forward and grasped the man's bicep. "Let the lady go," he said in his fiercest cop voice. "Now."

"Fuck off, asshole, this is none of your business," the man said but dropped his girlfriend's wrist and gave her an unnecessary push.

Meigs turned to her. "Everything okay here? Should I find a policeman?" If he *could* find a cop—so far he'd seen no sign of any law enforcement at all.

"I'm fine," she said, rubbing her wrist and then straightening her sunglasses. She turned to her friend and smiled tremulously. "I will see you later on the ship, George." She disappeared into the stream of shoppers entering Fast Buck Freddie's. The man scowled at Meigs and stalked off in the other direction.

Meigs blew out a breath and left Duval Street—so far the charm of the place was eluding him. He ambled over to the Sunset Celebration at Mallory Square—also mandatory in his host Laurent's mind. He slunk through a bevy of aggressive street performers with minimal musical talent, fended off a tarot card reader, and stopped by a crowd gathered around a slender man in ballet slippers and silver curls who directed a posse of mangy cats. Alice would have found this performance charming. But when the cat man motioned to Meigs to step into the arena to hold a flaming hoop, he fled.

The *Disney Magic*, a ten-story cruise ship decorated with white mouse ears on red smokestacks, was docked on the square. Meigs strode past her and on down the pier to a row of magnificent boats—racing sailboats with names like *Primal Scream* and *Big Booty*. *More like big money*, Meigs thought. Streams of spectators ogled the boats and their passengers. The largest yacht at the end of the line, the *Emelina*, got the most attention. On its upper deck, a four-man band banged out Buffett tunes for a group of elegant partygoers sipping fizzy drinks in glass flutes.

Meigs sat on a bench for a minute to watch the show. If he was ever worth a couple of million—a billion even—would he moor his ostentatious transportation steps from Mallory Square for every sun-sick passerby to moon over? No, he would not.

Voices floated across the water. "Why don't they move that stinkin' tub so we can see the sunset?" asked a handsome man from the rail of the party boat. He stabbed a finger at the enormous cruise ship across the water and frowned.

"Isn't it illegal to keep a cruise ship at the dock this late?" asked a woman with silver-lacquered nails and matching hair. A flash of sun glinted off the jewels in her belly button.

After the sun set to a smattering of applause, Meigs headed back toward Mallory Square. He stopped at a trolley bar for a Budweiser and leaned against the railing in front of the cruise ship. To his right, the cat man still pranced toe-heel like a misshapen ballerina, calling to the felines in falsetto French, now forcing a yellow tiger to leap over a scrawny black specimen and then through the flaming ring. The tipsy crowd gathered around him howled with appreciation.

Meigs watched the jumpsuited crew of the hulking *Disney Magic* prepare to launch, spooling enormous hanks of steel off cleats on the pier. Why had they been allowed to partially obscure the sunset—the ostensible excuse for this sideshow? Laurent at Notre Paradis had assured him this was rule number one on Bone Island (aka Key West): no boat shall be allowed to obstruct the tourists' view as the sun sinks into the harbor. And its corollary: tourists must and shall be encouraged to spot the green flash, said by Jules Verne to confer the power to read minds. Meigs doubted the minds here were worth the effort.

A heavy man with a bad sunburn and a loud flowered shirt tenting his gut paced down the gangway that opened from the belly of the ship, out onto the pier, and back. Meigs stiffened, recognizing him as the man he'd seen arguing on Duval Street earlier this afternoon. Two crew members dressed in cruise ship whites approached him, but he shrugged off the hand of the taller man, who'd reached out to pat his shoulder. The heavy fellow began to shout and wave his hands, but Meigs couldn't make out the words.

"Looks like one of the passengers forgot when their rig was setting sail," said a man next to him. Meigs turned to look him over—he seemed normal enough—blue golf shirt, sunglasses, a beer.

"Will they wait?" Meigs asked.

"Not for long," the man said. "They're fined for leaving late. And the docking fees for cruise ships are prohibitive to begin with."

Meigs watched the three men continue their heated discussion until finally the heavyset man disappeared into the hull of the ship. He emerged soon after, a porter tailing him with two suitcases, one brown leather, the other faded red denim with yarn flowers wired to the handle. The porter dumped the luggage on the dock and waited a minute for a tip, which was not forthcoming. The crewmen signaled to the workers manning the ropes, and the gangway was drawn up. The heavy man steamed up the pier with the luggage, sweating and cursing, and disappeared into the crowd.

"There ees a man who has carried few bags in hees life," said the cat man to Meigs as he packed his animals into small cages. Meigs nodded, surprised to hear him break character.

The *Disney Magic* pulled away from the dock, and Meigs went off in search of a carryout dinner. He refused to sit alone at a table for two at a café on Duval Street where every tourist who passed could feel sorry for him.

Next morning, Meigs carried his coffee and cereal out to the deck behind his lodging. He skimmed the front page of the *Key West Citizen*, loaded with typical small-town stuff—a push to recycle, a scooter/delivery truck crash, projected budget cuts in education and the police department. *This last bit of prudence,* Meigs thought, *would be a false and costly economy.* A small town populated by more bars per square inch than New York or New Orleans and a slew of transients and tourists made for barely contained chaos. They needed all the police officers they could hire.

He turned the page and perused the weather forecast—nothing but sunshine and super-humidity for the remainder of his stay. Could he possibly get out a day early? His eye caught on a small article in the crime report at the bottom of the page.

"Woman Reported Missing from Cruise Ship," the headline read. As Meigs studied the photograph accompanying the article, his fingers tingled. The clothes were different—a white shirt instead of the green tube top, the hair and makeup more formally styled—but he recognized the picture of the young woman he'd seen arguing with her friend yesterday. According to the paper, the girl's mother had reported her missing, and her travel companion confirmed the disappearance.

He took out his cell phone and dialed the police department's number but got a busy signal. He wondered if their lines were getting flooded with imagined sightings. In the end, rather than being taken for another attention-seeking fruitcake, he rented a ridiculous, souped-up, open-air golf cart to make the short trek to the KWPD. In person, with a badge in hand, he would be taken seriously. Besides, he'd rather kill time shooting the shit with cops than riding the Conch Tour Train or listening to female impersonators at the La Te Da Cabaret, both of which had been earnestly recommended by his lodging host this morning.

The police station was painted in muted pinks and greens and surrounded by a forest of palm trees. Meigs strode in and introduced himself.

"I'm a detective visiting from Connecticut," he told the officer at the front desk. "I may have some information on the missing person reported in today's newspaper. I'll speak to your chief if he's available."

Minutes later, an attractive man with a wide grin that showcased his even, white teeth against a deep tan emerged from the back and ushered Meigs into his office.

"I'm Chief Ron Barnes." He squeezed Meigs's hand, then sat behind his desk—a lot neater than Meigs kept his—and motioned to the chair in front. "Welcome to Paradise."

"Thanks. I guess." Meigs grunted and pulled the newspaper out of his back pocket. He laid it on the polished desktop and tapped the photo. "The paper said you're looking for this woman?"

"Sort of," said the chief. "This being Key West, we see more than our share of missing persons. Mostly they surface after they've slept off the booze or woken up in some stranger's pad. But Sheila Brown's mother wasn't satisfied with that explanation." He grimaced. "You have information?"

Meigs explained how he'd seen the woman on Duval Street yesterday, filling in as many details of the argument with her boyfriend as he could remember. "When that monster Disney cruise ship was leaving the dock, it looked as though someone was about to miss the boat. Her boyfriend—I'm assuming it's the same man—appeared quite distressed, or gave a good show of it, anyway. He ended up taking some luggage off the big boat, and that's the last I saw of either of them."

"George Vesper—the boyfriend—is coming in to touch base shortly," said the chief. "You're welcome to watch the interview from our observation room if you're interested."

Meigs was. A sergeant installed him behind a one-way mirror and, soon after, ushered Vesper into the room with the chief. Dressed in sharply creased khakis, a blue silk shirt, and an expensive-looking watch, Vesper appeared less disheveled than he had yesterday on the dock but even more sour. Chief Barnes asked him to recount the facts of yesterday's disappearance.

"Sheila wanted to check out the shops on Duval Street," Vesper said. "And when a gal wants to shop, I stay out of her way." He shook his head and grinned. "I'm not one of those panty-waist dopes who tags along to sit outside the dressing room and approve every damn purchase. I gave her a couple hundred bucks and told her to knock her lovely self out. This trip with Sheila wasn't going to be cheap"—he waggled his carefully groomed eyebrows—"but worth it, if you know what I mean."

"Were you and Ms. Brown experiencing problems with your relationship?"

Meigs noticed the muscles in Vesper's neck tighten. The thin hank of hair that had been combed across his sunburned pate trembled. He patted it down and frowned at the chief. "Not at all. She's a delightful girl, and the trip has been great so far."

The chief settled his elbows on the table and leaned forward. "What's your theory about her disappearance, Mr. Vesper?"

Vesper pursed his lips, the overhead fluorescents casting sallow shadows under his eyes. "Maybe she met an old friend and tied one on. I expect she'll show up later today. Frankly, her mother's a worrywart—it's a shame to squander your department's resources on this."

"Let's take down some basic information as long as you're here," said Chief Barnes. He opened up the small computer on the table in front of him. "Let's start with you."

Vesper reported that he was a businessman from Connecticut, age fifty-four, and this was his first cruise on the Disney line. He had been dating Ms. Brown for five months. They'd met in a local Mexican restaurant on half-price margarita night—she was a server in the cocktail lounge. Vesper owned four furniture stores along the Connecticut shoreline, and no, they did not carry crappy fiberboard pieces like the ones advertised by that buffoon on television. His outfit focused on high-quality wood and styles consistent with old New England fashion. He was divorced, two kids from a previous marriage that he seldom saw, even though he'd paid through the goddamned nose for prep school and college tuition.

"What about Sheila?" said Barnes, looking up from the keyboard. "What's her background?"

Vesper hesitated, patted his forehead with a neatly folded handkerchief. Despite their relatively short acquaintance, he said, he'd been swept away by both her physical presence and her personality. "A live wire with a very soft spot for a middle-aged man," was how he described her.

"Maybe she had a daddy complex, and maybe she didn't," added Vesper. "I can tell you that what went on between us was not parental."

Meigs rolled his eyes. What had Ms. Brown seen in this bozo?

Chief Barnes asked for contact information on the missing

girl, but Vesper was vague. He hadn't met any of her relatives, though she had made nightly calls to her mother, often in his presence. And she lived with a roommate—another waitress—when she wasn't staying with him. Vesper had already called her, but the friend claimed she hadn't heard from Sheila since they'd left Connecticut. He scrolled through his iPhone and found the friend's phone number.

"You're wasting your time, though," he said after reading it off.

Behind the mirror, Meigs jotted the number on his newspaper.

"Call us if you think of anything else. Were you traveling with friends?"

"Just us." Vesper refolded the handkerchief and stuffed it into his pocket. "I'm staying at the Marquesa Hotel. You can reach me there or on my cell." He shook hands with Barnes and left the room.

"He's got some dough," said Chief Barnes once Meigs was back in the conference room and the door clicked shut behind him. "No one stays at the Marquesa unless they're rich, famous, or both. What's your impression?"

"He's a liar," said Meigs.

Chief Barnes looked startled.

Meigs repeated how he'd seen Vesper and the girlfriend arguing on Duval Street, how she'd wanted some time alone. "So the trip *wasn't* going well, and he *is* the kind of pantywaist dope who wants to tag along shopping."

Chief Barnes laughed. "What else?"

"Most of the cruise ship disappearances I've heard about ended up with one of the parties murdered," Meigs added. "Didn't Vesper sound as though he didn't want you looking too hard for her?" Meigs tapped his fingers on the table. "But chances are, she got tired of this clown and bailed out. I imagine that cruise ship cabin could have felt awfully small after a few nights entertaining Vesper."

The chief laughed again. "You're right about that. I'll put one of my guys on it, ask around at Sunset tonight to see if anyone else saw her or talked to her. Thanks for stopping in," he added. "As you probably read in the *Citizen* this morning, the sailboat races are in town and we're stretched thin."

"I'd be happy to do some research," Meigs offered.

"We'll be fine," said the chief, his voice cool now.

Meigs motored back into town and stopped at the pink cement library on Fleming Street. He couldn't help himself—and what were the options? Alice would have wanted to tour Hemingway's house, have her picture taken at the Southernmost Point, order piña coladas, and watch the human interest show from a streetside bar on Duval. Dismal prospects without her.

Meigs settled at one of the computers in between a teenage girl with multiple eyebrow piercings and a shabby man whose odor suggested he hadn't put soap to skin in some time. He started by googling George Vesper. As Vesper had boasted, his four furniture businesses appeared to be doing well. Very well. An article in *Fortune Small Business* dissected his success and reduced it to customer service, quality manufacturing, and an aggressive marketing campaign that targeted wealthy homeowners along the Connecticut shoreline. For the article, Vesper had been photographed at his own waterfront home in Greenwich, which Meigs figured had to be worth eight or ten million. He also owned a "cottage" on Nantucket and a thirty-five-foot sailboat moored at a fashionable and pricey Cos Cob marina. During his limited downtime, Vesper enjoyed competing in local regattas. He appeared to have plenty of money and no problem flaunting it.

Next Meigs googled Sheila Brown and skimmed dozens of links about Sheila the artist, Sheila the fifth-grade teacher, Sheila the lawyer, Sheila the nature photographer. But nothing about Sheila the waitress.

Meigs then typed the Disney cruise ship's name into the search bar. The *Disney Magic* was a midpriced boat offering a standard western Caribbean winter break itinerary, including Key West, Cozumel, Grand Cayman, and Castaway Cay. He sat back in his chair, trying to ignore the homeless man next to him muttering as he rustled through a filthy knapsack. Meigs could definitely imagine Vesper steering by his genitals. But why on earth would a man with his alleged assets and sailing expertise choose a floating Disney city loaded with middle-class folks and their offspring? *Disney*, for God's sake. The girlfriend must have chosen it.

He logged out of the computer and returned to his B and B. Back on the deck, Meigs called the number of Sheila Brown's waitress friend and roommate, Maya Redkin.

"This is Detective Jack Meigs on behalf of the Key West Police Department." So it was a little stretcher—she'd never check on him. He explained about Sheila's disappearance and her boyfriend's worry.

"I haven't heard a peep since she left," Maya protested. "Oh, my gosh, did something happen to her?"

"That's under investigation," said Meigs, noting that for Sheila's alleged best friend, not getting involved came before concern. "She left the ship to do some shopping yesterday and didn't return. How would you characterize her relationship with George Vesper?"

There was a long pause. "He treated her well. Took her out to expensive restaurants and clubs. Bought her some nice stuff and sent some gorgeous flowers. Apparently he's loaded. What's not to like about that?"

"Would you say they were serious? In love? Was marriage in their future?"

Maya laughed. "Now that would surprise me, especially since

she has another boyfriend." She stopped and corrected herself: "Had one. And isn't Vesper a little old for her?"

"That would be her decision," said Meigs, bristling silently. He was the same age as Vesper without the big belly and the big bucks. Not that he wanted a girlfriend half his age but was he over-the-hill, too? "What about other family members? Friends? Anyone I can call who might know where she is?"

"She kept those numbers on her cell phone," said Maya.

"Was it Sheila who chose the cruise?"

"He planned everything—he liked to control things, you know? Listen, I have to get to work."

"Call us if you hear from her," said Meigs. "Save us a lot of trouble."

"Wait. What's the weather like down there?" Maya asked in a wistful voice. "It's ten degrees here and snowing."

"Incessantly sunny."

Meigs signed off and leaned back in his rocker. The roommate was definitely not concerned about Sheila. Nor was she impressed with the solidity of her relationship with Vesper. Both of which pointed to the likelihood that Sheila had fled rather than been taken by force. He let his thoughts wander to Vesper, his business in Connecticut, his flamboyant wealth. And this brought to mind a Connecticut entrepreneur who'd allowed his wealth to taint his judgment: Stew Leonard. Leonard had siphoned off cash from his high-end grocery shops in the 1990s with a sophisticated software scam and then served jail time for tax fraud.

Meigs grabbed his hat and sunglasses and hurried back to the pier at Mallory Square. A Carnival cruise ship had taken the place of the *Disney Magic*, and the cat man was setting up for the evening's performance.

"I'd like to buy one of your T-shirts," said Meigs. He pointed to a light blue shirt with "The cat man and his flying house cats" written across the chest. When he'd paid for the shirt, he showed his badge and handed him the newspaper photo of Sheila. "This woman disappeared yesterday, and I'm wondering if you happened to see her."

The cat man studied it and gave it back. "I can't be certain; they pass through here like herds of mutton."

"But maybe...," Meigs said.

"Eet was almost dark, but maybe she boarded the beeg yacht at the end of the pier." He pointed to the empty slip that yesterday had held the *Emelina*. "After the cruise sheep was gone."

Meigs thanked him, trotted back to Notre Paradis, and asked to use Laurent's computer. He googled the *Emelina*. One hundred and sixty-seven feet long, the boat had been sold in Monaco and was expected to winter in St. Barths. He jotted down the owner's information and tucked it into his pocket, then started off for the Marquesa Hotel. A chat with George Vesper was in order.

The Marquesa's lobby was caviar to Meigs's hotel's scrambled eggs. The soft hiss of a waterfall and the rustling of the uplighted palm fronds masked the scooter traffic outside. Vesper was splayed in a chaise near the poolside bar. He beckoned over a server dressed in blue Bermuda shorts and ordered a super single malt bourbon that Meigs had never heard of.

"Mr. Vesper?"

The man glanced up, his face blank.

"I'm Detective Meigs, Guilford Police Department. Following up on the reported disappearance of Sheila Brown."

Vesper pinched his lips together in a tight frown and said nothing. Meigs couldn't tell if he recognized him from the altercation on Duval Street. If he did, he wasn't acknowledging their connection.

"Do you happen to know the owner or the crew of the *Emelina*? That's one of the yachts that were moored a nine iron from your cruise ship yesterday."

The waiter approached and settled a drink on the glass table next to Vesper. Vesper didn't even look at the man, never mind thank or tip him.

"Can't say that I do," Vesper answered, taking a swallow of the gold liquid. "What does that have to do with Sheila?"

"Any chance that she would have had friends on that boat?"

"Sheila?" Vesper threw back his head and roared with laughter. "That girl lived from tip to tip. No way she'd have pals that wealthy." Then he sat up and scowled. "Why do you ask?"

"Might she have been connected with one of the crew members? Maybe cadged a ride out of town?"

Vesper's face turned from red to purple. "If that no-good bastard boyfriend..." He chugged the rest of the drink as he scrambled to his feet, now hulking over Meigs.

"Was anything missing from your cabin after Sheila went shopping?" Meigs persisted.

Vesper took off his glasses and glared. "Look, this has all been a big mistake. I should have told you right up front. We had an awful row that morning, and she said she was taking the first plane home, which was fine with me, only she took my ruby ring and the cash in my wallet, too."

"I'm sure Chief Barnes can radio the Coast Guard, have a chat with the captain, and see whether Sheila's on board. Insist she return your belongings."

"Never mind that," Vesper growled. "I can take it from here. I'll settle this with her at home."

"As you like," said Meigs, starting back toward the lobby. "I'll fill in the chief. He may wish to follow up. I would imagine the IRS might have some questions, too."

"This is none of your damn business," Vesper sputtered after him. "What's a Connecticut cop doing working a Key West case anyway?"

Meigs left the Marquesa, loaded back into his golf cart, and returned to the police station and asked to speak to the chief.

"I came across some information on that missing persons case," he said to Chief Barnes. "If you contact the pilot of the *Emelina* yacht, I suspect you'll find that Sheila Brown stowed aboard with a large sum of cash. The cash may have come courtesy of cooking the books at Vesper's furniture business. It's kind of a tradition in Connecticut." He smiled. "Stew Leonard, Martha Stewart, even former governor John Rowland. Some of the wealthy folks in our state aren't quite satisfied with what they've got. So they stretch the rules to suit them."

"That's an awfully big leap," said the chief.

"Not really," said Meigs. "Vesper just didn't seem like a cruise ship kind of guy. And the magic of Disney? I don't think so. Then I noticed the Grand Cayman Island was included on the itinerary. Suppose Vesper had made substantial illegal gains and intended to bank the money offshore. The Disney cruise would be a terrific cover. But his companion figured this out and disappeared with his cash. No wonder he was upset."

Chief Barnes shook his head. "That's a hell of a lotta supposition."

"Your cat man saw Sheila stow aboard the *Emelina* after sunset," said Meigs. "While he's working his felines, he watches everything."

On the way home from the police station, Meigs stopped at the Lost Weekend package store for a six-pack of Red Stripe beer. Back in his room, he changed into his cat man T-shirt and took a beer out onto the back deck.

Maybe this vacation thing wasn't so bad after all. Maybe tomorrow he'd buy a ticket for the Conch Train and another for a tour of the Little White House, in memory of Alice.

———

FOUR DAYS LATER, as Meigs finished packing for home, Chief Barnes texted him, "Coast Guard located the Emelina in the

British Virgin Islands. Sheila and bf onboard with 3 hundred K cash. Thx 4 the assist."

Meigs texted back, "ur welcome."

Then he called the taxi company for a ride to the airport, specifically requesting a bird-free cab. Still, he wasn't surprised when a golden retriever the size of a donkey lumbered out of the van's passenger seat and began to sniff his luggage.

"Don't you even think of it," he shouted.

# LAMBORGHINI MOMMY

## BY HARLEY JANE KOZAK

The party that led to the murder was held in December at Tina and Howard Skate's estate. The party's title, in florid font on the embossed invitation, should've clued me in to the kind of night I was in for; for starters, it was long—the Forty-third Annual White Alder Academy Holiday Gala for Major Donors. The party itself was longer and, until the last four minutes, remarkable only in its dullness. But that's the thing I have with galas, soirees, fetes—they seem like a good idea when I'm RSVP'ing and then the big day arrives and it's always, *What the hell was I thinking?*

Bunny, fellow mommy and my best friend at White Alder, wouldn't let me bow out. "You cannot un-RSVP," she said. "It's rude. Also, you need to socialize. You haven't had sex in two years."

"There'll be sex at this gala?" I asked.

"A prerequisite for having sex," Bunny said, "is meeting someone with whom you'd like to have sex. That won't happen at soccer practice. You need a party worth waxing for."

"What if my former husband is there? Or his ghastly grandmother?"

"That house is so big," Bunny said, "you could live in it three weeks and never meet the inhabitants. It's how the Skates stay married. If Stephen's there, you'll see his big head a mile away and move to another wing. But dress up, okay? Last week the fourth-grade room mom asked me if you were Jillie's nanny."

So I dressed up in a little black Vera Wang left over from my past life. I looked okay, and all evening I tried not to think about how I'd rather have been home playing Scrabble with Jillie. I glommed onto Bunny and Bunny's husband Rick and chatted up the headmaster and the other moms. I didn't see Stephen. I didn't have sex with anyone. The big excitement was getting lost on my way to a second-floor bathroom.

I was back downstairs in the foyer, making a respectable 10:30 p.m. exit, when I heard the line that would change my life.

"Well, well. If it isn't the hottest mommy in the Lower School pickup lane."

I turned. Several people were being handed coats by a maid, one of them talking to me—a tipsy one, judging from his flushed face and one-hundred-proof breath.

"Uh...," I said.

"Oh, yeah, play dumb." He grinned. "But you don't drive a car that sexy to stay under the radar."

To my surprise, I felt pink with pleasure. "You find Toyotas sexy?"

His smile faltered. "You're not—? You don't drive the Lamborghini?"

"Toyota Highlander." I added hopefully, "Hybrid."

"Wow." He was stunned. "You seriously look like someone else."

"Someone who drives a Lamborghini." I pointed outside. "Think I could convince the valet guy?"

"Heh." He laughed weakly. I started to introduce myself, but he was already looking past me, out to the porte cochere. " 'Scuse me. There's my BMW."

He squeezed by me out into the night, and I dropped my "Hello, I'm new to White Alder; it's my first year" smile. In fact, I frowned. In my peripheral vision, I saw Helene Hochstetter, my ex-husband's grandmother, burrowing into her mink. She'd no doubt overheard that exchange with her big Hochstetter ears. Who in Southern California needed mink? I thought, handed my own coat by the maid. I struggled with my sleeve, feeling wallflowery, wishing I'd carpooled with Bunny and Rick.

And then someone behind me was helping me into my coat. "I think you could convince the valet guy," a voice said. "Go on. Drive off in a hot car."

I turned again. This stranger appeared sober, although his tie was askew, flashing its Dolce & Gabbana label. I wanted to fix it. "I wouldn't know how to drive a Lamborghini. Do they come in automatics?"

"It's what's known as a supercar," he said. "And friends don't let friends buy supercars in automatic. But you wouldn't have to drive it. Pick me up hitchhiking, and I'll drive it for you."

"I don't pick up hitchhikers."

He buttoned my coat for me, three buttons, right up to the neck. He had green eyes. "Ah, but you used to. Back in your misspent youth. Didn't you? And I bet you hitched a few rides yourself. I bet you were good at it."

"I was. I did." I smiled involuntarily for the first time all night.

From the porte cochere, the valet guy called, "Ma'am? Your Toyota."

On impulse, I took the stranger's hand and shook it. Only he didn't let go, he pulled me in and kissed me on my cheek up by my ear.

"New kid on the block," he whispered, "don't be a stranger."

*Smells nice*, I thought. *Bet I never see him again.*
I thought wrong.

———

THE INVITATION TO Leighton Donaldson's birthday party popped out of the envelope in a burst of confetti that covered the front seat of the Toyota. "Come to my bowling party!" it cried in iridescent pink. "I'm turning double digits!"

I glanced at the rearview mirror at my daughter. "It's this Saturday. We missed the RSVP date. How long has this been in your backpack?"

"Leighton just gave it to me today in computer lab."

"I don't know Leighton. Is she a new friend?"

"Kind of. Can I go?"

"Yeah, if it's not too late to let them know. Sometimes they need a head count, for the bowling alley or whatever."

"It's not at a bowling alley, Mommy. It's at their house. And it's not a drop-off party. The parents are supposed to stay. Leighton told me."

My daughter was right on both counts. Leighton's mother called three minutes later while I was still in school traffic. "I'm Tracy Donaldson," she said. "I just need Julie's shoe size. We found the invitation wedged between the car seats, and Leighton felt terrible—she really wants Julie to come. And you come, too. I'll have grown-up food. Feydeau's catering."

Whoever Feydeau was. "Thanks," I said, staring at the license plate in front of me: TROFEE2. "We'd love to come. Oh, and it's Jillie, not Julie."

"Excuse me?"

"My daughter. It's Jillie, short for Jillian. People call her Julie all the time, though."

There was a long pause. "Oh."

—

AN HOUR LATER I was in the checkout line at Gelson's Market about to blow the rent money on organic grapes. "There was something weird about it," I said to Bunny in front of me. "What if she meant to invite a Julie, not a Jillie, and only on the phone did she realize her mistake?"

"Tracy Donaldson?" Bunny snorted. "She just doesn't like being corrected."

"What was I supposed to do? Have her call my kid Julie?"

"You were supposed to change Jillie's name to Julie." She nodded toward our offspring, doing homework in Gelson's café corner. "Wait until she sees how pretty Jillie is. This will get ugly."

"Why isn't little Richie going? Is it girls only?"

"Little Richie hates Leighton. She threw up on him in pre-school, and in first grade, he gave her head lice—intentionally, Tracy says—and now they shun each other." Bunny opened an unpaid-for Lindt chocolate ball, offered it to me, and then popped it in her mouth. "But I want to hear about the McMansion. It cost six million of Junior Donaldson's money and six years of Tracy's life, and the rumor is, now Junior wants out of the marriage, and Tracy's screwed."

"Why?"

"Prenup. Oh, and check out Feydeau. Tell me if he shows up himself or if it's just his staff."

"What's he look like?"

"Were you raised by wolves? He'll be in a toque hat. He looks like the Pillsbury Doughboy."

I was no more excited about this party than I'd been about the gala, but Jillie wanted to go and there was nothing I wouldn't do to make my nine-year-old happy, to foster friendships, to ease the "I miss my old school" melancholy. It wasn't just her school. She missed her old house. Her old life. But I couldn't fix everything.

As to the question of whether Jillie's invitation had really gone missing in the Donaldsons' car or whether we were last-minute guests, I forgot about it.

Until I saw the car.

———

THE LAMBORGHINI WAS yellow, the yellow of the rubber gloves my cleaning lady wore back when I had a cleaning lady. The dads approached it like it was Stonehenge, speaking in hushed tones of "aggressive graphic elements" and "maximum torque." It occurred to me that the way to get middle-aged men keenly interested in their offspring's parties was to park a supercar in front of an eight-car garage.

"Hey, Tracy!" a man called, but when I turned, a look of confusion replaced his smile. "Sorry," he mumbled, and Jillie and I kept walking across golf course–quality grass toward imperious doors. My daughter was uncharacteristically shy, forgetting herself to the point of holding my hand until we rang the doorbell. A maid took our wrapped gift and directed us to the backyard. We moved through rooms too grand to identify— ballrooms?—and outside. Canyons surrounded the house, making me want to sing "The Hills Are Alive with the Sound of Music," but I restrained myself because these people weren't show people. Or even showy people. The staff wore black, and parents were in weekend casual, ironed polo shirts and high-heeled sandals. We all looked overdressed against the stark backdrop, which was more Old West.

"Which Indians lived here in the olden days?" I asked Jillie.

She squinted up at me. "What?"

"Didn't you learn that for your California Mission report?"

"Mommy, this is a party. Chumash, okay?" She spotted her friends, and they yelled her name and she ran to them, relieved.

Across the fire pit, inspecting the lagoon, was the guy, my guy, the one from the Skates' gala who'd helped me into my coat. I was about to go hit him up for some snappy repartee when I saw Tracy.

It's disquieting to see your own double.

Watching her move toward me with my own disproportionately long arms and legs, I had the sense that if she moved her limbs, mine would move in response. Did she feel that, too?

"You must be Jillie's mom. I'm Tracy," she said with outstretched hand.

Sure enough, my hand stretched toward hers in a mirror image. "I'm Sarah," I said, but Tracy summoned a waiter, who slipped me a champagne flute. And the spell was broken. Her arms, legs, and midriff were bare and tan, and mine were not. Her nails were long, square cut, and French manicured. Our hair, long, black, poker straight, was parted on opposite sides.

"Try the lamb kebabs," she said. "I had to practically sleep with Feydeau to get them. He doesn't approve of winter lamb. I can't believe I haven't met you. You were at the major donor gala, weren't you?"

"Yes, I—"

"I enjoy that event. Much more intimate than the Spring Benefit or the Halloween Hoedown. Are you loving White Alder? What school did you come from?"

"Warner Avenue."

A tiny line appeared between her brows. "I don't think I know it."

"It's public," I said.

Her face froze. It was more even featured than mine with a straighter nose and better makeup.

"It's in Bel Air," I said. "So no gang violence or metal detectors."

"Oh." Her face relaxed. "You lived in Bel Air."

"Yes."

"Why did you move?"

"My husband got the house in the divorce."

"Really? You must not have had a good lawyer."

I never expected to feel protective toward my divorce lawyer, but there you go. "The house was a wedding present from his grandmother," I explained. "And he'd been living in it before our marriage, so I thought it would be rude to ask for it. Not that I had the money to buy him out."

"So he bought you out?"

This was an odd getting-to-know-you conversation, but boundaries were never my strong suit, so I plunged onward. "Not exactly. His grandmother said that if I let him keep the house, she'd pay tuition at White Alder. She's on the board of directors. I traded a great public school in a neighborhood I couldn't afford for a great private school out in the"—I almost said "sticks," but resisted—"countryside."

"So you moved to Calabasas. Gated community?"

"Townhouse." I may as well have said "trailer park."

Tracy regarded me thoughtfully, sipping champagne, leaving a trace of lip gloss on the flute. "So did you get anything out of the deal? Besides White Alder?"

I took a sip of my own champagne. I'm no judge, but I was guessing Cristal. "Full custody," I said.

———

SOME TOPICS, EVEN for those with weak conversational boundaries, aren't suitable for children's parties. Like the grim details of a marital demise. Like how it feels to take a hit in the face, to experience brain-numbing pain at the hands of a husband.

The first time it happened, my cheek swelled up but my thoughts flattened out to a mild *What the hell just happened?* curiosity. It was so odd being struck, so without precedent in my life that I considered it a freak accident, like when a tornado sends a tree through a house. Nobody's fault.

The second time it happened, I experienced no curiosity, only the calm certainty that there would be no third time. I left Stephen standing in the backyard. I walked inside, upstairs, and packed a suitcase for me and another for Jillie, who was at school. Through the open window came the sound of the blender making margaritas on the deck below, which was already becoming, in my mind, Stephen's deck rather than our deck.

I drove to the police station, told the desk sergeant what had happened, and asked him to photograph my face. I did not press charges, but I filed a report. Five days later I filed for divorce.

What died in me that month wasn't my faith in men—Stephen Hochstetter hardly represented half the human race—but my faith in me. If my own judgment was so wretched that I could love and procreate with a man like that, what else in life might I be screwing up?

Not that I said any of this to Tracy Donaldson. Not that I needed to. I followed her down hallways and up stairs as she did a commentary on her house that required no more response than does the audio headset tour at the Getty Museum. Wood beams salvaged from a château in Provence. Marble from Siena. Tile by local artisans. Furnishings: Pierre Deux, Henredon, Silk Trading Company. She had a proprietary way of speaking about "the work" that evoked images of Tracy herself upholstering love seats, wielding pickaxes, climbing ladders in France to liberate wood from ceilings. Perhaps she did. Her calf muscles were well developed. Her whole body was taut and toned and tanned and her clothes so tight it was hard not to stare. I wondered if she would, upon request, do a commentary on herself. Lasered skin by Arnie Klein. Nose by Alfred Blalock. Triceps by Billy Blanks.

"And the game room," she said, interrupting these charitable thoughts, "had to be done over four times before they got it right."

"How great to have a room for the kids," I said. "Keeps that Toys 'R' Us plastic out of the living room."

"It's not for kids. It's my husband's." Tracy opened massive double doors.

The skylit ceiling was twenty-four feet, high enough to accommodate the airplane in the middle of the room. It wasn't a big airplane, but still. Halfway up the walls, a walkway encircled the room, like in an English gentleman's library, giving access to bookshelves. The shelves held collections: cars, trains, swords, guns. One of the room's walls was made from the side of a caboose, yellow and red, from the Union Pacific Railroad.

Tracy looked around, then yelled, "Junior?"

"What?" a voice yelled back. I followed Tracy around the airplane to an alcove, where two taxidermy victims, a lion and a bear, stood poised to attack. Mounted on the wall between them was a flat-screen TV, showing a video game in progress.

Two men sat on an orange sofa, engaged in heated battle, holding steering wheels. I recognized one as a soccer dad. The other would be Junior Donaldson.

"Junior." Tracy's voice held no hint of conjugal affection.

"Son of a *bitch*!" Junior cried. "No! No! No!" He cranked his wheel to the right, and I watched the TV screen, which showed a simulated driving game.

"You're toast, Donaldson," the other guy said, then glanced at us. "Hey, Trace."

"Toast?" Junior rose from the sofa, college basketball tall. "Toast, motherfucker?" He aimed the racing wheel belligerently at the screen.

Tracy walked over, pressed a button, and the screen went black.

"What the hell?" Junior yelled.

"We are having a party," Tracy said. "You are the host."

"So? People can't find the bar on their own?"

The soccer dad stood. "I'll go give 'em directions." He lumbered past me and winked. "Don't get caught in the cross fire."

The maid appeared in the doorway and glanced from Tracy to me, then back again. "Miss Tracy? The lifeguards, they need to know, yes or no on diving boards?"

"God. Can no one make an executive decision? I'm coming." Tracy got right in her husband's face. "Junior, I put a lot of work into this party. The least you can do is put in an appearance. Sarah, escort him downstairs. Do not let him turn on that TV. No games."

And then she was gone, leaving me alone with her husband.

Junior hung the racing wheels on a wall tenderly, lining them up just so amid the electronic tennis rackets, golf clubs, and fishing rods. I wanted to leave—why was I stuck with the party pooper?—but my inner social director demanded I attempt conversation.

"You have Wii Boxing?" I asked. "How is it?"

Junior's face lit up. "You're gonna love this." He handed me a pair of boxing gloves fitted with remote controls.

I handed them back. "Tracy might yell at me," I said. "And I cry easily. Ix-nay on the video games."

"C'mere, then," he said and led the way across the game room, around a corner to a home gym better equipped than the one I paid a monthly fee for. Its centerpiece was a mannequin made of black leather, bulky and ugly, a human-shaped punching bag. "Ever work out with a dummy?" Junior asked.

I resisted a wiseass response. "Nope. Just heavy bags."

"I call him Pete. Go ahead. Hit him with your best shot."

I took a stance, then gave Pete a friendly left jab, then another, then a quick combination, three jabs and a right cross.

"Harder," Junior said, handing me a pair of real boxing gloves. "Pete can take it. Let loose."

It seemed impolite to refuse, so I slipped off my sandals and slipped on the gloves and went at Pete as Junior egged me on with "Drop your shoulders" and "Faster recoil" and "Swivel your hips."...I went from straight punches to hooks and uppercuts to Pete's leather jaw and then finished with a sloppy groin kick. Junior hit Pete, too, demonstrating the concept of upper body rotation on the hook.

"Better," he said as I tried it again. "You're a fast learner."

"This is a fun party," I said, breathing hard.

"I like you," Junior said. "What's your name?"

———

AFTER JUNIOR AND I rejoined the others, the ice stayed broken. Leighton, the birthday girl, led her guests from the indoor bowling alley to the outdoor lagoon to the putting green while a professional videographer captured it for posterity—until one of the moms complained. "A security breach supposedly," Tracy told me. "Ha. Like her kid's going to be kidnapped. Her husband wins two lousy Oscars, and suddenly they need bodyguards? Please. He's an *actor*." Tracy grabbed the hand of a passing guest, then snaked her arm around his waist. "Hi, Guy. Do you love my party? Tell me you love my party."

Tracy's tone was intimate, and Tracy's Guy was my guy, the one from the gala, and I felt a flicker of jealousy that was both surprising and unpleasant.

"Yours? I thought it was Leighton's party," he said, smiling.

"No, you didn't." Tracy smiled back, her face close to his.

"No," he said. "I didn't."

I wandered off across the perfect green grass to stare into the canyon, which is where Guy found me, minutes later.

"Like the view?"

"Except for that." I pointed to a neighboring estate on a hill. "Mausoleum? State penitentiary?"

"That's the Zoltan Pali–designed mansion of a renowned producer."

"What's he produce? Concrete?"

"Porn. Did you meet your Lamborghini?" he asked.

"Yes," I said. "It's very…yellow. So. Do you have a fourth-grader, too?"

"No, I have a fourteenth-grader. At UCLA. I'm not here as a guest."

"What are you here as?"

"I'm working."

"Are you a gigolo?"

"Are you in the market for one?"

"No, I'm on a budget," I said. "What are you really?"

But he wouldn't tell me, so we played *What's My Line?* and it took him twelve guesses to peg me as a singer doing mostly weddings and commercial jingles, whereas I still hadn't guessed him when the maid I'd seen earlier came to say Miss Tracy wanted him.

"Thanks, Maria," he said, and then to me, "We'll continue this next party."

"What if I'm not invited to the next party?" I asked.

"I know people."

I was hoping he'd kiss me again, but he just smiled and walked away.

Jillie, meanwhile, was in heaven. Leighton took her to the stables and lent her riding gear and afternoon turned to evening as four of the girls rode into the hills—with a servant, a certified EMT, Tracy assured me. My daughter was horse obsessed as only the preadolescent female can be, and when she was invited back the following weekend for a two-day riding clinic with Leighton's instructor, it was hard to say no.

"You'd be doing us a favor," Tracy said as the servant handed Jillie her party favor, a personalized bowling ball and matching shoes. "There's an extra horse I'm thinking of buying, and we're short a rider."

"Please, Mommy?" Jillie said. "Please, please, please, please, please, please? Say yes."

I did.

———

AND JUST LIKE that, we were part of the inner circle. The riding clinic led to twice-weekly lessons, because Leighton's instructor felt a partner would force her to focus.

"He said Jillie's a better rider, which will make Leighton competitive," Tracy explained. "I need to improve her dressage skills. She doesn't show well."

So Jillie and I spent two afternoons a week at the Donaldsons'. Tracy was rarely around, but Junior would inevitably pull me into the game room to box.

"If I could get you to stop apologizing every time you throw a punch," he said, "you could be a contender." Junior struck me as lonely. He didn't need to work, owned a house he had no reason to leave, and thus was socially malnourished.

"He's also a cretin," Bunny said, serving hot lunch with me one Tuesday. White Alder discouraged parental visits, so moms fought for the honor of spooning catered lasagna onto Styrofoam trays to spy on their offspring's educational experience. "Junior Donaldson," Bunny added, "has always had more bucks than brains."

I was cutting brownies into two-inch squares. "Why'd Tracy marry him?"

"Are you listening? More bucks than brains." Bunny squirted ranch dressing on a vat of iceberg lettuce. She spoke softly since we shared the lunch bungalow with three other moms and a dad. "Tracy comes from old money, which, after the market crash of 1987, became no money. She investigated the Donaldson automotive empire and decided Junior looked kinda cute. She needed an underwriter for her social life."

"But why am I her new best friend? I don't have breeding, bucks, connections—"

"—or a husband she can sleep with." Bunny nodded toward Fairuza Damadian, stacking napkins across from us. "Maybe it's your ex-grandmother. I saw them together at the Founder's Day Breakfast. Tracy's running for Volunteer Association president, so she's courting Hochstetter *Grandmère*."

"Yes, but Hochstetter *Grandmère* doesn't like me."

"She likes Jillie, Sarah. These people worship blood. Especially their own."

It was true. Helene Hochstetter considered my lineage pathetic, but offset, in Jillie, by Stephen's genetic contribution. "A great sire can overcome a mediocre dam," Helene said, "but nothing can overcome bad training." Which was why she'd lobbied for Jillie's transfer to White Alder—she didn't want her growing "marish," which I assumed was code for "like you, Sarah." And while I didn't love the horse analogy, my foal was getting a great education, so I sucked it up.

"Look." Bunny pointed out the bungalow window. "Our esteemed headmaster. Forced to court the nouveau riche to keep the school up and running, but he, too, longs for the old days when only The Best People's children were admitted, however dim-witted."

I stared, feeling my heartbeat quicken. "Bunny, who's that man he's with?"

Bunny squinted. "That's Guy Lasseter."

"What's he do?"

"Security consultant to the stars. He's installed half the surveillance cameras and bodyguards in the valley. Everyone uses him." Bunny tossed her vat of salad like it was an upper arm workout. "Hey, why'd Tracy change her hair?"

I dragged my gaze from Guy. "What?"

"A white blonde pixie. Very Annie Lennox. Is she going into the witness protection program?"

"She doesn't look like me anymore?"

Bunny took a brownie from my tray, looked around the bungalow, then ate it. "Sweetie, she never looked like you. I mean, height, weight, coloring. But no one who really knows you two would think so."

———

ONE WEEK LATER, I saw it myself. Not just Tracy's hair, which so altered her appearance that she hardly looked like either of us, but her pursuit of my erstwhile grandmother-in-law. They were lunching at the Four Seasons. The Hochstetter matriarch glanced my way, then pretended not to see me, and so of course, I made a beeline for their table.

"Hello, Helene," I said. "Tracy."

Tracy looked up, but Helene studied her place setting, her jewel-encrusted blue-veined hands caressing the flatware.

"Hello, Sarah," Tracy said. She was wearing a Chanel suit. "I've never seen you here before."

I held up sheet music. "Meeting a new bride."

"Yes, Sarah works," Helene said, making *works* sound like *turns tricks*. "By the way," she said, facing me. "You'll be interested to know that Stephen is seeing Isabel Taittinger. Excellent family. I've spoken with Isabel about Jillian, and she and Stephen are anxious to spend far more time with the child than the current arrangement allows. My lawyer tells me it's a simple matter of—"

"Over my dead body," I said pleasantly.

She raised an eyebrow. "I beg your pardon?"

"Over my dead fucking body."

———

TWO HOURS LATER, I dropped Jillie at the stable, then went for a run along the back trails of the Donaldson estate. I needed wilderness. And solitude. I told myself that my kind, ethical lawyer was a match for whatever shark Helene could hire in a custody dispute, but I felt panicky.

It wasn't that Stephen didn't love our daughter, only that anything that didn't involve drinking bored him stupid. And the less time he spent with her, the less they had to say to one another. He didn't want joint custody—this was all Helene and her obsession with bloodlines and legacies. And she wouldn't stop here. She'd go for full custody. She'd claim I was somehow unfit, drag me into court, and outspend me. No one who left the Hochstetters kept the silver, the real estate, or the kids, a onetime sister-in-law had warned me. I'd thought she was kidding.

I jogged distractedly until the scenery overtook me, the beauty of the canyon, stark, massive, pristine—

Except for the yellow Lamborghini parked a mile below me. What was it doing there, so far from the Donaldson garage? I could see a fire road nearby, which explained how it got there but not why. Maybe Tracy, like me, needed solitude. Bunny knew people with so much domestic staff they rented apartments just to be alone.

Or maybe Tracy was having afternoon sex in the Lamborghini.

I thought of witnessing that, then turned and headed back to the stables.

As I neared the estate, my cell phone picked up a signal and came to life with a message from Maria, saying Mr. Junior had something to show me. I was calmer now, fit for human company, so I jogged to the house and met Junior. "Come see what Tracy gave me today," he said, pulling me into the gym. "I call him Repeat."

Repeat, a new dummy, stood alongside Pete, enabling one to simultaneously fight two assailants.

"See?" I said, putting on gloves. "Tracy does love you. Surrounding you with dummies."

Junior laughed. "Save your breath. You'll need it." He had me do a long combination, over and over, until I was breathing hard and sweating harder. "What we really need," he said, "is a dummy who fights back. Work on your weak point."

"Which is?" I gave Repeat a last roundhouse kick. "Sorry, Repeat."

"Dropping your guard. Every punch you throw, your face is wide open."

"Huh," I said. "Do I have a strong point?"

"Yeah. You fight like you got something to lose."

It was the last thing Junior Donaldson said to me.

———

I HEARD THE news from Bunny the next morning as I drove Jillie to school.

"Not just dead," Bunny said. "Shot. Blood everywhere. Maria, the Donaldsons' housekeeper, told Celia, whose husband is our gardener Alfonso, that it happened in the airplane. Junior had an airplane?"

"Yes, yes, in the game room." I pulled off the road, shaking. "But it doesn't work anymore, it's just for show...."

"Like Junior," Bunny said. "RIP, of course."

"Mommy, why are we stopping?" Jillie asked from the backseat. "What happened?"

"Something bad," I said. "Leighton's daddy died yesterday."

"Gosh," Jillie said. "Like an accident?"

"It must have been an accident," I said.

"Mommy, are you crying?"

"It wasn't an accident," Bunny said on the phone. "It's on the surveillance cameras. Someone murdered Junior. And Celia says that Maria says there was so much blood they have to redo the wood floors."

———

THE COPS CAME to my house.

I figured they'd interview me since I'd seen Junior just before he died, but I didn't know they'd come that afternoon. To my house. And ask such creepy questions.

Like what I'd worn the day before. And whether I'd had sex with Junior.

I felt ill. I told them I hadn't had sex with anyone in two years and wouldn't, in any case, do it with a married man, especially one whose wife was a friend.

"You and Mrs. Donaldson are friends?" one detective asked me.

I thought of Tracy at the Four Seasons. "Not close friends. But—our daughters are friends."

"And you were friends with her husband."

"Junior. Yes." I started to cry.

"Why are you crying, Mrs. Hochstetter?"

"It's Miss Zaleski." I was crying out of sadness, I said, which was true. But also, I was scared.

The detectives asked to look around the townhouse and asked if they could take Jillie's gym bag, the one she used for riding gear. And my laundry. And then I was freaked.

"Why'd you do it?" one of the detectives asked me softly.

I stared at him, thinking I'd heard wrong.

"Surveillance footage," he said. "We saw the whole thing. Why don't you come with us to the division office and explain it?"

The room was spinning. I thought I would throw up. But I remembered my last conversation with Junior. "If you're arresting me," I said, "I'll come. Otherwise, I'm picking up my child from school."

They left. I called my divorce lawyer and asked if he knew any criminal defense attorneys.

———

MY NEW LAWYER was more basset hound than pit bull, but his retainer had been paid, he told me, and I wasn't to worry about money yet. Useless advice as his hourly fee was my typical week's take-home pay. He wouldn't say who'd paid the retainer, but I suspected Bunny and Rick.

"The police are building their case," he said. "Right now, let's just keep you out of jail."

"Keep me out of jail," I repeated. Our big plan.

When I went to get Jillie now, I felt stares from the other moms in the Lower School pickup lane. Jillie did, too. She wouldn't tell me what the kids were saying, but she wouldn't go to riding lessons, so I left messages at the Donaldsons'. No one called back. Bunny said that paparazzi were seen on campus, and the headmaster sent a mass e-mail requesting cooperation with increased security measures, expressing condolences to the Donaldson family, and offering counseling services to any student disturbed by The Incident.

I was disturbed.

Bunny gave me sleeping pills, but I was scared of them. I stopped eating. I was too upset to practice, and I tried to imagine doing vocal exercises in prison and wondered how I'd live without singing.

I wondered how I'd live without Jillie.

I stopped answering the phone for anyone but Bunny or my lawyer. I lay on the sofa, wrapped in a blanket.

On the third day, I emerged from my emotional coma and called Guy Lasseter.

———

HE OPENED THE door to his ranch house, greeted me without smiling, and led me out back to a guesthouse. A German shepherd lay on the threshold, thumping a tail in greeting. "Is he your security system?" I asked.

"She," Guy corrected me, "is the woman in my life."

The guesthouse was a studio, outfitted with computers, monitors, and electronic gadgetry. Guy clicked a remote and a flat-screen TV came to life, playing a silent movie.

On-screen, in the Donaldson game room, Junior sat in his plane. Straddling him was—me.

I wore tight, dark clothes. And gloves. Junior and I kissed for thirty-eight seconds, according to the counter at the lower edge of the screen. When Junior reached under my shirt to unhook my bra, I reached behind him, and then there was a gun in my gloved hand, abnormally long. I shot Junior in the chest. His body convulsed and twitched, but I sat calmly on his lap until he stopped moving. Then I climbed out of the plane, collected something from the floor, and left the room.

Guy replayed it three times. I watched in silence, fighting panic, piecing things together. I assumed that the gun had a suppressor attached and the object collected from the floor was a shell casing. I figured that Junior had mostly bled out his back as there wasn't much blood on his chest, facing the camera.

"The police have a copy of this?" I asked.

"Yes. Along with this." Guy clicked the remote and the Donaldson driveway appeared, showing my Toyota parked between Junior's Ferrari and the riding instructor's Ford pickup. "And this." He fast-forwarded to Jillie and me getting into the Toyota, post–riding lesson, and driving off.

"See?" I said. "I'm wearing different clothes."

"You're carrying a gym bag. You could've changed. They found blood in Junior's bathroom."

Claustrophobia overtook me, a premonition of prison. Cement floors. Caged rooms.

I turned to Guy. "I need your help. I need to convince the police that I'm not that woman."

"First," he said, "you need to convince me."

———

WE DROVE GUY'S convertible to the fire road behind the Donaldson property.

I talked nonstop. It was Tracy, I said. Tracy in a long black wig in clothes she later disposed of. She'd done it perfectly, looking natural while keeping her back to the camera. The average viewer—cop, jury—knowing Tracy only as a blonde, wouldn't recognize her.

Guy said nothing.

We drove onto the fire road, ignoring the AUTHORIZED VEHICLES ONLY sign. We drove until we reached the point where we could look up and see the Donaldson property. Then I tried to find the place the Lamborghini had parked off road.

I couldn't.

Deep in the canyon, every tree, copse, thicket looked like every other one. And what was I looking for, anyway? A yellow paint chip? A footprint?

"Okay," I said. "Wherever she parked, she hiked up to the property. It's steep, but she's athletic."

"I've got cameras covering the back of the estate," Guy said. "Motion detectors activate them. They weren't activated that day."

"But I was jogging there. And when I left Junior, I went out the back to the stables. The same path. Why didn't the motion detectors pick that up?"

"You tell me."

His face was impassive, but his tone was skeptical: I hadn't tripped the motion detectors because I was lying about jogging, about the Lamborghini. Tracy hadn't tripped them because she wasn't there.

"What's Tracy's alibi?" I asked.

"She was with a pillar of the community all afternoon."

My throat went dry. "Helene Hochstetter."

"Yes."

"Helene's lying."

He raised an eyebrow. "So it's a conspiracy."

"It's a tough crowd."

We studied each other. I said, "If I came in the front door and went out the front door, where's that footage? Where's me watching the riding lesson?"

"I have cameras in the barn but not the show ring."

"And the front door?"

He hesitated. "There've been installation problems. Those cameras weren't working."

"Or those cameras were unplugged."

Something crossed his face. "But you haven't suggested this to the cops."

"I just figured it out."

"What else have you 'just figured out'?"

The canyon was quiet, except for chirping birds. "She used you."

That killed his impassivity. I saw an opening and pushed it. "Doesn't feel good, does it? Gullibility. Finding out you're not as smart as you thought you were. That people can't be trusted."

Unexpectedly, he laughed. "But you trust me. You just pointed out some flaws, which I can now fix. What makes you think I'm not in on this?"

My heart stopped, but my mouth kept working. "What makes you think I'm not wearing a wire?"

His look of surprise would have been gratifying in other circumstances. But then Guy moved in on me. His hand grabbed my arm with enough force that I didn't think twice. I didn't think once.

I hit him with a left hook.

It wasn't a great punch, but it was okay. It broke his nose. And I dropped my guard, leaving my face wide open.

But Guy Lasseter wasn't Stephen Hochstetter. He was occupied with his nose, bleeding profusely. He said *son of a bitch* twice. Blood seeped through his fingers and dripped onto the grass and rocks.

I wasn't aware of my own reaction until he looked up, still holding his nose, and said, "What the hell are *you* crying about?"

"That felt awful," I said. "I'm never doing that again. I hate this. I'm sorry, I can't hit real people." I was edging toward hysteria, which only fueled my distress. I was thinking how Junior would tell me to suck it up, that there's no apologizing in boxing, that hitting's the whole point, and thinking of Junior produced spasmodic sobs. I took off my sweatshirt and gave it to Guy, who used it to stanch the bleeding.

"I'll live," he said. "I shouldn't have come at you like that. I wanted to see if you really were wired."

I cried harder. "I'm not."

He stared, as if meeting me for the first time. As if he were trying to picture me shooting a man at point-blank range, then waiting calmly on his lap, watching him die.

As if he couldn't.

———

I DROVE BACK with Guy riding shotgun, still bleeding. "I'll buy you a new T-shirt," I said.

"I'll let you."

I steered carefully along the fire road, avoiding ruts. High above on a hilltop, the concrete mansion witnessed our slow progress.

"That porn producer," I said. "Is he your client, too?"

Guy looked up. "He is."

"Does he have cameras overlooking the canyon?"

"He does."

"Do his work better than Tracy's?"

Guy looked at me.

"Sorry," I said.

In fact, the porn producer, a generous soul, gave us the whole week's footage, including, on Tuesday afternoon, 1.8 seconds featuring a yellow Lamborghini.

———

THE ANNUAL WHITE Alder Spring into Life Silent Auction and Benefit was held at the Four Seasons in May.

Absent and much discussed was Tracy Donaldson. The Volunteer Association's president-elect refused to resign her office unless she was convicted of murder, which, given the quality of her defense team, was no sure thing.

Few party guests doubted her guilt. None doubted her motive. This crowd understood prenups and how annoying they can be.

Helene Hochstetter was in attendance, wearing Scaasi. When confronted with the evidence, she'd told detectives she'd simply been mistaken about what time Tracy Donaldson had left her company. She was an elderly woman, her lawyer pointed out. There was no question of prosecution.

Maria, the Donaldson housekeeper, when threatened with deportation, had miraculously recalled giving bloody clothes and a wig to a cousin in east LA, something she always did with Miss Tracy's discards. The items were presumed to be in El Salvador. Maria was not invited to the Spring Benefit.

Guy and I left the party early, once he'd determined that his clients' bodyguards were appropriately dressed, their tuxes covering their firearms. We went home and played Scrabble with Jillie.

After Jillie went to bed, we changed the rules a bit and kept on playing.

# THE CONTROLLER

## BY DAVID MORRELL

Y ou don't have a first name?"
"I have one. I just don't use it. The less people know
about me, the better."

"Sure. The bodyguard with only one name. Cavanaugh. Like a trademark. Creates a mystique. Clever."

"Actually, Cavanaugh isn't my real last name."

"I don't understand."

"I try to be invisible, starting with my identity. What you called me just now—a bodyguard—that's not what I am."

"But I was assured you could help me."

"A bodyguard's what a mobster uses. His skills are limited to his size and his ability to inflict pain. I'm a protective agent."

"Okay. All right. Fine. A protective agent."

"If I take this assignment—"

"If?"

"I need to be assured of something. A man with your power and wealth. You didn't get where you are by being passive. It's your nature to take charge and assume control."

"I have three former wives who'll testify to that."

"Well, I won't risk my life for someone who'll put us both in danger by not doing what I tell him. The paradox of hiring a protective agent is that while you're the employer, I'm the one who gives the orders. Can you accept that? Can you follow my directions without question and allow yourself to be controlled?"

———

F. Scott Fitzgerald once wrote, "The rich are different from you and me," to which Hemingway famously replied, "Yes, they have more money." In Cavanaugh's experience, however, the true difference was that the extremely rich were able to shield themselves so thoroughly from the basic messes of life that after a while they forgot that messes existed. Problems with vehicles, plumbing, appliances, hot water heaters, furnaces, roofs, and so on, the sort of breakdowns that a person of ordinary income might lose sleep over or feel was a sign of impending doom, were unknown to the very rich. Fixing messes—that's what servants were for. That's what personal assistants were for. That's what money was for. Fires, floods, earthquakes. Inconvenient certainly, but while others took care of the mess, a Gulfstream V soared toward Rio or Nice or Dubai or one of many other resort locations. Of course, even the rich had dental problems, eye problems, bladder problems, but the best medical specialists in the world could correct those things if you threw enough money at them. Meanwhile, it was best to pretend that dental problems, eye problems, and bladder problems didn't exist.

Inevitably, even the rich encountered a problem so severe that it couldn't be ignored or fixed by wealth—a mortal illness, for example—and it always came as a shock that they weren't as entitled as they assumed. Something similar had happened to Martin Dant. At the age of twenty, he'd inherited his father's oil refinery business. Because of not-in-my-backyard issues, it was almost impossible to expand that business and build new refineries, so Dant invested in the broadcasting industry. Photogenic, he appeared frequently on news programs he owned, and after expensive instruction by several advisers to former presidents, he became—at the age of twenty-eight—a wunderkind public affairs moderator to whom politicians learned to pay court. At the age of thirty-five, he almost entered the governor's race in Georgia, but by then, his numerous affairs had jeopardized his first marriage (to a television producer), and he decided that the freedom to have a private life was more appealing than the nuisance of hiding scandals. Besides, he could gain far more power by using his wealth to influence politicians than he could ever gain by being a politician himself.

When Dant was forty-two, his second marriage (to a Washington political commentator) went the way of the first. By then, his empire included a motion picture company, which resulted in his third marriage—to a *Vogue* model, who aspired to be a movie star. She shared his interest in environmental issues, particularly wetland preservation, and in the pursuit of that goal, Dant acquired huge tracts on the U.S. eastern seaboard and in South America. His marriage to the fashion model lasted even fewer years than did his previous marriages, however, and at that point, Dant decided that connubial bliss was probably not something he was destined to achieve. Acquiring possessions and power was far more rewarding and long lasting.

Cavanaugh knew these details—and considerably more—because of a thick profile that his security company, Global Protective Services, had compiled. The extent of Dant's financial tentacles was even greater than Cavanaugh expected, but the strength of the man's ambition, determination, and sense of destiny didn't surprise him at all. Cavanaugh had provided security for tycoons on numerous occasions, and they all exhibited the same confidence, bordering on ruthlessness, when it came to generating wealth and getting what they wanted. Some had a degree of charm comparable to the Great Gatsby. Others made no effort to ingratiate themselves. If you didn't like the crude, cruel, or imperious way they treated you, well, tough shit. There were plenty of others who'd be more than happy to take your place.

Cavanaugh had no opinion. People without money could be crude, cruel, or imperious also. His business was saving lives, not making judgments. He protected the defenseless against predators, and sometimes even the very rich could be defenseless.

That was the case with Martin Dant. No one amassed an empire without making enemies. Over the years—Dant was now sixty-four—his enemies accumulated until it was impossible to keep track of them. One particular enemy had decided to get revenge. A month earlier, a sniper fired at Dant as he stepped from his limousine and approached his private jet at Teterboro Airport outside New York City. Dant heard the snap of the bullet passing his head and then its impact against the limousine. Two weeks afterward, as Dant and a female companion approached a boathouse at his Cape Cod estate, the building exploded, knocking them to the sand. Two days ago, a bullet shattered the window of a Grand Cayman office where Dant was negotiating to buy a struggling airline. Glass cut his face.

———

"Persistent," Cavanaugh said.

"More frequent," his partner noted. Her name was Jamie Travers. Trained by him, she was also his wife.

"Not good at it, though."

"Unless the idea is to scare Dant for a long time before killing him," Jamie observed.

"If so, the tactic's working," Cavanaugh said. "Whoever's doing this has definitely got Dant's attention. He's not twitching or sweating or pissing his pants, but I can see in his eyes how much strength he needs to appear calm."

"Right," she agreed. "For most of his life, he controlled everything around him, and now someone's showing him what it feels like to *be* controlled."

They got off the private elevator and reached the entrance to the penthouse of Dant's Fifth Avenue office building in Manhattan. In the marbled lobby, a guard had phoned to announce that Cavanaugh and Jamie were on their way up. The elevator had a security camera. So did the vestibule to the penthouse.

Two solid-looking men emerged from alcoves on either side of the elevator doors. They wore loosely fitted suits that Cavanaugh had no doubt concealed firearms. Their shoes were sturdy, presumably with steel caps. Their belt buckles had a design that Cavanaugh recognized, hiding knives.

"ID," the man on the right said, curtly adding, "please."

While the man on the left stood back a careful distance, Cavanaugh and Jamie complied.

"Are you armed?" the man on the right asked.

"Of course," Jamie answered. "But you already knew that. The elevator has a scanner, doesn't it?"

The sentries looked uncertainly at one another.

"You'll have to surrender it," the man on the right said.

"Don't think so," Jamie told him.

"No one gets in there with a weapon."

"I guess word didn't reach you. We're on the security team."

"Mr. Novak says there's been a change of plan."

"Mr. Novak?" Cavanaugh frowned. "Who's *he*? We're here to see Mr. Dant."

"Let them in," a voice said from a speaker next to the camera above the door.

"Yes, Mr. Novak."

The sentry on the left pressed buttons on a keypad. A lock on the door made a metallic sound as it was released. Cavanaugh opened the door, revealing a spacious room with a magnificent view of the city.

A tall, well-dressed man was silhouetted against the bright skyline. Cavanaugh took for granted that the wall-to-wall windows were bullet resistant and that the man's position had been chosen for dramatic effect. Crossing the room, he noted metal and glass furniture with rigid lines that matched those in several modernistic paintings. A rough guess put the value of the room's contents at ten million dollars.

The man at the window made his own assessment, shifting his attention between Jamie and Cavanaugh, although it was Jamie he mostly looked at.

"I'm Ben Novak, Mr. Dant's security chief." In his forties, Novak had a thin, stern face and short military-style hair. "I watched a monitor when you met with Mr. Dant yesterday, so I know who *you* are," he told Cavanaugh. "But I don't know who—"

"Jamie Travers."

"Pleased to meet you." Novak offered his hand.

When they shook, Novak held Jamie's hand a moment longer than necessary. "You have calluses on your thumb and your index finger."

"That's awfully personal."

"There's only one way to get calluses like that," Novak said.

"Definitely personal."

"How many rounds do you shoot a day?"

"Two hundred," she replied.

Novak referred to the calluses that a habitual shooter develops from repeatedly thumbing ammunition into a magazine and pulling a trigger.

He raised his eyebrows, reluctantly impressed.

"Good." Cavanaugh put a thick folder on a glass desk. "Now that we've gotten to know each other, here's our threat assessment. We have an appointment to discuss it with Mr. Dant."

"Yes, well, there's been a development," Novak said. "Mr. Dant decided you won't be needed."

"Oh?"

"He asked me to give you this check for your trouble." Novak indicated an envelope on the desk. "I think you'll find the amount satisfactory."

"It's hardly satisfactory if he gets himself killed." Cavanaugh turned quickly, addressing a security camera in the upper left corner. "Mr. Dant, you're making a mistake."

"I'll escort you to the—"

"Mr. Dant," Cavanaugh said more loudly toward the camera. "When we spoke, I told you a man doesn't acquire your power and wealth by being passive. I guess I was partly wrong. I didn't realize your management technique was *passive-aggressive.* Is this how you do business? You don't have the balls to deal face-to-face with an awkward situation, so you arrange for an employee to take care of it?"

A door opened. Martin Dant stepped from a room filled with computers, monitors, printers, and other electronic equipment. Men were occupied in front of screens that provided financial statements and stock market information. One of several security displays showed Cavanaugh, Jamie, and Novak.

Dant wore designer loafers, khaki pants, a blue linen shirt, a gold bracelet on one wrist, and a Patek Philippe watch on the other. He wasn't tall, but he exuded a power that gave him presence. His silver hair, healthily thick, contrasted with the golden tan that enhanced his television good looks. A square face, distinctive features, penetrating blue eyes. Even the half-dozen scabs from the flying glass that had cut his face reinforced the masculinity he projected.

His gaze rested on Jamie, then focused on Cavanaugh.

"If this is a question of ego," he told Cavanaugh, "remember you haven't actually been fired. After all, you never really had the opportunity to start the job. Nothing personal. I merely changed my mind."

"But we *did* start the job," Cavanaugh responded, "and you

might as well receive some value for that check you want to give us. We found some interesting items."

"We? If you mean Ms. Travers, I wish you'd brought her to yesterday's meeting."

"I was preparing your threat assessment," Jamie told him.

"The thing is, I already know there's a threat," Dant emphasized. "I confess I was nervous, but then I reminded myself that risk is a fact of life. It's just a question of keeping it away from me. So the answer is to increase my protection. Isn't that right, Mr. Novak?"

"Well, yes, sir, I think there's—"

"It's the control issue," Cavanaugh interrupted.

"Excuse me?" Dant asked.

"Yesterday, I wondered if you were willing to take orders from someone who worked for you. Now I have your answer."

"None of this concerns you any longer."

"Please look at the threat assessment," Jamie requested. "If it doesn't convince you, we'll gladly leave. After we tear up the check."

Dant paused. He glanced at the folder. He looked at Jamie. He considered Cavanaugh.

Absently, he scratched one of the scabs on his face, where the bullet through the Grand Cayman window had sprayed glass shards at him. When he lowered his hand from his cheek, blood was on his finger.

"Maybe I was wrong. Maybe we should begin again."

———

CAVANAUGH TOOK A page from the folder and showed it to Dant. "In the past five years, you had a seventy percent turnover on your protective detail. Mr. Novak is your fifth security chief in that same period."

Dant looked surprised.

"Surely you knew this," Cavanaugh said.

"Yes, but that's confidential."

"Apparently not, or else we wouldn't be discussing it with you."

"How did you learn this information?"

"I hacked into your computer system," Jamie answered matter-of-factly.

Dant looked more surprised.

"We have a lot of resources," she told him.

"The district attorney will want to know all about them."

Cavanaugh pointed at the file. "Here's the agreement you signed, authorizing us to use any means necessary to prepare a threat assessment."

"I'll plug the holes," Jamie assured him. "Then I'll hire a friend who's better than me to try to hack in. Meanwhile, the flaws in your computer security might have been how the person who's trying to kill you learned your schedule. Teterboro Airport. Cape Cod. Grand Cayman. You can't be followed easily, so that means somebody's ahead of you."

"Another thing that stands out," Cavanaugh said, pointing at the file, "is the absence of any female personnel on your security team. There hasn't been any in the past three years."

"I don't know why you think that's significant," Dant replied. "Men are obviously more suited for dangerous work. Besides, it's difficult to find properly trained female bodyguards, given that almost everyone in that business is a former member of a special-operations military unit. Isn't that right, Mr. Novak?"

"Not exactly, Mr. Dant. There's a female special-ops unit that—"

Dant cut him off, asking Cavanaugh, "Why do you think women should be on my security team?"

"The men in the lobby and outside your door showed more interest in Jamie than they did in me. So did Mr. Novak. So did *you*. In your case, that's a function of your fondness for female companionship."

"Which is none of your business."

"It is if your protectors need to accommodate that fondness. The team might be more objective if some of them are women. It's not that Mr. Novak or the men outside stopped being professional. On the contrary, I got the impression they were worried that a woman could be a greater threat than a man and that they weren't sure how to deal with that. A female protector would know how to handle the situation."

"I won't give up my social life."

"No one's asking for that," Cavanaugh emphasized. "But you can have patience enough to wait until background checks are made. Three years ago, you had female protectors. What happened? The unusually high turnover in your security staff? What do you suppose is the problem?"

Dant shrugged. "Maybe they find better money somewhere else. How would *I* know?"

"You pay higher than the standard rate. No, the problem is you treat them like bodyguards instead of protectors."

"Back to that again. I refuse to allow anyone to tell me how to run my life."

"Even if that's what's necessary to save it?" Jamie pointed at his face. "By the way, one of your scabs is bleeding again."

This time, Dant didn't touch it. "Whoever's trying to kill me won't have the satisfaction of making me cower. Tonight, I'm going to attend a charity benefit at Lincoln Center."

"But that gives us hardly any time to plan the security arrangements," Jamie objected.

"Mr. Novak has already taken care of that."

————

AT NIGHT, LINCOLN Center was one of Cavanaugh's favorite places in Manhattan. Its brilliantly lit, elegant buildings, spacious plaza, and spectacular fountain represented what the city could be at its best, never failing to impress him.

Except when Cavanaugh was working. Then all he saw were unlimited vantage points and uncontrollable crowds.

Dant's limousine arrived by an indirect route that might have fooled someone into thinking he'd changed his mind about going to the charity benefit. It was one of four that had left the basement parking area of Dant's Fifth Avenue building, their tinted windows making it impossible for surveillance to detect which of the limousines Dant had chosen to use. Near Lincoln Center, the vehicles had separated and approached all four entrances: Columbus Avenue, West Sixty-fifth Street, West Sixty-second Street, and Amsterdam Avenue.

Dant rode in the second limousine, sipping Armand de Brignac champagne. Cavanaugh sat in back with him while Novak sat in the front, using a scrambler-equipped two-way radio to communicate with the rest of the security team and coordinate Dant's arrival. Jamie had gone ahead.

The black of Dant's Brioni tuxedo made his thick silver hair seem more lustrous, emphasizing his photogenic features. Expertly applied makeup disguised the scabs on his face.

"Have you ever been shot at when you protected someone?" he asked Cavanaugh.

"A couple of times."

"Were you hit?"

"Once."

"Let me ask you something. It's obvious you don't like me, and yet you're willing to risk your life for me. Is the money that important to you?"

"I barely know you, so how can I have an opinion about whether you're likable or not? If it matters, I admire how hard you worked to build your empire. Not many people have your determination."

"I got that from my father." Dant didn't say it happily. He glanced toward the glow of traffic. "Would you risk your life for someone you absolutely couldn't stand?"

"Drug dealers have tried to hire me. Mob bosses. Corporate CEOs who aren't any better than con men, looting pension accounts. Financial advisers who cheat the investors who trusted them. Sometimes evil is obvious. Otherwise, it's not my place to judge. Most people muddle through their lives. All I can do is hope that if I keep them from dying a while longer, maybe they'll find a way to justify being alive. The truth is, I'm less interested in the people I protect than the bullies I protect them from."

"Bullies? Do I detect anger?"

"My father beat my mother."

"Ah, yes, fathers." Dant pointed through the window toward Lincoln Center. "Did you ever see the movie *The Producers*?"

"Sure."

"You remember the plot? Zero Mostel and Gene Wilder embezzle money from widows by getting them to invest in a Broadway play that they do everything to guarantee is a flop. The widows invest more than the play cost to produce, so Mostel and Wilder are guaranteed a profit."

"Yes, Wilder's an accountant as I recall."

"They dream up that plan at Lincoln Center. At night at the fountain. When the idea comes to them, the fountain gushes. I couldn't stop laughing when I was a kid and I saw that fountain gush. The first time I came to New York, the only place I wanted to see was Lincoln Center and that fountain." Dant looked amused. "I donated five million dollars for tonight's fundraiser. It underwrites cultural events at the center."

"Nice to have culture."

"I don't mind having that publicized. It isn't self-serving. What I *don't* publicize are the considerably greater amounts I donate to after-school programs, homeless shelters, food banks, day care centers, inner-city health clinics, and so on."

"You just gave me a lot of reasons to risk my life for you."

———

THEY USED THE garage entrance on West Sixty-second Street, proceeding past harsh underground lights to a guarded area that provided access to an elevator reserved for VIP donors. Cavanaugh and Novak got out first, joining six protective agents, three on each side, who shielded Dant as he moved from the vehicle to the elevator.

The lobby doors opened, revealing tuxedos and evening gowns, the drone of hundreds of conversations, lights glinting off champagne and cocktail glasses—and diamonds, lots and lots of diamonds. Uniformed servers moved through the crowd, offering canapés from polished trays. A string quartet played in the background.

For most attendees, the occasion seemed festive. For Cavanaugh, it was a nightmare. At the other entrances, security personnel presumably made sure that everyone who came through the various doors had an invitation, just as a guard now took Dant's invitations and the ones he'd arranged for Cavanaugh and Novak. But invitations were easy to counterfeit. Plus, there weren't any metal detectors. If Cavanaugh and Novak could enter with concealed firearms, so could someone with violent intentions. To add to the problem, while Cavanaugh wore a tuxedo, Novak did not. Nor did any of his security team. The rule was, Always match what your employer wore. Then not only did you blend with the environment, disguising your function, but also you might confuse a gunman's aim, making it hard for him to distinguish his target from similarly dressed people around him.

Dant merged with the crowd. Following, Cavanaugh watched him approach a woman whose blonde hair was combed above her head, emphasizing her statuesque figure. As she turned toward Dant and smiled, her movement had a dancer's grace. He kissed her on the cheek, so low that his lips almost reached her neck.

Cavanaugh stopped a discreet distance away.

"Champagne?" a server asked.

"No, thank you."

"Looking for a good time, lover?" a woman asked.

It was Jamie, who shifted in front of him so that he seemed to be focusing on her while he actually concentrated on the people around Dant a dozen feet away. She wore an evening dress that emphasized her green eyes.

"As long as you're with me, it's always a good time," he said, the murmur of nearby conversations floating over them.

"Well, I'll tell you one thing that's not good." ·

"You mean, apart from the fact that Dant's security team is wearing suits instead of tuxedos, so they can't move into the crowd without attracting attention?"

"Even if they did, their military haircuts would give them away."

Looking past Jamie's shoulder, Cavanaugh watched Dant whisper into the woman's ear. She nodded as if experiencing pleasure.

"He certainly has a way with the ladies."

"With her, he's had practice."

"What do you mean?"

"She used to be his second wife."

"What?" Cavanaugh concealed his surprise. "But she doesn't look like her photographs. She's too young. She ought to be in her late fifties by now."

"The kind of alimony she gets from Dant, she can afford the Elixir of Youth. That's the name of the office of her cosmetic surgeon. By the way, I got a look at the seating chart. Dant has a balcony seat. First row."

"Novak should have caught that. What else hasn't he checked? We need to—"

"I should have said Dant *had* a balcony seat. I arranged for him to sit behind you."

Cavanaugh's feeling of relief lasted all too briefly. "Wait a minute, what's he doing?"

Dant and the woman left the crowd, moving toward an exit.

Cavanaugh pressed a transmitter hidden under his cummerbund. Activating a microphone on his lapel, he warned the team that Dant was headed outside. He and Jamie followed, trying to disguise their urgency.

"Mr. Dant."

Dant turned, looking annoyed.

"Sorry to interrupt, but an old friend asked me to give you a message."

"Not now."

"He said the message was really important."

"It's too loud in here. This lady and I want some fresh air. It's been a while since we had a chance to talk."

Impatience with Cavanaugh's interruption made the ex-wife's features harden.

"You know it *is* loud in here," Jamie said. "I'd like some fresh air, too."

She and Cavanaugh followed Dant and his ex-wife into the nightglow of the plaza outside Lincoln Center. The blare of traffic replaced that of conversations and the string quartet.

Cavanaugh saw Novak and the rest of the security team coming outside. If they'd worn tuxedos, Dant might have been indistinguishable from his protectors, but as things were, he was conspicuous in his formal evening clothes.

"He's heading toward the fountain," Jamie said.

Cavanaugh hurried in front of him. "All you needed to do was tell us in advance what your plans are."

"Sometimes I don't have a plan."

"Look, just give us a half hour, and we'll make sure the area's clear."

"The opera's scheduled to start by then."

"Please."

"What good does all the money in the world matter if..." Dant shook his head bitterly. "I knew this wouldn't work."

Cavanaugh looked ahead toward the huge circular fountain. Lights shimmered under the water. A tarpaulin covered part of the fountain's curve. Cones stood in front of a sign: UNDER REPAIR.

"At least let me check the tarpaulin."

"Get out of our way."

The explosion had the force of hands shoving at Cavanaugh's chest. His ears felt slapped. Stumbling back, he closed his eyes from the glare of the blast. He winced as Dant and his ex-wife walloped against Jamie and him, all four of them crashing onto the plaza. Sickening smoke swirled around him. Bystanders screamed.

———

"How many fingers do you see?" the doctor asked.

Cavanaugh told him.

"What year is it?"

Cavanaugh told him.

"What's your social security number?"

"You're kidding, right? You expect me to give you my social security number?"

"Just wanted to see if you're alert. Are you sick to your stomach?"

"No."

"Are your ears still ringing?"

"Not as much."

"I wouldn't try to handle any heavy machinery." The doctor looked at Jamie, whom he'd already checked. "Otherwise, I think it's okay for the two of you to leave the hospital."

"What about Mr. Dant? Is he okay?" Jamie asked.

"The same condition as you. I released him twenty minutes ago."

"Released him? No. We need to talk to him."

"The police wanted to talk to him first. But even without them, I get the feeling it would have been impossible to keep him here. He definitely knows what he wants. Speaking of the police, there's a detective waiting to ask you more questions."

———

Two hours later, Cavanaugh and Jamie were escorted by Global Protective Services agents to a car outside the hospital. They were driven to the security firm's headquarters at a building in midtown Manhattan, on the fortieth floor, where they met with the hastily summoned heads of GPS's various divisions.

"Dant's been treating his protective team so badly, no one with any talent wants to work with him," Cavanaugh said, rubbing his forehead.

"You should buy a lottery ticket," the director of the Far East division said. "That close to the blast, you didn't get hit with shrapnel. All things considered, this was your lucky night."

"What about the other people in the area?"

"No serious injuries," the head of electronic security devices replied.

"Sounds like there wasn't *any* shrapnel."

"Maybe the idea wasn't to kill Dant as much as continue scaring him," Jamie suggested. "It prolongs the revenge."

Cavanaugh nodded, a motion that aggravated his headache. "And once again, whoever's after Dant had information that allowed him or her to know well in advance where the target would be."

"Yes, the charity event at Lincoln Center," the director of corporate security said. "But it's a big leap from knowing that Dant would be there and predicting that he'd go out to the fountain, especially when security was supposed to be tight. It would have taken a lot of trouble to hide the bomb where the repairs were being made. Maybe someone pretending to be part of the repair crew did it. But nobody would risk it unless Dant was sure to go out there."

"Dant has a thing about that fountain. The first time he visited New York, that's where he went."

"So whoever's doing this has personal information about him, more than just the sort of details available by hacking Dant's computer system and learning what his schedule is," Jamie said. "Really personal details. The sort of thing only someone close to him would know."

———

"I'm sorry, sir," the receptionist's voice said. "Mr. Dant isn't available."

"Then put me through to Mr. Novak," Cavanaugh said into the phone.

"He's not available, either. Would you like to leave a message?"

"Yes." Cavanaugh gave his name and phone number. "Do you know when they'll be free?"

"Not for quite a while. They're in Europe."

Neither Dant nor Novak returned his calls.

———

A client had a television tuned to a business channel. Jamie glanced in that direction and suddenly pointed.

"My God."

Above the stock market quotes streaming along the bottom of the screen, a photograph of Dant appeared next to a caption that said "Breaking News."

"...near this peaceful Greek island," an announcer somberly reported.

The television showed wreckage floating on water.

"According to Martin Dant's security officer," the announcer continued, "he went out for a moonlight sail. Despite recent attempts to kill him, Dant was known for being determined not to let threats control his life. He was alone when the bomb went off, completely destroying his boat. Windows were shattered within three blocks of the harbor. Local authorities are still searching for the body."

———

"FIVE ATTEMPTS ON his life," Jamie said. "Two with a rifle, three with explosives. Ever hear of an assassin who didn't specialize in a single method?"

"And that explosion at the Lincoln Center fountain," Cavanaugh said. "All flash-bang but no shrapnel."

———

SAUDI ARABIA.

Gunshots echoed across the desert. With Jamie beside him, Cavanaugh drove a Range Rover to a checkpoint. They showed their identification to a Saudi guard, who studied a list, nodded, and motioned for Cavanaugh and Jamie to get out of the vehicle. In the stark heat, other guards approached them.

The gunshots persisted.

Jamie wore the black cloak that all women in Saudi Arabia were required to wear. The head cover wasn't as strictly enforced for Western women. Even so, Jamie made sure that she had a black scarf in her pocket in case she was ordered to wear it. Meanwhile, a floppy-brimmed Helios sun hat covered her head while dark sunglasses concealed her eyes.

The vehicle was checked for weapons and explosives.

So were Cavanaugh and Jamie.

The guard motioned for them to get back in the Range Rover and proceed, but not before one of the guards slid into the rear of the vehicle, staying with them.

Although unpaved, the desert road was remarkably smooth, not surprising given that the area was owned by a member of the Saudi royal family. The gunshots became louder.

Buildings appeared ahead. Some were functional, containing what Cavanaugh assumed were offices, a lecture hall, a cafeteria, a dormitory, and bathrooms. Other buildings—mere shells—formed mock urban streets, along one of which a three-car motorcade was attacked by submachine guns and a rocket launcher. The motorcade slammed into reverse gear, pivoted 180 degrees, rammed into forward gear, and raced away, only to be confronted by more fire from submachine guns and a rocket launcher.

However realistic, it was a practice exercise using nonlethal ammunition.

The people engaged in the exercise were Saudis. The men supervising it were American, German, and Australian, all of them former members of special-operations units. Cavanaugh knew their backgrounds because he recognized all the instructors, having worked with them from time to time.

After a siren blared and the gunfire ended, a burly sunburned man in desert camouflage fatigues came over.

"Training a protective detail for the royal family?" Cavanaugh asked.

"A favored cousin." The accent was Australian. "The man you asked me about on the radio—he's over there."

Cavanaugh and Jamie approached the street on which the mock ambush had occurred. The man they wanted to talk to was explaining something to one of the drivers.

Sensing something, he looked toward Cavanaugh and Jamie, narrowed his eyes, finished his explanation to the driver, and reluctantly walked over.

"Novak," Jamie said in greeting.

Hardly pleased, Novak asked, "What brings you two here?"

"Old times," Cavanaugh said.

"Our feelings are hurt," Jamie told him. "After everything we've been through, you don't return our phone calls or answer our e-mails. It's enough to make us feel rejected."

"Look, you know what Dant was like. He did what he wanted. Half the time, it was impossible to get ahead of him and clear the way. What happened to him wasn't my fault. He insisted on taking that sailboat out, and short of restraining him, I couldn't have stopped him."

"We want to talk to you about your girlfriend," Jamie said.

The smell of burned gunpowder hung in the air.

"Girlfriend?" Novak asked.

"You've been in Saudi Arabia only two weeks, and already you forgot the woman you've been living with for the past year?"

"Sure. Right. My girlfriend."

"Dant was smart enough to have a woman on his security team until three years ago," Jamie pressed on. "Laura Evans. Used to be in the army. In a special-ops unit for women who accompany members of Delta Force on some of their missions—the kind of missions that involve infiltrating a foreign country by posing as tourists. A young married couple on a holiday blends easier than a man traveling alone."

Novak nodded. "I know about that female unit."

"Haven't had the pleasure of meeting Laura yet. She seems to have wanted to drop out of sight, and she's doing a good job of it." Cavanaugh stepped closer. "But Dant's computer records indicate that she was the last woman hired to protect him. Why do you suppose that was?"

"I have no idea, but I bet you're going to tell me."

"We contacted agents who worked with your girlfriend on that assignment," Jamie said. "Seems that Dant treated her as a bodyguard instead of a protector, or maybe it's more accurate to say he treated her as a body. Kept trying to strike up a relationship with her. Wanted to take her to dinner. To have a drink with her. To be alone with her. Wouldn't let her do her job. Pissed her off so much that she quit before the way he distracted her might get both of them killed."

"Okay," Novak said, "I see where this is going."

"You and Laura crossed paths on an assignment a year and a half ago. You started dating and eventually moved in together."

"I don't deny it. Not that we see each other a lot. When I'm working, she isn't—and the other way around."

"We know Laura *wasn't* working when a sniper fired at Dant at Teterboro Airport," Cavanaugh said.

"Hey, that's an awfully big accusation you're—"

"You complained to her about the way Dant wouldn't follow directions to keep him safe," Cavanaugh continued. "In turn, Laura complained about how he treated her when she worked for him. She said, 'If anybody ever tries to kill the son of a bitch, if he gets the hell scared out of him, he'll appreciate what his security people do for him.'"

"You're dreaming," Novak said. "There's no way to prove a conversation like that ever happened. If you went to the police, they'd laugh at you."

"We're not the police."

Novak pointed toward drivers getting into the motorcade vehicles. "Look, we're about to start another exercise. I don't have time for this."

"You told her when Dant would be at Teterboro," Jamie said. "It's a small airport, mostly for business jets. Not hard for a professional to infiltrate. Laura shot at him, deliberately missing. Later, the two of you enjoyed the practical joke. Hell, there was even the possibility that he might pay you extra to increase his security."

"Bullshit."

"You enjoyed it so much that you couldn't stop," Jamie insisted. "The bomb in the Cape Cod boathouse. The sniper attack in the Caymans. The two of you were determined to see Dant sweat. But I'll give him credit. He didn't."

"I've heard all I'm going to—"

"We have hotel receipts and witnesses that prove Laura was in Grand Cayman when the sniper took another shot at him. We figured she wouldn't risk bringing a rifle into the country, so we asked around and found the drug dealer she bought it from."

"The police won't believe a goddamn drug dealer."

"But I told you we're not the police," Cavanaugh emphasized.

The fierce sun had terrible force.

Novak studied them. "Dant's death wasn't our fault. We had nothing to do with it."

"Sure sounds like a practical joke that went bad."

"The first three attempts..." Novak sighed. "Okay, that was Laura and me. Wanting to get him to come to his senses and realize how important his security was."

"The bomb at the Lincoln Center fountain?" Jamie asked.

"As big a surprise to us as it was to you," Novak replied. "After that, I was scared. Believe me, I tried everything I could to keep Dant off that fucking boat. I have nightmares about it. In a way, I did kill him. Because somebody got the idea from Laura and me. The difference is they wanted to do it for real. God knows he had a lot of enemies. Look at how his empire collapsed after he was killed. The bastard couldn't stop doing whatever he wanted, taking chances regardless of the risk. He borrowed against one corporation to prop up another, then borrowed against *that* one to save yet another. He even raided pension funds to meet his payroll, but nobody realized it because he had a genius for cooking the books. He ruined a lot of people. Maybe one of them realized what was going on and decided to get even. Or maybe..."

"Maybe what?"

"Maybe Dant couldn't bear the idea of going to prison. Laura and I wondered if maybe he killed himself, going out as dramatically as he did everything else."

A siren blared.

"I need to get back to work," Novak said.

"Don't bother," Jamie told him. "You and your girlfriend aren't protective agents anymore."

"What? But this is the only thing I know how to—"

"You swore to risk your life for Dant. You accepted money from him. Then you attacked him. You make me sick," Cavanaugh said. "We don't have enough proof to go to the police. But we've got plenty enough proof to convince the agents who depend on you to watch their backs. If we ever hear that you're on another protective detail, we'll spread the word about what you did. You won't like what happens to you."

The siren blared.

———

"I believe him," Cavanaugh said, driving away.

"So do I," Jamie told him. "But we're not any closer to finding who killed Dant. He had so many enemies, it could take years to investigate them all."

"Maybe it isn't a question of who hated him most. How about, who benefited most?"

———

THE PACIFIC ISLAND was so out of the way that it didn't have regular aircraft or boat service. In Hawaii, Cavanaugh—who had a pilot's license with multiple ratings—chartered a two-engine seaplane with extra fuel tanks that gave it an extreme range. He and Jamie, accompanied by two protective agents and a special passenger, took four hours to reach the island with palm trees, white beach, and gentle surf that seemed like a vacation poster when seen from above.

After touching down in a sheltered cove, Cavanaugh guided the seaplane toward a dock. Beyond it, a village nestled among the palm trees.

Puzzled natives waited for them.

"Does anybody speak English?" Cavanaugh asked as he and Jamie and the agents tied the aircraft to the dock. "*Français? Español?*"

No one responded.

One agent guarded the plane while the other agent and the special passenger followed Cavanaugh and Jamie past the villagers toward the end of the dock. Beyond the soft beach, they reached the grass huts of the village.

The sound of engines guided them to electrical generators and numerous barrels of fuel. The primitive facades of some huts contrasted with their sophisticated interiors, which included air-conditioning, a stove, a refrigerator, a freezer, satellite television, computers, even a wine cooler.

"Where *is* he?" Cavanaugh demanded of the natives.

They looked dumbfounded.

"Fine. We'll get him. It'll just take a little longer."

The island was eight miles long and four miles wide with a ridge along the middle. Plenty of spots in which to hide.

Not that it mattered. The special passenger was a bloodhound.

Cavanaugh let the bloodhound sniff the interior of the master hut. When the dog found a scent, it barked repeatedly, ran outside, and led them toward the interior of the island.

The trees became thicker, the undergrowth dense. They made their way to a stream and took fifteen minutes to find where the scent emerged a hundred yards to the left on the other side of the water. They squirmed over fallen trees and reached a steep, rocky slope, the start of the ridge that formed the island's spine. Sniffing along the bottom of the slope, the dog stopped in confusion, circled, came back to the same spot, and again was confused.

"Dant couldn't just vanish," Jamie said. "How did he hide his scent?"

She and Cavanaugh looked up, noticing a tree branch above them.

"He jumped up, grabbed the branch, squirmed toward the slope, and touched down several feet above where the dog could smell him," Cavanaugh said.

They lifted the dog onto the slope. Instantly it retrieved the scent and scrambled upward with Cavanaugh, Jamie, and the handler working to follow. They reached a bluff and hurried along it. Sweat stuck their clothes to their skin. Along another slope, the dog again lost the scent.

But this time, there wasn't a tree branch above them to explain how Dant could have lifted himself and fooled the dog.

"Well, if he didn't go up and he didn't go forward...," Cavanaugh said.

"He backtracked and jumped off the trail," Jamie concluded.

They ran back the way they'd come and almost passed the cave before they realized it was there, camouflaged by bushes. The bloodhound barked frantically, wanting to charge in.

The handler restrained it.

Cavanaugh wiped sweat from his face and unclipped a canteen from his belt.

"Dant, are you thirsty?" he yelled toward the cave. "You covered a lot of distance in a hurry. I've got water." He shook the canteen so that Dant could hear the water sloshing.

The shadowy cave entrance was silent.

"Or maybe you planned for an emergency," Jamie said, "and stocked the cave with food and water."

Cavanaugh raised the canteen to his mouth, taking several swallows. Although the water was unpleasantly warm, his parched tongue absorbed it.

"Fine. We'll set fire to the bushes and smoke your miserable ass out of there."

He and Jamie gathered dead leaves and branches, stacking them in front of the bushes that obscured the cave.

He struck a match.

"Stop," a voice said from the enclosure.

The bushes rustled. Gradually a figure emerged.

But he didn't look anything like Dant. He was bald and bearded. His nose had a bony ridge. A scar disfigured his neck.

"Never heard of anyone getting cosmetic surgery to look ugly," Jamie said. "Since you went to all this trouble, why didn't you try to pretend to be someone else when we arrived?"

"I was prepared to until I saw you getting off the plane." Dant's expression was sour. "I figured I could fool anybody, except people who spent up-close time with me and are experts at paying attention."

"Yeah, those camera-friendly blue eyes of yours are hard to disguise," Jamie said. "Tinted lenses might have done the job, but I suspect you forget to put them on day after day when only the natives are around to see you. Even with tinted lenses, you wouldn't have fooled us, though. Your cosmetic surgeon told us what you look like now."

"But..."

"Yes, I know—you thought you'd guaranteed his silence by promising him a quarter million dollars a year. The trouble is, the second check you sent him bounced. Worse, he believed what you told him about how well your companies were doing. To impress his clients, he said he had a stock tip that couldn't go wrong. They invested heavily. When your house of cards collapsed, the clients blamed him for their losses. His practice is ruined."

"There are plenty like him," Cavanaugh added. "Thousands of people lost their jobs because of you. Their pensions are worthless. They can't pay their mortgages or feed their families. Their lives are destroyed. All because you did whatever you wanted whenever you felt like it."

"Big gains require big risks."

"Keep telling yourself that in prison. Did you figure the first three attempts to kill you were only the beginning? Novak was behind them incidentally. He couldn't stand you any more than anybody else does. Did the explosion at your Cape Cod property give you the idea to arrange for the last two explosions on your own, so when your boat blew apart, people would decide you were blown apart also and finally give up searching for you?"

"Something like that." Dant glared. "How the hell did you find me?"

"Once we figured out what you were doing, it became a matter of asking the right questions," Jamie answered. "Naturally you'd want to change your appearance. After that, you'd want to hole up someplace remote for a couple of years until you felt it was safe to return with a new identity. What property did your companies own that would be acceptable, particularly in terms of your appetite for female companionship? We spent months going through your records. One of your shadow companies bought this island just before your empire started to teeter. That seemed a good clue. So did the half-dressed native women."

"Damn it, why couldn't you leave me alone? I gave you a generous check."

"Which bounced. But that's not what pissed me off," Cavanaugh said. "I told you protecting people is a very personal thing for me, and yet you treated it like a joke."

"I needed to. It was part of the act. I had to show I was so determined to do what I wanted, so controlling, that even the best bodyguards couldn't have kept me from getting on that boat."

"Not bodyguards. Protective agents."

"Right. Whatever."

"Now *you're* the one who'll be controlled."

# POETIC JUSTICE

## BY CAROLYN MULLEN

I f it hadn't been so hot that summer, I sometimes wonder if I, a hard worker, good neighbor, loving mother, and grieving widow, would have committed murder. But it was hot that summer of ninety-six with a muggy, steamy heat that weighs down your body and softens your brain, dampens your compassion, and kindles your hatreds. So, it was to be.

"Oh, praise the Lord, it is hot," Miss Pinkett said, fanning herself with her order book. I said nothing, though for once I agreed with her prattle. The dust and grit from the mill's smokestacks mixed with the sweat coursing down my neck, and my petticoats were already damply sticking to my legs, although it was only ten in the morning. But I had other worries than the heat wave that had settled over our little corner of Baltimore like an invisible evil spirit, sucking out any of the meager energy and pleasure that we might have enjoyed. I was looking through the cheaper fabric selections, hoping I could afford enough to make my daughter's birthday dress. It wouldn't be the satin frock of her desires, but at least it would be new.

"Make up your mind," Miss Pinkett said. "You can see there are other customers waiting." I ignored her remark as it was clear that Mrs. O'Casey and Mrs. Reeley, who were plodding their way through catalogs of dress patterns they could never afford, were in no hurry. But then Miss Pinkett rushed to look out the door. Her two sullen young assistants started giggling, and the catalogs were dropped quickly as my neighbors joined Miss Pinkett.

"Oh, look, he's come to town," she said while beckoning me to join her. "Come see how handsome he looks." Reluctantly I looked out the front window, but the sun reflecting from every surface momentarily blinded me. And then, there he was, emerging from the sun, striding down the pavement as if he owned it, which of course he did, along with everything else in this town.

And he was very handsome indeed, his slim, tall frame fitted out as the gentleman that he claimed to be. He was wearing a long fashionable sack coat over a silver waistcoat, but appeared to be unaffected by the oppressive weather. He stopped to say hello to our butcher Mr. Brooks and tipped his top hat at a woman who appeared frozen in place as he passed. *Who wears a top hat during the day anymore?* I thought, but why care about that when I was looking at the man I damned to hell in my nightly prayers. A colored man approached him but quickly stepped off the pavement; there was no tip of the hat for him. At this point, Miss Pinkett appeared to be having the vapors as she twittered uncontrollably. "Mr. C's crossing the street, and I think he's coming here."

As I watched him approach, the sunlight shifted so that his rings and pocket watch sparkled and even the blond hair not hidden by his hat glittered like the gold he must have stashed away. I looked down and busied myself, going through the fabric in the remnants bin, hoping I would not have to put on a civil face and mind my tongue.

I needed to get to my cleaning job with Mrs. French, so I looked over, hoping that he wouldn't stay long. But he talked and talked while Miss Pinkett nodded or shook her head in agreement like a sideshow puppet. He was speaking quietly, but

I heard fragments about northern radicals stirring up workers in the city. But when he said, "We businesspeople need to stick together on this," I let out an unintended snort. As if little Miss Pinkett was a comrade-in-arms with the man who owned all the mills in this town and her store and her house. He noticed me then and looked my way. "Hello, Mrs. Morris," he said with a solemn air, "so sorry about your husband—what an unfortunate accident. He was one of my best workers."

I was standing so close to the man responsible for Tom's death and all I did was respond, "Thank you."

I was stuck in place when he suddenly looked at me again. "Aren't you Rose Morris's mother?" he asked softly with a gleam in his light blue eyes. "How is she doing? She is certainly a beauty." I pictured young Jane McMahan, who had worked occasionally in Mr. C's mansion, packed away in shame to some relative up north, then dying in childbirth. She was beautiful, too.

"She's only fifteen," I said, but the gleam was still there.

As he started to leave, he turned to Miss Pinkett. "By the way, one of my maids has run off somewhere and I'm looking for someone reliable to take her place. So if you know of anyone..."

"I could come and work for you." The words blurted out before I could think of why I was offering them. "I can get you references if you want."

"Not necessary, start Monday," he said with a small smile that chilled my soul while my body still sweltered. Then he left.

My head was swimming as I tried to understand what I had just done, when I heard Mrs. Pinkett sigh, "I think he has an eye for your Rose. Just imagine what it would be like to be the mistress of Calvert Hall. She'd be richer than a queen." I quickly left the store, forgetting to buy any fabric because, as the hot air coming off the sidewalk enveloped me, I was beginning to think of murder.

———

I HAD BEEN working at Calvert Hall for about a week and still had not seen all the rooms in the house. With the exception of the reception room, which was bright and airy, the rooms I cleaned were surprisingly dark with small mullioned windows that permitted little light to enter. The dining room and parlor, which were my particular responsibility, were filled with massive black oak furniture—imported from England, I was told—that seemed to swallow most of the existing light. I had only glimpsed his bedchamber; just the chosen were allowed to enter there, the young and pretty who were foolish enough to believe that this could be theirs someday. From what I did see and hear, even in the daytime, sunlight was not welcome in this room; the shutters were kept closed at all times.

So there were not the rumored golden fixtures in the bathrooms to polish, but the rooms were filled with urns and vases and pictures and candlesticks that had to be kept spotless. There were even several full suits of armor that loomed like ghosts in the dim gaslit hallways. The help lined up each morning to hear a lecture from Mrs. Hastings, the head housekeeper, reminding us how valuable everything was in Calvert Hall, followed by a detailed list of our shortcomings discovered the previous day. By her nervous demeanor, I was sure that she had already received a sterner lecture from Mr. C. I was careful not to appear on that list so that no fault could be found with my work. I needed the time to make my plans.

At the end of the week, I was trying to polish the large dark sideboard in the dining room—no easy task with its ornate carvings and dull finish—when the front door knocker sounded. Mr. C did not have a butler; the gardener and the stable hands were the only men he employed, so the job of greeting visitors normally fell to Mrs. Hastings. She was dealing with some crisis in the kitchen and no one else was around, so I rushed to open the door to a pleasant-looking man with a lush reddish mustache. He came into the foyer and stuck out his hand, but it took me a moment to understand that he wished to shake hands with me. I was flustered and embarrassed; my hands were rough and red and might seem coarse to a gentleman.

"I'm Mr. Robinson and I'm expected, and who are you?"

"Sarah," I managed. Not one visitor to the house had asked me that before.

"Well, Sarah," he said, "take me to a room where I can make myself comfortable. I've known Dickie since our days at Harvard, and he has never missed an opportunity to make someone wait. He knows I'm arriving today on the noon train, so don't worry about me. I expect that I'll be seeing you often as I plan to stay a week or so while I'm talking with a publisher in the city."

Mr. Robinson seemed different than most visitors to the house—he actually looked at me. Feeling flustered and a bit uncomfortable, I led him to the ground-floor reception room. I wanted to be noticed as little as possible, and while he seemed nicer than most, I worried whether his presence would be an added complication.

He stood looking out the window at the green lawns and lush gardens that mirrored the colors in the stunningly beautiful painting by some French artist that's on the wall opposite the great fireplace. Guests all seem impressed with its cost. "How does he keep his lawn so green?" he asked. "This damn heat has burned most living things in this area to a fare-thee-well."

"You haven't offered our guest a drink? Now that's no way to treat such an esteemed writer." I had not heard Mr. C enter the room; the silk Chinese slippers he always wore would slide across his carpets with only the slightest telltale sign that he was behind you.

I started to stammer a reply, but Mr. Robinson jumped in,

"Dickie, it's fine; it's only just noon, and that's a bit too early to imbibe—at least up north where I come from."

"Sarah," Mr. C added in the particular soft but sharp tone that I had learned preceded a rebuke, "you did not turn on the electric lamp." He turned to Mr. Robinson. "It's an Edison," he said, his pride of ownership saving me from a further tongue-lashing. I dutifully turned it on, though any glow from the lamp was washed out by the sunlight pouring through the windows. That, of course, was beside the point.

"And Sarah, were you going to allow my guest to swelter, why is the ceiling fan not turned on?" He was also proud of this fan—the only one that existed in Baltimore, or so he often claimed.

As I started to comply, Mr. Robinson once again stepped in. "Why don't you show me around this huge barn of a place, Dickie, so I don't get lost." Mr. C looked disappointed, but to my relief, they both left; I, however, did not. Once I was sure they were elsewhere in the house, I took off my shoes and let my feet sink into the softness of the blue and gold oriental carpet. It was unlike the carpets in the other rooms that were of a dark red color that reminded me of the dried blood on the butcher's apron. I then turned on the fan and stared at the painting, imagining that I was in that peaceful yet wild garden under a kinder sun, until the layers of heat had peeled away and I felt, for at least the one moment, free from all thought.

I didn't see much of either man for the next few days, and though I was working ten hours a day and was worn out from the unrelenting heat and the long walk up the hill to Calvert Hall each morning, I could not sleep but lay awake soaked in sweat in the airless bedroom I shared with Rose. These nights were filled with unanswered—and maybe unanswerable—questions. How could I, meek Sarah Morris, be thinking of committing such a dreadful sin? Would I really be capable of taking the life of a living, breathing human being? What would happen to Rose if

I were caught, and since I was not that clever or experienced in criminal ways, was not that a distinct possibility?

I thought of talking to the priest, but I remembered Tom's words. "Everything here belongs to the company, Sarah. The church, the police—none of them are on the side of the working-man." So wasn't it just better to curse my lot in life and accept it? My husband was dead and was going to stay dead, and Mr. C had everything in life a person could wish for. Not fair, but as my mother used to tell us when we would complain, "We're just plain folks and that is the way it is, so stop your whining and get on with it." With a welcome rush of relief, my mind was made up—I was not a murderer. I would work at Calvert Hall until I could arrange other work to put food on the table, and then I would forget Mr. C and the past so Rose and I could have some kind of future.

But after only a few days of peace, events occurred that changed my mind. Mr. Robinson, who was always kind when I brought him a drink or cleaned his room, needed to stay an extra week to work with his publisher. One still oppressively hot afternoon, I was bringing iced tea to the reception room where he and Mr. C were talking. The large ceiling fan was making quite a racket so they did not hear me approaching, and I heard my name mentioned. I ducked out of sight into the hall, but leaning close I heard Mr. C say in a grave manner, "It was a terrible accident... very unfortunate. No one knows what really happened. It was at night, and he was alone fixing one of the machines when he fell. Must have been instant, poor fellow. Not to speak ill of the dead, but he was a careless workman and shouldn't have gone in at night alone. We'll never know what he was thinking. Anyway, he was also a bit of a troublemaker, always stirring the others up; we probably would have let him go in any case."

I could not move and only in time caught the tray as it began to fall. Mr. C knew why Tom was there that night. How dare he concoct such lies.

Somehow I gathered myself and served the iced tea. I noticed Mr. Robinson looking at me thoughtfully, but I left quickly before anything could be said.

The next day was even worse. Again I was bringing cold drinks to them, this time to the side terrace, when I felt the ground drop away. Sitting at the table next to Mr. C was Rose, lovely and radiant, laughing at something that Mr. C whispered in her ear while he lazily fingered her lovely long flaxen hair that I had helped her brush that morning. She saw me and turned scarlet.

"Momma, I just came to bring you some of the banana bread I just made." Rose is sweet, but there is no way she would have made the trek up that hill to give her hardworking mother a treat.

"Thank you, but you can stop bothering these gentlemen and go home right now." I spoke more sharply than I intended, and Mr. Robinson gave me a quick glance.

"It's no bother," Mr. C said while favoring me with a small smile. "Let me show you around the house and gardens first, Rose, since you so graciously came all this way."

He saw I was about to protest when he pulled Rose up and started immediately to lead her away. "No need to worry, Sarah. I'll take good care of her; you stay here and take care of our guest." He was still smiling that smile that fluttered the pulses of so many young girls, and not-so-young girls, as they went into the house.

"How did your husband die, Sarah?" I jumped, having forgotten that Mr. Robinson was still there. Fighting a strong urge to run away, I remained still and the story spilled out.

"He died at the mill eight months ago. The mill foreman came by in the middle of the night and demanded that Tom go in right away and fix some equipment so it would be ready for the morning shift. Tom wanted to refuse, but..." I swallowed hard, guilt almost smothering me. "I told him not to give management an excuse to fire him, because he had stood up to them too many times already. In the morning, the knock came at the door. Someone on the morning shift had found him lying dead on the carding room floor. They said he must have fallen and fractured his skull while trying to untangle some wires near the ceiling, but I don't know."

"You're not sure what really happened, are you?" Mr. Robinson looked at me intently as though he had more questions, but I had to look away. I was fighting the urge to tell him everything, to share with a fellow human being the intense rage that had kept me so isolated from others. But I knew that he must not have suspicions about my motives for being in this house.

"It's just hard for me to talk about, that's all," I said and fled inside.

The next day, I once again heard the two men talking as I walked past the library. One voice, Mr. C's, was slurred although it was only four o'clock. That was nothing out of the ordinary. But what held me in place was the other voice. Mr. Robinson, who was always so soft-spoken, was shouting. "You are going to do what?"

"I said I am going to fire them all. I give them a job and their homes, and what do they do...? They listen to some radical from the Knights of something or other who tells them to join his union because I'm their enemy. Me...who gives them turkeys at Christmas and pays for their kids' confirmation dresses."

"But you can't do that!" Mr. Robinson responded. "They've worked at your mill all of their lives, and where would they live? Besides, if you fire most of your workers, who is going to make your precious cloth?"

"I can do whatever I want; I own these people. Haven't you figured that out by now? And besides, all I'd have to do is hire a bunch of coloreds. I can pay them less, and they won't talk back. And as for that damned organizer, we'll take care of him and his buddies."

"What are you talking about, Dickie?"

"Well, Eddie, I'm just saying, we may be the Line State, but we still know how to dish out southern justice."

At this point, Mr. Robinson barged out of the room without seeing me standing there. His face was pale and he looked ill as he almost ran to the side door that led to the garden. I felt sick, too, and wished with my whole being that I had not heard that threat, so I could just go about my day without carrying the burden of this terrible knowledge.

———

AND SO IT came to pass—I knew what I had to do, and there would be no backing out. I did not save my husband, but I would save Rose. And I would save the innocence of the other young women who Mr. C would have lured into his den. And the lives and livelihoods of those who, like Tom, were trying to give the mill workers a fair wage for their long day's work. Now, my former moral qualms were quieted. All I wrestled with now were the more practical matters. How would I accomplish this? Find some mushrooms and poison him? Sneak up behind him and hit him over the head with one of his medieval lances? It was ludicrous. After all, what did I know about murder?

But I was surprised how easy it was once the final decision was made. Within two days, I had both a plan and the means, and all I needed was the opportunity and the will. And then it happened.

It was a fine summer night. The heat wave had finally broken, and a cool breeze welcomed us when we had a chance to step outside. Mr. Robinson, who had made himself scarce since the argument, was off to a party in the city. "Don't expect me back until late," he had said.

It was Gertie's night off, and I had been told to stay later to do the evening cleanup. The rest of the help had either gone home, if they had other homes, or were hanging around the kitchen smoking and telling terrible jokes because they knew that Mr. C always spent the evening drinking in the library and rarely emerged before midnight when he staggered to bed.

Because Gertie was not there, it fell to me to bring Mr. C his nightly mug of hot chocolate before I could leave for the night. How easy it was to stir in several capfuls of the sleeping powder I had obtained to get me through the sleepless nights since Tom's death. Then, wearing the gloves that I used when doing particularly dirty work (*how apt*, I thought), I entered his bedchamber for the first time, walked to the canopied bed, put my hand under the mattress, and found the gun that all the help knew was there. "He keeps a loaded pistol there," laughed Mazie, who, young and pretty as she was, had the privilege of joining him in his bedchamber. "He's really afraid that some large masked intruder will break into his room one night and take off with some of his valued treasures." I was neither large nor masked, but I guess he did have some reason to fear.

All I had to do then was go back to the library where Mr. C was slumped over snoring, a circle of dim lamplight illuminating little but his golden hair. Hardly the fine figure of a man so admired by the fools of the town. Grunting like a small pig, with spittle running down his chin, smelling of the brandy he had been drinking for hours, he looked almost pathetic. But pity was no longer in my vocabulary. I lifted his right hand, fixed it around the pistol, and moved it to his temple. He opened his eyes in confusion. "Yes, Mr. C, it's Mrs. Morris. You took my husband, but you can't have Rose," I said softly. I put my finger over his on the trigger and fired. *It's really over*, I thought numbly, and then I heard the library door click closed.

It was that soft click, rather than the booming retort from the gun, that reverberated in my ears and in my heart as I stood there not knowing what to do. I should scream. I should hide. I should run. Instead, I took off my gloves and placed them in my pocket, picked up the mug, walked over to the large gilded mirror, and stared at my reflection to see if I had somehow changed into someone else and then walked slowly into the hall.

Mr. Robinson was there just down the hall. He stared at me for a moment and then remarked in a quiet and somewhat apologetic voice, "The party was dull, and I came back early." We both stood there silent for a few moments, and then he said, "So you best be off home, Sarah. I think I'll turn in myself now."

As I walked toward the main door, still carrying the mug, he added, "You need to show up here on time tomorrow." I turned to reply, but he was already walking away.

———

I REMEMBER LITTLE about the walk home except that I was shivering with cold though the night was warm and balmy. I must have fallen deeply asleep as soon as I reached our home because the next thing I remember is Rose frantically shaking me awake. I was still in my work clothes, and I only had time for a quick wash. There is no point in recounting the anguish I felt while climbing the hill to Calvert Hall that morning. I believed I deserved whatever torment my demons would dish out. However, I was almost paralyzed with the fear of leaving Rose to face the world alone.

By the time I arrived, three police wagons were in the courtyard, their horses churning up the manicured front lawn, and several policemen were dashing in and out of the front door, one of them dragging a red-faced young man who was shouting that his editor would not like one of his *Morning Herald* reporters being treated like a vagrant. "That Mencken is always poking his nose where it doesn't belong," said another, older policeman. So the word was out, I thought. I was allowed to enter after Mr. Robinson came out and gave his okay.

Inside, it was chaos. Police were everywhere, and I could not help feeling anxious about the muddy footprints they were leaving on Mr. C's fine oriental rugs. Our councilman was there doing nothing useful that I could see, but managing anyway to look puffed up with importance. I joined the group of servants who were chattering excitedly, some with disbelief, others with proclamations that they had seen signs that such a tragic event was coming. Two of the pretty but silly young things, who had frequented Mr. C's bedchamber and who probably had imagined a life far above their station, were crying and snuffling rather loudly. But Colleen, who apparently had discovered the body, was sitting on a chair white-faced and silent. *I am so sorry, Colleen*, I thought to myself, but I, too, said nothing.

Mr. Robinson was talking to a stout man in a fancy uniform. I heard only snatches of what he was saying, something about possible despondency over gambling debts and a woman in New York City. The man nodded solemnly and looked over at us and then at one of his men.

"These people are just in the way. Pick one or two to clean up the mess, and send the rest to their rooms or homes or wherever."

I was surprised that he did not want to speak to any of us, but perhaps he figured that we could not possibly have anything useful to add. I left quietly, knowing with a certain satisfaction that this was the last time I would see Calvert Hall.

My memories of the week that followed are blurred around the edges and reminded me of riding on the carousel as a child, catching quick glimpses that whirled by before you understood what you were seeing. Of course, wherever I went—on the streets, in the shops, and among the servants in the homes where I collected the dirty laundry that I was again washing—nothing was discussed but this unexpected event. It seemed that almost everyone had their own special insight into what actually transpired, with talk of gambling debts, a married mistress in New York, and even blackmail of some sort. I drifted through these conversations silently, my refusal to speak of Mr. C often taken as a sign of deep and heartfelt grief.

Just before the public memorial service that was being held to honor the man who was, in the words of the flyer posted everywhere, "our foremost citizen, whose grace and generosity touched all our lives," I heard murmurs that snapped me out of my trance.

When I was picking up the laundry from my newest employer, the cook, Katie, told me that Mrs. Bartlett in the haberdashery heard from Mrs. Brown, whose husband worked as a janitor in the police station, that the police were not convinced that such an important and distinguished well-off personage would depart this world voluntarily, especially without leaving a note. The possibility was being raised that some malcontent agitators from the city might have been involved.

"No, no, they mustn't think it's murder," I said before I realized I had spoken. Luckily, Katie, a big, softhearted girl, interpreted this as further evidence that I was in mourning and insisted that I sit while she fetched me a glass of water.

Then later while telling me that he could not let me have any more meat until I had paid off my bill, not even the ham bone I would have used to flavor our greens for that night's supper, the butcher turned to his assistant and excitedly informed him that the police were still not convinced "that things were really as they seemed."

Given these rumors, I was not sure that I had the strength to attend the memorial service and in the end went only because Rose insisted that we pay our respects. My soul still bore the weight of what I had done, and my head was heavy with images of the cold jail cell that might await me, but this was lightened because Rose, while saddened, seemed not emotionally scarred by the event. Maybe we could get through this, I thought.

———

THE TOWN HALL was full. In the back rows, I saw many workers from the mill with their stained work clothes and dusty shoes, shuffling uncomfortably and receiving sharp glances from Mr. Sullivan, my husband's foreman, who must have herded them there. Appearing more proper in the front rows were the shop-keepers and their staffs, looking quietly pleased at this recognition of their higher status. And seated at a raised table in front were the town notables—church leaders, police chief, and other mill owners.

Our councilman, of course, was in the center, clearly pleased as punch with this chance for such public attention. When he began to speak of how much our town would miss this great man, I saw my Tom's face instead. The councilman was followed by the parish priest, representatives from other mills, a Baltimore City Hall official, and a few other worthies, all recalling the virtues of the late departed but exhorting us to carry on in spite of this grievous loss.

"And now," said the councilman, "we are honored in our little town to have as our last speaker, the world-famous poet, Edwin Arlington Robinson, who, as it happens, was a friend of the deceased and one of the last to ever speak with him. He has written a poem especially for this occasion, and we will be the first to hear it." He was clearly flustered, not knowing whether to shake hands or what, and sat down abruptly. I went rigid and must have been gripping Rose's hand too hard, for she gave me a quizzical look. I put my hands back in my lap but could not make myself look up while Mr. Robinson started to speak.

"I am honored to be here to speak of my late classmate.... It would be an exaggeration to say we were actually friends," he started. "But still it is fitting that, as a guest in his house at the time of his death, I should memorialize this awful event. Therefore, I beg your indulgence and will read the short poem I have hurriedly written in his memory."

It was difficult for me to hear most of what was said over the buzzing in my head and the pounding of my heart. The phrases came by like fish darting around in a bowl: "quietly arrayed," "glittered when he walked," "richer than a king," "schooled in every grace," "wish we were in his place."

He then paused, and somehow I knew he was looking at me. I could not help but look up to meet his gaze, my chest so tight that I thought I could never take another breath.

He cleared his throat and then continued with his eyes searching my face, "So on we worked, and waited for the light, and went without the meat, and cursed the bread." An even longer pause and then, "And Richard Cory, one calm summer night, went home and put a bullet through his head."

And amazingly, that turned out to be that. Life, as hard as it was, just went on. No more police investigations. No more images of Rose fending for herself while I lived out my life in a cold, dank cell. No more rumors of murder. Because, after all, everyone knows that a poet would never lie.

# HAPPINE$$

## BY TWIST PHELAN

When you're rich, the help comes to *you*—dress designers, hairstylists, masseuses, personal trainers. The scripted embroidery on this gal's lab coat read *EverYoung Botox Clinic.* Cosmetic dermatologists, too. It would take a hell of a lot of paralyzing bacteria to erase the lines on Breezy Taakall's face—lines she got from worrying about losing all her money.

"Thank God the paparazzi didn't see you," Breezy said to the Botox lady as they walked down the hallway to the master bedroom. At precisely 6 p.m. the master bedroom would belong to the feds.

I could have stopped them, but I decided to let them go. Breezy wasn't the defendant, and technically she had the right to be here, at least for a few more hours.

I went to find Don—he's the other marshal. He was babysitting Nicky and his lawyer in the living room. Today we were doing the walk-through, Nicky's last chance to gaze upon some of his booty—the penthouse on East Sixty-fourth and everything in it. He'd been under house arrest at a friend's apartment during the trial, and the judge had allowed him to continue living there until he had to report to prison. This was the only time he'd been back to his place since the indictment.

Nicky was due at the Big House first thing tomorrow morning. Don and I had two other jobs today in addition to tagging everything for the asset sale and making sure the Taakalls didn't take anything they weren't supposed to: first, keeping a moderately arthritic middle-aged guy from escaping, and second, making sure none of Nicky's victims got close enough to take revenge.

The penthouse's living room was big enough to seat the New York Philharmonic and still leave plenty of room for dancing. The walls were papered with linen and covered with beautiful artwork. I recognized Picasso, Matisse, Renoir, and Monet, and that was just what I could see from the foyer. Through the alcove was a dining table that would seat at least twenty.

There were red tags attached to everything. Don was refastening one to a silver hairbrush. I heard that Marie Antoinette used to own it. No kidding.

I asked him where Nicky and Gerald were. Gerald Karius was one of the legal laundrymen the financial crowd called in when they got rings around their white collars.

Don looked like a turtle, with a neck that disappeared into his shirt collar. "Lawyer's out in the hall on his CrackBerry," he said. "I thought Nicky was with you." He hunched his shoulders to pull his head back farther into his shell.

I got a funny feeling, like I used to get when I was a cop. I sprinted down the hall toward the master bedroom. The double doors were shut. I opened them.

Nicky was in a lounge chair that had been pushed against the wall. His trousers had ridden up; above a purple silk sock I spotted the electronic monitoring device. His trademark unbuttoned French cuffs hung out beyond his jacket sleeves. He gripped the arms of the chair while Breezy pulled his shirt collar away from his neck. The Botox lady was bent over him with a syringe in her hand.

Breezy looked up at me, her violet eyes wide. The Botox lady steadied her wrist on Nicky's collarbone. The needle was aimed just to the right of his Adam's apple. A double dose of that stuff will smooth away a lot of wrinkles—and paralyze a person's breathing muscles in less than a minute.

What Breezy was doing was no big surprise. Maybe you don't remember that Enron guy—he dropped dead from a heart attack *after* the jury convicted him but *before* he was sentenced. A dead financial felon can't file an appeal. No appeal means the conviction is legally void—like the trial never happened. No conviction means no fine. If Nicky dies today, all Breezy's problems go away—the marshals, the red tags, the forfeiture sale. She keeps everything, including her husband's corpse with its handsome face as smooth as her own.

I sprinted across the room, grabbed the Botox lady's wrist, and twisted it. She whimpered and dropped the syringe. I pulled her away from Nicky.

"What the hell are you doing?" Nicky said. "Have you lost your mind?"

He pushed himself out of the chair and examined his image in the ornate-framed mirror over the mahogany dresser, turning his head right and then left.

"Let go of Miriam so she can get back to work. I don't want these crow's feet on tomorrow's news." His tone was the same commanding one he used in that TV commercial. You know, the one where he got out of the helicopter and told us if we gave him our money, we'd end up rich.

I shook my head. Here I am thinking I saved his life, when really I just saved his wrinkles from extinction. Well, my job was to make sure Nicky got safely to prison, even if all he cared about was how he looked on the way.

"Mr. Taakall," I said in as cool a tone as I could manage. "You're here for a walk-through, not a spa day." I picked up the syringe from the carpet and dropped it into the Botox lady's open case. "Let's go," I told her.

"You people just won't stop trying to humiliate us!" Breezy said. She turned to Nicky. "Don't worry, darling," she cooed. "My Chanel foundation will do wonders." She stroked his silvery hair. "Trust me, baby. We'll take care of each other."

Gerald Karius appeared in the doorway, resplendent in a dark suit, white shirt, gold and gray striped tie tied in a double Windsor knot, and black Italian shoes buffed to a brilliant shine.

"What's going on here, Marshal?" Gerald said. "You know you're not allowed to talk to my clients when I'm not present."

"Fine," I said. "So tell your clients they have one hour until we lock up the place." I pushed the Botox lady past him and out of the room.

I never knew what to expect from the Taakalls, even though I'd gotten well acquainted with Nicky over the past few months. Actually, I'd mainly gotten to know his stuff, which is practically the same thing. From the time the judge entered the pretrial asset seizure order, we'd been cataloging everything he owned so it would be ready for sale if Nicky was convicted.

There are the Haves and the Have Yachts, and the Taakalls are the latter. They had enough stuff to keep me and Don and two other forfeiture guys busy for six weeks. Add Nicky himself to his list of prized possessions. I'd tagged drawers full of stuff devoted to keeping him perfectly trimmed, clipped, and buffed, plus racks of shirts and suits to make the man.

We also tagged fifteen vacuum cleaners. Who needs fifteen vacuum cleaners? Turned out Breezy was nuts about the carpets being perfectly smooth. She had to have them vacuumed right after anyone walked through a room. I'm not talking about getting rid of dirt. She wanted her carpets to look as well-groomed as the Yankees' infield grass. So there was a vacuum cleaner on every floor of every house—the New York penthouse, the Jackson Hole ski lodge, the Connecticut farm, the condo in Florida, even the jet—plus a housekeeper to run each one. That made the hundred-thousand-dollar road grader at the Connecticut place seem almost logical. It was a present from Nicky to Breezy, so she could always have a comfortable ride on the fourteen-mile driveway to the country house, whether she was in the Range Rover or the yellow phaeton with the calash top Nicky had given her for her last birthday, along with the two gray hackney ponies to pull it.

I have nothing against the very rich. As a matter of fact, I've made a study of them. Having money does something funny to people, and having a lot of money does something even funnier. It sounds great to be able to buy whatever you want, no worries. But it puts you on a treadmill of wanting more, more, more. You spend so much time wanting and getting, you don't have any time left to be a person.

Nicky had made enough money legitimately that he could have retired years ago with his family fully provided for as long as they lived. But for people like Nicky, it wasn't about enjoying what money could buy. It was about getting more. Nicky was like a mountain climber who thought if he stopped to enjoy the view on the way up, he'd fall. Me, I'd be happy to make any higher ground. I'm living so far beyond my income, we're in different zip codes.

After Nicky made all that money with his Ponzi scheme, he could have moved to someplace like Switzerland or Brazil where they wouldn't have cared how he got rich. Instead he stayed here, making a big show, until somebody ratted him out to the U.S. attorney. Before you knew it, Nicky was indicted and Gerald was negotiating a plea.

Despite the "Jail to the Thief" headline in the *Post*, he ended up with only seven years for securities fraud, mail fraud, wire fraud, and every other fraud the U.S. attorney could think of. Gerald got him a light sentence in return for the names of the other players in the scheme. I don't know who was footing the lawyer's bill. Nicky's accounts were frozen, and Gerald Karius didn't work for free.

Nicky also had to pay a pretty hefty fine—a hundred million bucks. So far we'd collected about fifty million in money and stuff. Grayson—she's the assistant U.S. attorney on the case— said there was a lot more, but I didn't think so, especially after we found Nicky's account in the Caymans with the six million in it. He'd left the account number taped to the underside of his desk drawer.

Grayson went back to court after we found Nicky's secret stash. She said Nicky's deal should be revoked and the judge should give him twenty years, like the other defendants. But Nicky testified he had forgotten about the account and that's why he hadn't listed it on the inventory sheet. He said something like, "I don't keep track of the small stuff. It's dollars to you and pennies to me." I don't know if he was telling the truth or not. If he was trying to hide the money, pretty dumb to stick the bank info on a piece of furniture we were going to seize.

It's got to be hard to walk into your home and see red tags attached to everything—your furniture, your clothes, even your electronic toothbrush—all that stuff you sold your soul to get. In cases like this, we seize everything in the apartment, including the apartment itself—three floors on Fifth Avenue overlooking the park.

Ten thousand square feet per floor, a total of thirty-eight rooms filled with antiques from Sotheby's—Don calls it the rich man's eBay—and modern art. The library had a gold leaf ceiling that came from a palace in Italy. There was even an indoor pool with silver stars spangled across the bottom, so when you launched yourself off the board, it's like you were diving into the sky. A lot of things are upside-down in the super-rich world.

All Nicky's loot was heading to auction. The Taakall name was the new hot label. Every pair of socks, every spatula would go for ten times what you could buy it for in the store. I wondered if Nicky would be proud when his branded stuff fetched top dollar.

The same press that vilified her husband paid Breezy grudging respect for standing by her man. I wondered if Breezy was fonder of Nicky or of everything his money bought her—the biggest, fastest, newest, and best. There were rumors in the *Post* that Nicky had a girlfriend, but nothing came out in court. Maybe the fact that Breezy hadn't tried to kill him a few minutes ago was proof she really loved him.

The strain on her was starting to show. The skin under her violet eyes looked tight and bruised, and I didn't think it was from a session with the Botox lady. No doubt about it, she was still a pretty woman. From the way he looked at her, Gerald knew it too. For a lawyer, he had a bad poker face.

I put the Botox lady on the elevator. When I came back into the apartment, Louis Taakall was in the hallway between the family room and the kitchen, along with his two daughters. They'd just arrived.

Nicky, Breezy, Louis, and Gerald were the starring cast for the walk-through. Husband, wife, son, and lawyer—the modern nuclear family. Louis was Nicky and Breezy's only child. He and his wife owned an art gallery on the West Side. The owners were actually Nicky's unwitting investors—it came out in court that the gallery was dependent on cash infusions from Louis's dad. I'd tagged the gallery inventory last week.

Louis was in his early thirties. His face was pale, and he had twitchy fingers. He'd been just as antsy last week when he came by the penthouse to collect the things his grandfather had left him in his will. He'd been storing them there. They were the only items in the place that weren't bought by Nicky with other people's money, so they were exempt from forfeiture.

His daughters were real cuties. Katie was about seven, a blonde with round peachy cheeks. Jen was a few years older, a thin brunette. She had an overstuffed pink knapsack slung over her shoulder, like a Sherpa. Both girls had their grandmother's violet eyes.

"Daddy, we have to go to my Mandarin lesson," Jen was saying. "I don't want to be late. We're learning personal pronouns— *wǒ, nǐ, nín, tā,* and *tāmen.* I have to be there."

"Gammy!" Katie shrieked and bolted toward Breezy.

She and Nicky were walking toward us from the direction of the bedroom. Neither seemed to be in any danger from the other. Breezy had regained her composure—her blond hair was smooth, her steps precise in high heels. The skin on Nicky's face looked five years younger and several shades tanner. Breezy knew how to wield a makeup brush.

Louis could have used her help. A decade of hard living had left permanent bags under his eyes, and red veins had bloomed on his cheeks. His gallery's parties always made the tabloids. He was known for caring more about getting his picture in the paper than selling the pictures in his gallery. No surprise, he'd dropped out of sight after Nicky's indictment.

"I wanted the girls to see their grandfather before he...goes away," Louis said to me. "Besides, we had to let the nanny go six months ago. Vanessa finally found a job, so I've been Mr. Mom."

He looked the part. His khakis and faded polo shirt were straight out of the L.L.Bean catalog. His hair looked like he cut it himself—no more slick razor cuts like in the tabloid shots of his party days.

Everyone walked to the family room to the beat of Jen's

backpack bumping against her leg. Breezy took a seat next to Gerald on a sofa. Katie squirmed between them and began recounting the tale of their crosstown trip.

"The train smelled like pee, Gammy."

"It's a subway, dummy," Jen said.

"I'm not a dummy! Anyway, I hate the train. I don't want to go on it anymore."

"There's nothing wrong with the subway, Katie," Louis said. "I think it's a lot more fun than taking a cab. I think we'll take it more often."

Jen cast a beseeching look at him. "Daddy, we're going to be late."

"We won't be, sweetie. Now go say *hi* to your grandy."

"Jen's always mad at me," Katie said in a stage whisper to her grandmother. "We have to share a room at the new apartment and she says I touch her stuff but I don't."

Jen dragged her backpack across the carpet to where her grandfather sat on one of the silk brocade sofas.

"Hi, Grandy," she said.

"How are you doing in math?" Nicky asked.

"I just got an *A* on my quiz."

He grunted. "You're very good with numbers, Jennifer," he said. "That's the most important thing."

The Taakall charm was famous, but Nicky was keeping it mostly under wraps today. Jen stood for a minute, uncertain, then plopped down on the carpet and unzipped her backpack.

I ran through the rules for Louis. Basically, a Taakall could keep anything of sentimental value that was worth less than twenty dollars.

"Twenty dollars?" He swept his arm in an arc that took in the furniture, the art, the possessions stacked on the dining table. "I don't think you could find anything here worth less than twenty thousand."

"It usually means photos or letters," I said.

"Then I'd like this one." Louis picked up a photo from among the cluster on the sideboard. He wore a graduation cap and gown. Nicky stood on one side, his arm thrown over his son's shoulders. Breezy, on the other side, smiled brightly.

"You can have the photo but not the frame." I removed the photo from the gold-plated frame. According to the appraiser, it had been made for John Singleton Copley by Paul Revere. I handed it to Louis.

He looked at the photo and sighed.

I glanced over at Nicky on the sofa. His legs were splayed out before him, his eyes were closed, and his head was back against the cushions. Jen sat at his feet, working on her math homework—I could see the large block numbers.

"The only other things I want are my daughters' drawings and the schoolwork they gave their grandparents," Louis said.

"They're all yours," I said. "What about any more photos?" I showed him the twenty-plus frames I had collected from Nicky's home office. Each one was a study in wealth and power—Nicky hoisting the mainsail of his Hinckley, Nicky sitting in a new Spyker with the car's doors extended like raven wings, Breezy dancing with a celebrity gate-crasher at the White House.

"So I can remember all of Dad's toys that he bought with investors' money?" Louis said. "I'll pass."

I felt a little sorry for him. Louis hadn't chosen to have his self-worth replaced by net worth. Now he had to start over and not even with a clean slate. It would take time for people to forget who his father was, and for Louis to forget the taste of the silver spoon. Having money and losing it can be worse than never having it at all, especially if you never earned it.

"Excuse me," I said to Louis. Breezy and Gerald were walking among the tables where her jewelry was laid out. I wanted to keep an eye on them. It was our responsibility to make sure nothing of value was taken from the apartment. Breezy wouldn't be the first person to slip a pair of diamond earrings into a pocket.

"Da-ad." Jen stretched the word into two syllables. "My Mandarin lesson?"

"I'm getting your stuff, baby. Then we can go." He was already on his way to the kitchen.

"Daddy, I want to come with you!" Katie wriggled off the sofa and ran after her father.

I'd finished tagging everything in the kitchen this morning. Four-star restaurants were run out of smaller spaces. When I cleaned out the fridge and freezer—a tin of caviar, two bottles of champagne, and a flacon of Joy perfume went on the inventory— I noticed the ice cubes were in the shapes of Ns and Ts. The rich were into personalizing. They wanted to be sure you knew they owned everything, even the ice cubes.

Silver service for dozens was spread out on the nearby table, and there were stacks of paper-thin china on the granite counters, each dinner plate bearing a gold crest and *Taakall* in bold script. Breezy didn't pronounce her last name the way Nicky did anymore. After the newspapers started making fun of *Take-all*, she adopted *Tack-all*—accent on the *all*—as the correct version. Maybe she just wanted people not to make the connection. It's got to be tough for her and Louis. They didn't have anything to do with what Nicky did. But they're still villains to the public.

I signaled Don to keep an eye on Nicky and Breezy while I followed Louis and Katie to the kitchen. Louis was in the butler's pantry, staring at the various papers stuck with ivory-topped pushpins to a corkboard set into an antique Venetian frame. Neither Nicky nor Breezy had paid any attention to the colorful mass of artworks and test papers.

"You want all of them?" I said.

Louis jumped as though I'd startled him. If he'd taken something to calm down, it wasn't working. He was still as twitchy as when he'd arrived.

"Sure," he said.

I started unfastening the drawings. Katie had signed the picture of a horse. Or maybe it was a camel. Jen had done well on a math quiz. There were a few teacher corrections in red and a big red *A* at the top with a circle around it.

I handed Louis the evidence of his children's talent and brilliance.

"Daddy, I want to see my drawings!" Katie said.

"Can you say *please*?"

"Pleasepleasepleasepleaseplease."

Louis smiled—the first one I'd seen from him—and made his arms into an easel for the drawings.

Katie paged through the stack, announcing the subject of each one. The horse-camel was really a deer.

The next drawing was smaller than the others.

"I like this lady! She's a pretty dancer," Katie said.

"Okay, that's enough," Louis said. He arranged the drawings back into one stack and put the math quizzes on top. "Katie, let's—"

A commotion erupted in the family room.

We got there in time to see Breezy yanking on one sleeve of a fur coat. Don held on to the other—a determined snapping turtle. Jen watched with her mouth open. Nicky still sat on the sofa, oblivious to the ruckus, sorting through photos Don had removed from their frames. He wasn't really interested in anything that didn't involve making money.

"I have to go out for milk for Jen! She's thirsty and there's nothing left in the house," Breezy said. "You're inhuman! It's November, and I need a coat!"

"I'm sorry, ma'am," Don said, "but you can't take this outside. It's not on the permitted list."

Breezy's jaw tightened. "For God's sake, it's only a mink!"

To someone with a pair of sables appraised at eighty grand each, I suppose a five-thousand-dollar mink jacket would be the equivalent of a Costco windbreaker.

"I'm sorry, Mrs. Taakall," I said. "All the furs are part of the sale. They can't leave the apartment."

"Don't worry, Mom," Louis said. "We're leaving soon."

Gerald put a hand on Breezy's arm. "Forget about the coat; it's part of the past. You have to let that go."

"How can I when it's all laid out in front of me like a garage sale!" Breezy wailed. She dropped the coat sleeve and let Gerald lead her to a chair.

"I'll get you a glass of water," Gerald said. He looked at me and I nodded. He headed for the kitchen.

"Time to go, sweetie," Louis said to Jen.

"Fiiiiiiiiiiiinally," Jen said.

Louis bent over and picked up one of the folders Jen had taken from her backpack.

"Daddy's going to borrow this, baby." He put the papers from the corkboard into it.

I noticed one of Katie's drawings had been framed and hung beside the entrance to the family room. I took it off the wall and started to disassemble the frame. The tape didn't want to come off as easily as it had on the other pictures in the house.

Gerald reappeared with a brimming crystal glass mono-grammed with a *T*, its red tag still attached. When I'd managed to extract Katie's drawing, I smoothed out the creases where it had been folded so it could fit into the frame. This one showed a dog...or maybe a beaver?

Katie saw what I was doing.

"That's mine!" she cried and ran full tilt toward me. Gerald tried to sidestep, but he wasn't fast enough. Katie collided with him at knee level. The water in the glass arced through the air, dousing Louis's folder.

"Damn it, Katie! You need to watch where you're going," Louis said.

He gingerly opened the folder. The first few documents were damp. The water had turned the marks on Jen's math test into smears of red.

Katie stared in shock at her father for a moment, then burst into tears.

"Baby! I'm so sorry." Louis dropped the folder on the table and knelt beside her. "Daddy said a bad word. And he didn't mean it. Sorry, baby." He hugged her gently and patted her back.

"Daddy," Jen said. "She made a mistake."

"Who did, sweetheart?" Louis asked, still cradling Katie. The little girl had stopped crying.

"Mrs. Forgiani." Jen held up the math quiz marked with red. "She wrote in the wrong answers."

"Sometimes teachers do that, baby." Louis tucked Katie's hair behind her ears. "Feeling better, sweetie? I really am sorry."

Katie's eyes glistened, but she nodded.

"Okay, girls, say good-bye to your grandparents and let's go." Louis closed the folder and put the wet papers on top of it. He picked up Jen's backpack.

"I'd like to keep that," Nicky said, nodding at the math quiz that had been splashed with water.

"But, Grandy, it got wrecked," Jen said.

"Doesn't matter, Jennifer," Nicky said. "Give it to me."

Louis picked up the folder and the wet papers. "Dad, I'll make sure Jen brings you"—he caught himself—"that I bring you Jen's next test." Louis smiled at his daughter. "Another one with an *A* on it, right, baby?"

"Louis, I said *that's* the one I want." Nicky's tone was sharp, like crystal being struck.

Jen backed away from her grandfather. She looked confused and a bit scared.

"Dad, I said I'd bring you one later." Louis's tone was as forceful as his father's. He reached for his daughter's hand. "C'mon, baby. We don't want to be late for your Mandarin lesson."

"*Louis*—" Nicky got out of his chair and started for his son, but Don stepped into his path.

"Easy there, Mr. Taakall." Don put a restraining hand on Nicky's chest while Louis herded the two girls into the foyer. I followed them. I had Katie's drawing, the one I'd just removed from the frame.

"May I have the folder, Louis?" I said. He had stooped down to help Jen slip her backpack onto her shoulder.

Louis slowly straightened. "The folder?" He turned to face me.

I held out my hand. Louis glanced at the front door, as though he was contemplating making a run for it. Then he looked at his daughters, blew out a breath, and handed it over.

"Here," he said without looking at me.

I took out the math quizzes and Katie's drawings, so the only thing left in the folder was the sketch. The dancing lady looked a lot like some of the drawings I'd been tagging in the apartment all week. The ones signed by the famous name.

I turned the sketch over, and there was the familiar signature with the big *P. Picasso*.

"I don't think you meant to take this one, Louis," I said. "I think you meant to take the drawing that was hanging in the foyer, the one that didn't quite fit in the frame."

He looked at me now but didn't say anything. His breathing was ragged, as though he'd just finished running a marathon.

I handed him Katie's dog-beaver. "This is the real masterpiece."

I think I saw tears in his eyes as I handed him back the empty folder. He slipped Katie's drawings and Jen's math quizzes into it.

"Daddy, can we *please* go to Mandarin now?" Jen said.

Louis kneeled beside her. "What do you say we skip it and go to Dylan's Candy Bar instead?"

Jen frowned. "But I'm supposed to go to class."

"You don't have to go, baby. Today can be"—he searched for the right words—"like a snow day. Our own personal snow day."

"Really?" Jen said. She let her backpack slide off her shoulder and drop to the floor. "Can I have Peeps?"

"Me, too!" Katie said. "I want Peeps, too!"

"We can all have Peeps," Louis said.

The girls cheered and raced to be first to the elevator button. Louis picked up Jen's forgotten backpack.

"I just imagined Dad's tombstone," he said. "*Here lies Nicky Taakall. He knew the price of everything, but the value of nothing.*" He turned and walked away to join his daughters.

After I watched them get into the elevator and the doors shut, I went back to the family room. Breezy sat on a sofa, a handkerchief pressed to her mouth. Gerald hovered beside her.

"Breezy isn't feeling well," he said when he saw me. "The stress of today..."

Breezy moaned.

"Mrs. Taakall, do you really not feel well?" I asked.

"My stomach..."

I didn't want her to be sick on the Turkmenian rug. I picked up the plastic trash can that was beside Nicky. It was half full of corrugated paper from the photo frames Don had dismantled for him.

I put it at Breezy's feet. She leaned forward; her hair hung like a golden curtain.

Suddenly she screamed. I jumped back to avoid getting splattered.

Breezy reached into the trash can and pulled out a small black and white photo. "It's *her*!"

I glanced at Don, who was turtled into his collar more than usual. If he could have withdrawn his head all the way, I think he would have.

"You said it was over!" Breezy yelled at Nicky.

He crossed his arms and looked annoyed. "It is," he said. "I forgot that photo was in there."

"What are they talking about?" I asked Don.

"There were photos of two women in one of the frames," he said. "One was behind the other. Nicky said to toss that one, it came with the frame."

Breezy launched herself at Nicky. For a moment, I could have been watching *The Jerry Springer Show.*

"I trusted you!" she screamed at him. Spittle flew from her lips. "I said I'd wait until you got out. You promised we'd have our old life back!"

She was crying now. Nicky grabbed her wrists. Blood seeped from where her nails had scraped his cheek. So much for all that nice makeup work.

"I told you—it's *over*. It's been over for a long time. For chrissake, Breezy, she was the one who turned me in. Why the hell do you think she did that?"

"Do I look stupid, Nicky? I'll be sixty when you get out! That little bitch won't even be thirty. I bet you told her you'll still be rich so she'll wait for you!"

Don helped Gerald pull a still-ranting Breezy off Nicky and back to the sofa. I opened my cell phone and dialed Grayson's office.

"I think you want to come down here and talk to the Taakalls," I said. "Why? To ask them how they were going to be rich again as soon as Nicky got out. You don't have to call Karius. He's already here. Only thing is, I think he's going to need a lawyer, too."

I closed the phone and regarded the couple.

"Grayson is coming over. And by the way, it is just like on TV—the first one to talk gets the better deal ninety-five percent of the time."

It took the rest of the week to sort out everything. Breezy talked first, just as soon as she hired a new lawyer. Her jealousy over Nicky's affair had turned into anger during the months of public humiliation in the tabloids. Anger that trumped even her desire for a return to the good life seven years from now.

Gerald had helped Nicky set up the Cayman account as a red herring. They figured we would stop looking once we found it. So they made it easy by taping the account number to the bottom of Nicky's desk drawer. They stashed the big bucks elsewhere.

Breezy traded her testimony for immunity. Gerald got a year and disbarment. No big loss to the legal profession there. Nicky is facing additional charges—perjury, for starters, but I'm sure the U.S. attorney will think up a few more.

No plea for him this time—he's going to fight it out at trial. I guess the aggressiveness that made him rich is all he has left. The judge already invalidated his existing deal and sentenced him to a full term. So he'll have lots of time to think about the women he's pissed off—the girlfriend who turned him in to the feds because he wouldn't pay her off and the wife who found out about the affair.

What about the big money? Well, the account and password numbers were too long to memorize. So Nicky wrote them on Jen's math quiz—the teacher corrections in red ink—right after he was indicted, before he was kicked out of the penthouse.

Why didn't he just give the numbers to Breezy? He isn't saying. Maybe he wasn't sure he could trust her, maybe he was testing her to see if she'd stick by him through the bad times—the tabloid headlines, the trial, losing all their stuff.

Breezy's only chance to pick up the account info was during the walk-through, because she'd had to move out after Nicky's indictment, too. But she got distracted by the fight over the fur coat. Nicky never considered the possibility that Louis would take the papers off the corkboard. As a matter of fact, Louis cared about his daughters' work only because that's where he'd hidden the Picasso sketch when he came to get the stuff from his grandfather the prior week.

But I think he's different now. When Grayson picked up the math quiz, he wished her luck finding the money. "Don't bother to let me know how much there is," he said. "I don't care."

I got the announcement last month. Louis and his wife are opening an art therapy practice for poor kids. Enclosed with it was one of Katie's drawings.

I taped it to my file cabinet. It's a bear—or maybe a rhinoceros. Just to remind me of what happened on East Sixty-fourth Street that afternoon. Some of it was about money, but most of it was about what's left after the money's gone.

# ITERATIONS

## BY S. J. ROZAN

The morning sun squeezed in the window and poked him in the eye. He rolled over, but he knew it was there and that was enough. He flopped onto his back, yawned, stretched. Yup, there it was, that sunshine, loitering at the edge of the drapes. Of course, he didn't have to put up with it. The nifty control panel beside the bed had buttons for the blackout blinds right next to the ones for the heat, air-conditioning, lights, TV, DVD, and stereo. He supposed, with his money, he could probably hire a plane to haul a cloud across the sun until he was ready to get up. The hell with it. He got up.

While he shaved, he thought about checking his schedule for the day, but he wasn't interested. Since he'd sold the business— no, scratch that because it wasn't true. Since it became obvious to him—screw what everyone else could see—that the processes were going to succeed, that the principles behind the processes (principles he'd patented as soon as he'd dreamed them up) would revolutionize this corner of the information industry— well, around then he'd begun to lose interest. It had been slow, because for a while, there was still a lot to keep him involved. First, they had to design and build the damn hardware to run the damn software to prove the damn principles actually worked, because the world was full of idiots who'd stand under a falling piano until it proved it would actually hit the ground.

That hadn't been so bad, though. He enjoyed the iterations, the refining: first, you get this bug out, and the hole it leaves reveals that one, so you get it out next. Better and better each time, until all the bugs were gone and the system was perfect. He'd never given a damn about the actual apps, but as long as the proof demanded devices, he'd patented them, too. In the beginning, he'd have been happy just selling his formulas, principles, software, and if anyone had been smart enough to buy, they could have saved themselves a lot of money. That the skeptical world had insisted on seeing it all in action first only meant that in the end he had more to sell. When he'd finally unloaded the business, it was to a consortium of his rivals. He'd forced those moronic behemoths to pull together for the first time in their sludgy corporate lives because they all feared him more than they loathed each other. He supposed that was an accomplishment in itself, one the business trades never mentioned in any of the glowing articles on him, but who cared? He'd never been in it for the fame, and the fame was part of the irritation now. By the time he sold it all off, he was thoroughly sick of it all. The fun was long past. He'd walked away from the business with no regrets and with more money than all but about a hundred other people on the planet.

That was kind of the problem, though.

Maybe money couldn't buy you love, but it could damn near buy you everything else. Which meant there wasn't really a lot of use for *you*. Until and unless he came up with another project, he had nothing to do, which would have been okay; he'd always been real good at hanging out. Except the people he got a kick out of hanging out with had to make a living. He could buy them off—sure he could, set his buddies up for life so they could play air hockey and go skydiving—but anyone who let him do that, he wouldn't cross the street with.

And those hundred others like him, what they called the super-rich, the ones who—like him now—needed bodyguards and security sweeps and had to build home theaters and gyms and be trapped behind their own walls?

A self-impressed crowd of arrogant, skills-free assholes. Them he wouldn't even stand on the corner waiting to cross the street with.

Screw it. He tapped the touch screen in the bathroom console; heard Belinda's patient, "Yes, Ray?"; and told her, "Cancel everything. Tell Tony to bring the car."

"Ray, you have—"

"I don't care. Reschedule. I'm going out."

He clicked off, knowing she was sighing, gritting her teeth, and doing what he told her: calling Tony, rearranging and rescheduling and canceling. Well, he didn't care; that was why she got the big bucks. And that was it right there. Ray Derring didn't have to care.

He was lacing up his black oxfords when the surround sound blasted Belinda's ringtone: she was Robyn Hitchcock, "I Got a Message for You." He hit the button, said, "Yeah?" into the air.

"A reporter, Ray. From *Scoop*."

"What are you talking about? Hello? I don't do reporters." Belinda had been with him for years. Maybe she needed a vacation.

"He says—"

"Who cares what he says? How did he even get as far as you?"

"Amy thought this was one you'd—"

"Amy was wrong." Maybe Amy needed a vacation, too.

That was the one thing Ray shared with the rest of the super-rich hundred: a loathing of these tabloid bloodsuckers, leeches who'd photograph you taking a crap, write the story up, and make it front-page news.

Ray got out of the private elevator in the garage to find Tony lounging against the black-windowed Lexus. To rearrange the garage and put the elevator in, Ray had had to buy the building. Not to mention combining the top two floors into his giant skybox apartment and the next two down into apartments for his staff. Staff! Jesus Christ. Tony and Belinda, great; but who the hell needed all those other people, especially the security guys? Damn! Tony was trained and armed, though, and the car was hardened, so when he went out in the car he left the bodyguards home.

Besides, he was the boss. He could leave anybody anywhere he wanted to.

They exchanged greetings, Tony giving Ray his usual amused nod. Ray had interviewed a lot of drivers and most of them were good, but Tony Aletto was as good as any and got the job because he didn't seem impressed that he was being personally interviewed by Ray Derring.

"Where to?" Tony grinned. He opened the door and got in the shotgun seat. Ray slid behind the wheel and smirked back as he steered the car up the ramp. Tony turned out to have been a good choice; he was impressed by pretty much nothing, even by the fact that Ray liked to drive.

And he could keep a secret.

———

THE TAXI GARAGE was crowded, waiting for the shift change, but Ray Derring's slot was empty as always when the Lexus pulled in. "Hey, Tony," the guys around the poker table said, nodding but keeping an eye on their cards. They hadn't been expecting Tony, but they hadn't not been, either. Derring, like a lot of rich guys who lived uptown, sometimes got driven downtown. A bunch of them paid a monthly fee to keep their cars off the street and give their drivers a place to hang between when they dropped them off and picked them up. Otherwise, the drivers would have to drive home in the fancy car, then maybe turn right around and take it out again, exposing it to cabbies like them and all those drivers from Jersey for what? The rich guys chipped in for extra security, and the fleet owner liked that, but the drivers thought it was a crock. Like some mook was going to come in here and screw with a rich guy's car. With them there? They were the real security. Especially for Derring. None of them had met him— of course not—but at both Christmases since he'd started here, Tony had shown up with envelopes for each and every one of them. He brought big bags of chocolate eggs for their kids at Easter and rosewater jellies for the Pakistani guys at the end of Ramadan. Those rosewater jellies were awful unless you were a Pakistani, but the point was, they all agreed Ray Derring was a stand-up guy, even if he had more money than God.

"Everybody has more money than God," Tony'd said once at the poker table, where he sat in with the guys going on and the guys coming off while he waited for his call. He lifted his glasses theatrically and squinted at his cards, like they might look different that way. "God don't need money. He just points a finger at you. Zap! You're rich. Or you're toast."

Today was pretty much the same as always. Tony played okay. He wasn't a hustler at the poker table, mostly playing the cards he had, bluffing just often enough so they'd know he sometimes bluffed, so he could sucker them in when he did have cards. Some days he came out ahead, some days behind. It was like anything.

None of the other rich guys' drivers were there today, though, so Tony got all the rich-guy ribbing. Happened like that sometimes.

———

"HEY, TONY, WHAT'S with your boss? I hear he flies kites on his roof; the guy don't have nothing to do?"

"That so? Then I was you, I'd invest in kites." Tony swept in the pot he'd won.

"Hey, Tony, Derring really dating Joy Jones, that actress? Papers keep seeing her going up to the penthouse."

"How would I know? You ever see me going up to the penthouse?"

"You'd think he could get himself some hot young broad. Jones has gotta be forty."

"And she's got, what, three Oscars? Maybe he don't like 'em young and stupid. You in or out?"

"Hey, Tony, what the hell you mean, you're folding? You work for the richest guy in America."

"Yeah, well, funny, he don't let me play with his money."

"What do he let you play with?"

With a satisfied grin, Tony nodded at the Lexus. "Lots of his other toys."

———

CLOSE TO TWO hours after Tony arrived—he was up about forty dollars—the dispatcher wandered back to the poker table. "Any you jokers want lunch?"

"Pizza."

"Curry."

"Chinese."

They argued, agreed, threw their money in. The dispatcher went back to the booth to make the call. Usually he didn't come back again until the food arrived, but today he did.

"Tony? Someone wants you up front."

Tony looked around the table. None of the other guys had any light to shed. "What the— Okay, these suck anyhow." He threw in his hand. "Keep your paws off," he said, pointing to the pile of chips at his chair. Not the biggest pile on the table but probably second. Three of the guys made as if to reach for them. Tony snorted and walked away.

No one was waiting at the booth, but a skinny guy in a leather jacket stood in the shadows at the top of the ramp. Tony strolled up to meet him. "This better be important, pal, because I got a hot streak going."

"It's important." The guy was young, pale, with a nasty grin.

"I'm waiting."

"Andy Traynor. From *Scoop*."

Without a word, Tony turned and walked back down the ramp.

"I wouldn't," Traynor called after him.

"I don't give a shit what you wouldn't."

"It's not about your boss."

Tony turned back. "What?" he said sardonically. "It's about me? You guys at *Scoop* so out of ideas you gonna run a profile on Ray Derring's driver? Buzz off, kid."

"It's not about Derring's driver. But it's not about your boss."

"What the—"

"Ray Derring," Traynor said, "will be pissed off if you don't hear me out."

"I doubt it."

"I guarantee it."

Tony gave him a long look, then a grin. "Okay, kid. Twenty bucks says whatever you got to say, Derring won't give a shit."

"There's a lot more money involved than that. But if that's what it takes to get you to listen, you're on." Traynor pulled a twenty from his wallet, waved it in the air.

Tony walked back up the ramp. "Go ahead."

"Good move."

The kid's smarmy grin almost spun Tony around again, but instead he looked at his watch and folded his arms.

"It's not about Derring's driver and it's not about your boss, because nobody gives a damn about Derring's driver and you're the boss."

"You wanna say it in English?"

"It'll be faster if you don't bullshit, but okay. You're Ray Derring. The disguise is good, the glasses and all, the brown contacts. And the accent, the stoop, the whole posture thing. You learned all that from Joy Jones, right? You're not sleeping with her, you're taking acting lessons. Or maybe you are sleeping with her. I couldn't care less. The point is, I could write it up for *Scoop*, or you could give me five hundred thousand dollars. One way, all your friends here, and wherever else you go to be just a regular Joe, they all hate you; the rest of the world laughs at you; and your game's over. The other way, you don't even miss it."

Tony stared, then busted out laughing. "Kid, you're fucking nuts!"

Traynor, with the creepy smile, pulled out his phone. He showed Tony photos: the car pulling out, two figures behind the dark glass. Interesting but meaningless. But the photos kept going: a guy getting out of the shotgun seat at an Irish bar uptown or with a fishing rod at the north end of Central Park. Tony with a couple of the other rich guys' drivers at a Knicks game, way up in the nosebleed seats. And then a couple of photos of bottles and cans.

"What the fuck?"

"Picked them up here and there, where you went, where he went," Traynor said casually. "I had them tested for DNA. He's Tony Aletto. You're Ray Derring."

"This is bullshit."

"No. This is my meal ticket. I've been following you for months, racking this stuff up. Wouldn't stand up in court, you were arrested for something, but it's enough to spoil your game and get all your little friends mad at you. Look, Derring, I don't know what the fuck is in your head, but you obviously get off on hanging with the common man and who am I to spoil your fun? Unless you make me."

Tony started to say something, stopped. After a long moment, in another voice, he said, "You're a cocksucker."

"I know. That doesn't solve your problem."

"All right. Suppose I pay you off. What am I buying?"

"The photos. The DNA tests. The whole thing, it's all here on the phone. You can buy the phone."

"I'll smash it."

"You buy it, it's yours; do what you want."

"And then you're back next week with the backups. And the week after and the next week, too."

"Jesus Christ, you think I'm crazy? This is my one shot. You pay me, I disappear. Guy like you, obviously you could come after me if you wanted to. My goal is to make paying me off less trouble than anything else. Why do you think I only asked for half a mil?"

That grin again. Tony almost punched him, but Ray nodded. "I assume you want cash?"

"Damn right. Mixed bills, nothing bigger than a hundred. That just about fits in a briefcase."

"You have it all worked out, don't you, kid? Okay. The park on the west side by the river. Tonight at 2 a.m., second pier south."

Traynor shook his head. "Awfully deserted and dark down there."

"Fuck is the matter with you? You think Ray Derring's going to hand a briefcase to a jerk-off at high noon in Starbucks? How about the middle of Times Square, that make you happy?"

"Come in disguise. Use your acting lessons."

"Kid," he said with exaggerated patience, "I got to be who I am by knowing exactly what I can do. Of course I'm going to come disguised, but it would be too big a risk, taking this act out in public. I'm not that good."

"Well, doesn't have to be you. Send someone. The real Tony how about?"

"I see that grin one more time, I'm gonna slam it down your fucking throat. Anyone I sent would wonder what's going on, and even if you don't tell them, which I doubt you could manage because you're so fucking proud of yourself, even if, they'll know someone got one over on Ray Derring. Then it would never end. You're the one who said you want paying your ass off to be less trouble than anything else. Only one way that'll be true. The pier at two, or I'll take my chances. And you can take yours."

Traynor went gratifyingly pale. A brief silence, then bravado: "You got it."

"Bring the phone. And make sure you don't use it between now and then."

Traynor raised the phone, wagged it, and risked the grin. "No worries."

Ray Derring nodded. He turned around, walked out of the shadows and down the ramp, and with a "Which one of you assholes stole my money in the meantime?" Tony Aletto returned to the poker table.

———

DESERTED AND DARK down here, that was the truth. Ray stood in the shadows by the railing. He was early. He was always early, even though he'd been told and told he was too important to let other people keep him waiting. He wasn't interested in playing those games.

He played other games.

Here came Traynor. He was early, too, though probably not, like Ray, to get the lay of the land. Quick steps, hands in pockets, head swiveling—he was early because he couldn't wait to get his hands on his half mil and outta here.

Outta here for sure.

Ray considered springing out screaming to see if the guy would poop his pants, but why add complications? In a soft voice, he said, "Kid. Over here."

Traynor jerked around, then relaxed when he saw Ray. His nasty grin lit up the night. "Good disguise. You look just like Ray Derring in Harley gear."

"Give me the fucking phone."

"Give me the fucking money."

The compromise: Traynor held the phone, screen lit to show one of the garage photos, while Ray, his leather-gloved hands gripping the briefcase, opened it to show Traynor the money. Traynor pawed through, picking up a couple of stacks and riffling them with his thumb as though he'd know real bills from phonies. When he nodded, Ray released the briefcase and Traynor handed over the phone. Ray dropped it and, staring into Traynor's eyes, stomped it under his Doc Marten. Traynor shrugged and turned. He walked away.

Ray gave him two steps, then took a silent stride forward, yanked Traynor off balance, and slammed a six-inch hunting knife into his liver.

"What the—fuck! You son of a—!" Ray, holding Traynor hard, snaked the knife around to make sure the cut wasn't so clean the blood would start clotting. Traynor was still howling when Ray tumbled him over the railing into the river. Ray wasn't worried. Lacerated liver, internal bleeding, icy water—the kid wasn't coming back. He heard him splashing around for a time, but not a long time, while he took off his own new, street fair, cash-bought leather jacket and tossed that into the river, too. From the phone debris, he carefully picked out the memory card and held it over the flame from a Bic, melting it into uselessness before he chucked that in along with the rest of the plastic shards. Using the Bic was probably overkill, but he hadn't gotten to be Ray Derring by neglecting details.

Did Traynor think he was stupid? That he'd believe it would be only this one payoff, that a call wouldn't come in six months from Cancún, from Ibiza, from Bali? And another, six months after that?

And how stupid, for that matter, was Traynor? He really believed keeping his mouth shut about Ray's masquerades was worth half a million dollars?

Ray leaned over to pick up the briefcase. If Traynor's death spasm had frozen his hand to it, Ray had been prepared to part with that, too, but the asshole had dropped it. Ray swung it, grinning, as he strode along the empty pier and back to the Lexus. He knew for a fact it was a better grin than the kid's.

———

RAY PARKED THE Lexus, rode up in the private elevator, slipped into the skybox apartment. Well, slipped. He was the boss. He hadn't told the security guys he was going out, hadn't told Tony he was taking the car, but he didn't have to, did he? He put the money back in the second safe, the one even Belinda didn't know about. He'd have to get rid of the briefcase tomorrow. Not that he was worried about the kid's prints being on it. He'd wiped it down with a damp cloth, just being belt-and-suspenders. But it was anomalous, Ray Derring with a bulky briefcase, and the cleaning people or Belinda or someone might see it sometime. If they did they might not care, but he didn't like to leave even tiny details hanging. He hadn't thought about the briefcase and he should have and he did now, considering ways to dispose of it.

As he undressed to shower, he discovered a couple of spots of the kid's blood on his jeans. Damn. Not a problem: he'd rinse the jeans out now, let them dry overnight, then toss them in the laundry. But it shouldn't have happened. Maybe he shouldn't have wiggled the knife. But then how to make sure the wound was messy? A serrated knife? That might have worked better.

Ray showered, slept, woke when the sun snuck in past the blinds and jabbed him in the eye. He rolled over, yawned, and stretched. After he did all his morning bathroom stuff, the stuff any tabloid parasite would have creamed to have photos of, he tapped the screen and told the kitchen people to send him a pot of coffee. It arrived as he finished dressing. He took it out on the terrace, where he sat surveying the city and going over last night.

It was all good in all the large parts. He couldn't find any flaws here in the light of a beautiful day, except for the briefcase, and the jeans, which implied a problem with either the knife or his technique. It was also possible, on reflection, that he'd parked too far away; even that late, he might have been seen walking with the briefcase. Not very likely, but possible.

Drinking coffee that had been not only blended and roasted to his specs, but shade-grown to his standards on a Costa Rican estate he'd bought, he thought for a while. Not too long, because when decisions were obvious, why belabor them? He tapped the touch pad in the table side console.

"Yes, Ray?"

"Belinda? What's on for today?"

She told him, with an unspoken warning in her voice: *Don't make me rearrange again.* He could, of course, and of course she would, but he was feeling pretty laid-back. Why not? So sure, he'd meet today's people, listen to their proposals and ideas, most of which were likely to be stupid; he'd get reports from his own people on things he'd set in motion himself, which were not stupid and didn't need him to oversee them. "Okay, fine," he said and smiled as he sensed Belinda's relief. "And listen. Tell Amy: all those pain-in-the-ass reporters? Tell me which one's the biggest pain. The most obnoxious. Don't, for God's sake, send him up or anything. Just his name."

"That would have to be Traynor from *Scoop*."

"No, not him," Ray said. "The second-biggest pain, then."

Belinda clicked off to go check with Amy, and Ray finished his coffee, got ready to go downstairs for his first meeting of the day. Amy would tell Belinda, Belinda would tell him, and there he'd be. Iterations, refining. Better and better each time, each bug that was removed revealing new ones. Then those removed, too, until all the bugs were gone, and the system was perfect.

# RICHIE AND THE RICH BITCH

## BY JONATHAN SANTLOFER

The first time I work for Marcos he has me steal this painting from a private home—snazzy place out in East Hampton. I don't know how he got to me and I don't want to brag, but long before I met Marcos, I had a reputation as an independent operator who could get anything in and out of anywhere, and he came to *me*, not the other way around. Anyways, Marcos gives me the address and describes the painting and says he don't need to know the details of how I'm gonna get it, just says he doesn't want anyone to get hurt.

So I go and watch the house. I learn the guy's routine. He's a bachelor, older guy, gray hair, distinguished, maybe a widower or something. I don't know, don't really care, but for three, four days I watch his house—not so easy—but I got a talent for being invisible. I keep a log of every move he makes—when he goes in, out, where he goes. Then I do a little test. I put on my workman's uniform, go up and knock on the door, say I gotta check the gas meter. The maid lets me in and I get a chance to look around, and there it is, the piece of art Marcos wants me to steal, about the size of a notebook, of the American flag painted in mushy gray, looks to me like finger painting. Stupid, I think, and wonder why this one and not the others because there's art everywhere—on the walls, floor, even hanging from the ceiling. But I don't think about it too much, because more important, the alarm system is in the basement right next to the gas meter (often the case), and convenient. I see it's turned off, so I figure the guy only turns it on when no one's in the house, logical. I know he runs on the beach every morning from 6 to 7 a.m., and the maid—I also know from watching the house—doesn't come in till 8 a.m., and I'm wondering if he bothers to set the alarm when he goes for his run. So I wait till the next morning. I see him leave the house in his running gear with one of those little heart things strapped around his chest, like maybe he has a problem, though he looks pretty fit for a guy his age, fifty or so, and better than me, even though I'm ten years younger, but I'm not the exercising kind. I wait till he disappears over the dunes; then I creep around to the back of his house, which is huge, sixteen, seventeen rooms with an ocean view like out of a magazine, and there's big glass doors and one's not locked so I slide it open an inch then go back to my van that says "LILCO" on it—that's Long Island Lighting Company, which I had hand painted to look just like the real LILCO vans. An expense, but every job has expenses. Now I wait to see if the cops are gonna show, but they don't, so I know the alarm was off. Not only that, but the guy doesn't even bother to lock the fucking door.

So the next morning, when he goes for his run, I slip in through the glass door, walk upstairs and pluck the American flag painting off the wall, put it in my van, and drive off. I meet Marcos in the city, just like we planned. I have the painting in a briefcase and hand it over to him. He gives me the $10K he promised. Not bad for less than a week's work.

But then, a few days later, I read in the newspaper that the little flag painting is by someone named Jasper Johns, which I think must be some bullshit made-up name, like actors have, but I'm wrong; the name's legit and he's famous. And here's the kicker—that stupid painting is worth over a mil. Now who feels stupid? So, I go to see Marcos. I say, Marcos, you fucking kidding me? A million-dollar painting and you give me a lousy $10K? Marcos looks at me, says, Richie, we had a deal, we're in business, no? I look at him, I say, But— He cuts me right off; says, Richie, you're not listening. Let me explain it in a way you will understand. Then he takes a minute, smooths his hair back, which don't need no smoothing there's so much gel it's like concrete, and he's staring at me the whole time, face like chiseled marble, good-looking but something unreal about him. Finally, he says, Richie, you have a choice. You can go away and be happy with your $10K, or I can have you killed. I burst out laughing, but Marcos just stands there, black eyes on me like two hard pieces of coal, and I don't think he'd actually kill me. He's a rich guy, too, all decked out, Armani suit, loafers with a gold chain like the people he steals from and sells to, so I figure he's not gonna get his hands dirty, but I see he means it and I figure, in his line of work, he knows plenty of people who will do the job for him. So I say, Hey, I'm happy with my $10K, and that's that.

But next time Marcos calls me for a job, I say, I'd like a percentage of the take. Marcos laughs, says, Richie, how are you going to know what the work is worth so you can figure out your *percentage*? I say, I won't know, not right away, but I'll find out. And Marcos laughs again, says, Richie, I underestimated you. He tells me not to worry; he will make it worth my while, and ever since he pays me good money, gives me a deposit then, when he unloads the art, pays me the rest. We done a lot of deals since then. Last time, he paid me a hundred grand, so I figure the painting I stole must've been worth three, four mil, but I was happy with my hundred.

The way it works is Marcos fences the art. Not on the street, he's too classy for that, and it's next to impossible or I'd do it myself. Think about it, unloading a hot Rembrandt, or what have you. Where you gonna go with a famous painting? Nowhere. Like I said, next to impossible. Marcos has his buyers lined up ahead of time. *Commissioned theft*, they call it. He shows them pictures, or maybe he knows who wants what, or they ask him to get them a certain piece of art. It's like Dial-a-Painting. You want it. He gets it. A Michelangelo or one of those stupid Andy Warhol soup cans. It's all crap to me, but expensive crap.

We'd been working together awhile, though we'd never, as they say, *fraternized*, until a month or so ago. It was after a big payout; Marcos was all happy, flush from the sale, giving me my $100K like it was two bucks, and he says, Richie, let's celebrate. I'm a little surprised because he's my employer and in another class from me, but I say, Sure. We go to a hotel bar, and after a few drinks, Marcos starts telling me how one time he delivered a painting to a Japanese guy who's got a walk-in vault in his basement, all decked out with velvet on the walls and spotlights on the paintings, a museum for his eyes only, all art stolen to order. No shit, I say, not that I'm surprised, but I want to keep up my part of the conversation. No shit, says Marcos. Then he tells me about some clients in Switzerland who have the art he's stolen for them just hanging on their living room walls. I say, That doesn't worry you, Marcos? He looks at me with those coal black eyes, says, No, Richie, it does not. You see, in Switzerland, if you have the art in your possession for three years or more it becomes *yours*, and my clients never display anything until they've had it for at least three years. I say, Hey, let's move to Switzerland, and Marcos laughs.

So this time, Marcos hooks me up with this rich bitch. He's already talked to her but says she wants to meet the *handler*. Marcos doesn't like the idea and tells her so, but she insists. So I say to Marcos, It's okay. I'll meet the rich bitch. He sighs, says, Keep it simple, Richie. I say, How else would I keep it? So I meet the rich bitch, only something about her doesn't quite strike me as a *real* rich bitch. She's too showy. She's dressed like every other Upper East Side bitch—cashmere sweater, straight skirt, low-heeled pumps—but her hair's all wrong, bright blond like you need sunglasses to look at it, and her makeup's troweled on, and she's got those long fake nails like beauticians in Queens. But I don't get the feeling she's a cop or a fed, so either she's new money or got no taste or both.

What she wants is for me to steal a dozen paintings, like Marcos already told me, but I play dumb. I ask, What kind of paintings? She says, What's it to you? I tell her I like to know my merchandise, same way she wanted to meet the *handler*. She gives me a look like I'm lower than a roach, but says, Old Masters, and that's all she's gonna say. But it's enough. A dozen Old Masters… I'm thinking Marcos is gonna make megamillions, must have his clients all lined up by now—no way Marcos would take a chance being stuck with hot paintings. I wonder how much he's paying the rich bitch since he's already agreed to pay me two hundred grand, good money, but now I figure while I'm here doing his dirty work and taking a risk by showing my face, I'm entitled to a little extra, right? So I tell her there's an additional fee. How much? she asks. I throw out a figure—fifty grand—and she agrees just like that, so I know I underbid. But what the hell, I'm gonna make $200K from Marcos, so this is gravy.

The rich bitch explains she's got keys to the place, a townhouse on East Seventy-ninth Street, and assures me it'll be empty, no maids, no one, that it'll be real easy, and I start to think it sounds *too* easy and wonder if she's having her own paintings stolen for the insurance? Don't laugh, it happens. But I don't care if she is, long as I get my money.

So, I do the job, and it's just like she says, easy. I deliver my van full of paintings to Marcos, and he gives me $10K and tells me he'll get me the rest of my money once he gets paid for the paintings, like usual. But two days later, Marcos is on the phone screaming so loud I can't make him out. What'sa matter? I ask. They're fakes! he says. I say, What? He says, The paintings, they're copies, forgeries. I say, Holy crap. He says, I can't do shit with them. I say, What about the rest of my money? He says, Richie, did you hear me? The paintings are fakes, worthless. I can't sell them. There is no money—but you can keep the deposit and consider yourself lucky.

But I don't feel lucky. I feel pissed. All I got is the $10K from Marcos. Then I get a little paranoid. How do I know Marcos is leveling with me? Could be bullshit. He's never pulled something like that on me before, but the economy sucks and maybe he's hurting.

So I put the word out, ask around to see if anyone's trying to fence any Old Masters like the ones I stole—Titian, Courbet, Corot, Delacroix. I read the labels on the backs, very big-deal art, and I know my stuff. After that first job I did for Marcos, the one where I didn't know that Jasper Johns guy, I figured I'd better get smart; so ever since I been taking art history courses at the New School, continuing ed, they call it, and I've learned plenty. Anyway, turns out there are a few Old Masters on the market, but not the ones I took off the townhouse walls. So I believe Marcos. Then I realize there's nothing in the news about the heist, very unusual, so now I'm pretty sure whoever I robbed didn't report it, and I think the rich bitch is definitely screwing with me—and with Marcos. I'm figuring she had to know the paintings was fakes or she coulda sold them at auction; something else I know about—I got every Sotheby's and Christie's catalog going back ten years. I'm also figuring that the person I stole them from—if it wasn't the rich bitch herself—knew they was fakes, too, or they woulda reported the crime, right? So it looks to me like Marcos and me was set up to help them unload a bunch of forgeries. I figure Marcos knows this, too—he's no fool—and so the rich bitch is as good as dead, but I want my money before that happens.

I get in touch with her. I say, There's a problem. She says, What problem? I say, With your paintings. She says, Like what? I say, I'll tell you when I see you. She says, Forget it. No one can see us together. I say, Sister, you'd *better* see me. I tell her to meet me at midnight in this little park practically under the George Washington Bridge just beside the Hudson River, and she says okay. But it's her husband who shows up, a real rich-boy Ivy Leaguer with a pink sweater tied around his neck, you know the type. I tell him what Marcos told me, that the paintings are forgeries, and he says, You're insane, and sniffs like I smell bad, and I say, Believe it, and I want the rest of my money— the $200K Marcos was gonna give me. He sniffs again, says, Dear fellow, I do not have that kind of money, and that's when I grab his hand and bend his fingers back till I hear the bones crack. He starts screaming and crying, and I tell him to shut the fuck up or I'm gonna break more than his fingers, and he says, I lost all my money with that Madoff guy. I say, That's convenient. And he says, No, really. I tell him, Tough shit, I want the money. He tells me it was his wife's idea; he just went along because he'd lost all his *capital*. I say, So you knew the paintings was fakes? He says, No, I swear I didn't. They're my mother's paintings, and no way they could be fakes. I pull him close and say, Now you listen to me, Joe College, they *are* fakes, all of them, and he's hugging his mangled fingers and crying, snot running down his face, and says, I have to get to a hospital. I say, I want my money, and you got two days to get it. Then I take his wallet, his gold Rolex, and his college ring. I know it's not worth much, but I never had a college ring and it fits me good and I like the way it looks on my finger. I ask, What college is this from? He looks at me all funny, standing there sniffling and crying, and says, Yale, and I feel like I just got an honorary degree. I repeat, Two days, and send him on his way.

I figure Marcos must have his own plan. After all, he's got a reputation to uphold, and he's just tried to fence forgeries, which doesn't make him look too good to his clients, who must be real disappointed. Then I wonder if two days is too long? So the next morning I get in touch with the rich bitch. First thing she says is, There was no reason to resort to violence, to hurt my husband. I say, He's alive, ain't he? Then I tell her I changed my mind, I want the money right away, and she tells me the same story, that they lost all their money with that Madoff guy, the Ponzi schemer, and I tell her tough shit, but I say, Okay, I'll give you till tomorrow.

Then I do a little research, easy because Madoff's investors, all the people he swindled, are listed on the Internet, and sure enough, their name's on the list. Still, I know rich people like that got *assets*, homes and shit, and they can come up with $200K like you and me can come up with ten bucks. I tell the rich bitch, I want my money no matter what, and now *she* starts crying, really bawling, telling me how she's a really good person and has donated money to all sorts of charities over the years and now here she is broke and I say, Well, I'm your next charity, bitch. But she swears they're flat broke. She says, Get it from my mother-in-law, she's the one whose paintings you stole, and she's got plenty. I say, If she got so much money, how come her paintings was all fakes? She says, How would I know? I say, You still got a day to come up with my money. But I figure what the hell, I'll go see the old lady.

I stand outside her townhouse all day. I see her coming and going, one of those skinny rich ladies, starving to death on the Upper East Side, legs like sticks, face like a skull all stretched, Martian-like. I see a maid go in with groceries and leave at the end of the day, and I go ring the bell and the old lady opens the door and I say, Your son, Oliver, sent me. She looks at me like I took a dump on her shoe, says, About what? I push past her into the townhouse, my hand over her mouth, look around at her naked walls and say, You lose some paintings? Then I say, I'm gonna take my hand away and I'm not gonna hurt you unless you scream, and she nods and I let go and her eyes pop a little but the rest of her face doesn't move. I say, Why did you have forgeries on your walls? She says, Who *are* you? I say, A friend of your son's, I told you. She says, I know my son's friends, and you are not one of them. I show her his ring on my finger, and she says, What have you done to Oliver? And I say, Not much, not yet, but I will. Then I tell her it was her darling son, who she's so worried about, who set up the heist. The whole time her face is as placid as the moon, but I think it must be Botox because no one is that cool. When I finish she says, My son would never do such a thing. It was that wife of his, Enid. She did it to hurt me. I ask, Did Enid know the paintings was fakes? She says, No. Then she tells me she sold all the art privately when her husband died a few years back because he didn't leave her as well off as she expected, but she had copies of the paintings made first because she didn't want anyone to know, especially her son's climber wife, that's what she calls the rich bitch, a *climber*. She says, I don't want that little climber to inherit one penny of mine when I die, so I cut my son off, took him out of my will. I ask, He know that? She says, Of course. I'm an honest woman. I gave him a simple choice, Enid or his inheritance. He chose Enid.

I explain to her what went down and how I'm now out $200K and that I want my money, and she just looks at me with that mask face. Then she asks if I want a drink, and I'm thinking she's nuts. I say, No. She mutters, That dreadful girl, that dreadful girl, shaking her head. Then she says, I will get you your money, but I want you to take care of Enid—I want her punished. I just look at her, this skinny old lady, who's as big a bitch as the young one. I don't tell her about Marcos—that he's gonna punish her daughter-in-law plenty. I just say, That's not my line of work, and she says, But you must know someone who does that *sort* of thing, and I say, Maybe I do, and she says, Good. I say, You get me the money I'm owed, and I'll find somebody for the job. I ask for half, $100K, as a deposit, and she says, Can I write you a check? I laugh. I suppose not, she says, tells me she'll get me the cash in the morning.

That night, Marcos calls and I tell him I leaned on the rich bitch and her husband, but I don't tell him about the old lady because I want to get the money from her. He says, Richie, leave them to me; it's all taken care of. Then he tells me about another artwork he wants me to get for him right away, an oil painting, a Goya, small enough to fit under a jacket, in a little museum outside of Seville; that's Spain. He tells me the museum has shit security and where he'll meet me for the pickup and that he'll pay me $100K, and I write everything down, thinking this just keeps getting sweeter and sweeter.

Next morning, I call the old lady, tell her I found someone for the job, but I need all the money up front, $200K, half for me, half for the guy who's gonna take care of her daughter-in-law. She asks, How can I trust you will do what you say if I pay you first? I say, You're gonna have to trust me. And she says, Okay, come to my place at noon, and I do, and she hands over the money, all in hundreds, and says, I surely hope I can trust you. I say, Don't worry, that rich bitch daughter-in-law of yours is as good as dead—and I'm not lying because I know Marcos has put a contract out on her. The old lady says, I don't want Oliver to get hurt. I say, Of course not, thinking, *Too late for that.* She says, And I never expect to hear from you again, you understand? I say, Aww, gee, and here I thought we was gonna have tea every other Tuesday, and she gives me a look like she's trying to lift an eyebrow, but her face doesn't work so it's just her eye that's opening wider and wider. By the way, she says, What happened to my paintings? I say, They was fakes, who cares? She says, I'd like them back. I say, Too late, I already dumped them in the river. I don't want to tell her I was just the middleman. She says,

Oh, but my walls look so naked. I say, Have someone paint more fakes. And she laughs, I think; her face doesn't move, just a little bark comes out.

After that, I go buy my ticket to Spain and I splurge, I buy first class, why not, and the girl at the ticket counter gives me a funny look when I pay cash but doesn't say anything.

Next thing I know, the *young* rich bitch gets in touch with me, says she has my money. I almost faint. I'd given up on her. I already got the old lady's $200K plus another $100K coming from Marcos, and now the young rich bitch is coming through with *another* $200K. I'm in shock. She asks, Will you leave us alone if we pay you? And I say, Hell yes, I'm leaving the country. I tell her to bring the money to the fleabag hotel off Times Square where I been staying because I want to see the look on her rich bitch face when she's standing in a dump like this.

Then I go out and have a good meal, steak and potatoes au gratin at a French bistro and three glasses of red wine, and after that I buy a needle and thread and a travel bag and come back to the fleabag hotel and start sewing the $200K into the lining of the bag. I do a meticulous job, too, because you can't be too careful with airport security these days, and I don't want to explain why I'm traveling with so much cash. I have half of it sewn in when there's a knock on my door, so I stash the bag under the couch. It's the rich bitch and her Ivy Leaguer husband, hand all bandaged up, and I ask him, Why are you here? Rich bitch answers for him, says, Did you think I'd come here alone? God knows what you would do to me? I say, Lady, you flatter yourself. The rich bitch is cool as ice, arms folded across her chest, looking at me like I'm scum, but the Ivy Leaguer is all nervous, sweating. I say, You have the money? She says, Yes. I say, So where'd you get it, I thought you was broke? She says, I sold my diamond ring, and looks all pained like she's gonna cry, and I say, Boo-hoo, gimme the money, and she opens her big canvas bag, and next thing I know she's slammed something against my gut and the Ivy Leaguer's got a grip on my arms and she does it again and I feel it like ice and see this big kitchen knife and blood leaking out of my gut, and I say, You fucking rich bitch. And she says, Oliver, get your ring and your watch. I'm curled up on the floor and the Ivy Leaguer is tugging the ring off my finger, saying, Oh, my God, Oh, my God, and the rich bitch says, Shut up, Oliver, and he says, But, but—And she says, But *what*? You think anyone is going to miss a man like *this* in a place like *this*? She tells him to wipe the doorknob and to look around for anything they might have touched, and he's still saying, Oh, my God, and now my gut is on fire but I'm freezing, and I hear the Ivy Leaguer say, What's this? Everything is starting to blur, but I see he's got my travel bag, and I hear the rich bitch say, Oh. My. God. There must be a hundred thousand dollars in here. No, wait, there's more sewn into the lining. Then she leans down to me, her face with all that makeup like something out of a bad dream going all fuzzy around the edges, and says, Thank you, we can certainly use this. And I want to say, You better use it fast, bitch, 'cause your days are numbered, but I can't speak. She says, Oliver, see if he has your wallet and anything else that might link him to us, and the Ivy Leaguer starts going through my pockets, and my eyes aren't working right and I can't hardly feel my legs, and my whole body is shaking and I hear the rich bitch say, Is that a plane ticket? And she leans down to me, and I feel her breath on my face and she says, "Oh, I just adore Spain and I so need a vacation; this whole affair has been *such* a strain, and then she laughs. And everything is swirling around, going in and out of focus, and I know for sure that I'm dying, but I'm thinking, You ain't going nowhere, you rich bitch.

# PAPARAZZO

## BY ELAINE TOGNERI

Here they come," I muttered, one of a swarm of photographers loitering on the Arrivals Level of Terminal Four at LAX. My height allowed me to see the crush of passengers heading our way before everyone else. I scratched my beard, hoisted the portable recording camera to my shoulder, and peered in the viewfinder for the shot.

We all waited for Monday's American Airlines flight from JFK anticipated to arrive at 8:40 p.m. Rumor had it movie star Galazy Reinhardt would show her hot body in LA for the first time since her celebrated split with Sean Penn. I focused the camera, using the face of a man hurrying toward the luggage carousel. For some reason, America wants to see the rich and famous as they stroll out of the spa, rush to a restaurant, or in this case amble through the airport. I don't understand this fascination, but I don't complain about it, either. The candid video clips I take don't earn me much, but I have something to prove.

Passengers massed around the brushed-steel luggage return. I saw a leggy, long-haired blonde and started filming until I focused in on the face. Permanent frown lines pegged her as older than Galazy. I scanned the crowd huddling around the conveyor belt. Two husky men, a brunette in distressed jeans, and a short, older woman cast curious glances our way. My fellow paparazzi grumbled and spread out. I turned off the camera. Bags lurched round and round on the belt. Men and women retrieved their luggage and hurried off.

The flood of passengers slowed to a trickle and stopped. I'd stared at the revolving carousel for so long I had sea legs. Only one worn black suitcase with a yellow tie on the handle remained. I doubted it belonged to Galazy. Finally, an attendant collected it. Anyone who was somebody had come and gone, and Galazy wasn't among them.

The swarm left LAX in search of a new queen. Some to catch celebrities leaving a movie premiere. Others headed to the night-clubs to photograph the rich at play. I didn't have gas money after paying the rent and had bummed a ride to the airport with Harry, the owner of NewsUrWay, a website with high hopes he'd talked his rolling-in-bucks father into funding.

"Hey, Skip," Harry called. "Want to grab a beer?"

That sounded great, except for my empty wallet. "Only if you're buying."

"Sure, business expense." Harry matched my long stride as we headed for the parking lot. At five foot eleven, he's five inches shorter but all leg. He's what I call a friend, if it's possible to have one in this business. It doesn't matter that we've known each other since high school. If we saw a celebrity, we'd ditch each other in the second it took to get into position for the camera shot. Neither of us mentioned Galazy's not showing. We're used to leads fizzling out.

My car's a used Dodge Caravan with a hundred thousand miles. It doubles as my studio on the road and a place to sleep when necessary. Harry drives a black BMW Z4, another gift from Daddy. We slid into the roadster's leather seats, both ratcheted all the way back with the hopeless idea of accommodating our legs. Still a ride was a ride, and Harry was buying.

"Which bar?" I asked as he drove north on the Pacific Coast Highway.

"I've got this thing I promised my dad I'd show up for. At Marina del Rey."

"So much for a beer. I'll stay in the car." Probably wouldn't be allowed in anyway with my faded jeans and T-shirt, not to mention the facial hair. I brushed a hand over the beard my mother hated.

"You can't dislike free. All you can eat and drink. Come on."

"Which restaurant?"

"It's casual. A private party at the Californian." Harry shrugged. "No big deal. We're almost there."

"Even worse."

Harry pulled in the drive, laughed, and pointed. "Read the sign and weep. Valet parking and no cameras. Do you even remember how to talk without that thing in front of your face?"

I growled as I grabbed my camera bag. "Does this piece of junk have a trunk?"

Harry popped it open, and we both stowed our gear. Harry handed the valet his ignition key.

We approached the hostess, a blonde with a sprayed-on tan and lots of cleavage. She said, "Welcome, gentlemen. The bar's on the patio, and the buffet's inside. May I check you in?"

"Arkling Junior and guest," Harry said, breezing by.

When I followed him, he said, "Got to show my face. How about you score us some beers?"

The patio bar overlooked the marina and had lights shining on all those pretty sailboats. A light breeze trickled the ocean's tang into the night air. I ordered two drafts, grabbed the chilled mugs, and found a spot at the rail. The first beer went down quickly. Since Harry wasn't in view, I started on the second. Sipping this time, I studied the crowd. It's a built-in phenomenon when you have my job. Mostly California surfer girl types and guys equally tan but older. A broad-chested man dressed in a business suit walked among them, nodding at all. He stopped to talk to a well-preserved brunette who looked like Sophia Loren. Her laughter at whatever he said confirmed the identification. I reached for my camera and cursed.

The car. I needed Harry to open the trunk. Where was he? Wait, the sign said no cameras. But I had my cell phone with its built-in shooter. My hand closed around it in my pocket. Oh, yeah! This was going to be an exclusive. Harry didn't need to know. Sophia sauntered inside and I followed, waiting for the shot with the best lighting. She disappeared into the ladies'.

I stood close by. The picture would be even better after she freshened up. I pulled out the phone and flipped through the options, setting the highest resolution possible. Anybody would think I was checking my messages instead of getting ready to take a photo. Five minutes later, she still hadn't come out. I pointed the phone lens at the door across the hall to take a practice shot. The doorway opened, revealing a conference room with two men huddled over a laptop. They looked up as I snapped the picture, a terrible shot as the reflection from the computer screen lighted the window, casting their faces into shadow except for a glint from the guy with the glasses. A waiter appeared in the doorway, carrying an empty water pitcher.

"Shut the door," a gruff, accented voice called.

I turned away, slipping my phone in my pocket. Still no Sophia, but Harry walked right toward me.

"I couldn't find you on the patio. Where's my beer?"

"Sorry, dude. Got to let some out," I said, pointing at the bathroom. "I'll meet you at the bar." I pressed on the door.

"Right behind you," he said, following me in.

Crap! I would probably miss Sophia, or he'd see her and there would go my exclusive. I couldn't leave without explaining, so I hurried.

"Dad's dating one of those chick-lets," he said. "Introduced me to her. Looks younger than Susie."

Susie was Harry's last girlfriend. If I remembered right, his dad hired a detective to see if she was after his money. She got so mad when the guy broke into her Facebook account and questioned all her friends and family, she had tossed all Harry's stuff from her apartment's bedroom window.

"Bummer!" I said, thinking more about missing Sophia. I stopped outside the ladies'. "You waiting for someone?" he asked.

"No, well, I did want a phone number." I grabbed my phone and positioned it just in case of a miracle.

The door across the hall opened again, and one of the men came out. He had a dark mustache and olive skin that reminded me of an actor who did character parts. I pressed a button to snap his picture. The man at the laptop glared. "Are you taking pictures?" he yelled, standing and slipping off his glasses. His skin was pale, but his muscles bulged under the white tailored shirt. Again I noted a slight accent.

"No, no, just checking messages," I said, striding away. "Harry, ready to go?"

Harry's face hardened, and he whispered, "You lying SOB. Don't get me in trouble with my dad." He grabbed my arm and waved at the guys. "No worries. We're just leaving." We rushed to the door. Harry handed the valet a twenty for quick service, and in short order, we roared away. I saw the pale guy staring after us. He reached for his wallet. The valet was making a killing tonight. He didn't know me, but for another tip would blab all he knew about Harry.

"What the hell were you thinking taking pictures?" Harry asked.

"That's my job. It's how I relate to the world at large."

"Bullshit! I'm tired of your little act. Who did you think you found?"

"I don't have a clue."

Harry shook his head. "Don't call me for a ride again. In fact, I'll drop you at the Metro. Get home on your own."

————

ONCE I FINISHED the long trek to my apartment, I chugged a beer before going on the computer. I Bluetoothed the pictures into a folder on my laptop and duplicated them on the USB drive I kept on my key chain. I'd learned the hard way not to let pictures sit in the camera and to always make multiple copies. While I checked e-mail, I drank a few more brews. My eyes kept closing, or I would have finished the six-pack.

I tossed my keys on the kitchen counter next to the coffee machine, set the cell phone on the small table by my bed, and undressed. Too tired for anything but sleep, I dropped on top of the covers. I floated in a beer buzz until my bladder complained. That's the major drawback of beer. What goes in must come out, usually at inopportune times. As I debated ignoring nature's call and sleeping some more, I heard a click, like a door had eased shut. I reached for my cell. I didn't know if I was going to call 911 or just see what the hell time it was. Couldn't do either. The phone had disappeared.

I slid off the bed and snapped on the overhead light to verify what my hand had discovered. No cell phone. Not on the table, not on the floor. Had I left it in the other room? No way. I remembered the noise that woke me. My pulse quickened. Was someone in my apartment? I crept to the door and put my ear to the flimsy panel. A quick glance at the floor showed my bare feet cast a shadow. If anyone was in the living room, they'd see me behind the door. I flipped off the light, feeling like a horror flick victim who'd descended the basement stairs with a faulty flashlight. Too damn stupid to live.

I stood listening. My pulse thumped over the stillness. A car door closed. I raced to the bedroom window. Nothing in the rear parking lot. I ran to the door. I threw it open, and the knob crashed into the wall. That repair would bankrupt my security deposit, but I had bigger problems. Nothing moved in the living room or mini kitchen. I sped to the front window. A motor started. Grabbing a night-vision zoom lens and screwing it on my camera, I focused on a moving vehicle and kept snapping until the car vanished into the dark.

Breathing heavy, I stumbled to the light switch and flicked it on. The cable that chained my laptop to my desk lay on the floor cut in two pieces. An open expanse yawned on the desk, my laptop gone. I fumbled through the desk drawers and made sure my photo-editing software was still there. My camera equipment looked untouched. Thieves who ignored thousands of dollars in merchandise. They stole my cell phone and my laptop. What did those two items have in common? Still fuzzy from the beer, the only thing I could think of was the photos of the men at the Californian.

I checked the front door. Locked, but that didn't mean much. Just turning the latch could bolt it behind you. I peeked through the peephole. No one in the hall. I opened the door. Scratches around the handle, on the doorframe, and all over the door itself with a layer of dirt covering them. They could have been there for years.

I didn't want to call the police. No rental insurance to put a claim in on anyway. Too little in my checking account to pay for replacements. I could ask Mom for a handout, but the possibility she'd turn me down was 99 percent. The deal was I had to make it on my own. Plus, how would I make the call? I'd lost my phone.

I locked up and pulled a blanket and pillow off the bed. Settling on the floor in the living room near my remaining possessions, I tried to sleep again. Seconds later, I jerked awake. My keys? I found them in the kitchen where I'd left them. The USB drive still attached. I had a copy of those photos. I gripped the keys tightly the rest of the night.

———

BY MORNING, NOTHING made sense, but I had a plan. A friend worked at Loyola's Keck Computer Lab. He could give me access to a PC. I headed to LMU intent on identifying the guy in the pictures.

Face recognition software would have helped, but you need a photo for comparison and the money to purchase the application. All I had was my picture, my brain, and Google. First task, download the pictures I'd taken of the car and save them to my USB drive. Second, save everything to a new Internet account. Third, blow up and print the pictures. Last, find the guy. After a couple of hours on the computer, I came up empty, so I broke down, begged my buddy for his cell phone, and called Harry.

When he answered, I said, "Hey, it's Skip. Sorry about that situation last night. I wanted to try my cell phone camera." I paced the hallway as we spoke.

"Did you get a new number?" he asked.

"No. Dead battery." Why was I lying? Maybe because if he thought there was trouble, he might not be so forthcoming.

"Why are you calling me?" he asked.

"You're right. I'm holding out on you. I took a picture of that guy with the mustache by the john. I thought he was a Latino character actor, but I can't find him."

"Wrong!" Harry sang out.

He loved besting me. "So you know who he is?" I turned toward the wall and leaned on it with a scrap of paper I'd taken from the lab.

"Of course, but he's not a money picture." Harry's voice dripped disdain, like I should know better.

"Crap! Who is he?" I uncapped my pen.

"Some mucky-muck with International Accountants. They do business with my dad's firm."

Maybe I should have paid more attention to financial types when I had the chance. I scribbled the company name. "Listen, I've got a shot of the President's dog you can use on your website if you want some filler. No charge."

"That doesn't change the fact that you still owe me."

"Understood." After we hung up, I returned to the computer and visited the International Accountants' website. I clicked on officers. Sure enough Harry was right. I found a smiling picture of Pedro Hernandez, one of the company's many VPs. So big deal. Why did the pale-faced nerd on the laptop care if I took Pedro's photo?

I thanked my friend, grabbed my camera bag, and headed out for a day's worth of stalking at one of LA's luncheon hot spots. Lunch turned into dinner, and by the time I stopped at the library for more free PC access, I had a few clips of minor leaguers. Enough for gas money anyway. Using my e-mail and PayPal accounts, I sold the shots and then took the Metro home, my eyes closing so often I almost missed my stop. When I finally entered my apartment, I was ready for only one thing, bed.

The chunky man with a shaved head who lounged on my blue leather sofa had other ideas. When he stood, I matched his height, but every other part of him outmatched me. He smiled, his lips so large his teeth barely showed. "I hope you don't mind," he said. "We need to do some business."

"This isn't how I do business," I said, turning to examine the shelves of camera equipment above my desk. They looked untouched. I needed a new lock. One with a dead bolt.

"You take pictures for a living, right?"

I turned to him. "You from the IRS?"

"I want to buy some of your work." He pointed to a canvas satchel on the sofa. "For cash."

"Not IRS then." I shrugged. "What are you looking for?"

"The pictures you took last night. All copies."

"Tell Sophia not to worry. Her secret's safe. I didn't capture her on film."

He stepped closer. "Don't be an idiot. Make the deal."

"How much?"

He gave a tentative smile. "That's better." He looked at the sparse furnishings in my apartment. "A thousand bucks."

A lowball offer because he thought I was hurting. Probably counting on telling his client it cost more and pocketing the difference. I shook my head. "Tell Pedro my laptop's worth more than that. All I want is my phone and computer."

"Two thousand."

Still greedy. "Phone and laptop," I repeated. I walked to the door and opened it. "Negotiation's over." I held my breath, hoping to brazen it out.

The man grabbed the bag and stopped next to me at the door. He stood so close I could feel the heat from his bulky body. When he reached into his pocket, my stomach flinched. I hoped my baggy T-shirt hid the reaction, because all he did was hand me a business card. "I'll check on the phone and computer," he said, nodding. "Call me at noon tomorrow."

I closed the door behind him, set the card on my desk, and went to the window with the same camera and lens I'd used the night before. A couple of cars drove by. I took some pictures. They probably wouldn't amount to much. The ones from last night hadn't. Once I'd satisfied my need for action, I returned the camera and looked at his card again.

He must have created business cards with the pbskids.org History Detectives website template and chosen "expert" as his classification. I noticed his name right away, Mike Porpine, and that sounded familiar. The next morning at the pay phone outside Starbucks, I confirmed my suspicions with Harry's ex-girlfriend, Susie.

"Yeah, Old Porcupine screwed up my life," she confirmed. "Let me know if you need any help trashing the bastard."

I wasn't sure if she meant him or Harry's father, but the father was who I focused on. His business manufactured and supplied airplane parts to Lockheed Martin. The library and Google were becoming my best friends. I hiked there, settled in at a computer, and found the company. Some employees had posed for pictures available online. This time I searched for the muscle-bound nerd with the glasses. No luck. I tried Lockheed Martin. Maybe they were doing a secret business deal, and if I released those photos, it would compromise the announcement. My eyes blurred from hunting for employee pictures. The odds against me mounted, but I sloughed on. I only had until noon.

I called it quits at eleven, returned to the pay phone, and called Harry. "It's Skip."

"Oh." His clamming up meant he knew something.

"Someone stole my phone and laptop after our party the other night."

"Not me."

"Yeah, but you're how they got my address. Who'd you give it to?"

"Nobody. Just Dad. He wanted to send you an invitation to another party. You and your mother."

That hurt. He knew my family situation.

"You're acting like an idiot," he said. I thought he was quoting my mother's last conversation with me, until he went on. "I can't believe you were stupid enough to believe that was Sophia Loren at the party."

"What do you mean?"

"Hello! It was a look-alike. Sophia doesn't do commercial gigs. Come on. She hasn't worn that painted-on mole since 1960. You're proving yourself a dilettante. You don't even know the business."

Like he was a hotshot paparazzo? Pretending his little website was a top media outlet. How did he even know I saw her? "You're in on it," I said.

"I've still got my hand in the paternal wallet. What did you think, Skip? Be smart for a change. Just give them the pictures." He disconnected before I could ask another question or, more likely, cast another allegation.

I was missing something big-time. I strolled into Starbucks and breathed in the bracing brew of hazelnut, vanilla, and coffee. A cup of Komodo Dragon would get my brain working. Once the steaming beverage arrived, I sat at a table by the window and looked at the first picture I'd taken. The one with the two guys in it. Studying faces once again didn't get me anywhere. I stroked my beard.

What if it was something else? I examined the blown-up photo from edge to edge. Beige walls, tan carpet, a table, chairs, computer. Nothing out of the ordinary. I stared at the blurry reflection on the window from the computer screen. A small red and white square with what looked like a cross on it. A flag. The Red Cross flag. So they were making charitable donations at the party? Who would care if they were seen doing that? Unless they didn't want other people coming after them for money. That happens to rich people a lot. But surely that wasn't incentive enough to steal my phone and laptop. They could have just asked me to keep it under wraps, and I would have agreed.

A half hour before I was due to call Porcupine, out of ideas, I ordered another coffee. "Hey," I said to the attractive young woman filling my cup. "Pretend you're on *Jeopardy!* and the answer is the Red Cross flag."

She glanced at me. "What flag was developed from the Swiss flag by reversing the colors, using a red cross instead of a white one?"

Out of the mouth of babes. I dropped a five into the tip jar and dashed to my table. She was right. It wasn't a red cross, but a white one. The Swiss flag. I stared at the reversed letters on the window. BLS—Bank Lullin Swisse, the main competition to UBS. UBS had just settled a tax fraud suit with the IRS. They admitted to collaborating in tax evasion, paid a large fine, and turned over account information for cheating clients. Maybe Bank Lullin Swisse had similar practices. Porcupine could wait. I needed to talk to Mom.

———

SOME THINGS ARE better done in person. Convincing Mom to let me violate our agreement without consequences was one of them. I filled the van's tank with the cash from the shots I'd sold yesterday and drove to Malibu. Mom lived in a stunning beachfront estate with a walled driveway, ocean views, and her own private fruit orchard. I understood the attraction of the pool and lanai. Why she needed eight bedrooms and three guesthouses stumped me, but I knew better than to broach the topic.

I parked my van in front of the garage. She could tell neighbors I was a repairman for all I cared. A new housekeeper answered the door and escorted me to the pool, maybe to verify that I was actually the son of one of the richest women in America.

Because of the sunny day, Mom lay dressed in her bathing suit but in the shade to protect her skin. She slipped her Armani sunglasses down her nose and looked over them at me. Her hair shone, its luster a tribute to the product she developed that brought all those millions. A smile crept across her face. "Have I won?" she asked.

"No, I need a favor." I pulled over another chaise and sat on its edge.

"Prescott, I'm not inclined to grant one."

"Skip." I hated my real name. "My name's Skip now."

"Okay, Skip. You've got two more months to live your fantasy. Go! Enjoy them." She pushed her glasses back up and leaned into her lounge chair.

I almost stood and left. I should have turned over the pictures and forgotten about them. Instead, I stared at her, seeing the businesswoman who donated a million to Haiti earthquake relief and then a million to Chile's, too, because it was the right thing to do. I was about to put the rest of my life at risk because it was the right thing to do. All rich people aren't money-grubbers, only half of us. "Mom, I need your advice."

She turned her head away, looking across the infinity pool toward the beach. "I gave it to you ten months ago."

She'd allowed me one year to prove I could earn a living pursuing my dream of being a photographer. If I succeeded, I'd have a lifetime. Otherwise, I was sentenced to a year working at Vanvell Shampoo before she signed over my trust fund.

"Remember International Accountants?"

Her head snapped back to me. "Those idiots who audited Uncle Ferdinand?"

"How would you like a little payback to one of their VPs?"

Her eyes gleamed. "So what's the favor?"

"A contact at the IRS and access to my trust fund."

"The first is no problem, but the second means you've lost."

"I'm only moving the money to another bank, not spending it, so the deal should still be on."

"You've got to give me something." Her eyes narrowed. "Patti called me the other day."

"No way, Mom. I am not going on *The Millionaire Matchmaker*. Think of something else."

She rubbed her chin. "How about this?"

I sighed and ran a hand over my beard, a good-bye caress. "Okay, deal."

———

OLD PORCUPINE RETURNED my laptop and phone when I gave him the photos. "Don't know what the big fuss is anyway," I said when I handed them over.

He just said, "Keep it that way."

But I had other plans.

I called Harry. "Now that I know what's going on, I want in."

"What about your deal with your mother?"

"I'm sick of living in that dump. Listen, she's signing over the trust fund and some extra on the side. I need that invitation you bragged about."

"I'll talk to my dad."

"Why does he have so much influence?"

"Why do you think, dummy? A sideline. We get a commission for bringing in clients." It figured. Harry always worked the angles at school. Guess he could blame his genes. It took a week to set everything up. My mother had her lawyer document the conditions of the release, bought me a tailored Italian suit, and even arranged for a barber to shave me at her place. I sensed a lack of trust at that last part but didn't complain, especially when she gave me the Cartier Tortue diamond-encrusted, rose gold watch. She'd been amazing.

Harry came through with an invite to the next yachting event.

I arrived at the country club in a limo, also courtesy of Mom. I drank a couple of club sodas, afraid I'd blow my role if I had even a single beer. While I waited for my appointment, I watched the crowd, my fingers tapping the side of the glass, a totally inadequate way to dispel pent-up tension. No look-alikes today. I wondered where Sophia was.

My worst fears came true when I finally entered the conference room to meet with the private banker, and the pale-faced, muscular guy with the glasses from the Californian shook my hand. What if he recognized me in spite of the clean shave and fancy suit?

"I'm Peter Gruekir. Nice to meet you, Mr. Vanvell." He had a slight accent with a European flavor.

I settled into the plush brown chair next to his. "Call me Prescott." I thanked my mother for the pretentious name. "I'll get right to the point. Taxes are killing me."

"We certainly hear that a lot. Have we met before?" He stared.

Did he recognize me? Sweat moistened my chest beneath my jacket and shirt. "No. About my tax problem, you don't know the half of it." I handed the check from my trust fund to him.

"There are a number of strategies—"

I interrupted, "Think income when I say, 'You don't know the half of it.'" To keep him off balance, I leaned forward, the gold stud in my tie keeping it in place. "I need somewhere I can safely put that other half." I thought about winking but restrained myself, not wanting to overplay the part.

"I don't know what to say, Mr. Vanvell."

Crap! He wasn't going for it. I added a rich man's frost to my voice. "Then I'm in the wrong place." I rose.

His mouth dropped open. "No, please. There are other options, entirely at your risk, but you'll need to fly to Switzerland."

I dropped back into the chair. I hadn't expected that. It wasn't illegal for BLS to do business in Switzerland. I frowned to look suitably distressed. "Impossible. My father died in a plane accident. I don't fly in respect of my mother's wishes." I'd finally found my calling, the biggest liar in the state of California. I hoped he didn't know that what dear old Dad had been flying in when he crashed and died was his Mercedes. I waved my arm to make sure Peter spotted my Cartier watch. "I have to admit I'm new to this, but can't I bank over the Internet?"

He pressed a couple of buttons on the laptop, and the Swiss flag appeared. "First, we must create an account for you, yes? This will be a secret between you and the bank alone."

I smiled. "Excellent. Put it under the name Skip." I leaned into the chair, making sure my tie pointed at the laptop to capture the procedure. I wondered if the IRS would let me keep the camera tie tack that was broadcasting the evidence they needed. A small reward for catching BLS and all those tax evaders with secret accounts.

Peter typed. He hesitated, then hit enter, and frowned.

Now that I'd said my nickname, the code word, I couldn't wait until the justice department and IRS agents busted in. I put my hand in my pocket and closed it around the small digital camera waiting there.

The screen responded with the message "account established." Peter turned and stared at me. "Why the name Skip?"

I froze. How stupid was it to use something he would recognize? I wished the camera I clutched could morph into a gun.

Peter examined the check I'd given him. He studied me again.

I held my breath, certain I could hear his brain clicking, putting it all together. Peter slipped off his glasses and rubbed his nose.

Dissembling? Sure I was used to fighting paparazzi to position myself for the best photos, but I used my elbows, not my fists. Where the hell were the IRS agents?

Someone yelled. Footsteps pounded. Peter looked toward the door.

I dared to breathe again. Oh, yeah! My pictures would be an exclusive. I would sell them to the real news. The hell with paparazzo. I was graduating to photojournalist. Winning the bet with my mother, the final satisfying victory. I pulled out the camera. Ready, set, smile. Here they come.

# DAPHNE, UNREQUITED

## BY ANGELA ZEMAN

t 11:45 on a spring night, Daphne March unlocked her Greenwich Village apartment door. She entered, her gown swirling at her ankles, still drifting in the otherworld of her thoughts. The heavy fire door swung shut, eclipsing the outer hall light. She dropped her keys with a musical clatter into the dish on a dimly lit table. And in the darkness of her living room, her eyes registered a shadow that didn't belong.

She twisted and backed against the table. "Who's there!"

"Hello, darling Daphne." The man's tone was creamy, appreciative.

Her heart thudded in her throat, nearly choking her, but her expression remained unruffled.

"Lord," the voice continued, "who knew you'd grow up to be a queen." A flare of light and a metallic snap indicated he'd lit a cigarette.

"Joseph." She began stripping off her long gloves, the only evidence of emotion in the trembling of her fingers.

"No other flesh than mine."

She asked lightly, "How did you get in?" She let her gloves

drop to the Persian rug and strode toward him, flipping on light switches as she advanced. The lights illuminated a cozy room, upholstered in chintz peonies of pink and peach against forest green moiré silk–covered walls and white painted French doors. Her apartment was small, half the penthouse floor of a twenty-story prewar building. Only one bedroom, but bright from many mullioned windows. A wraparound terrace offered views of the street below and the Hudson River farther west.

He waved the hand holding the cigarette vaguely toward the door. "It's a very old lock."

Tall with fair hair and a deep tan, his slender, bespoke-suited body weaved slightly. He opened his stance for balance. His smile was full of awareness of his own charm.

"How much did you pay Max to let you in?"

"Your noble guardian of the door? You besmirch his—"

She stopped, still ten feet away. "You're drunk."

"Well, yes. Liquid courage was required."

"To bribe Max?"

"Aaah, no. That was easy. Noble Max came ignobly cheap, to be frank."

Daphne considered him. Despite her forty-nine years, her features were unlined and her figure only slightly fuller than in her youth. The hair she kept pulled into a simple coil was more golden blonde than his, but she avoided the sun.

"You couldn't be upset at the blind item in my column. Everyone knows about your marriage aspirations."

"Now that—" He stabbed the air with his cigarette. "That's the problem."

"That people know?"

"No, darling. My aspirations."

"Your marriage plans?" She squinted with incredulity, but her breathing eased. "Are you sure you want to continue this discussion? With me?"

"You mean, because you might print what I say in tomorrow's paper? Nope. Not worried." His lips quavered. "I'm in love."

She said, unimpressed, "In love with her father's reputed billions."

"Not reputed. Real. Did a thorough check." His smile brightened.

Daphne said, impatience edging into her tone, "Then pardon me if I'm being dense, but what..."

"Why? Weary from scrounging tittle for the huddled masses yearning to be me? Nobody's waiting up for you. I know for a fact you're practically a virgin. Lovely with the light behind you. What color is that dress? Peach again?"

She said plaintively, "Joseph."

He sighed. "Okay. I'm not free to marry the girl—yet." He dragged unsteadily on his cigarette. A column of ashes fell to the rug.

"But you are free. Or did I lose track after you divorced the Olympic skier?"

"Her Shpanish papa gives not *un poco euro* abou' the skier. Or the others. No, darling Daphne, the problem is you."

"We divorced twenty-five years ago." No emotion flickered in her brown eyes. "I was your first."

"Sure were," he said softly. He swayed again and repositioned his feet. "Remind me...oh. Yesh—well. Remember Father George, presided at our wedding?" His head drooped and bobbed. "Bishop now...but you lunch with him Thursdays; no reminder needed, is there?"

Sour knowledge filled her eyes. "Oh, dear. Teresa Rosa De La Paula, late-life apple of her devoutly Roman Catholic papa's eye. To them, you're still married. To me."

"In—." He hiccuped. "Indeed. Daily mass, daily malarkey. You, all over again." His tone was bitter.

"Joseph. That child will expect—things—from you. She'll

interfere with your—your habits, and you hardly need her money! With your family's wealth, you could buy castles."

"Don't want cashels."

She said impatiently, "You know what I mean! Why invite such—fuss?"

"Fuss? Scrutiny of bad behavior, you mean. Tactfully put. I suppose it grows—goes—wi' the job." He pulled himself straight again. "You wouldn't understand."

Watching him, her curiosity sharpened. "I heard a rumor. May I run it past you for comment?"

He flung out a palm in invitation.

"You've informed your government pets: you wish to fill the upcoming vacancy, ambassador to Spain."

His shoulders moved, as if he'd stifled a retort.

She sighed. "So that's how you attracted this girl. You promised she'd be madam ambassador in her own country. I did wonder, but I never believed you'd"—she smiled painfully—"disturb your customary lifestyle with actual work."

"Service to my country," he said defensively.

"Service to your family business," she corrected sharply. "The Institute for Air and Space Safety opening in Barcelona. Rouchard International Limited sells weapons; now you want to profit by defending against them. You want the IASS defense contracts. Her illustrious papa's blessing would give you entrée, make you an insider at the institute."

"So it would. But your best chum, Bishop George, says he'll block any petition for an annulment. Don' know why."

"You know exactly why," she said flatly.

"I'll expand the dynasty in grand style. Children," he said sullenly. "Everything. Not my father's son anymore. But me."

"You!" Daphne couldn't help the astonished laughter that exploded from her.

Joseph shrieked, "Shut up!" Suddenly he looked old and

emaciated instead of slender. His scrawny neck extended, tendons like ropes, as he shouted, "Bastard knows all about me! You told him everything in those goddamned confessionals! I *knew* I couldn't trust you! I can just see you, jabbering away like two little girls!"

Daphne demanded shrilly, "And you learned this how! You threatened him?"

"He threatened *me!*" He flung his cigarette aside.

He strode forward and grabbing Daphne by her shoulders swung her around. Now the light was in her eyes. He towered over her. She struggled, thrust her arms between his, trying to break his grip. He hustled her backward, both of them stumbling. In seconds, they burst through the French doors onto the terrace, splinters and glass exploding into the night. Their feet tangled in her long skirt, and both fell heavily amid the shower of glass to the stone floor. Blood oozed from tiny cuts on their necks and arms.

She squirmed frantically to get out from under him.

"This is going to be easier than I thought," he snarled. He pushed his groin into her. "Oh, my, maybe I should fuck you first. Keep struggling, I don't often get a hard-on like this...."

Her bloody wrist slipped from his grip, and she struck his face hard. The blow made him pause.

She said in an enraged hiss, "You'll never get away with it!"

"I won't? You must've learned by now, people like me get away with just about everything. Did any of my young friends complain?"

"You crippled Peter; that scared the rest! But I'm not scared." She flailed at his face. "I have powerful friends! They know you! They'll figure it out!" She beat at him, but his body kept her pinned.

"You mean *my* friends? You think they'd finger me? For *you?*" He laughed. "You're not one of *us.* Poor Daphne, fooling herself all these years that she 'belongs.' She loves everyone, but nobody loves her back."

She gasped and went limp. "You're wrong! After all these years—"

"Years of writing sickly anecdotes instead of exposing the nasty bits. You think you've won their affections?"

"They're good to me!"

"Like their cocker spaniel. Pats and yum-yums for Darling Daphne, who loved them unconditionally. And protected them when they needed it, in print." He paused, as if considering something. "Yes. Exactly like a dog."

Tears flowed down her cheeks. "They *do* love me!"

"Darling, people like me don't befriend people like *you*. Not when it counts. We *use* you."

"NO!" She heaved against him. They rolled, and she managed to pull herself to a sitting position, pushing him back.

"Poor Daphne," he crooned at her, head lolling carelessly in the crunching glass. "She cares so much." He laughed again, his voice high and drunk.

"Stop it!" she shouted. She swung at his face, catching only his ear.

He lifted a leg and kicked her, knocking her sideways. For a few more seconds, they grappled, but he managed to stand. He hauled her up with him. Despite the chill air, he was sweating heavily.

He used his body weight to slam her against the parapet edging the terrace. He bent her backward over the thicket of dormant ivy stems, grinding her against them. He pushed her farther and farther backward, over the rounded top. Her breathing, ragged and desperate, made misty clouds illuminated by the streetlights. Traffic sounds drifted up from the street below.

Grinning, teeth bared, he said, "Oopsy daisy, over you go." He grunted with effort as he bent to get an arm under her legs.

"Tragic, they'll say." He huffed. "Jealousy drove you to it. You do envy us, Daphne." He lifted, and now her feet dangled over the edge, skirts flaring gracefully in the breeze. She sobbed, scrabbled desperately at the ivy, the bricks. Suddenly she pulled a brick loose.

She slammed it against the side of his head. He staggered backward, dragging her off the parapet. She dropped out of his arms as they hit the terrace floor hard. Pulling back both legs, arching her feet, she kicked his knees with the spikes of her heels.

He gave a sharp cry and collapsed backward. They lay apart for a moment in the darkness, both panting, neither moving.

Finally, she pulled herself up and crawled to his side. She leaned over him and, gulping air, felt for a pulse at his neck. "Joseph?" she whispered.

His eyelids lifted. He looked at her, poised above him. He smiled faintly. "You're a fool."

"*You're wrong!*"

He groaned, then weakly crooned, "Nobody cares about Daphne." He chuckled.

She lifted the brick with both hands and slammed it once, twice, again...into the dark red pulp that had once been a face.

Daphne stopped. She dropped the brick and crossed herself. Over and over she crossed herself.

———

MOMENTS LATER, DAPHNE scrambled to her feet. She ran to the intercom by the door, pressed a button, and cried, "Max! Come upstairs!" She waited, trembling, until an eon later, she heard a knock.

Max Kovalevski, her doorman, burst through the door when she opened it. "Miss March!" He stared at her, aghast. "Wha— what happened! Are you all right?" Max was a short, powerfully built Russian man in his fifties who liked the night shift, which meant that due to her late hours, he saw more of Daphne March than many of her neighbors. He'd worked in the building almost as long as Daphne had lived there, twenty years.

"Is that *blood*?"

She looked down at her torn, bloody hands and ruined gown as if surprised at their condition. Instead of answering, she turned and led him into the apartment. As they passed through the living room, he bent to scoop a smoldering cigarette from the carpet. The air was foul with the smell of charred wool.

Max followed her through the terrace doors, which hung crooked and smashed. She stopped and faced him.

"What the hell?" He stepped gingerly over the litter of glass to see deeper into the shadows. His mouth opened wordlessly as he scanned the scene, the body. The cigarette in his fingers continued sending up spirals of smoke until Daphne snatched it and flung it over the parapet. Max twisted to look at her.

"Is that...?"

Daphne's eyes were wild and huge, glistening in the dark. "He tried to kill me."

"*Kill* you?" Max wrapped his thick arms tight across his chest. "*Kill* you!" He shivered. After a long pause he said, "I—I could take him downstairs before I call the cops. I'll tell 'em he got here, I mean the lobby, like that. Said he was looking for you."

"How could he go anywhere in that condition? How could he talk?"

He exhaled. "Right. Right." He scrubbed a calloused palm across his mouth. "I'll say—I'll say I told him to get out, wouldn't let him in, too drunk."

Daphne stared. "You knew he was drunk?"

Max looked away, blinking rapidly. "I'm sorry. I'm so sorry, Miss March." He continued miserably, "I'll say, I told him to get out and refused to get him a cab. Told him get his own cab. And that's the last I saw 'im. 'Til I found him out back by the trash when I took my one a.m. break." He glanced at his watch. "Twelve fifteen now. You should get yourself to the Hamptons, Miss March. Like as if you'd gone earlier." He swallowed. "As if you wasn't here when he came. Any luck, nobody'll look up here."

Daphne dropped her eyes. Nodded. She said sadly, "We'll see how it goes."

"This—this'll take me a while. I'll get rid of—" He groped for a word, failed. "Clean up," he finished.

She followed him back to the front door.

Max paused before he passed through to the hall. "They'd believe he'd come to you for help. Everybody knows his, uh, reputation. And that you never hold a grudge."

She looked at him with a blank expression, as if unable to take in his words. In her mind, she heard: *Poor Daphne, loves everyone.*

While Max took away Joseph's body and hung a blanket across the broken doors, Daphne showered and dressed.

She went to a small room off the kitchen, unlocked the door, switched on the lights, then traced a finger along the labels of file cabinets that filled one wall. She found the drawer she wanted, pulled out a manila envelope fat with photos and papers and tattered with age. She relocked the door, went to the table in the foyer, and slid the envelope into a drawer. Then she left her apartment by the back stairs.

———

TWO WEEKS LATER, Alice Winchester shifted a few crucial inches in her chair, effectively cutting off a bellowed monologue from a ruddy-complexioned man on her right, whose donation of Communist Chinese photography to the Museum of Modern Art was being celebrated tonight. She leaned closer to the young man on her left. She whispered, "Forgive me for neglecting you—" She waved a hand to express duties owed to the guest of honor at her own party, who sat blinking, taken aback at his sudden loss of audience. "Did you get the brand of scotch you prefer? Do you need a refill?"

He whispered back, "Yes, thank you, and no, thank you. You're more attentive than I deserve." Straightening, he stated loud enough to be overheard by several guests, "Mr. Baughlander's stories are mesmerizing!" He beamed at the elderly, confused man.

Alice giggled. "It's all right, Wayne wouldn't hear a cannon go off in his ear. His wife's my greatest friend. She'll tell him what you said. He'll be happy; he believes anything complimentary about himself." Alice was a redhead, forty years Cory's senior. Remnants of her once-striking beauty had been preserved by surgery and the cut of her Dior dinner gown. She settled more cozily in his direction.

"What sweet eyes you have." She tapped the back of his hand with two fingers. "As if you'd never seen a shocking thing in your life. But if you're a friend of Daphne's—which you must be, since you're her 'plus one'—that can't be true. Who are you, darling?"

"Cory Sandhurst," he replied. He put down his dessert fork with relief, released by the etiquette of conversation from eating the rest of his plum tart. He hated pastry, but he knew Mrs. Winchester's private chef, Edie, would soon be called out from the kitchen for bows and applause. Mrs. Winchester required enthusiasm for Edie's skills from guests who desired return invitations to her monthly dinner parties, and Cory desperately wanted to return.

He hesitated, then said, "Wonderful room. Grander than I'd imagined. I'm thrilled to get a chance to see Stan Renard's work. The choice of details, your walls liquid with color. The curtains. Perfect setting for the Monet lilies."

Alice listened, a faintly puzzled looked on her face.

"I was at school with your grandson, Bret." As per Daphne's script, although the statement was true.

"With my Bretsy?" cooed Alice, delighted.

"Yes." He recalled how Bret cringed at his grandmother's pet name.

"You're not—" She hesitated, brow furrowed. "Not the son of Astrid Lenoire Sandhurst?"

He nodded.

"And your father—John Sandhurst, the banker? My God! I know you!" she cried. "Your mother's a genius; we saw a placement of hers in a Berlin museum. You have her eyes; I knew I'd seen them before! God, you're such a hunk, as we elders used to say. Still say, obviously!" She laughed, and Cory leaned back in his chair. The move drew Alice closer. Daphne had told him about that.

"But—how do you know our darling Daphne?"

"We met through PEN."

Alice continued, "We always say that, you know. 'Darling Daphne.' She is so dear. She says only the nicest things about us in her columns."

Daphne had kept an eye on him all evening. He'd been trying not to look at her but hadn't been able to prevent an occasional glance her way, like a nervous tic. He looked again. She'd pushed her chair back from the table and sat, legs crossed, one leg exposed by the slit in her narrow skirt, rolling a frosted glass of champagne against one cheek, as if she liked its coolness against her skin. Not drinking it. One drink per night was all she allowed herself, she'd said, and she'd shared that with him in her office prior to tonight's dinner.

Daphne was seated at the second of Alice's three round tables, each of which seated eight. He stared, helpless to look away. Despite the uncomfortable eighteenth-century French chairs, she radiated an air of reveling in her surroundings, of glorious enjoyment of the evening and her companions. A blonde goddess in pearl lace, she'd thrown her head back to laugh, exposing her creamy throat.

"Look at her," he found himself saying. "She belongs here."

"She's allowed here," corrected Alice. She smiled up at him, for he was tall, and she was a petite woman. "You don't see any other press here, do you?"

Suddenly Daphne shot Cory a droll wink, then turned to speak to someone.

For a second he forgot to breathe, feeling his heart jump into his throat. *We're off,* he thought.

Alice continued, "PEN. That's the literary organization. You're a writer?"

He nodded, swallowing hard. "A journalist. Press, like Daphne." He plucked a full wineglass from the table, disregarding whose it was. Daphne had explained to him that a full glass in a journalist's hand, in place of the alarming microrecorder or notebook, psychologically freed people to talk.

"Oh, but not *press* press, you're one of *us!*"

Cory said, puzzled, "Us?" His eyes lifted to scan the room.

Alice frowned slightly. "Your parents, dear. Two of our best families."

"Oh, yes. I'm *good goods*. Daphne brushed me up. Mother opted out of society somewhat thoroughly when she left my father."

Alice chuckled. "The privilege of artistic genius. You escorted none of the debutantes when you were younger, either; I would've remembered. You heard about Jojo, of course?"

He blinked. "Jojo? No...oh, Joseph Rouchard. Daphne's ex, yes. Terrible."

Alice shuddered. "*He* was at Le Bal Crillon in Paris this winter. Where he met his fiancée. Stunning, and I don't mean her inheritance. What was Jojo, practically sixty? She couldn't have been more than twenty! Came out with the Josselen girls; he was there to escort their poor widowed mother, Lula Winter-Josselen, for God's sake! More his age, but you know these empire builders and their arm candy. I'd be less shocked if he just, well, you know. But he intended to marry that child! Well, why I bore you with this…Oh, yes. The subject was society. Your father is on the board of my foundation." Her eyes narrowed.

"My mother supports my choice of career," he said, knowing he was answering several questions at once.

"Male writers embody danger and romance to my mind— Hemingway, Miller, Fitzgerald." Alice sighed, fanning her face mockingly with her napkin. "You're not seeing Daphne romantically, are you? Her name hasn't been linked with a man's since—"

He cleared his throat. "She's retiring, have you heard? To write her memoirs."

She chattered on as if she hadn't heard his interruption, touching his hand again. "I'm giving darling Daphne's birthday party soon, at Dianna's Cafe. You'll come, won't you? It's an annual event. I vary the guest list each year. One hundred is really only fifty, you know"—her speech slowed—"and she knows just everyone.…" She stopped.

He forged ahead. "The column published on that Friday, the day of your party, will be her farewell to her reading public."

Alice stared at him.

Cory repeated, "On her fiftieth birthday in two weeks, she retires. Friday, at your party. April first." Journalists repeat key lines. Good journalists, anyway.

Alice's fingers curled into claws. He felt her nails unintentionally gouging into his skin. He waited, expression pleasantly expectant.

One of his best traits, Daphne had said during his job interview. His emotions stayed hidden always. His father had railed for years, accusing him of having no warmth, no feelings for others. He did. Just not—outwardly. He wished his father could've heard Daphne explaining it. Until she had, he'd believed himself a selfish, cold fish. His father's term.

Daphne said his feelings were so overly empathic, he'd learned early to hide them in self-protection. She asked if his father had been emotionally abusive. Then, eyes soft, she told him not to answer. Daphne reminded Cory of his mother, who'd done her best to protect him from his father.

"People confide in you, don't they," Daphne had said, not a question. "Because they sense that you care. So few people care. Are you sure you want this job?"

Cory's mind returned to the present. "She leaves for Maine the morning after the party. Her apartment's already on the market."

He saw the information finally lodge in Mrs. Winchester's mind. Relief washed over him. *Done*, he thought.

Almost giddily, knowing he'd lost his audience, he added, "I'm replacing her at the paper by the way." *Hired by a wink, seconds ago.* She might remember these words later. Or not.

Daphne had informed him with daunting certainty that when Alice caught sight of him at her predinner cocktail hour, his gray eyes, auburn hair, and quarterback stature would gain him a seat at her left, prior seating arrangements notwithstanding. He'd been skeptical, but here he was. "Beauty's a power," she'd said in her office, "but short-lived. Beauty, intelligence, and presence— that's good for the long game. You're the whole package." He stared at her—a blonde with dreamy wide eyes and the controlled glamour of a mature Grace Kelly—and seeing nothing of himself in her description said thank you anyway.

When she explained why she'd sent for him, he'd been shocked. Her column was more than a job. He would be stepping into a life.

Tonight had been his final hurdle. He'd won. By God, he'd won. But what had he won?

He focused again on Alice, who was beginning to sound shrill. "I'm giving her birthday party! Does that mean nothing to her?"

He answered patiently, "Quite the opposite. She wants to spend her final night with her closest, most loved friends—"

Alice reared back, then jumped up, and rushed away to huddle in conversation with members of her inner circle.

Exactly as Daphne had told him to expect.

When Edie was brought out, bashfully wiping her hands on a vast snowy apron, he applauded with everyone else.

———

FOR THE NEXT few days, Cory suffered what seemed to him a blend of assault and drowning as Daphne drilled away his assumptions and fine-tuned his work habits. He reminded her he'd written for the *Star News* police desk in Hartford, but she'd scoffed. She kept asking him if he wanted her job. And he did. He thought so, anyway.

———

THE MONDAY BEFORE her retirement, he stepped into Daphne's office. She glanced warningly at him from her phone conversation. The caller, Cory soon overheard, was Alice Winchester.

With the phone still at her ear, Daphne handed Cory her calendar and a pile of pink slips—phone calls to return. She whispered, "Yours now," and smiled warmly at his surprise.

She said into the receiver, "I *do* understand, Alice; calm yourself, dear." (She made a wry face at Cory.)

Cory heard Alice exclaim, "He's glued to his daughter's side, and one stumbles over them just everywhere! It would be over the top if they crashed the gate and made a scene. Policemen might crash in right behind. Better to invite them, we can only hope her father *might* calm himself. The man should count his blessings, escaping Jojo for a son-in-law. Monumental awkwardness for your birthday, darling—but—of course you understand. Of all people, you would. Has that wretched man been arrested yet?"

Daphne said, "What wretched man?"

"The jealous one. From your building, darling."

"*Jealous!* Max just tends the door, Alice."

"People are whispering—but I suppose it's untrue, or you would've written about it—oh, what am I saying? You'd hardly treat Jojo's murder as a social event. Sorry, darling, so frazzled. Tell me about your book—how is your memoir progressing?"

"It's not. I won't start until I'm moved into my new country house. Yes, in Maine." She listened. "No, dear, I'm not acquainted with Stephen King, but wouldn't that be thrilling?" She listened again. "My publisher? Pegasus. Fitzgerald's my editor."

Cory heard Alice exclaim, "Fitz? I'm so happy for you. Now listen, I hope you're excited for your party!"

Daphne said, "You know I am, Alice."

"We've expanded the guest list, taken the whole restaurant."

"You did?" Daphne's eyes softened.

"Oh, my goodness, it's an occasion, you retiring from our midst. We must give you a good send-off!"

"But—the menu?"

"It's all managed. Your favorites: tournedos of duck breast with cherries, the mushroom tart. Wayne will be bringing fresh morels, as always, from his Connecticut estate. Perfect weather this year, he says he'll have plenty. Edie will run over and supervise; we couldn't do it without Edie, she'd never forgive us. And Ted—you know Ted Tibedeaux, always does the rooms—he's very excited to do the entire restaurant this year."

"All of Dianna's?"

"We love you; what else could we do?"

After Daphne hung up, Cory watched her but couldn't decide if she looked sad or happy. Silence reigned over the room for a few moments. Then she waved him out.

———

Thursday morning, Daphne invited Cory to her apartment. After arriving, he followed her outside to the terrace, where coffee and pastries waited on an iron outdoor table.

Cory examined his surroundings, curious but intimidated, having learned how few were admitted to her private space.

Her apartment was a jewel with a terrace wide enough for benches, chairs, and a large round table. From the buds peeping out among tangles of brown stems, Cory saw that vines and flowers would soon frame her majestic views. Indoors, a sprinkling of antique chairs and tables, worn and comfortable, sat dappled with sunlight.

To his surprise, after pouring coffee for them both, she lit a cigarette. She smoked only rarely, he had noticed in their few days together, and only when disturbed.

"What's wrong?" he asked.

Her eyebrows rose in surprise. "Nothing." She stood up to look over the parapet, smoke drifting from the cigarette between her fingers. The Hudson River glittered in the distance.

The spring air was still crisp. Cory shivered. He drank half the coffee in his cup to warm himself. "You like Maine?" he asked.

She laughed. "Well—I probably will. I've never been there. It'll work out."

"You're coming back?"

"Back?"

"To see your friends. They'll miss you obviously."

She smiled. He shivered inwardly at the despair in that smile. "You must know my story."

He nodded. She'd married into the Social Register. Marry in, divorce out. Not "seen" anymore. Socially invisible. His mother had explained these details before he'd decided to take the job.

Not *them*, he suddenly remembered. *Us*. He felt a swift stab of anxiety. "I heard somewhere: 'bastards occur like eclipses—once every few years, scaring hell out of the superstitious.'"

Daphne pointed at him with her coffee cup and laughed. "Witty. Write that; they'll love it."

*They.*

On his way out, Cory stopped at a small cabinet made of what appeared to be glass shards. He said, "Wow! Outstanding!" He glanced around at the chintz. "In several ways."

Daphne grinned. "Know what it is?"

"A portable bar?"

"Made from a collage of broken mirrors from Studio 54."

Cory's mouth dropped open.

She giggled. "I couldn't resist! Think of the stories it represents."

Cory said, "Imagine how much coke you might find in all the little cracks!"

"The prior owner raised the price because of that."

Cory laughed.

She opened a side door. "Scotch goes here; Alice told me you're a scotch man. Ice bucket, tongs, glasses." She pointed out where everything went, then considered him speculatively. "You take it."

He gasped. "I couldn't!"

"It deserves someone who appreciates it. Besides, the movers will just break it. A gift to launch your glittering future. Really."

"I—I'll keep it safe for you."

"No. Then maybe you'll forgive me for giving you these." He trailed her across the foyer to a door in her kitchen. Stacked inside an otherwise empty room were file boxes. "All yours," she said, waving her arm grandly.

He looked at her blankly. "What is it?"

"Your...it might be appropriate to call it your birthright, but your mother wouldn't approve. Your job. Well. Strictly speaking, my job until tomorrow. But these will help you do your job."

Suddenly he knew. "It's all here, isn't it? I'd heard that about you, that your research was golden. You never wrote what you couldn't prove! It's true?"

"Twice confirmed, preferably." She lit another cigarette.

"So—you want me to dispose of this for you?"

"Don't be silly. You'll need it. This information will give you a head start on anything that comes your way."

He gaped. "Like what?"

"If I answered that question, it would spoil your fun. Take it away before the movers arrive. Money can buy a lot of satisfied curiosity, better to avoid tempting them."

He started counting, "Five, ten—"

"Thirty-seven file boxes, for God's sake. I did this job twenty-two years. It accumulates. Don't store it at the newspaper, if you don't mind some advice."

He watched her exhale a long column of smoke. "Couldn't you have scanned this into a computer?"

"I did." She thrust a box of DVDs into his hand. "Backup and backup."

He hastened after her as she strode toward her foyer. "Aren't you keeping a set for yourself? For your memoirs?"

"Sorry to abandon you, I have a lunch with the bishop."

She pulled her coat out of a hall closet. "Oh, my gloves. Cory, would you mind? They're in the bedroom on the bed." She pointed. "Through there."

When he obediently went where she pointed, she took the manila envelope from the table and, darting to the portable bar, pushed the envelope into a section and latched its door securely.

When Cory returned with her gloves, she was buttoning

her coat. She tossed him a set of keys. "Call Max. He'll help you."

"The infamous doorman?"

Her smile was wry. "He didn't murder Joseph. You should talk to him. No, I mean it. Talk to him." She pulled on her gloves. "Leave the keys with Max, won't you? The movers come at two. Oh, and I wouldn't let anyone touch the portable bar if I were you."

"Carry it myself."

"Good." Daphne gazed around at the apartment. "It will be nice to be relieved of everyone's skeletons." She glanced up at him, smile brilliant beneath her glistening eyes. "I'm going to love being free."

"You mean being retired?"

"...Yes."

Cory didn't watch her leave. He went back to the room and hefted one of the boxes. He couldn't help wondering what it contained.

———

THAT NIGHT, AFTER a wearying day, Cory sat in his own Murray Hill apartment, which before the influx of boxes had been sparsely furnished. He admired the bar, which had settled well into his retro-hip decor, then turned on his computer.

The thought of doing this had tantalized him all afternoon. He slipped in a DVD and waited. When folders appeared on the screen, he selected a file at random and opened it.

He read, eager, his attention sparking whenever he ran across a familiar name. Sometimes a frown flickered across his face. He opened other files. Suddenly he drew back, repulsed. Then involuntarily he exclaimed, "No!" Shaken, he scrolled, read more. No longer amused, he put in another DVD. Again at random, he opened a file. He read, then clicked onto other files. Sickened, he shut the lid of the computer.

Cory went to a window and gazed out, leaning on a stack of boxes, no longer drawn to open them. The street below was quiet. Murray Hill had nothing compared to the glamour of a neighborhood like Daphne's.

Distracted, he went to his new bar and unlatched the doors. In with the scotch, he saw a manila envelope. Drawing it out, he hesitated, then opened it. When he saw the name on the first page, he froze. Then he read.

His hands shook as he poured himself the drink he'd wanted. Then he called his mother. She was in Milan this week.

"*Cory!*" Her voice sounded pleased. "I've been wondering—"

One hand holding his glass, he dropped into his desk chair and shifted the papers to his lap. "How's the show going?"

"Ho, don't kid me, kid. I hear the cubes knocking around in that cut glass tub. You didn't call about my show. What's wrong?"

He set the glass on the desk. "Right. Life-changing question: Did I make a wrong turn, replacing Daphne March? Is this a job I want?" He explained about her memoirs and files and Alice's comments. While he talked, he flipped open his computer lid, clicked onto the DVD again. He glanced at the papers in his lap for reference, hunted and found the scanned material on the DVD. He clicked the file open.

"And Mom, listen to this." He began reading to her from the print on his screen.

"Stop," she cut him off. "Believe me, sweetie, I know what it says."

Cory clicked on "select all" and hit Delete. "Mom. I'm sorry, but you should know I read it. And Mom, nobody who knew the facts could blame you."

"Thank you, sweetie. Many find it convenient to blame me, but only your opinion matters."

He put in the backup DVD, repeated the search, select, and delete. "Mom, whether I keep the job or not, I can't leave her now."

"So don't. Cory, you've dreamed all your life of becoming an investigative reporter."

"Yes." He took another drink, ice cubes clinking as he tilted the glass, then sat thinking. "Yes, but society gossip. I'd imagined political intrigue. Murder."

His mother gave a wry laugh. "Oh, you'll find that in your present company, and more."

"Is Daphne's—material—true? Could these people have been so ruthless?" he asked plaintively.

"To protect such privileged lives? Cory, there's a price tag on that high plane of advantage. Only a special few survive intact. Look at me. I escaped, but barely. Cory, Daphne needs a friend. You have advantages she never did. Use them. Be as courageous an investigative reporter as she was. Gossip, I would say, is not how I would describe the job ahead of you. If you're up for it."

———

Cory didn't find Daphne all the next day. He finally dressed and went to Dianna's.

Although the evening had just started, the party had spilled out onto the sidewalk, gate-crashers swelling attendance beyond comfort.

Cory pushed through smokers gathered under the green awning. Their conviviality had attracted nonsmokers and the party had spread down the sidewalk both ways. Waiters were pouring drinks, lingering to chat. Guests and restaurant staff had known each other for years, Dianna's being treated by the patrons almost as a private club.

Inside, he heard Ted Tibedeaux shouting, "Two extra places at each table—that's it, for God's sake!"

Alice collided with him. "Oh, Cory! Have you seen these? I had the menu engraved on cards." At Cory's blank look, she insisted, "Keepsakes."

"Where's Daphne?" he demanded.

Alice ignored his question and hurried off. Only when people began seating themselves did Cory find Daphne. Wearing a shimmering pink dress, she stood leaning against the velvet curtain framing the doorway, watching the guests.

He stepped close behind her. "Mother sends her most emphatic love."

Daphne glanced up over her shoulder at him. She was smiling, but her eyes glistened. "I always admired Astrid."

The room was overheated from too many bodies. Daphne kept watching, kept smiling. Cory dabbed at his perspiring forehead with a napkin. He thought he'd choke from the perfumes and cooking odors.

He blurted, "Let's get out of here!"

"Leave my party? Why?"

"Your memoirs! They're terrified of what you could write. They'll hate you. I think they already hate you. Your reputation for finding proof to back everything—you're in danger!"

She said, her voice untroubled, still watching the guests, "In my entire career, I've never written anything to hurt them. I'm their Darling Daphne. Why would they think I'd change now?"

"Because that's what they'd do if they were you! They have no understanding of someone like you!"

She folded her arms.

Cory gripped her shoulders, pulled her around. "You're daring them to do it, aren't you? You *know* what's going to happen!"

"What's going to happen?" She wouldn't look at him, but her body was rigid, arms stiff. "They made my special morel tart, you know. They do it every year. Edie makes it just for me."

"You know the truth about them, how they really feel about you, but you still cling to your hope. You want more than anything in your life, more than your *life*—to be wrong. But in spite of all that wishing, you're still Daphne March."

"Wayne brings the morels fresh from his Connecticut estate. Picks them himself." She twisted away.

"Others would just tell themselves happy lies, but that's not good enough for Daphne March. Daphne March, who documents everything, who never prints a word without confirming it twice. You want proof that they accept you as one of them. You need it! Proof!"

As if he hadn't spoken, she strolled into the room, waving and greeting guests as she wound her way through them to the head table. Alice waited for her there with her great friends, the Baughlanders, and others.

Cory stood in the doorway, too devastated to join the party. Waiters rushed in and out, some muttering at him for being in the way, but he couldn't move.

At the end of the long evening, he saw Edie edge into the room through the kitchen door, flushed and sweating, ready for her accolades.

Daphne rose to her feet. Glasses rang gaily as spoons tapped for silence. Gradually the chatter quieted. With hands extended toward Edie, Daphne led the applause. She said loudly over the noise, "You surpassed yourself, dear Edie! Thank you, Alice!" Alice stood, beaming. The crowd burst into cheers, which went on for a few minutes.

When Daphne crumpled to the floor, at first no one but Cory seemed to notice. He pushed through the crush of guests to get to her. The crowd hushed; then voices and noise swelled to a deafening level.

———

AFTER HER VOMITING and convulsions subsided, Daphne was taken from the emergency room and installed in an intensive care suite on the seventh floor. The unit lay on the other side of swinging doors, through which visitors needed an electronic pass to enter. Outside and to the right of the ICU door, a dazed Cory found himself sitting in a private, luxurious waiting room. He had no idea how many hours had passed. Alice, Edie, and a handful of Alice's friends sat around him on the long sofas. Arrangements of flowers sat on every table, crushed together.

Abruptly Cory stood, like a diver lunging for air. "Too many flowers."

Alice said soothingly, "Of course." She signaled for the attention of a male aide. "Take these flowers elsewhere. The cancer ward will do."

He said, "Yes, Mrs. Winchester," and took two arrangements away.

At Cory's look, Alice said, "What else are donations for?"

Then a doctor burst through the ICU doors and entered the waiting room. He stripped off his gloves and said directly to Alice, "Unconscious. She might last until tomorrow." Everyone stood up and gathered close.

Cory said, incredulous, "She's going to die? From what? How?"

"Accident, clearly. Still, the police will check, Alice. Have to look into any sudden death, and under the circumstances, youngish woman, good health." He shrugged.

Alice said firmly, "Thank you, John. My nephew's been called." She said in an aside to Cory, "My attorney, darling."

"What accident?" demanded Cory.

The doctor's voice sounded aggrieved. "You can't imagine how many deaths we get every spring. Ridiculous mushroomers so sure they'll never make a mistake. Mr. Baughlander brought in morels from his estate, I hear. Who knows what Edie cooked in those tarts of hers. Madness, trusting amateurs."

Edie, eyes popping, exclaimed, "I know mushrooms, good from bad, every sort! I'd never make a mistake like that! Never! Madam! You believe me, don't you?"

Alice said, "Well, there will be publicity, but it'll be controlled." She touched Cory's arm possessively.

The doctor left, striding toward the bank of elevators. Edie trundled after him, moaning.

Before Cory could collect his thoughts, raised voices came from the hall. Cory darted to the doorway and saw a man in a suit and a uniformed policewoman standing in front of the elevators, trying to hush the shouts of a tall nurse, who clutched Edie's hands in both of hers. Edie sobbed where she stood.

"Those people!" the nurse exclaimed to the man, obviously a detective. "My Aunt Edie, never in all her years of service would she say a word against them, even when they more than deserved it. But this!" The tall nurse put an arm protectively around Edie. "My aunt could tell you plenty—if you could get it out of her." She shot a venomous look at the waiting room. "After forty years of cooking mushrooms, calling this death an 'accident'? As if she'd make a fatal mistake with mushrooms! Especially ones picked by that old loony! They think they're above paying for their sins; they like to pretend they haven't any. They use people like my Aunt Edie."

Cory, trembling with rage, realized everyone had clustered at his back to watch. He heard Alice mutter in a low tone to her friends, "Edie won't say a wrong word. We'll be fine. I promised her—well, let's just say she won't be sorry, even if they send her somewhere for a while."

Cory turned to face the group and blurted, "Take the blame, you mean."

Alice touched his chest. "I meant poor, poor Edie will never lack for job security. Could you print that for us, Cory? Daphne would've wanted you to say it that way. Dear Cory. I'm so grateful you're one of our own and not an outsider. Who else could understand people like us? People who matter."

Alice continued, "By the way, Daphne's book. Have you read it?"

After a pause, Cory said, "No. I didn't get the impression she'd written it yet."

"Are you sure?"

The Baughlanders at Alice's side repeated, "Are you sure?"

Cory studied their faces. "I could look for it."

"Yes," Alice said. "Do. Go through her things."

"Sure, if Max will let me in."

Mrs. Baughlander chuckled. "She could inspire loyalty in some surprising people, our Daphne."

"Darling Daphne," said Alice, as if correcting her. Then she turned to Cory. "Let me know."

"Ah," said Cory. "Excuse me. I must speak to the detective with Edie, make sure he gets the details right. I am, after all, a reporter."

# ABOUT THE AUTHORS

**Ted Bell,** a native Floridian, is a graduate of Randolph-Macon College in Virginia. He has an honorary doctorate in fine arts from Kendall College in Michigan. Ted spent most of his career in the advertising business, located in New York, London, and Chicago. He was president of the Leo Burnett Company and retired as Chairman of the Board and Worldwide Creative Director of Young & Rubicam in New York, at that time the world's largest ad agency. Subsequently, he began a career as an author. His Alex Hawke series of espionage novels have all been *New York Times* best sellers. He also writes historical novels for young adults, the Nick McIver series, which are also *New York Times* best sellers. Ted is on the Advisory Board of George Washington's home at Mount Vernon, serving under former Secretary of the Army Togo West. He is married to political consultant Page Lee Hufty and lives in Palm Beach, Florida, and Aspen, Colorado.

**Peter Blauner** is the author of six novels, including the Edgar Award–winning *Slow Motion Riot* and the *New York Times* bestseller *The Intruder.* His most recent novel is *Slipping Into Darkness.* A native New Yorker, he has also been a crime reporter for *New York* magazine, a Good Humor ice cream salesman, and a staff writer for the *Law & Order* television franchise. He lives—within his means—with his family in Brooklyn.

**Karen Catalona** lives in San Francisco, California, with her husband and two children. As a Deputy District Attorney, she has prosecuted a wide range of criminal offenses, most recently felony gang crime. She is working on her first novel.

**Tim Chapman** is a former forensic scientist for the Chicago police department and currently teaches English composition and Chinese martial arts. He recently earned a master's degree in creative writing from Northwestern University. His fiction has appeared in the *Southeast Review* and *Alfred Hitchcock's Mystery Magazine*. His story "Downsizing" was a finalist in the World's Best Short Short Story Contest. He wishes he could play the saxophone. He lives in Chicago with his lovely and patient wife, Ellen.

**Lee Child** was born in 1954 in Coventry, England, but spent his formative years in the nearby city of Birmingham. He went to law school in Sheffield, England, and after part-time work in the theater, joined Granada Television in Manchester for what turned out to be an eighteen-year career as a presentation director during British TV's "golden age." But after being let go in 1995 as a result of corporate restructuring, he decided to see an opportunity where others might have seen a crisis, bought six dollars' worth of paper and pencils, and sat down to write a book, *Killing Floor*, the first in the Jack Reacher series. It was an immediate success and launched the series, which has grown in sales and impact with every new installment. Lee spends his spare time reading, listening to music, and watching the Yankees, Aston Villa, or Marseilles soccer. He is married with a grown-up daughter. He is tall and slim, despite an appalling diet and a refusal to exercise.

**Michael Connelly's** twenty-second novel, *The Reversal*, was released in October 2010 and reteamed lawyer Mickey Haller with LAPD detective Harry Bosch in another fast-paced thriller. His books have been translated into thirty-five languages and have won the Edgar Award, Anthony Award, Macavity Award, Los Angeles Times Best Mystery/ Thriller Award, Shamus Award, Dilys Award, Nero Award, Barry Award, Audie Award, Ridley Award, Maltese Falcon Award (Japan),

.38 Caliber Award (France), Grand Prix Award (France), Premio Bancarella Award (Italy), and the Pepe Carvalho Award (Spain). Michael was the president of the Mystery Writers of America organization in 2003 and 2004 and edited both the MWA anthology *The Blue Religion* and the Edgar Allan Poe anthology *In the Shadow of the Master*. He lives with his family in Florida.

**Frank Cook's** mystery short stories have appeared in New England crime fiction anthologies published by Level Best Books, and his non-fiction pieces have appeared in print and Web publications worldwide. He has authored two business development books, including the bestselling *21 Things I Wish My Broker Had Told Me* for real estate agents, and has coauthored two additional titles. He is completing his first novel. Frank resides in New Hampshire, where he serves on the board of directors for Portsmouth public television.

**David DeLee** is a native New Yorker. He holds a master's degree in criminal justice and is a former licensed private investigator. His previous short stories have appeared in DAW's *Cosmic Cocktails* anthology and consecutive volumes of *Strange New Worlds*, published by Pocket Books. He currently lives in New Hampshire, where he's working on a novel featuring bounty hunter Grace deHaviland.

**Nelson Richard DeMille** was born in New York City on August 23, 1943, and moved as a child with his family to Long Island. In high school, he played football and ran track. He spent three years at Hofstra University, then joined the army and attended Officer Candidate School. He was a first lieutenant in the United States Army (1966–1969) and saw action as an infantry platoon leader with the First Cavalry Division in Vietnam. He was decorated with the Air Medal, Bronze Star, and the Vietnamese Cross of Gallantry. Upon his return to the United States, he went back to Hofstra University, where he received his degree in political science and history. He has three children—Lauren, Alexander, and James—and still lives on Long Island. DeMille's earlier books were NYPD detective novels. His first major novel was *By* *the Rivers of Babylon*, published in 1978 and still in print, as are all his succeeding novels. He is a member of the Authors Guild, the Mystery Writers of America, and American Mensa. He holds three honorary doctorates: doctor of humane letters from Hofstra University, doctor of literature from Long Island University, and doctor of humane letters from Dowling College. He is the author of *By the Rivers of Babylon*, *Cathedral*, *The Talbot Odyssey*, *Word of Honor*, *The Charm School*, *The Gold Coast*, *The General's Daughter*, *Spencerville*, *Plum Island*, *The Lion's Game*, *Up Country*, *Night Fall*, *Wild Fire*, *The Gate House*, and *The Lion*. He also coauthored *Mayday* with Thomas Block and has contributed short stories, book reviews, and articles to magazines and newspapers.

**Joseph Goodrich** is an alumnus of New Dramatists and an active member of the Mystery Writers of America. His plays have been produced across the United States and in Australia and published by Samuel French, Playscripts, Applause Books, Back Stage Books, the Padua Hills Press, and others. His script *Panic* was awarded the 2008 Edgar Award for best play.

Agatha Award–winning author **Daniel J. Hale** holds degrees from Cornell University, Southern Methodist University, and the Bowen School of Law. A former French resident and a recovering attorney/ mountain biking addict, Hale served as the executive vice president of Mystery Writers of America in 2007. He's now an instructor with Southern Methodist University's CAPE Creative Writing Program.

Clinical psychologist **Roberta Isleib** is the author of eight mysteries, including *Six Strokes Under*, *Deadly Advice*, and *Asking for Murder*, all published by Berkley Prime Crime. Her books and stories have been short-listed for Agatha, Anthony, and Macavity awards. She lives in Connecticut with her family but is lucky enough to spend winters in Key West.

**Harley Jane Kozak,** a sometimes actress, lives with her family in California. Her debut novel, *Dating Dead Men*, won the Agatha, Anthony, and Macavity awards. Its sequel was *Dating Is Murder*, followed by

*Dead Ex* and *A Date You Can't Refuse*. Her short prose has appeared in *Ms. Magazine*, *Soap Opera Digest*, the *Sun*, the *Santa Monica Review*, and the anthologies *Mystery Muses*, *This Is Chick Lit*, *A Hell of a Woman*, *Butcher Knives and Body Counts*, and *Crimes by Moonlight*. She blogs on The Lipstick Chronicles (http://thelipstickchronicles.typepad.com/the_lipstick_chronicles/). None of Harley's former husbands resemble the one described in "Lamborghini Mommy."

**David Morrell** is the award-winning author of *First Blood*, the novel in which Rambo was created. He holds a PhD in American literature from Penn State and was a professor at the University of Iowa. His numerous best sellers include the classic spy trilogy, *The Brotherhood of the Rose* (the basis for an NBC miniseries that premiered after Super Bowl XXIII), *The Fraternity of the Stone*, and *The League of Night and Fog*. The protagonists in "The Controller" previously appeared in *The Protector* and *The Naked Edge*.

**Carolyn Mullen** works as a freelance health policy consultant after an almost twenty-year career in the federal government. She has long hoped for the chance to write something more compelling than the bureaucratic prose this career necessitated, and this story is her first foray into fiction. She lived in New York City, Atlanta, Reno, London, and San Francisco (where her heart still resides) before settling in Baltimore. She and her husband, who both have grown to love Baltimore, share their house with three bossy cats and a one-eyed dog.

A Stanford graduate and former plaintiff's trial lawyer, **Twist Phelan** writes critically acclaimed short stories, suspense novels set in the business world, and the legal-themed Pinnacle Peak mystery series. While a lawyer, she asked a Ponzi scheme defendant why he'd done it. "I'd heard money doesn't make you happy," he said. "But I wanted to find out for myself." Read more about Twist and her work at www.twistphelan.com.

**S. J. Rozan,** a native New Yorker, is the author of twelve novels. She has won the Edgar, Nero, Macavity, Shamus, and Anthony awards for best novel and the Edgar Award for best short story. She is a former Mystery Writers of America national board member, a current Sisters in Crime national board member, and president of the Private Eye Writers of America. In 2003, she was an invited speaker at the Annual Meeting of the World Economic Forum in Davos, Switzerland. In 2005, she was guest of honor at the Left Coast Crime Convention.

**Jonathan Santlofer** is the author of five novels, including *Anatomy of Fear*, recipient of the Nero Wolf Best Crime Novel Award. He is a highly respected artist whose work has been written about and reviewed in the *New York Times*, *Art in America*, *Artforum*, and *Arts* and appears in many public, private, and corporate collections. He serves on the board of Yaddo, one of the oldest artist communities in the country. Santlofer lives and works in New York City.

**Elaine Togneri** has thirty published short stories in markets ranging from webzines and anthologies (*Blood on Their Hands*) to major magazines (*Woman's World*). She has also published nonfiction and poetry. Elaine holds an MA in English from Rutgers University and has taught courses in English composition, technical writing, and short fiction. She is a member of the Florida Writers Association, Mystery Writers of American, and Sisters in Crime. The founder and a past president of the Sisters in Crime–Central New Jersey chapter, Elaine relocated to Florida in 2007.

**Angela Zeman's** short stories often appear in anthologies and magazines. In 2010, "Chanel, 1927" appeared in *Adironacks Mysteries I (North Country)* and "Skip Trace" appeared in *Back Alley* webzine. In 2011, "The First Tale of Roxanne" will appear in the International Association of Crime Writers anthology *A World of Crime and Mystery*, edited by Douglas Preston; and "May" will appear in *Adirondack Mysteries II*. "Green Heat," first published in Jeffery Deaver's anthology *A Hot and Sultry Night for Crime*, was selected by Nelson DeMille to be included in Otto Penzler's annual collection *Best American Mystery Stories of the Year* (Houghton Mifflin).